The Fearance
by Rob Badcock

ISBN- 978 1 909 425 54 5

Also by Rob Badcock

Big Frog - Book One of the Meskitoe Trilogy

1

When you wake up from a faint, you have absolutely no idea where you are, or even who you are. Nothing around you makes sense. Someone is staring into your face, usually a woman with a reassuring smile who tells you everything's going to be all right. This woman slapped his face with a 'Wake up, we're here!' and moved on down the aisle. Still tasting the bitterness of the wakewafer on the back of his tongue, Rib Meskitoe stared at the red light flashing on the panel above his head.

'Will passengers in pod numbers 2540 to 2590 please assemble at the rear of the ship for transfer?' It wasn't really a question. 'Please make sure you have all of your belongings with you.'

He checked his pod number. 2542! That was him! As he unstrapped himself and grabbed his bag from the overhead locker, the announcement from the flightcom slowly permeated his befuddled brain. Transfer? What transfer? He thought he was on a direct ticket. Memories of a previous faulty booking powered panic through his veins and he tried to attract the stewardess' attention. But she was engaged in heated argument with the occupant of pod number 2539, directly in front of his.

'I've paid an extra two thousand dollars for Priority Fast-track and I don't see why I have to wait to get off this goddam awful ship,' drawled the fat Texan, prodding the stewardess on the shoulder with each word. She promptly reached up to prod the call button, at which a guard appeared from nowhere to prod the

Texan on the nose with the muzzle of a Kalashnistun. The occupant of pod number 2539 sat down. With a false smile, the stewardess politely informed him that he would be the last to disembark. The Texan opened his mouth to protest, then thought better of it, the whiff of gun-barrel oil lingering in his nostrils.

The stewardess returned to duty with a vengeance. 'Move on down the aisle, please. Quickly now. Move it!'

The guard played his part by waving his gun in the face of anyone who looked as if they were going to complain. He gave Rib a shove in the back. 'You hoid what da lady said,' he grunted in guttural Bronx.

'OK, OK, I'm going,' said Rib. Stumbling along the aisle, he turned to venture a question. 'What was it she said about transfer? This is the right ship for Tycho, isn't it?'

'Yeah,' the guard laughed, 'if you're lucky,' and gave him a final nudge, this time with the rifle butt by way of encouragement. The passengers from pod numbers 2540 to 2590 were herded down to the rear of the craft into a small, windowless cabin. The guard blew a kiss as the door slid shut with a heavy clunk. The bulkhead now safely closed, Rib raised a single digit. They found themselves in some kind of airlock, pressed tightly together like sardines in a can. They waited uncomfortably for what seemed like an age. No-one looked each other in the eye. The human race was rather good at this, having honed the act to perfection in elevators over the course of the previous hundred years. A heavy rasping of metal from the wall of the hull signalled that something was about to happen and the crowd shuffled forward. Would they have elbowed their way to the front of the queue if a firing squad awaited them on the other side, wondered Rib. His thoughts were broken by the airlock door sliding open. Passengers pushed and shoved to get to the front. The surge slowed to an abrupt halt as the scene before them unveiled itself. To a person, passenger list 2540 to 2590 stepped back in disbelief.

They were being herded from the sleek, sanitised interior of the lasership into what could best be described as a shitbucket. And a tiny shitbucket, at that. The unmistakable odour of an unloved latrine wafted over their heads. Being at the rear of the queue usually gives you the advantage of being the first to back away. No thank you, I'll catch the next one.

But not this time. The blow to the back of the skull knocked Rob to his knees. 'And that, you little toid, was for da finger. Doncha fink we got scans in space, huh?'

Rib pondered a reply, but tasted blood where he had bitten his tongue. His instinct was to stay stum and stay kneeling. His, however, was not to decide and he was picked up by the scruff of the neck and hurled into the shuttle, where he landed sprawling on the floor. He stood up unsteadily, rubbing the back of his head.

Two stewardesses were ushering nervous passengers to their seats. The younger of the two gestured Rib to the only one left vacant, right at the front. 'Please take your seat. The shuttle is due to depart any minute.' He did as he was told.

The flightcom crackled: 'This is your Captain speaking and I'd like to welcome you aboard Shuttle 495 on this 26th day of June, 2043. My name is Johnny "Peaches" Bannister and I am joined today on the flight deck by co-pilot Haruki "Ginger" Yashimoto, who will be taking us down to Tycho today. The weather on the ground is a fine 20 degrees, with a light south-westerly breeze of 2.7 knots, and our estimated flight time is … ahem … 37 minutes. Your stewardesses on board are Doris and Chardonnay. Now please settle back and … enjoy the flight.'

The younger woman was already seated facing Rib, right at the front of the cabin. She was soon joined by the older stewardess, who would best be described as battle-scarred. Such was the thick layer of orange make-up covering her face, seemingly applied with a trowel, it was difficult to determine her true features. Seriously scary-looking, with the manner to go with it. 'Make sure your seatbelts are securely fastened,' she barked. Rib tugged on his own and noted that the leather strap was frayed in the middle. Little chance of that helping much in an impact, he thought. The badge on the lapel of the older stewardess said Chardonnay and the younger one's name was Doris. Surely they must have got them mixed up? Doris wore no make-up but maybe should have. Her pale, drawn face wore a terrified expression

A grating noise from the rear of the shuttle signalled that they were disengaging from the lasercraft. It was just as well shuttle 495 had no portholes. Rib was spared the looks of utter horror etched on the faces of every single man, woman and child on the lasercraft watching the rusting scrapheap move slowly away from the mothership with short blasts from its portside rockets. To a person, they all mouthed to themselves, 'Oh my God! Have we got to go in THAT?'

Still a bit woozy, thanks to the parting gift from the Bronx, Rib looked around the shuttle. It was even worse than his first impression: the seats were bare, scratched metal; trickles of rust-coloured water ran down the walls; and a stench – a mixture of urine and vomit – made him want to gag. How could this be? Why hadn't the lasership landed on Tycho itself?

The thrust from the main rockets pinned Rib back in his seat. The roar was deafening. The whole craft shook as it began its descent. Rib tried to focus on the number of rivets in the metal-plating hull beside his seat. He stopped counting when it registered that one in every four had popped out.

Co-pilot "Ginger" Yashimoto came over the address system. 'We shall shortly be entering the atmosphere of Tycho. You may experience a discomforting degree of turbulence. You are to remain seated at all times with your seatbelts fully fastened. If you are wearing dentures, please remove them immediately. If you are pregnant, suffering from epilepsy, heart condition or a bad back, you are advised to keep your fingers crossed. May your God be with you. In the meantime, just sit back, relax and enjoy your flight.' Fortunately, "Ginger" Yashimoto spoke with such a pronounced Japanese accent that only a few words of his message were decipherable.

Chardonnay then unbuckled her belt, moved unsteadily to the middle of the aisle and screamed at the top of her voice, 'Will all passengers please adopt the brace position. Now! Please do not be alarmed,' she added, 'this is normal, routine procedure.' While the senior stewardess checked that everyone had their heads between their knees with hands clasped around the back of their necks, Doris crossed herself and screwed her eyes tight shut.

On entering the planet's atmosphere, Shuttle 495 went into uncontrollable spasm. Rib was sure all his teeth would be shaken out. A rivet popped out from the hull wall just above Doris' head. It landed in her lap, swiftly followed by another. She screamed. Chardonnay staggered back down the aisle and slapped her in the face. It was too late. The whole cabin decided that this was a good time to follow Doris' example. It's not easy to scream from the brace position, but that didn't stop the passengers of Shuttle 495. Then, in an instant, the shaking stopped, the screaming stopped. They were through. An Armenian in seat twenty seven cheered.

'You may now resume your normal positions,' said Chardonnay. 'We have entered the atmosphere of

Tycho.' The Armenian cheered again. The cabin heaved a collective sigh of relief and reached forward for the in-flight magazine to peruse the duty-free.

On cue, the engines cut out, tried to restart, spluttered fitfully to life, and stopped again.

This time for good.

'Will all passengers please adopt the brace position!' shouted Chardonnay as calmly as she could. In doing so, Rib sneaked a look at Doris, who was now sobbing uncontrollably. Chardonnay put an arm around her. 'C'mon kid, it'll be OK. We'll get through. Trust me.' This approach seemed to work better than the slap and Doris stopped crying. The cabin went eerily silent. Not a word was said, not even a prayer offered, as the bent-double passengers of Shuttle 495 put their faith in a captain called Peaches and a co-pilot named Ginger. All that could be heard was the whistling rush of air, as the craft plummeted like a stone towards the planet's surface. After what seemed like an eternity, a grinding noise came from the rear. Something mechanical opening, thought Rib. Wings? Flaps? Undercarriage? Almost immediately, the shuttle pulled out of freefall into a steep glide. Everyone screamed, but only for a second, on account of their stomachs touching their tonsils. The whole ship was now vibrating . Two metal studs pinged out from the cabin plating and landed on the floor between Rib's feet. The liberated rivets bounced up and down, dancing an Irish jig in celebration of their new-found freedom, before disappearing down a grating.

The shuttle juddered into a steep dive to the left. Someone a couple of rows back was being violently ill. Then another, this time across the aisle from Rib. He didn't notice. His eyes screwed tight, his hands clenched together behind his head, he whispered, 'This cannot be it. This cannot be it …'

An engine fired. The shuttle slowed and seemed to hold altitude. If only there were portholes, then they would get an idea of how far they were from the – BANG! They smacked down onto the tarmac and bounced twice before coming to a skidding halt at the very end of the runway. The forty nine passengers and two stewardesses of Shuttle 495 cheered, whooped, clapped their hands and cried with relief. All except the Armenian who was wondering how he was going to stand up with a trouserful of poop.

The intercom crackled. 'This is your captain speaking. We have now arrived at New Gatwick Airport. We apologise for the slight turbulence on today's flight. I am pleased to announce that we have arrived 15 minutes early due to our ... revised flight path.' Like hell, thought Rib. More like engine failure causing the thing to fall from the sky like a stone. 'Before leaving the shuttle, please make sure you remove all bags, coats personal possessions, domestic pets, livestock, firearms and children from the overhead lockers. On behalf of the flight crew, Co-pilot Yashimoto and I wish you a pleasant onward journey and look forward to seeing you aboard BrianAir again.'

'I should effing cocoa,' came the collective response of the crowd, now fighting its way to the exit. Rib waited until the last passenger had stumbled past him before he grabbed his bag and got up to leave. Chardonnay and Doris were standing at the top of the steps.

'Thank you for such a memorable flight,' he said.

'Our pleasure,' said Chardonnay with a fixed smile. 'Thank you for flying BrianAir.' Doris burst into tears and the older woman reverted to default mode, dealing her a resounding slap on the kisser.

Rib paused on the second step down to take in the scene spread before him. A number of passengers lay prostrate, kissing the ground. The pilots had somehow already disembarked and were now doing high fives with men in orange bodysuits, presumably the ground crew. Peaches put a hip flask to his lips and drank deeply before passing it to Ginger. They've earned that, thought Rib. Still standing on the steps, it took him a couple of seconds to take on board what was different. It was the air. He breathed deeply. It was so fresh and sharp that it cut into his lungs like a knife.

'Please move along, sir,' requested Chardonnay at his shoulder.

'Oh, sorry,' he mumbled as he carefully took the steps down to join the file of passengers heading towards the terminal building some hundred metres away.

The temperature was a warm twenty degrees Celsius. A light, south-westerly breeze drifted across the airfield at 2.7 knots. It was a beautiful day.

2

He sprinted to catch up with the guy at the back of the line. 'Hiya,' he said. The short, balding man with a walrus moustache returned the greeting with a grunt. Undeterred, Rib pressed on, 'How come the lasercraft didn't land on Tycho? Why did we have to risk our lives in that piece of shit?'

The walrus shrugged his shoulders. 'I dunno, just bloody glad we made it at all. Look over there ...' he added, pointing to some sort of enclosure at the far end of the runway. The glare of the bright sun combined with the heat shimmer made it difficult to see what the man was pointing at. Shielding his eyes, Rib worked his way around the perimeter of thick, lush woodland peppered by a few huts, until a low compound came into view. It struck him that, in the brief time he had been on the planet, the only structures he'd seen were wooden. What grabbed him, however, was not the construction of the compound, but its contents.

It was a scrapyard. Not a scrapyard filled with cars, mopeds, buses. It was a scrapyard piled high with space shuttles. Twisted wreckage. Mangled remains of miscarried missions. Rusting, broken hulks. Twenty or thirty of them. Maybe even more. His eyes were drawn to blackened gouges in the runway, about 50 metres to his right. Deep scars of countless crash landings. Shit, he whispered to himself.

'Just bloody glad we made it at all,' repeated the Walrus.

He was right. Somehow, they had survived where hundreds, maybe thousands hadn't. Why? Suddenly, Rib felt very tired. Too tired to think, too tired to stand. All he wanted to do was lie down on the tarmac, put his rucksack under his head as a pillow, and go to sleep for a year or two.

The sign on the terminal building read "Welcome to New Gatwick". On entering the vast wooden hangar, it became immediately clear that the place was anything but welcoming. The building bore closer resemblance to a refugee camp than an arrivals hall. More people were crammed in than Rib had ever seen gathered in one place before. He couldn't begin to guess how many, standing in queues waiting to be served food from huge trestle tables, lying on row upon row of crude timber beds, either sleeping or talking to neighbours, or standing in line for what appeared to be a medical station, a Red Cross flag hanging limp above its entrance. The subdued hum of the gloomy interior stood in such stark contrast to the bright world outside. Here it was humid, fetid, almost menacing. Wherever he looked, there were guards. Armed guards. Armed not with guns, but black truncheons, swinging from their belts. Welcoming it was not.

'Shuttle 495?' barked one of the uniformed men, this one armed with a clipboard. He waved Rib's group over to him.

A passenger at the front piped up, 'Excuse me! Where do we go to file a complaint? We have been subjected to what can only be described as appalling treatment. We have – '

The guard, whose yellow badge told the world he went by the name of Dirk van Vliet, raised his sizeable left palm to within an inch of the man's nose. 'Listen, you're here, yeah? You're here ... yeah? Did your ticket say First Class?'

The man shook his head.

'Did your ticket say Return Journey?'

He shook his head again.

'Did you read, understand and thereby agree to the small print of the booking terms and conditions?'

This time, they all shook their heads.

'So, you're here, yeah? Now move on!'

They all interpreted this to mean move on as in come to terms with it, get on with the rest of their lives. Dirk van Vliet meant move on as in get your arses out of the reception area where you're standing in the way. 'Move on!' he bellowed, pointing to a door marked "Immigration". This time they got the message and obeyed without a murmur.

The new arrivals pushed their way through the crowds to a doorway leading them into a narrow tunnel which sloped downwards about twenty five metres, until they came to a barrier, where an official told them to have their papers ready. One at a time, they were gestured forward to booths, where they were interrogated as to the purpose of their visit: whether they were a terrorist or not, whether they suffered from mental illness, whether they held a criminal record, whether they enjoyed regular bowel movements. Daunting as these questions were, the real challenge lay in your ability to keep both feet behind the thick white line as you stood at the head of the queue. If you so much as placed a toe on the line, a thick-set guy wielding a big stick appeared from nowhere to hurl oriental invective in your face until you stepped back. Which you did ...

Once over this hurdle, Rib joined another line, this time taking him along a narrow, upward-sloping tunnel. He had expected the next stage to be the customs check, followed by the arrivals hall, where he would run the gauntlet of a dozen unhappy-looking 57-year-old private taxi chauffeurs – all with their hair dyed boot-polish black – holding up a tatty piece of cardboard with a businessman's name written on it in scratchy blue felt-tip. If only.

What they faced at the top of the passage filled them with horror. They emerged out onto a mezzanine, where they stood dumfounded staring at the scene below. A massive hall, far larger than the first, stretched some hundred metres into the distance. Spread before them was a mass of humanity, shuffling forward inch by inch in one long, continuous line, snaking tightly back on itself to pack in as many people as possible. On closer look, the serpent was broken by areas where people were sleeping or eating, similar to the set-up in the first hall. What was totally different was the atmosphere. Here, it was almost totally silent. Every now and again, the deathly stillness was punctuated by a tannoy announcement or the cry of a child. Suddenly, just below them to the left, something was kicking off. Two guards were dragging a man out of the queue. A further two were restraining a woman, presumably his wife, who was struggling and screaming. After some thirty seconds, she too was led away, but in a different direction. Nobody moved a muscle to help them.

Rib was torn from this disturbing scene by a guard telling them to move along. An elderly woman at the front of their group asked him the question they all had on their lips but didn't dare to ask. 'How long will it take for us to reach the end of the queue?'

The guard laughed. 'Do you want the good news or the bad news?'

'The good news. We could do with some good news, for Christ's sake!'

'OK, OK. Keep your pinny on, Grandma. The good news is that it will take 72 hours.'

A gasp was all the woman could utter. Nobody wanted to hear what the bad news was, but they were going to hear it anyway, whether they liked it or not.

'And the bad news is ... that it could take a lot, lot longer,' he said with a grin.

'That's outrageous!' the eighty-year-old cried. 'We've travelled half way across the universe, crawled from the wreckage barely alive back there , and you're telling me that we've got to wait SEVENTY TWO BLOODY HOURS to get through Immigration?' she screamed in hysterics.

'Listen, lady ...' the guard leaned forward and looked her in the eye. Rib knew what was coming next and he was right. 'You're here, yeah?'

The message to all new arrivals was coming over loud and clear:

1. You are one of the privileged few members of the human race to have experienced Watershed and lived to tell the tale.

2. You are one of the privileged few members of the human race to have experienced the journey from Planet Earth to Planet Tycho and lived to tell the tale.

So shut the fuck up ...

3

How long had they been in the hall? He looked back to see how far they'd come. Twenty metres. Maybe twenty five at a push. What did it matter? It was slow. Painfully slow. Made worse by the heavy pall of foreboding that hung over the place. Back on Earth, a queue was a place where people struck up conversations, normally to moan about the reason for the queue in the first place. More often than not, such exchanges were uninvited, even unwelcome. But they represented some sort of spontaneous connection between members of the same species.

But not here. Men and women shuffled forward, avoiding eye contact, with vacant expressions on their faces. Couples, families, huddled together as if to seek protection against their new, alien environment. This place reminded him of somewhere, but he couldn't put his finger on it. Yet of one thing he was certain. This was not what he had expected. This was not what he had signed up for. This was not his new future, his new life. His thoughts served only to take him back to what he had left behind. Mum, the refuge, his mates. This wasn't helping at all.

What must have been an hour passed. Then another. They reached the first food and drink station. It was unbelievable how happy it made them all feel to reach this milestone. How many hours since they'd last eaten? And how many calories had the near-death shuttle flight taken out of them? And how many of them had emptied the contents of their stomachs on the floor of said rustbucket?

So, the basic fare of soup, sandwiches and water arrayed before them on large, rough-hewn trestle tables was nothing less than manna from heaven. Rib didn't realise how hungry he was. A scabby cat wouldn't have stood an earthly. And it all tasted so good. So very, very good – a rich lamb broth with beads of pearl barley at the bottom of the bowl, succulent chicken with crisp iceberg lettuce, sandwiched between two doorsteps of thick white bread, beakers of water, tasting as pure and clear as if newly drawn from a mountain stream. All served by three little girls, not one of them a day over ten, full of dimples, freckles and smiles.

'If any of you would like to rest for a while, you can lie down over here,' said one, pointing to a line of beds, each with a blue blanket folded neatly at its foot.

'Er, no thanks,' said Rib. 'But thanks, anyway.' He was confused. Nothing seemed to stack up. Tycho was one big contradiction after another: the sleek spacecraft against the death-trap shuttle; the fresh, clean air against the cloying atmosphere of the hangar; the cynical aggression of the guards against the innocent smiles of the children. Something wasn't right.

They merged back into the slow-moving queue, shuffling forward, shoulders hunched, barely a word between them. Within a matter of minutes the welcome break of the food station had faded into distant memory. The whole scene was surreal, a scene on a film-set where a long serpent of a thousand extras with no lines were waiting for a cue. Only there were no cameras, no director's chair, no make-up assistants. This was real all right. And yet something was nagging at the back of his mind. It wouldn't let him go. He wouldn't let it go. And when he finally dragged it up from the darkest, deepest recesses of his soul, he wished he hadn't.

Sweat began to pour from his brow. He looked around. Everything he saw confirmed his suspicions. The nightmare of all nightmares. A film. He had seen something like this in a film. At College. In History. What had set his mind racing? The man roughly escorted away by armed guards. A family separated. He swallowed hard. The Nazis. The Jews. The concentration camps. This was no new beginning at all. In fact the very opposite. He had to get out of there. And fast.

A big hand clamped onto his shoulder. 'Will you kindly come this way, sir?' The quasi-request came in a distinctly Afrikaans accent. Rib twisted and wrenched himself free and made a break for it. Straight into the arms of two waiting gorillas, who wasted no time in restraining him, one by means of an arm lock, the other a crunching headlock. Struggle as he might, he couldn't move a muscle.

'Let me go you bastards!' he swore as they forced him down into a bent-double position.

'Sir, it is in your interests not to resist,' said the guard who was squeezing his head as if it were a lemon. Rib refused to co-operate and made it as difficult as possible for his captors to manhandle him over to a door marked "Shower Block H". On seeing this, Rib redoubled his efforts to kick and bite his way free, but to no avail. The guards bundled him through the now open doorway and dumped him without ceremony onto the floor. He lay there, breathless, face down. He heard the heavy door slam shut. Not prepared to give up without a fight, he flipped himself on to his feet in a backwards somersault and swivelled on the balls of his feet to face his assailants.

They were nowhere to be seen. He whipped round

again to make sure they were not behind him. They had disappeared. To his astonishment, he was totally alone. Totally alone in Shower Block H. This could mean only one thing. He sprinted to the door. It was locked. There was no handle on the inside. There was no way out. He stood with his back pressed against the door, gulping in air. The only sound was his heart trying to hammer its way out of his ribcage.

He was in a short corridor, no more than ten metres long. There was no sign of showerheads, no tell-tale whiff of gas. In fact, it looked nothing like a gas chamber at all. Thickly carpeted, the corridor was painted in a pleasant matt light-blue eggshell colour and decorated with colourful Impressionist prints. This was becoming even more surreal, he thought. In a matter of moments he had moved from Schindler's List to Alice in Wonderland. He sidled cautiously along one of the walls, hoping the door at the end would not begin to shrink before his eyes. Should he knock? Don't be stupid! Jannes and Piet were probably on their tea-break on the other side ready to resume their kick-shit-out-of-the-kid-routine at the slightest provocation. This door did have a handle, which he turned gingerly and pulled. It wasn't locked. It opened without a sound and he stepped through, bracing himself against attack.

He was met with a smile from a six-foot tall African woman of indescribable beauty. She glided over to him, carrying in one hand a silver tray with two glasses on it. She leaned forward and kissed him on both cheeks. Her scent was intoxicating. He looked into her eyes, tried to say something, but couldn't. She gave him one of the drinks. It was champagne.

'Welcome to Tycho, Master Meskitoe,' she said.

4

When he learned from the tall beauty that he had been singled out as a Priority Landing Passenger, courtesy of High Commodore Zeta Meskitoe, he exploded. 'Where is she? I want to see her! Now!'

'I am afraid the High Commodore is not available to welcome you in person,' said the African woman, Uzuri, who listened patiently as the boy standing before her ranted and raged, cursing at his grandmother for giving him preferential treatment.

He was seething. How dare she presume without even asking him? This was his new life. A new life based on new terms, not family favours. What sort of person did she think he was, leaving his fellow travellers behind, consigned to days of purgatory in that shithole of an immigration hall?

Uzuri listened calmly, allowing him to give full vent to his anger. Then she said softly, 'Rib. May I call you Rib?'

He mumbled yes. It was difficult to say no to someone so amazingly attractive.

'I can understand how you are feeling, but let me assure you that High Commodore Meskitoe wanted only to help. She wanted to be absolutely sure that you would arrive on Tycho safe and sound and that your onward journey would go smoothly. That's all.'

'Safe and sound!' Rib scoffed. 'Does she know how

close we were to being wiped out on that shitbucket of a shuttle?'

Uzuri took a deep breath. 'I need to tell you that Captain Bannister and Flight Lieutenant Yashimoto are among the finest in our fleet. They were removed from active service duty to fly your shuttle, Shuttle 495, on the specific orders of the High Commodore. As I said, she only has your interests at heart.' She paused. 'Now, would you like to taste this champagne? It's Bollinger. I think you'll like it.'

'No, I wouldn't like to taste the champagne and no, I wouldn't like it!' he snapped back.

'That's fine,' she said quietly, putting the tray down on a side table. 'Am I to understand that you wish to rejoin the line in the Immigration Hall? Guards Heynckes and De Boor are standing the other side of that door awaiting further instruction. The High Commodore was very specific that the choice had to be yours. So, Rib, the choice is yours. A sip of champagne or a kicking in the corridor. What's it to be?'

'Well,' faltered Rib. 'If you put it like that ... I am feeling a little thirsty.'

***

The stagecoach journey to Stonyville took almost two days. Just forty hours. But to the young passenger squeezed in between his fellow travellers in the six-horse Wells Fargo wagon, it seemed as if he were crossing ten time zones.

The seven other new arrivals in the carriage spent the first six hours of the trip sharing horror stories of long waits and bad treatment at Immigration.

'We had to wait over seventy hours, didn't we Henry?' wailed the thin woman dressed in green sat next to Rib.

'Seventy? Who's the lucky one? We were there for five days, weren't we, Charlie? Five whole days!' countered the fat woman in pink sat by the window.

Rib's VIP status as Priority Landing Passenger had swept him through in two hours forty-seven minutes. Including a champagne break. He decided not to share this piece of information with the rest of the carriage. Instead, he spent the journey looking out of the window as the stagecoach bumped its way northwards, rocking from side to side along rutted tracks. An unfamiliar landscape of pastures and cornfields, lazy rivers and rolling hills flashed by as he tried to adjust to his new surroundings. All he really knew about Tycho was that it was an exact clone of his own planet. But surely Earth could never have been like this? They passed through small settlements, where people came out of their houses to wave. Some threw their hats in the air. They made a stop at a place called Kingston to change horses.

'Be back on the coach in half an hour,' said the driver, who went by the name of Zeke, without giving them any clue where they could get something to eat or go for a leak. Zeke headed off into 'The Frontier Hotel', an imposing three-storey wooden building. The passengers followed.

Rib stood for a few seconds, shielding his eyes against the sharp rays of the sun. A couple of lacklustre stretches did little to ease his stiff limbs. Down the main street – and there appeared to be only one – a horse stood tethered to a rail outside a ramshackle bar with a large sign over the door saying "The Gold Nugget". Opposite it, a more substantial building declaring itself in formal lettering to be the First National Bank. A single, dusty street, lined by wooden buildings, each with a boardwalk and an awning over the windows. No sign of life, save the sporadic sound of muffled laughter coming from The Gold Nugget. He managed a surreptitious pee behind a tree. He needn't have worried – the place was deserted. There was no-one to see him. It was a one-horse town. He was keen to be first back to the stagecoach, so that he could claim his window seat. When the others returned, more than one had the smell of alcohol on their breath.

Zeke was joined up front by a grizzly-looking guy. The sort of guy you wouldn't cross.

'Zak will be riding shotgun for the rest of the trip, folks,' said Zeke.

Shotgun? I didn't see any shotgun, thought Rib.

Shadows lengthened as they raced through open countryside. Dark hedgerows scraped against the side of the coach where the road narrowed. Zeke pressed his team of horses on with a crack of the whip and shouts of 'Yaar! Yaar!' It was almost dark when they stopped again, this time an overnight stay at a roadside rest place. Zeke led them to a long, single-storey cabin which he called a bunkhouse. He pointed out the location of latrines and mess hall before hotfooting it to the bar, accompanied by Zak.

Once they'd dumped their bags on beds in the bunkhouse, the travel-weary group made a beeline for the mess hall, where they joined a line at the food counter. The thin woman dressed in black, who hadn't said a word through the entire trip, elbowed her way in front of Rib. She had been drinking, he reckoned. Her turn came and she stood, swaying slightly, ready to place her order with the gawky, gap-toothed boy wearing a blue and yellow checked shirt behind the counter. A chalkboard propped up against a drum of cooking oil advertised soup and a roll at a price of ten dollars, which seemed extremely reasonable.

'What's the soup?' the thin woman slurred.

'Clam chowder,' said the boy.

The thin woman recoiled in disgust. 'I'm a vegetarian. Do you not have anything else?'

'Don't you eat fish? Clam is a kind of shellfish.'

'I know perfectly well that a clam is a kind of shellfish, thank you. And no, I do not eat fish.'

'I could grate some cheese over it for you?' offered the boy, in a misjudged attempt to be helpful.

The woman gave him an incredulous stare. 'No, that would not work at all! It would still be clam wouldn't it? Just do me a roll with some grated cheese and that will have to do.'

The boy paused, playing over in his mind what he had to say next. He pointed at the chalkboard. 'Sorry, ma'am. We don't do cheese rolls. We only do clam chowder and a roll.' He paused again. 'Ten dollars.'

It was the ten-dollar straw which broke the camel's back. The thin woman let out a gurgling cry, stomped round the counter and grabbed a large chef's knife from the chopping board. The boy, named Seth, flinched with fear, taking protective hold of his gonads. Miss Ginsoak did nothing more, however, than hack herself a hefty chunk of cheddar, help herself to a roll and stride over to a table in the far corner of the mess hall, where she sat glowering out of the window.

Seth opened his mouth to ask her for the ten dollars. He felt a hand on his arm.

Rib shook his head at him. 'Don't …'

The clam chowder was good. Very good. Simple, natural ingredients cooked perfectly. By the time Rib had mopped up the last drop from his bowl, it was dark outside. He was shattered and decided to turn in. Easier said than done. The cavernous bunkhouse was lit only by a single lamp just inside the entrance, so he had to grope and fumble his way down to his bunk right at the far end. Having stubbed his toe against at least three beds, to the clear annoyance of their occupants, he finally felt the familiar shape of his bag and stowed it under the bed. Not being a great one for taking his clothes off in public, even in the dark, he climbed straight in. The roughness of the coarse blanket against his cheek was the last thing that registered before he dived down a hundred fathoms into a deep, black sleep.

5

The wart-crusted hand of Shotgun Zak shook him hard by the shoulder. 'Wakey-wakey! Hands off cocks, on socks! We leave in two minutes,' he added as he strode out of the bunkhouse.

'My hand wasn't on my cock and I've already got my socks on,' muttered Rib, blinking in the sharp sunlight shafting through the window. He threw off the blanket, catapulted out of bed, went over on his ankle, lay in a crumpled heap on the floor and said shit six times.

Not only was he last on board the stagecoach, he was clearly late, confirmed by the overt display of sighing, tut-tutting and raising of the eyes to the heavens by his co-travellers. He was forced to squeeze in beside Miss Ginsoak, who had already dropped off and became seriously, seriously annoyed at being awoken before the coach had even started. Zeke cracked the reins with a 'Yaar! Yaar!', the team of horses sprang forward and the stagecoach jolted out of town leaving a trail of dust in its wake.

Reluctant to engage in eye contact, Rib gazed out of the window at the landscape rolling by. At times thick forest, then meadows filled with red, yellow and blue flowers, open heaths covered with prickly-looking bushes, then back to dense, lush woodland again. Such a different world from the dense, steaming rainforests he'd left behind.

Mid-morning, it was under the cool canopy of such a wood that Zeke deftly steered the horses to a halt in the middle of a ford, which crossed a fast-running river. The team clearly relished the ice-cold water cooling their hot hooves and pranced in appreciation.

'Whoa, boys, whoa!' soothed Zeke, jumping down from his seat to go amongst them, stroking and whispering horse-talk words of affection. He had lived with them for five years and loved them more dearly than he had ever loved any two-legged critter.

The critters of the two-legged variety did little to improve his view of the human race as they tried to disembark the coach.

'Why have we stopped here? I'll get my feet wet!'

'That figures,' said Zeke. 'It's a river.'

'Drive forward, my man! You can't expect us to get out here!'

'I stop here for the comfort of my horses, not you. The wagon is staying put. If you don't want to get out, don't get out.'

Rib needed no encouragement to get out. He took off his shoes and socks, splashed over to a boulder, where he sat with his feet dangling in the cool current. Zak came round with a wicker hamper containing muffins and smoked-ham sandwiches. A number of the party turned their noses up at such basic fare, but Rib woofed his down and said yes please when the man named Shotgun offered a reload. As he polished off his second blueberry muffin, he gazed upstream at the babbling weir, the source of the currents and eddies swirling round his feet. He wondered what kind of fish swam there and how big they were. Again, he was the last to take his seat when it was time to go. He didn't want to leave and, as the horses climbed the incline back onto the highway, he wondered whether one day he would ever find his way back to that beautiful spot.

Conversation in the stagecoach was sporadic. Rib did not take part, but couldn't help keeping one ear open to the polite exchanges. The entertainment came soon after they had changed horses at a settlement named Aylesbury. The fake-tanned man called Clive addressed his wife so loudly that it was clearly meant to be heard by all present.

'At least we managed to get in our holiday of a lifetime before all this bloody Watershed business kicked off.'

This was a cue for someone to ask him where they had gone on their holiday of a lifetime. Nobody did.

Undeterred, Clive confirmed. 'Oh, you should have seen the food and drink. It was an all-inclusive package deal, so we didn't have to pay for anything once we were there. Everything you needed was on the resort. Of course there were excursions to World Heritage Sites of Special Interest and all that sort of thing, but they cost extra. No, we had all we needed on the resort, didn't we, Bev?'

'Mmm,' Bev nodded.

'And the buffet! You could fill your plate up and go back for as much as you wanted, couldn't you, Bev?'

His lard-arsed wife, clearly the type to pile the plate high, nodded again. Clive looked around the carriage and paused, preparing to deliver the climax of his thrilling travelogue.

'I'd recommend Fuck-It to anyone!' he said.

Miss Ginsoak had appeared to be fast asleep throughout. Without opening an eye, she said, 'I think you'll find it's pronounced Phu-Ket.'

And that was the final word on the subject. Indeed, the last word to be spoken at all for the remainder of the journey.

(Appearances can be deceptive: the thin old woman had once enjoyed an illustrious career as conductor of the Halle Orchestra, had sponsored from her own personal funds the building and running of a school in a poverty-stricken African village and won a silver medal in the luge in the 2006 Winter Olympics. She lost everything in Watershed: her husband, Derek, her three beloved children, Sam, Harry and Fiona, and her twelve cats. So she had every excuse for opening a fresh bottle of Plymouth Gin at 5:30 each morning. And had Rib Meskitoe known this, he would have been thoroughly ashamed of taking her for an ill-tempered, drunken old shrew.)

6

The sun was sinking fast as they pulled into the town called Stonyville, their final destination. The travel-weary, buttock-bruised occupants of the stagecoach climbed out, collected their bags and followed Zak into a less-than-grand-looking building declaring itself to be The Grand Hotel. All except Rib were staying there and they formed a queue to check in.

Shotgun tapped him on the arm. 'Mr Meskitoe?'

'Yes.'

'You're staying at the Waterloo, over the road, Flat 3,' and handed him a piece of wood with a key attached. The piece of wood had "Flat 3" burned into it. Rib held it in his hand and stared at it as if it were the key to the meaning of life.

Zak broke the spell by picking up his bag. 'You see the building over there? The one with Waterloo Brewing Co. on the front? The entrance is the door on the right. You go up two flights of stairs and your room is at the top. It's got a three written on the door.'

'Thanks,' said Rib, took his bag and set off across the street.

'Whoa! Hold on a second!' Zak darted into the hotel and re-appeared holding a lamp. 'Here, you'll need this.'

'Thanks,' said Rib, taking the lamp from him.

'And remember to turn it off when you go to bed,' were Zak's parting words.

'OK, thanks again.'

Zak hopped back up onto the stagecoach and walked the team along the road some fifty metres before turning left and disappearing from sight. Presumably the stables were somewhere around the back of the hotel.

Rib stood in the empty street, wondering how the hell he would turn the lamp off. He decided to save that one for later and walked across the road. There were no lights on in the Waterloo Brewing Co., but he found the entrance easily enough. Negotiating the two unlit flights of bare wooden stairs up to the top floor was harder, scraping his bag against the walls and almost tripping over twice. How he managed to keep the lamp steady was a miracle. He unlocked the door, stepped inside and put the lamp on a table in the middle of the room. Flat 3 was big. Massive compared to the citidome pods he'd been used to. In the half-light cast by the oil lamp, he could make out a bench, two more chairs, a bed, a wardrobe and what seemed to be a kitchen area. A large set of French windows opened out onto a balcony above the street.

Time for bed, he yawned. He'd explore tomorrow. There was a chipped, white enamel jug of water on the table and he carefully poured half into a bowl, also of chipped, white enamel. He ferreted around in his holdall for far too long until he found his wash bag, then went through the motions of splashing water on his face and brushing his teeth – the armpits could wait until tomorrow. Sleep foremost in his mind, he undressed and slipped into bed. He closed his eyes. He opened them again, staring at the flame from the lamp on the table.

'Shit,' he muttered as he climbed out of bed. 'How the hell do you put this thing out?' He sat down on one of the chairs to get a better look. There was a small wheel sticking out from the base of the lamp. This must be it. He gave it a full clockwise turn. The flame flared up, half-blinding him in the process. 'Shit, shit!' he swore, jumping up and knocking the half-full jug off the table, soaking his left leg. 'Shit!' he swore again as the flame was now smoking with menace, blackening one side of the glass. He gave the wheel another turn, this time the other way. The wick went down. The flame went out. The room went dark. Rib Meskitoe crawled back into bed feeling like he'd wet himself.

7

The bright sunlight streaming through the windows told him it was morning. He had slept deeply and soundly. The upturned jug and water stain on the floor reminded him of where he was. Sitting up in bed, he slowly surfaced into the world of the living. The previous night's first impressions had been right. It was a large room, plainly furnished, with a blue-check tablecloth (wet) to match the blue-check ceiling-to-floor curtains fluttering at the French windows. He must have forgotten to close them. He got out of bed, stood unsteadily for a second or two, ignoring the protests from his legs: 'Why don't you get back into bed?' they pleaded.

The keen freshness of the morning air drew him out onto the balcony. The first thing that struck him was how high up he was, having completely forgotten the previous night's perilous ascent. From the balcony of Flat 3, you could see the entire length of the town's main street, most of which was still in shadow, broken only by criss-cross strips of early sunlight asserting themselves through the gaps in the buildings. Being so high up, the balcony was already bathed in the brightness of the new day, forcing Rib to shield his eyes to take further stock of his new surroundings. Directly opposite stood the Grand Hotel, still sleeping. There was no sign of life anywhere along the wide dusty road.

He had no idea of the time, but it must be really early. Really, really early. Maybe he should go back to bed?

He took one last lungful of cool clean air before going back into the half-darkness of the flat. Time to explore, he said to himself, looking forward with a real sense of excitement to seeing what was out there. A new life. His new life ...

A wash and dental hygiene session was off the menu on account of the empty white enamel jug on the floor. He picked it up and put it back on the table. He ran his tongue round the front of his top set of teeth, gave his armpit a scratch, threw on his clothes, pulled on his boots and stepped out onto the landing, closing the heavy wooden door quietly behind him. He tiptoed down the wooden stairs, trying to make as little noise as possible, through the vestibule and out onto the street. To be precise, out onto the raised boardwalk, which seemed to be a common feature at the front of all the buildings. One look at the deep ruts in the dry road gave him a clue as to the need for such walkways – in the rainy season, the street must be a mudbath.

Which way to go first? The Waterloo was located half way along the main street, which he later found out was called Main Street. There was no street sign. There didn't need to be. It was the only main street in town. Rib turned his gaze back in the direction from which they'd entered Stonyville the night before. At the very outskirts, the road climbed a hill on which stood a white wooden church with a spire. Hill-walking did not appeal at such an early hour, so he elected left instead. But before he set off, he wanted to get a better look at the place where he was lodging and stepped off the boardwalk out into the street. He looked up at his balcony on the top floor, followed it down a level to a similar balcony on the first floor, nailed to which was a big sign with "Waterloo Brewing Co." burned in large black lettering. Below that, a canvas awning covering the boardwalk. At street level, shuttered windows ran the whole width of the frontage. A sign hanging from the inside of the door said Closed.

A cool breeze blew straight down Main Street, still empty of life. Somewhere, a dog barked. Footsteps on the boardwalk would make too much noise, draw attention to him, which he didn't want. So he risked the ruts of the road. Dust and grit crunched beneath his feet as he set off along the street. On the corner of the first block he stopped to look in the window of the Stonyville Trading Post. The display, if that was the right word, was a jumble of brushes, shovels, mousetraps, pots and pans, rope coils, candles and a number of cartons bearing a skull and crossbones label. In all his life, he had never touched – let alone used – a single one of those items in the window, except a less-than-successful recent encounter with an enamel jug. He moved on.

Across the street, next to the Grand Hotel, was a two-storey building painted black. Above the door in silver letters was painted "Sheriff". Sheriff as in Sheriff? wondered Rib, stepping into bright sunlight as he crossed the intersect. Looking down the side street to his right, he could pick out a few shops, all shuttered. After a couple of blocks, they gave way to an open tract of scrubby wasteland. Beyond that stood a long low building, the sun in his eyes preventing him from making out what it was. He continued down Main Street, now back in the cool shade, passing a clothes store, followed by a saloon bar with the strange name of The Florence. Over the road he noticed the Stonyville Bank and, from the shop next to that – Bettina's Buns – came the unmistakeable, tantalising aroma of bread being baked. At least someone else was up. Rib couldn't help a licking of the lips. He passed more shuttered shop-fronts until he reached the edge of town, where

Main Street narrowed into a raised causeway, barely a wagon's width across. The road dog-legged to the right, disappearing from view behind the block at the very end of town. For some reason, he felt more than curious to see what lay around the corner and upped his pace. When he reached the last building, a barber's, he stopped and gasped in amazement. The causeway curved round another hundred metres before crossing a wide river over a stone bridge, where it then climbed up a steep hill on the far bank. But what made Rib's jaw drop was not the fast-flowing river sparkling bright in the morning sun, not the beautiful three-arched bridge with turreted passing places, not the sheep-dotted meadows to the left of the causeway flanked by weeping willows. What smacked his gob was the enormous structure which reared up from behind the buildings on Main Street to span the river some fifty metres downstream from the stone bridge. It looked for all the world like a huge, rickety roller-coaster, a colossal construction of timber trestles, tiers, spans and struts somehow meshed together to form a megalithic climbing frame of a bridge. It was as if a giant had spent twenty years of his life painstakingly gluing together twenty thousand logs to make the biggest matchstick structure in the world.

Did Tycho have its own Seven Wonders? If it did, this must be one of them, he thought, and broke into a run. He just had to get a closer look. In no time, he was standing on the stone bridge. The river carried a cool breeze which said hello to his hair. He leant on the parapet, drinking in the monster bridge. It was simply awesome. Unable to take his eyes away from the colossal structure, a number of competing questions battled in his brain. What sort of bridge was it? How many men had it taken to build it? How on earth did they put it all together? How on earth did it all stay together?

Further examination gave him the answer to the first question. On the opposite side of the river, the bridge butted against the hillside some twenty metres up from the bank. He could clearly make out a single track which climbed up and over the hill. It was a railway! His eyes followed the track in the other direction back towards the town. Through a gap in the trees, he could see how the track ran in a dead straight line parallel to Main Street behind the buildings he had just walked past – the bakery, the saloon, the bank – to the point where it came to the long, low building he had spotted before. That must be a railway terminal or depot, he thought. Another insistent woodpecker of a question tapped away at his brain. If Stonyville has a north-south railway running through it, why the hell had he sat for the best part of two days in a bone-breaking stagecoach?

A loud swishing sound from behind made him duck down beneath the parapet, from where he craned his neck skyward to see two swans fly over the bridge. On the other side, they swooped down to skim the surface before disappearing under the middle trestle of the wooden bridge in an impressive aerobatic display. The sudden appearance of the swans was a call to action. Smoke now rose above the roofs from the town's chimney pots. Stonyville was stirring. He should probably be heading back …

Shutters were being pulled back, awnings unfurled, boardwalks swept. And there were people on the street. It was as if the whole town had been holding its breath, waiting for him to pass, before coming to life.

The first guy he approached greeted him with a broad smile.

'Hiya,' said Rib.

'Howdee,' said the man.

An elderly lady brushing the frontage of her shop looked up to acknowledge him.

'Howdee,' said Rib.

'Good morning,' she returned.

A man trotted out from a side street on a light-brown horse with a white mane.

'Good morning,' said Rib.

'Hiya,' said the man. Saying hello in Stonyville was like playing scissor-paper-stone and losing every time. But people seemed friendly enough.

By the time he made it back to the Waterloo, Main Street was buzzing. Now it felt OK to use the boardwalks. In fact, the increasing horse traffic made it unwise to do otherwise, carts and wagons carrying cargo of all kinds: bales of hay, sacks of grain, logs, more logs. He grabbed the door handle to the entrance hall, but instead of going in, paused to look at a crowd gathered some thirty metres down the street. He decided to check it out. The neighbouring property to the Waterloo, a liquor store, announced itself as Diamond Dan's by way of a large playing card propped up against the door. Next to that was a small square, slightly set back from the main drag. In the middle stood two stone horse-troughs. Behind them, a wooden hoarding covered with printed sheets of paper. That was where the crowd was, reading articles pinned to the wall. Every now and then, a shout would go up and a huddle would press forward to one section of the wall. Someone burst out laughing, another swore and stormed off down the street. It certainly seemed to be the place where the townspeople of Stonyville came together early of a morning. Behind the wall, a large shed stretched back quite some way. The middle double-doors were open and he could just make out people setting out stands and market stalls in the dark interior. A few tables spilled out onto the square, where coffee and pastries were being served by a girl in a red-checked dress.

The aroma of the coffee said good morning to his saliva glands and he was sorely tempted to sit down and order something for breakfast. No, said his sensible side, you haven't even checked in yet. How do I check in? he asked his sensible side. I don't know, it said, but there's bound to be a clue back in the flat. Sounds sensible, reasoned Rib, and he strode purposefully back past Diamond Dan's. Ah! The Waterloo's shutters were now open. That was promising. Maybe there'd be someone there he could ask. He stepped into the lobby and was halfway up the first flight of stairs when he heard his name being called.

'Mr Meskitoe?'

The voice was deep and hoarse. A voice of a man who sounded as if he gargled with gravel. 'Mr Meskitoe?' the gravel gargled again. Rib turned to look down at the owner of the voice. All he could see was the silhouette of a man, a big man, blocking out most of the sunlight in the lobby.

'Mr Meskitoe?' came the third time of asking.

'Oh – er, sorry, yes,' said Rib stepping back down the stairs.

He was met with a huge outstretched freckled hand which shook his in an iron grip.

'Todd. Sunset Todd. I'm the landlord. Pleased to meet you.'

'Oh – er, howdee … hiya … good morning,' spluttered Rib as he withdrew his crushed hand to the safety of a pocket.

'Breakfast?'

Breakfast sounded great. 'Breakfast sounds great,' he said, following the big man named Todd through the entrance door to the Waterloo, a saloon which bore no resemblance to any bar he'd seen before. The dominant feature was the bar itself, running the whole length of the room. It was made out of some sort of metal, hammered into shape and polished to a fine shine.

'Ah, I see you're admiring my pride and joy, then.'

'Yeah. It's brilliant. What's it made of?'

'Copper,' said Sunset. 'Managed to salvage it, and a few other bits and bobs from, you know, the final days...'

The beauty of the bar stood in stark contrast to the dire state of the other furniture: two large brown leather sofas, both ripped with springs sticking out; bar stools, some dozen in all, every single one with chipped chrome pedestals on which perched black vinyl cushions, again all ripped open to reveal dirty yellow foam. From the ceiling hung an array of flagons and glasses.

The man named Sunset seemed to read Rib's thoughts. 'Did me best to save what I could. And the trip was a bit on the ... hairy side,' he added.

'Tell me about it.' Rib followed the shuffling figure of the landlord round the far end of the bar.

'Time for the guided tour later,' he said, pointing to a large wooden trestle table in the far corner which had been set for breakfast. 'Take a pew,' he offered, before disappearing into what smelled and sounded like a kitchen – sizzles and spits from a pan, coffee bubbling in a pot, toast toasting. On the table stood salt and pepper cellars, a tube of mustard and a large red plastic tomato. Rib picked it up and nearly dropped it when a hatch flew open to reveal his landlord's unshaven face.

'Careful with that, boy, it's a genuine antique. Nicked it from the Wimpy Bar in Wood Green High Road when I was a kid. Those were the days – days I'll always remember. Don't squeeze on it too hard, or you'll have the ceiling covered in ketchup,' he laughed.

'OK,' said Rib, carefully returning the loaded tomato to the table.

The landlord had withdrawn back into the kitchen. 'I notice you've already taken a morning constitutional,' he shouted, 'so I hope you've got the appetite for a Full English?'

'Great, thanks!' shouted Rib, having no idea what a Full English was.

'How do you like your eggs?'

'Er, whatever's easy for you.'

'Easy it is, then.'

'Thanks,' said Rib, mystified.

'Tea or coffee?'

'Erm, a cup of tea would be great.'

'Right you are. I'll boil the tea and put some more toast on. Mind if I join you?'

'Of course not.'

He soon appeared carrying an oval plate on which was piled what Rib realised to be a Full English: blackened pork sausages, crispy back bacon, tomatoes, baked beans, two fried eggs, a round black slice of something, fried potatoes and toast. It didn't touch the sides. Must have ranked amongst the best breakfasts he'd ever had.

'Well done, my son,' said the big man, taking his plate. 'Any more?'

'No, I couldn't possibly, Mr Todd,' said Rib.

'Call me Sunset, son,' he said on his way out to the kitchen. He turned in the doorway. 'I don't mean, call me Sun-Set-Sun. That would make me sound like a South Korean footballer, wouldn't it?' This brought on a wheezing fit of coughing which went on for a good twenty seconds as he busied himself noisily with the pots and pans in the galley.

Suddenly, Rib needed to pee. 'Excuse me, Sunset. Could you tell me where the toilet is?'

'Follow the bar round back to where we came in. The door with Bogey on it is the gents.'

A toilet door with a bogey on it? How disgusting was that! Rib got up from the table and walked back into the main saloon. Behind the bar was a glass window, through which he could see a collection of huge metal vats with dials and taps. This must be where the brewing goes on. He wanted to linger but the need to pee was now paramount and he hurried towards two doors at the far end of the room, each covered with a life-size black and white poster. On the left door, a picture of a buxom blonde stood over a grating trying to stop her skirt from billowing up, and on the right door, a photo of a gangster type with a suit too large for him and a cigarette hanging from the corner of his mouth. That one must be the gents, he decided.

The first thing he noticed as he entered was that someone had left a heap of grass and dried leaves on the floor. That came as a surprise, because the rest of the establishment, come to think of it, was spotless. His body told him that it needed a poo too and he squatted on the pedestal. Being a boy, he could only concentrate on one thing at a time. After five minutes of intense effort, his gaze fell on a sign pinned to the wall:

"PLEASE DEPOSIT THE ARSEGRASS IN THE BIN PROVIDED. DO NOT FLUSH THE ARSEGRASS DOWN THE TOILET."

S. Todd. Proprietor

Arsegrass? What's arsegrass? He then noticed another, smaller sign above the heap of grass and dried leaves. It read: "ARSEGRASS". Rib groaned out loud as the realisation dawned that he had to wipe his bum on this stuff. He did his best, which wasn't very good. He swore to himself that he would be rationing his bowel movements from now on in.

Back in the dining area, Sunset was nibbling on a piece of toast. 'Mmm. God bless raspberry jam. Can I get you some?'

'Thanks, but no thanks,' said Rib, his appetite dulled by the arsegrass episode.

'How did you find your room?' asked Sunset between mouthfuls.

'Oh, it's fine. It's great,' said Rib, wondering whether now was the time to own up about the jug. Maybe later ...

'There's a board coming loose up in the ceiling, but apart from that I think you'll find it's in good order.'

'No, it's fine, just fine. And I really like the balcony.'

'Yes, you're right there, my son. Nothing better than sitting up there lazing on a summer's afternoon with a pint in your hand watching the world go by.'

The reference to a pint turned Rib's thoughts to the large vats he'd seen behind the screen. 'Do you brew all your beer here?'

Sunset seemed pleased to be asked. 'Yes I do, as a matter of fact. All with my own fair hand. Learnt my trade in Belgium where I served my apprenticeship in the Artois Brewery. Specialise in IPA's, blondes, stouts and barley wines. What's your tipple?'

'Er ... I'm easy,' said Rib, not really understanding the question.

'Well, I can see that we are going to have to give you a tasting session later, then,' Sunset laughed. He then went all serious. 'Now, down to serious talk for one moment. You plan to stay for one month, is that correct? And thank you for forwarding the deposit in advance. Duly appreciated. I have to take a deposit, you understand, for breakages ...'

Poop, the water jug, thought Rib.

'... but you seem a trustworthy lad, so I'm sure there won't be a problem on that front. Do you have any ideas what your plans are, going forward?'

'Well,' faltered Rib, 'I'd like to take it one step at a time. You see, back on Earth I had a bit of a ... traumatic ... experience, and ...'

Sunset raised a hand to interrupt. 'OK, let's stop right there. None of my business to ask in the first place. We've all got our history. We've all got our past. Now, if you'll excuse me, I've got a row of raspberry canes that requires my undivided attention. Why don't we meet up this afternoon in the bar and I'll let you sample the wares, OK?'

'Yeah, that sounds great. I'll look forward to that.'

'Good! That's settled, then. Now, down to practicalities. There's a Market Hall just along the street and you've got your own kitchen in the flat. Just let me know if you need anything.'

'Thanks.' Rib stood up to leave the table. 'And thanks again for the breakfast. By the way, what was that round, black thing? It tasted good.'

'Ah, that was the black pudding. As everything else, locally sourced. You've never had it before?'

Rib shook his head.

'So you don't know where it comes from?'

Another shake of the head.

Sunset paused. 'I'll tell you later.' With a grunt, he got up and walked over to the kitchen door. Just as he was about to disappear, he turned round in the doorway and scratched his head. 'Just one more question.'

'Yeah?'

Sunset smirked. 'How did you get on with the arsegrass?'

8

Arsegrass ...

Rib smiled to himself as he looked back on his first two weeks in Stonyville. It seemed an age since he alighted from the stagecoach and saw the town for the first time. Then, his first impression was that he'd ended up on a Wild West film set. And, in a way, that still held true. It looked, felt and smelled like the Wild West. It had cowboys, horses, wagons, rodeos and the street architecture was so High Noon. But there the similarity stopped. There were:

- No gunfights
- No lynchings
- No gold in them thar hills
- No bank hold-ups
- No cheroot-smoking stranger riding into town
- No Enrico Morricone soundtracks
- No bar brawls (well, not many ...)

In fact, it was more Mild West than Wild West.

But for a fifteen-year-old ready to make his mark, eager to plough his furrow, willing to wet his whistle, Stonyville was the perfect place to be. A true frontier town, packed with pioneering spirit. At every turn there was a dollar to be made, a deal to be cut. The townsfolk were welcoming, open and friendly. That's not to say that the living was in any way easy. People led tough, physical lives. They worked hard, they played hard. Which meant that sometimes there was an unpredictable edginess about the place, but that made it all the more exciting. Most importantly for Rib, he felt safe in Stonyville.

After the month-long period of recuperation from the near-fatal crossbow wound from Besk on the balcony of his Mum's animal refuge, it had been time for a heart-to-heart. Both he and his Mum knew that he couldn't stay, much as he loved her and the place. He'd already run away from home once and, this time, he wanted to be open with her. He was surprised how receptive she was to the idea of him taking off again. He hadn't expected that. What she didn't tell him was that she harboured serious concerns about his future safety on the citidome. She didn't believe for one moment that Besk had been alone and dreaded the moment when one or more of his associates might be knocking on the door looking for her son. So she readily agreed to him joining the Exodus to Tycho. Of course, neither of them knew the dangers of the journey ahead, or he would never have taken the ride. The Protectorate had its reasons for keeping the new planet shrouded in a cloak of secrecy.

Rib had also been more than happy for his Mum to take the responsibility for the bulk of the two hundred million dollars he'd received from his Gran. Naturally, he never told her where he'd really got it from. They both remained content with the lottery win version of events, sharing an unspoken pact not to dig more deeply. Alice Meskitoe had friends she could trust and, having secured the future of the refuge, the funds were spread in a number of safe havens.

And so it was that Rib Meskitoe ended up in Flat 3 on the second floor of the Waterloo Brewing Co.

9

Opening hours were 12pm to 9pm. Pints served till 8:45, growlers till 8:59. Nowhere was to be seen a notice stating this. People just knew. Sunset certainly did, and he was strict about it, too. 'All right boys, let's roll,' was the closing-time call, and the boys invariably rolled without a murmur.

Occasionally, a stranger would alight from the southbound noon stagecoach, stick his head through the door and ask, 'Excuse me, are you open?'

'All day and most of the night,' Sunset would say.

'Really?'

'No, I was having you on. But we are open now. What's your poison?'

The bar was seldom empty but never crowded on account of its licensing conditions, which were explained to Rib one afternoon.

'Well, it's like this,' the landlord said, polishing a glass with a tea-towel. 'The Waterloo is not a public house. Nor is it a saloon. It is the tap room of a micro-brewery. Which means that people can't come here and drink as they would in a normal pub, they can only come and sample the beers.'

'I don't get it,' said Rib. 'You serve pints – I've seen you.'

'And so I do. But have you not also seen my chalkboard?'

'No.'

'Punters are allowed only three drinks during the

course of a day. So each time anyone has a beer, I have to chalk it up on the board.'

'So, let's get this right. They can have three pints of any strength?'

'No, I was careful to say three drinks, wasn't I? The really strong beers and barley wines are served only in these small glasses.'

'That's a snifter?'

'Correct. And one of these little devils counts as one drink.'

'So you can have three pints, two pints and a snifter, two snifters and a pint or three snifters.'

'Right in one!' laughed Sunset, putting the glass back on the shelf.

'And what are those flagons hanging from the ceiling?'

'They're the growlers. Reusable, carry-out containers, holding a quart. For your picnic, barbecue, hunting or fishing trip.'

'A taproom, eh?' mused Rib. So that's why it looks like a ...' he tailed off, realising that he had gone too far.

'No, you're absolutely right. Let me explain. If the Sheriff were to come in here, sit on my sofa and remark, "Mm, I do like the plush feel of this comfortable three-seater. And my! I do so admire the matching chintz curtain," I would be in deep mire. He'd be down on me like a ton of bricks. He'd suspect straight away that I was running a saloon and close me down before you could say Bob's Your Uncle. That's why the décor is deliberately spartan.'

Rib sat silent for a moment. 'But what I don't understand is why you don't apply for a full pub license? Then people could have as many drinks as they wanted and you'd take in much more over the bar.'

Sunset smiled. 'Good question. And don't think I haven't considered it.' He started to buff the surface of the bar with a soft yellow duster. 'But I like it just the way it is. My customers don't come here to get drunk. They come here for good company over a fine ale or two. Sure, they can get nice and mellow, but I don't have to deal with drunks every night. Who needs that? I certainly don't at my time of life.'

'I can see that, but what's to stop people going somewhere else first and coming on here after they've had a skinful?'

Sunset reached down behind the bar, took a small tin of Brasso and carefully dripped a couple of drops of the murky liquid onto the bar before rubbing it in with a dirty grey cloth. 'Another good question,' he said as he began to polish with the yellow duster. 'The fact of the matter is, it never works that way. If you want to have a session, you always start with the drink that's most pleasant on the palate. If you then want to get hammered, you move onto the cheap bottled cockspiss they serve up at the Florence, or you drown your sorrows in sour mash and gin. Never the other way round. And what's more,' he added, 'noon 'til nine's enough for me. Gives me time to do a bit on the allotment every day. Now, which one today?' He pointed to a board above the taps where all the beers available were displayed. Above the name and strength of each brew was a badly-drawn picture, coloured in. 'Try this one.' He pointed to a drawing of a grizzly bear wearing a wig and a short red skirt. 'Big Bear Blonde,' said Sunset, with a note of pride in his voice. '5.7°, plenty of character,' he finished.

Plenty of character, thought Rib, I should say so. Wouldn't like to meet her up a dark alley. He took a sip of the expertly poured pint. It tasted good. Nice and smooth ...

Sunset was now in full flow. Talking about beer. His beer. Rib had had the guided tour four or five times already, but it didn't matter. The old guy was in his element.

'Then there's Dog's Dribble IPA, 4.8°,' he said, pointing at the head of an evil-looking hound with drool dripping from its snarlcurl lips. 'Plenty of bite. Clean finish. See the two buttocks, there? That's a particular favourite of mine – Peaches Amber, 6.2°. I won't tell you who inspired that one. Fond memories, fond memories …' He drifted off into a world of his own and, for a moment, Rib thought he was going to escape the full narrative. It was not to be.

'Piss Poor Porter!' he suddenly barked.

Rib nearly spat his mouthful of beer back into the glass. 'Come on, Sunset, what sort of name is that. How can you call one of your beers Piss Poor?'

'Ah, well, young man, it's like this. It's an ingenious marketing stratagem of mine. Firstly, there's not a single customer who doesn't want to say the words "Piss Poor Porter" out loud. The alliteration is seductive, don't you feel? They can't help it. And once they've ordered it, they cannot resist taking a sip and then coming out with the smart-arse comment, "You know what, Sunset, this really is a piss poor porter!" I then come back with something equally witty and before you know it, an unbreakable bond between barman and punter is forged. In the trade, it's what we call banter. It goes without saying, of course, that it's a very fine beer indeed and they always come back for more.'

He moved onto the next. 'Now for the snifters.' The picture of the Brickhills Barley Wine was of three trees on a hill. The trees looked like they'd been drawn by a four-year-old, but Rib kept the observation to himself. What was convincing was the 15.8° writ large beneath the sign.

'Wow! That sounds strong,' said Rib.

'You're not wrong there my son. I would not

recommend you have three of those. Journey into Space ...'

Suddenly, the door burst open as if it had been kicked in. The frame of an enormous man filled the doorway, then walked slowly into the taproom, spurs jangling in rhythm with each deliberate stride. A cool breeze followed him into the bar from the street. The temperature seemed to drop ten degrees.

Sunset let the duster fall from his hand and signalled Rib to stand up. 'Good afternoon, Sheriff. How are you today?' he said with a tense smile.

10

The giant of a man now standing before them was a formidable sight. A cross between a black American heavyweight and something out of Terminator 12, he must have weighed in at 150 kilos at the very least. The floorboards of the taproom groaned in their new-found function of bathroom scales, not liking it one little bit.

There didn't appear to be an ounce of fat on him. His exposed torso glistened its statement to the world: "I am big. I am strong. Do not mess with me. Or you will regret it." The only article of clothing on his upper body was an unbuttoned black leather waistcoat, on which was pinned a bright, silver-star badge. He wore shades, which must have made it difficult for him to see in the dark interior of the bar, but that didn't seem to trouble him. In fact, he didn't appear to be a man who would be troubled by anything. But what stood out, quite literally, about this colossus was his haircut. He supported a magnificent mohawk – it must have stood six inches high. And it was bleached white!

Now, ordinarily you would reckon that a black man who's bleached his mohawk white would be a figure of fun, the butt of endless jokes, wouldn't you? Not this one. The nearest the townsfolk came to calling him a name was to refer to him as "Mister T." But always behind his back. Never to his face.

Booker T. Amps, Sheriff of Stonyville, slowly removed his shades and replied in a deep southern drawl, 'And a good afternoon to you, Mr Todd.'

'Can I offer the Sheriff something to drink?'

The man known behind closed doors as Mr T now turned his stare to Rib, who ventured a nervous smile. The smile was not returned. Keeping the look firmly fixed on Rib, as if he were the trigger-happy outlaw about to go for his gun, he said, 'Yes please, Mr Todd. I'll have a pint of your Piss Poor Porter.'

'Certainly, sir. One Piss Poor Porter coming up,' said the landlord, who took a glass from the shelf, held it up against the light, and gave it a buff with a cloth in readiness for the pouring. He held the clean glass at an angle as the black cream poured in a smooth flow from the tap. All the while, the Sheriff kept his eyes on Rib. Before he realised what he was doing, Rib found himself engaged in a staring contest with 150 kilos of rippling muscle. He was like the rabbit in the headlights, the only thing on his mind being sphincter control. Seven seconds passed before Rib threw in the towel and blinked six times in rapid succession. A frown came over the face of the Sheriff. Was this runt of a kid winking at him?

The unintended stand-off melted away as Sunset handed the perfectly-poured pint to Booker T. The man-mountain scrutinised the creamy head, held the glass up to the light and then downed its contents in one.

Sunset stood stock still, hands pressed flat on the bar, awaiting the verdict.

The Sheriff wiped his mouth on his forearm. Rib couldn't help staring at the creamy smear standing out on the black skin. The empty glass was placed carefully on the bar. 'Mr Todd,' he said, 'you know, that really was a piss poor pint of porter,' and burst out laughing. Sunset joined in, tears rolling down his cheeks, wheezing as though he was about to bust a gut. Rib entered the mirth melee with a high-pitched laugh of his own, which didn't come out quite as he intended. Meant to be a gentle chuckle, it sounded more like the cry of a hyena being castrated. The laughter stopped as quickly as it had begun. The Sheriff glowered at Rib, as if to say, 'Who the hell invited you in on the joke?'

The big man turned to Sunset. 'Thank you, Mr Todd. An excellent beer, as ever.'

'Another, Sheriff?'

'Thank you, but no. Not while on duty. Which brings me to the purpose of my visit.' Sunset visibly tensed. Booker T's gaze returned to Rib. Sphincter control time again.

'I assume, Mr Todd, that this new arrival is in possession of all the necessary papers?'

Sunset nodded rapidly, thinking HolyfuckIshouldhavechecked!

'And I assume, Mr Todd, that this boy is of legal drinking age? I don't need to tell you the consequences of serving intoxicating liquor to a minor, do I?'

Sunset now shook his head rapidly, thinking holyfuckIhopehe'sfourteen! He knew the consequences only too well. Straight to jail. Heavy fine. And worst of all, loss of licence. The sun would set on the Waterloo Brewing Co. ...

'Well?' the Sheriff asked.

'Well?' Sunset asked Rib.

'Oh, er, yes, the papers. Yes, I've got the papers,' he laughed nervously, emptying the contents of his pockets onto the bar. One wallet. One over-used, off-white handkerchief. One not-used-at-all condom, which had somehow slipped out of his wallet. Shit. He swore to himself, staring at the offending rubber. He'd forgotten it was there. He tried to remember when he had bought it. The use-by date stamped on the side told the sorry tale. It had expired over a year ago.

'Ahem,' coughed the Sheriff, interrupting the boy's tragic train of thought. 'The papers ...'

'Oh yes, I know! I've got them upstairs in my bag. Shall I go and fetch them?'

'Yes!' screamed Sunset.

Rib gave the Sheriff a wide berth as he left the taproom. He sprinted up the stairs two at a time, emptied the contents of his bag on the bed and went into a blind panic, unable to find the papers anywhere. Then he remembered the zip pocket on the side and, to his mighty relief, there they were, neatly filed in a blue plastic wallet. He bounded downstairs to find Mr T sprawled across one of the leather sofas. Sunset was still standing stock still, hands pressed flat against the bar, staring into space as if in a state of trance. Rib passed his ID papers to the Sheriff, who took them without a word and started to scrutinise them with a serious frown on his face, the serious frown which appears on the face of every single policeman, bartender, night-club doorman, immigration officer, girl behind the supermarket counter serving scratch-cards. How long does it take to read a name, date of birth and look at a photo? Do all of these people have learning difficulties? And why do they put on this 'Oooh, I-don't-know-about-this' expression? After much furrowing of the brow and not a little snorting of air through his wide nostrils, the Sheriff handed back Rib's legitimation documents.

'Hm, they appear to be in order,' he said as he rose from the sofa. 'Just make sure, Mr Meskitoe, that we have no need for any ... difficult conversations during your stay here. Do you hear?'

Rib nodded. Mr T slowly ambled out of the tap room. He turned in the doorway, Columbo-like. 'Oh, just one more thing ...'

The two held their breath.

'Mr Todd, are you going to chalk that beer up to me?'

'Ab-ab-absolutely, Mr Sheriff!' Sunset stuttered. 'Just about to,' he said, turning to write on the board with trembling hand.

The Sheriff left the bar without a further word. Rib heard him stride, spurs jangling, along the boardwalk towards the Market Hall. He stopped to raise his fingers to his lips. A piercing whistle rent the air. Rib crept over to the window, staying low so he couldn't be seen. A tremor turned into a rumble turned into a seismic episode, which dislodged a picture of the 1981 Tottenham Hotspurs team from the wall and sent it crashing to the floor, Garth Crooks' chubby little face smiling up through the cracked glass. Still trembling, Sunset busied himself at the taps.

A massive horse thundered to a halt outside on the street. Twice the size of a normal horse, it had a sleek, jet-black coat. Its flowing mane was pure white. The big black sheriff with a white mohawk mounted the big black horse with a white mane and they trundled off down Main Street, leaving a trail of dust in their wake.

Silence.

Broken after ten seconds by Rib whispering, 'What the hell was that?'

'Shaft,' replied Sunset, back still turned. 'The Sheriff's shire horse.'

'Why is it called Shaft?' asked the innocence of youth.

'I'll tell you later.'

A clink of glasses made Rib turn round. On the bar were lined, in a perfect row, six snifters of 15.8° Brickhill Barley Wine. 'Three for you and three for me. That, my son, was what is known in the trade as a close call.' His hand shook as he raised the first glass to his lips. 'Cheers.'

'That was seriously scary, 'said Rib, staring back out of the window.

'Mr Pleasant he ain't . When he does his little rounds we all have watch out. Even me ...' he trailed off. 'Nobody messes with the Sheriff of Stonyville. If ever Marshall Amps blows a fuse, it's time to hit the deck.'

11

Planet Tycho.

Largest of the inner planets of the Alfalfa-Beta system. Lower atmosphere consisting largely of nitrogen and oxygen, an ozone layer in the upper atmosphere serving as a protective shield against its sun's harmful radiation. Equilateral diameter of 1,275 kilometres, orbit period of 366 days, approximately 70% of its surface covered by water. In other words, an exact clone of Planet Earth. Every mountain a mirror image, every river, every stream the exact replica of its old-world counterpart. The perfect new home for the survivors of Watershed.

For those who made it through Immigration, the Protectorate enforced a strict repatriation policy. All incomers were assigned to the location corresponding to their place of domicile on Earth. 'Whoopee!' whooped those from Windermere. 'Twats!' cursed those from Canvey Island. Although, it has to be said, that the clean, crisp air of Canvey-sur-Tycho soon improved their mood.

Accordingly, each new settlement was named after its match on Earth, with the prefix "New" before the place name, much as the Pilgrim Fathers had done when they settled in America: New England, New York, and so on. This came as a mixed blessing for people suffering from a speech impediment. For example, all Geordies now joined them in stuttering New-Newcastle and ceased to mock their affliction. The downside came for those who had finally managed to conquer their impediment after years of therapy. (This policy was clearly bonkers and place names reverted to their original form within a matter of months).

Things did not go well for the first settlers of New Milton Keynes. They set up camp at the exact same location co-ordinates of their home back on Earth, on top of a windy hill. Early signs were, however, promising – they felt a real sense of community, of homecoming, and enjoyed great views of the surrounding countryside. The settlement began its life as a collection of shacks and tents, connected to the main north-south highway by a single dirt track running down the hill.

They decided to call a meeting to discuss how they were going to establish their new town. That was a good idea. They asked for volunteers to form a committee. That was a bad idea. The people who volunteered were the sad kind who had sat on committees all their lives. Accordingly, they held a certain view of what should be done and, more importantly, how it should be done. It was invariably the wrong view.

At the first public meeting, held in a timber shack grandly called the Civic Offices, an agenda was pinned to the door. People read it as they filed in. It said:

AGENDA
NEW MILTON KEYNES PLANNING COMMITTEE

('I don't like the sound of that for a start! The whole point of Planning Committees back on Earth was to prevent things happening, not getting things done!')

1. **Election of Committee Members**
   ('Look at them, sitting up there at the top table. They've already voted each other on, self-interested bastards').

2. **Apologies**
   ('I'm sorry I came, that's for sure.')

3. **Matters arising from previous meeting**
   ('I thought this was the first meeting?'
   'Have they already met behind closed doors?'
   'How do you get your doors to close? I can't keep mine shut in this fucking wind!')

4. **Transport Strategy**
   ('That shouldn't take long. Buy a horse!')

5. **Growth Plan to 2097**
   ('2097? I don't know what I'm doing next week!')

6. **Any other business**
   ('I'm gonna ask them where we're gonna get our food from.'
   'And what about a roof over our heads?'
   And where's the new football stadium going to be built?')

The meeting was acrimonious. A core of diehards on the committee did everything in their power to limit the debate to grid roads.

('Gridroads? There are only seven hundred of us in the whole town and you want us to spend three years putting together a Grid Road Transport Infrastructure

Plan Consultation Document? You've got to be having a laugh!')

And so it went on. The new town's population grew rapidly as new arrivals landed on the planet, but things didn't improve. Any discussion on how to move forward became gridlocked in bitter squabbling. Life on top of the windswept hill was particularly harsh. It was a long trek down to the highway and the nearest source of fresh water was a good kilometre away. It made people wonder why the original City Centre had been built on top of a hill in the first place.

Then, one hot and sultry August night, there was an incident which brought matters to a head. Chesney Wold was at his wit's end. An infestation of red squirrels in his loft was driving him nuts. On that fateful night, he decided to smoke the little bastards out. The roof slats were dry as parchment, scorched by the hot sun and dry west winds sweeping over the warm Cotswold Hills. Each dwelling was like a tinderbox. All it needed was one spark. The fire took hold immediately, devouring the stash of arsegrass stored in the roof void. Flames licked round the edge of the cabin, before leaping over the short gap to the next. Within a matter of minutes, every single building was engulfed in a terrible conflagration. It was a miracle that nobody perished in the Great Fire of Milton Keynes. Apart from one migrant Polish squirrel, that is. His name was Zbigniew and his final words were 'Niech to szlag!'

The townspeople salvaged as much as they could and camped out in a hastily erected shanty town on the west-facing slope of the hill, waiting for aid to arrive. Surely someone would come soon. After three days, help did arrive in the shape of a big black man with a white mohawk riding a big black horse with a white mane. People surged forward to get a closer look at the stranger. The huge horse evacuated his bowels and people backed off to put distance between them and the steaming pile of manure.

The Chair of the Planning Committee stepped forward. 'Welcome. I am Charles Windbag. ('Windbag by name, Windbag by nature,' shouted someone at the back.) Undeterred, Windbag went up to the young man on the horse and held out his hand.

Booker T Amps ignored it.

'I had rather expected the Protectorate to send a multi-national force of aid workers, possibly even a camera crew.'

Amps dismounted and walked over to a smouldering roof truss, picked it up and then threw it to one side. The crowd gasped. 'Now,' he said wiping his hands on the back of his pants, 'let's get this place cleaned up and re-built. I've got timber on order, it should be coming up the hill in a couple of days.'

There was a nervous silence.

'Well?' he demanded.

A voice from the back said. 'We don't want to live here no more ...'

'You don't want to live here no more?' retorted Booker T in disbelief. The horse gave a snort of scorn and pawed the ground with a hoof the size of a plate. 'But, but, you people don't know how goddam lucky you are. You're here, yeah?'

'We don't care,' came another voice from the crowd, now growing in confidence. 'We don't like it here. There's no water, it's windy all the time and we have to walk all the way down the bottom of the hill to the stagecoach route.'

'Yeah, and the fucker don't even stop!'

Amps raised his hands. 'Now just hold on there a minute. The law clearly states that people from the old Milton Keynes on Earth have to settle in the exact same place, New Milton Keynes, on Tycho. And that place is here!'

The crowd began to get restless. They didn't like this young whippersnapper and they didn't like the message he was giving. They edged forward. Things looked as if they might turn ugly, until the big man walked over to his horse and produced a bullwhip from his saddlebag. He cracked it over their heads.

The crowd went quiet.

'OK, OK, I hear where you're coming from. But you folks wanting to up sticks and put your roots down somewhere else, that's beyond my jurisdiction. I'm gonna have to put that one upstairs. Where shall I say you want to go to?'

'Down there by the river.'

'No, over there. We can dig a canal.'

'A couple of miles to the east would be a great place for a motorway!'

Booker T Amps shook his head and whistled Shaft. The soundtrack of his favourite film. He then whistled for his horse. 'I'll be back in three days.'

The crowd murmured its disapproval and inched forward. The young man on the horse reached for his bullwhip. The crowd inched back. 'Three days,' he shouted behind him as he rode back down the hill.

And sure enough, Booker T Amps was as good as his word. This time, he stayed on the big white shire horse, bullwhip buckled to his saddlebag for all to see. 'I have some good news!' he announced. 'The Protectorate have granted you permission to relocate, on the condition that it is no further than 8 kilometres from this spot. So, have you folks made your minds up where you want to go?'

They hadn't.

The practical pioneers wanted a sheltered, flat tract of land near a river, where they could grow crops, raise cattle, fish for trout. A vociferous minority of MK fundamentalists wanted to remain loyal to their roots of grid squares and roundabouts. Over the next twenty four hours, the young man kept his cool and his right hand firmly on his bullwhip as he played the role of peace envoy, negotiator and miracle worker all rolled into one.

Of course, he'd seen all this coming and had taken the opportunity at Protectorate HQ to seek the counsel of a couple of old timers in the Estates Directorate, Kirstie and Phil, who had given him the low-down on availability, accessibility and value of land in the locality.

As he was leaving, Kirstie had thrown up her hands. 'This is an impossible brief. They don't know what they want!'

'But Kirstie,' smooth-talked Phil, 'it's our job to try and help them find what they want.'

'A hundred dollars says they won't go for it,' she said.

Booker T held out his hand. 'Shall I take your money now, Ma'am?'

Phil smiled. It reminded him of the good old days ...

Under Booker's skilful stewardship, a compromise deal was now thrashed out, to the satisfaction of all parties. The small group of MK fundamentalists moved to a place four kilometres to the east of the windy hilltop. They named the new settlement Milton Keynes Village, overjoyed that they had returned to their roots. 'It's heritage, heritage!' they chorused as they sat around the table at the first meeting of the Joint Community Infrastructure Development Committee to vote on growth plans for the period through to 2097.

The other 527 inhabitants of the newly-charred new town chose a strip of land eight kilometres to the northwest of the blasted hill. It was the mirror-image of the site where the coaching town of Stony Stratford had stood on Earth, the place where wagon drivers would exchange exaggerated cock-and-bull stories of events back down the road. The Protectorate had supported the relocation based on the need for a watchful presence along this unprotected section of the north-south rail line. They appointed Booker T Amps as the town's sheriff, who named the place Stonyville.

'It's location, location!' cried the new settlers in joy as they herded their sheep out onto the verdant riverside meadows for the first time.

Marshall Amps spent his winnings on a silver horseshoe which he nailed above Shaft's stable door.

12

Rib became an avid reader of the Wall Paper. He loved it. Back on Earth, he'd shown little interest in news programmes or current affairs features on the Trawl. They were boring. But the Wall was something else.

The articles appeared in no particular order. Breaking news of a major catastrophe would appear beneath a report on the local high school hop. The early morning read became part of his routine. Walk down to the meadows, take a dip in the river, dry off watching the swans and geese, walk back to town, pop into Bettina's Buns for a bag of donuts or muffins, head up Main Street for a coffee and a read of the Wall. On wet mornings, he'd skip the swim and have breakfast on his balcony, watching the passing wagons slither in the mud.

The headline this particular morning was a weekly question-and-answer feature by the town's acknowledged gardening expert, Green-fingered Gertie:

Dear Gertie,

Q: What is the moss-like stuff growing all over my back yard?

A: It's moss, you dickhead.

From further afield, dramatic tales of railroad incidents and accidents featured regularly:

RAILWAY BRIDGE BURNS AT WALTHAMSTOW

Mr Martin Geraghty walked into the Tottenham Hale railway depot on Thursday morning to report a near-fatal incident. From his veranda overlooking the valley, he noticed that the trestle bridge had caught fire. Flames were fanned by the fresh south-easterly and soon the whole structure was ablaze. Menfolk from the town formed a bucket chain, but it was too late to save the bridge. Two of Mr Geraghty's neighbours, Messrs Pullen and Jones, rushed to plant red danger flags up the track to warn oncoming crews of the peril ahead, but the 10:45 from King's Cross thundered past. On seeing this, Mr Geraghty then committed an act of extreme bravery by standing in the middle of the track, arms waving. The crew managed to brake the engine to a halt only a few feet from the precipice and they were very grateful to gallant Martin for saving them from certain death. A hog roast was held in his honour at the Walthamstow Town Hall that following Saturday.

Hip-hip hooree for Mr G!

13

The offices of the town's newspaper stood right opposite the Waterloo, next to the Grand Hotel. The hallmark of any civilised society is an independent media and press, free from potential bias and ownership influence. And that's exactly what they had in Stonyville. Under the strict censorship of the Protectorate.

Early each morning, a good half-hour before dawn cracked, the news events of the previous day were pinned onto the Wall. It shouldn't have been a surprise that folks called it the Wall Paper, but it really was something that really pissed off the proprietor of The Stonyville Chronicle, Al Faraday.

The newssheets were printed in purple ink on brown, recycled paper. The technology used was primitive – an old, converted Banda machine that had sat forlorn and forsaken in a school caretaker's store cupboard, until somehow finding its way on a flight to Tycho in a container along with a collection of museum pieces. It had passed the "They don't make them like this anymore" test, which bought the squat little machine not only a ticket to a new planet, but a new purpose in life.

Of course, resource rationing meant that the mass production of hundreds of newspapers each day was out of the question, hence the daily output of just one A1 format edition, pinned to the Wall. This task, come rain or shine, hell or high water, befell Dorothy Spigot, printer, aged

79. Clocking in at 11 pm for a briefing with the editor and team to agree content and layout, she would then work through the night until the morning's edition was done – normally around 4:30 am – when she'd leave the premises, cross a deserted Main Street and pin the sheets to the Wall. From there she'd walk the fifty metres down to 2nd Street, take the staircase up the side of the building to her one-bedroom flat. She would then boil up some coffee, dark and strong, pour it into a white bone-china cup and take it with her into the toilet. There she would sit for ages, sometimes dozing off. She was in no rush and her bowels certainly weren't. Dorothy's diet consisted almost exclusively of dried-beef jerky and pumpernickel bread. If it wasn't for the strong black coffee, she probably wouldn't have gone to the toilet at all.

Dorothy Spigot lived on her own. If you'd asked her if she was happy, she would have looked you in the eye and said, "Yep, sure am!" If you'd conducted a poll amongst the 750-strong population of the town, using the following question:

- Dorothy Spigot, sweet old lady?
  or
- Dorothy Spigot, grumpy old cow?
  the outcome would have been as follows:
- Sweet old lady   :   0
- Grumpy old cow   :   749
- Spoiled voting slip   :   1 (Dorothy's)

She wouldn't have given a fig. Figs, unfortunately, were something she didn't keep in her larder.

But Dorothy Spigot did have that special something which set her aside from the rest of the community. Something which they all would have given their eye teeth for: a supply of toilet paper in the form of the previous day's newssheets. As the good townsfolk struggled with arsegrass, Dorothy enjoyed the luxury of a wipe with the sports page. There was one downside, however. If anybody had stopped her in the middle of the street, asked her to pull down her breeches, lift up her skirts and bend over, they could have read the result of the previous night's 8:45 greyhound race at Catford Stadium imprinted on her left buttock. Thankfully, nobody ever had ...

Another occupational hazard suffered by Dorothy was the print ink. It was indelible. Hours spent each night toiling over the Banda when everyone else was tucked snugly in bed left her hands with an immovable purple stain. It was like she was wearing purple gloves. To give a degree of balance to her appearance, she sometimes experimented with the ink to concoct a thick purple mascara. Instead of distracting attention away from her hands, this served only to elevate her position in the town as a figure of fun, the butt of all jokes (even though no-one had been exposed to the greyhound results).

Two sections of the community were especially guilty in this respect. Second Street joined the main drag opposite the town's school, and whenever Dorothy walked past, the younger schoolchildren would rush up to the railings and taunt her without mercy. This involved chanting rude rhymes at her, typically featuring the words "inky" and "stinky". Walk on by, was Dorothy's maxim, not once allowing herself to be dragged into an exchange with the little shits. You could say she turned the other cheek (not the one with the 8:45 Catford results). But this would not have been entirely true. For she was saving her cold dish of revenge for another day ...

Her other constant source of harassment was the town knife-sharpener, an odious low-life by the name of Judd Scoter, a man with the look of Wile-E-Coyote about him. Each day he set up his stall on Main Street, just along from the Market Hall: a grinding wheel standing beside a table laden with an extensive assortment of used knives, scissors, scythes, lawnmower blades. Nobody could walk past without being accosted by a "Sharpen your knife for fifty cents?" A "No, thank you" would then elicit the most sarcastic "Have a nice day" on the planet. If you were lucky. Fixed to the grinding wheel was a harmonica holder, which held a mouth organ, used by Scoter to taunt people who said no.

The widow Hansworthy was a big woman. Ever since the death of her husband, Hank, she dressed herself in black. Black boots, black skirt, black shawl right down to the ground, black bonnet. When Hank shuffled off this mortal coil, people said, "Blessed release." Not that he had been suffering from any drawn-out, terminal illness. No, Hank had been suffering from being married to the most domineering virago of a wife imaginable. To say he was hen-pecked would be an obscene understatement: the poor man was also hen-scratched, hen-kicked and hen-shat-on every single day of his miserable life. So when the black-bonneted widow glided down Main Street like a hovercraft battleship and rudely refused Scoter's kind offer to have her knives sharpened, she did not receive the sarcastic "Have a nice day." He waited until she was a safe distance past, licked his lips, leaned forward and played the Darth Vader signature tune on his mouth harp:

Daa-daaa-da-da

Daaa-daaa-da, da, da, da,-daa

The widow Hansworthy would turn, spit a curse in his direction and threaten him with her black umbrella. Scoter would pause to laugh, then carry on playing. Water off a duck's back …

But Dorothy, beyond all trace of a doubt, was his favourite victim and she fell foul of his cruel harmonica humour on a regular basis.

'Sharpen your knife for fifty cents, Miss Spigot?'

'No, thank you.'

Scoter would then lean forward and play the opening chords of the classic Prince hit before singing 'Purple Stain, Purple Stain ...'

Her time would come, she told herself, her time would come.

This apart, Dorothy Spigot was a happy woman. She loved her work, the solitude of the nightshift suiting her down to the ground. She was also a woman of unwavering routine. Each morning, when the print run had been put to bed, and the office locked up, she'd spend the next hour carefully pinning the newssheets to the Wall, replacing yesterday's papers. Sometimes she would then sit down on the bench next to the horse trough and wait for her first readers to appear. To see a crowd form and engage with her work gave her a deep level of satisfaction. She didn't care how they responded, whether they laughed or cried, clapped or cursed. Hers was not the content – that was down to Hetty, the journo. Dorothy's was the printed sheet, the paragraphs, the lines, the words. She connected with this gathering of men and women reading the Wall Paper, day in, day out, come rain or shine. They were the closest she had to a family.

14

Dorothy Spigot maintained a polite, professional distance from her two colleagues, Hetty Huxtable and Al Faraday, the owner-editor. Hetty and Al were good friends and saw a lot of each other outside work, often seen sitting in one of the booths in the rear lounge of the Grand. For Dorothy, work was work and she kept herself to herself. She liked it that way.

So when, on the eve of the first anniversary of The Stonyville Chronicle, Al summoned Hetty and her to a meeting at eight to discuss "Something Important", Dorothy was both appalled and horrified at such an infringement of her personal routine, at such a violation of her equilibrium. Nonetheless, she turned up, concerned to see what this "Something Important" might be. She walked into Al's office at eight on the dot. Dorothy was always on the dot – and was surprised to see Hetty already there. Her eyes fell on a spread of food and drink on the table and she immediately attacked the kettle chips, pouring herself a glass of the red.

'Er, good evening, Dorothy,' said Al, who had intended to deliver his message before inviting them to eat. Anyway, that was Dorothy for you, he thought, before pressing on. 'Hetty, Dorothy, thank you so much for coming in this evening. I know you both lead full and busy lives and I'm sure I've dragged you away from something exciting this – '

'Al, could you say that again?' interrupted Dorothy. 'I couldn't make out what you said.' She couldn't make out what Al said, owing to the fact that all extraneous sound was drowned out by the echo of kettle-chip-crunching inside her skull.

Al decided to ignore this request and continued. 'It is, of course, our beloved newspaper's first anniversary today. And how better to celebrate than to break bread and share a glass of wine with dear friends.'

This time, Al was interrupted by Dorothy erupting in a violent coughing fit. Hetty started to thump her on the back and Al offered her a hastily poured beaker of water. Dorothy's eyes bulged big as she shook her head.

'Has something gone down the wrong way, dear?' asked Hetty unhelpfully. It was just as well Dorothy was not best placed to respond.

The offending kettle chip was called Kenneth who, not fancying the idea of ending up in the old biddy's stomach, had wedged himself firmly against the walls of her windpipe like a climber negotiating a rock-face chimney. Only when Hetty gave Dorothy a mighty thwack between the shoulders was Kenneth forcibly ejected. Covered in mucus, he flew out of her mouth and landed splat in the bowl of guacamole dip. 'Oooh, this is nice,' he thought as he lay back, enjoying the soothing spa. 'I could get used to this. I wonder what time the seaweed wrap is?' Kenneth's life of luxury was short-lived. Dorothy picked him up, scooped a dollop of guacamole onto him, and popped him back into her mouth, this time taking care to crunch and chew before swallowing. And that was the end of Kenneth ...

'Are you sure you're OK, Dorothy?' asked Al.

'Yes, absolutely fine. Do go on.' She finished off her glass of red in one and poured another.

'OK, er, where was I?' floundered Al.

'Our anniversary,' said Hetty, wishing that it was.

'Oh yes,' said Al, now back on track, 'our anniversary.' He raised his glass, 'Cheers!'

'Cheers!' said Hetty who took a dainty sip of her wine.

Dorothy glugged hers down and grabbed the bottle for a refill.

'But, my friends, there is also another reason for me bringing us together this evening. I want to consult with you on giving our newspaper, on this historic day, a new name.'

Dorothy looked at him in wide-eyed surprise. Hetty shifted uncomfortably from foot to foot. She already knew, figured Dorothy. 'I've got two questions,' she said.

'Fire away,' said Al.

'Firstly, what's wrong with the Stonyville Chronicle? And secondly, why do you need our opinion? You're the owner. If you want to change it, change it.'

'Thank you for those helpful questions, Dorothy. Let me try and answer. Firstly, you must be aware that our current name is often shortened by our good townspeople to "The Chronic." I find that quite hurtful. Others just call us "The Wallpaper", which again is not as I would wish. So I think it's time to rid ourselves of those negative associations. And as for your second question, Dorothy, I would like to think that my management style is open, consultative and team-orientated. I genuinely want to give you, my co-workers, a say in the important decisions round here.'

Like, how much you pay us? thought Dorothy. No, she answered that one for herself.

'So this is what I propose. We're gonna stay here all night until we come up with a new name. I'm gonna lock the door now,' he took a key from his pocket and waved it in the air, 'and nobody leaves 'til we're done.' An electric spasm went up the inside of Hetty's left thigh at the thought of being locked up in Al's office all night.

Dorothy's mind was on other things as she eyed the buffet table. 'OK, Al, if that's what you want, that's what you want. You're the boss. But if you expect me to hang around here all night, I'm gonna need some fuel inside me.'

'Sure,' said Al. Dorothy's apparent mood of compliance was unexpected. 'So what'll it be?'

'How about some chicken wings, ribs and jalapeno peppers. That OK with you, Hetty?' Hetty nodded, saliva glands already in full flow. 'And the wine's looking a little lonely there, Al. How about a couple of growlers of Big Bear Blonde from the Waterloo and a bottle of Wild Spatchcock from the Florence?'

Al hadn't foreseen his wallet taking such a hammering, but hell, it wasn't everyday he enjoyed the company of his team, so why not? 'Why not?' he laughed. 'While I'm fetching the provisions, why don't you ladies start to get some ideas down?' He handed them each a small slate. 'If we begin by making our own suggestions first, then we can come together and agree a shortlist.'

As he strode along the boardwalk, Al had every right to feel good about how it was going. Dorothy was not the easiest of people to work with. In fact, he probably would have sacked her before now if she hadn't been the only person in town who could tame the Banda beast. And he had to admit she was damn good at her job. They didn't call her the Cyclostyle Queen for nothing. Quite simply, he couldn't do without her. His train of thought continued in the Waterloo, waiting to order the growlers. Did tonight signal a turning-point in his relationship with the crotchety old spinster? It really seemed so, and he felt so impressed by his person-management skills that he knocked back a snifter of Brickhill Barley Wine in celebration.

Al's euphoric sense of well-being was unfounded. The first thing that happened when he left the office was Dorothy rifling through the drawers in his desk.

'What are you doing?' cried Hetty. If anybody was going to feel around in Al's drawers, she was the first in line.

'I'm looking for the answer,' growled Dorothy.

'What do you mean? The answer to what?'

Dorothy stood up straight and looked Hetty in the eye. 'Listen, sister, are you really that gullible that you're taken in by all that co-worker consultation crap?'

Hetty opened and shut her mouth like a fourteen-stone goldfish out of water.

'Al knows all well and good what he's going to call the paper, and that's what I'm looking for. He must have written it down somewhere.'

'Dorothy Spigot, I think that is so mean of you!' protested Hetty. 'Al is a good man and, and ...' her eyes welled up with tears.

The old woman walked round the desk and placed a hand on the now heaving shoulder of Hetty. 'Oh, come on now. I didn't mean to get you all upset. Come on, let's dry your eyes and start thinking up some newspaper names, huh? You sit here at Al's desk and I'll work over here. OK now?'

Hetty snuffled, 'Yes, thanks,' and sat down at Al's desk. She started to scribble on the slate tablet, shielding what she was writing with her left forearm as she did so. Dorothy poured the dregs from the wine bottle into her glass and took it over to the layout table against the far wall of the office.

Half an hour later, Al returned laden with the food and booze. He carefully transferred the precious cargo from his canvas knapsack to the table. 'Tuck in, ladies!'

he said, closely avoiding being knocked off balance by the stampeding Hetty, quickly followed by Dorothy, rolling her sleeves up to dive into a bucket of chicken wings smothered in hot buffalo sauce.

Al uncorked the bottle of Wild Spatchcock, poured himself two fingers of the rough rye, and sat back at his desk to survey the feeding frenzy before him with a sense of satisfaction. It somehow felt ... wholesome ... that his team, his family, were at long last sharing each other's company. Yes, Dorothy had her ... routines. Her own way of doing things. Easily agitated if people disrupted her patterns. Some folks labelled her autistic, although Al wasn't sure. And anyhow, what if she was? She was the best printer he'd ever worked with. Sure, it was a well-known fact that her habits ran like clockwork – 11:30 was apple-eating time, come hell or high water, followed by her midday dump. Heaven help the man who inadvertently got in the way. Her routines were immoveable and absolutely not up for negotiation. Ever. There was one thing, however, guaranteed to override her obsessive habits. Free food and booze.

Which was why she was now as happy as a pig in a trough, up to her armpits in sticky barbecue ribs and pouring rye down her neck like it was going out of fashion. Between mouthfuls, she paused to throw a question in his direction. 'Al, aren't you going to write your proposals on a chalkboard, too?'

'Sure am,' he said. 'What time do you make it?' Hetty looked at her watch, tapped the glass, then tapped her head. Nothing worked on Tycho.

'Mine's stopped.'

Dorothy didn't need to wear a watch. She always knew the time of day, or night, without the aid of any timepiece. And she would always be right without 5 minutes. 'I would say it's 9:15,' she said, biting on a jalapeno.

'I've got 9:16,' said Al, 'so that must be right. Let's work through to 9:45 then bring our thoughts together. We should then be done and dusted by 10:30. OK?'

At precisely 9:45, the three sat together round Al's desk. 'Who's going first?' he asked.

'I'll go, but they're not very good, I'm afraid,' said Hetty. Her list read like this:

> *The Stonyville Story*
> *The Stonyville Scoop*
> *The Stonyville Gleam*
> *The Stonyville Gazette*
> *The Stonyville Bugle*
> *The Stonyville Zephyr*
> *The Stonyville Mercury*
> *The Stonyville Meteor*

> *Signed*
>
> Hetty Huxtable, aged 37$^1/_2$

'Excellent!' applauded Al. 'Such productivity! Such creativity!'

Such bollocks, thought Dorothy.

'Thank you, thank you,' Hetty blushed.

'You next, Al,' said Dorothy, getting in first.

'Erm, OK then. Here's my humble list.'

> The *Stonyville Sentinel*
> The *Stonyville Inquirer*
> The *Stonyville Vindicator*
> The *Frontiersman*
> The *Gleaner*
> The *Truth*

Dorothy nearly projected a mouthful of Big Bear

Blonde at the last one. Since when had they printed the truth? 'Yes, very good Al,' she lied.

'Thanks,' he said. 'And now, pray be silent for the verdict of Dorothy Spigot.'

MY LIST

The Stonyville Juggernaut
The Cake
The Stonyville ☼ *Sunbeam*
The Stonyville Arsewipe
The Daily Bun
The Muck-Spreader

Silence ...

Al forced a smile. 'Thank you Dorothy, for your wonderfully ... quirky compilation.'

Half-an-hour's discussion, at times verging on the heated, narrowed the ideas down to a shortlist of three: one of Al's, The Frontiersman; and two of Hetty's, The Stonyville Bugle and The Stonyville Zephyr. None of Dorothy's made it through the first round of votes. She felt hard done by, having never favoured a first-past-the-post electoral system. Under proportional representation, the Muck-Spreader would have still been in with a fighting chance.

At 11:30, they were still locked in stalemate. Hetty liked Al's Frontiersman, Dorothy liked Hetty's Zephyr, and Al liked Hetty's Bugle. Now distinctly the worse for wear after seven sizeable shots of Wild Spatchcock, Al slurred 'Hetty, I really do like your bugle, you know.'

'I like your bugle too,' she giggled, pissed as four farts.

Dorothy noticed what looked like a chewed spare-rib lodged on Hetty's ear like a pencil. The tell-tale trail of coagulated barbecue sauce down the side of her colleague's cheek confirmed her suspicions. For her part, having despatched a bottle and a half of red wine, four pints of Big Bear Blonde and five down-in-one Wild Spatchcocks, Dorothy could feel herself slipping into mellowness. But the nagging thought at the back of her brain that they all had to go to work in the morning was holding her back. For her, that meant in half-an-hour's time ...

Something had to give.

'OK, I've changed my mind,' she suddenly announced. 'I vote for the Stonyville Bugle.'

'Really?' said Hetty, so happy that she burst into tears.

'Really?' slurred Al, blinking at her with one eye open, trying desperately to focus.

'Yep, and that gives us a winner,' said Dorothy. 'Here's to the Stonyville Bugle,' she raised her tumbler. 'God bless her and all who sail in her!'

'Cheers!' her cut colleagues mouthed.

The formalities over, Dorothy now sprang into action. 'Al, we'll need a new logo,' she said as she scratched an image on her board.

'How about this, Al?'

Al was having serious difficulty focussing.

'Looks good to me,' he said, unable to formulate anything more complex.

Although Dorothy was in a hurry to get stuck into the morning edition with its new banner, she was only too aware of the strict authorisation checks the editor had put in place. Al insisted that any news story of major importance or feature of a controversial nature could not go to print without his written approval. Dorothy reasoned that a change of newspaper name qualified as a story of major importance, so she handed Al her slate with the sketch of a bugle. 'Al, Al! Wake up!'

Al stared at her through one uncomprehending eye.

'Al, I want you to write the new name of our paper above the picture and then sign below. OK?'

'OK,' he mumbled and started to scrawl on the slate.

'Thanks,' said Dorothy. 'Well, that's that then. We've got a new name. Halleluyah! Hetty, do you think you could escort our esteemed leader back to his flat. I need to get on with the print run. I'm already nine minutes late.'

Hetty sobered up in a flash and it wasn't long before her arm was wrapped firmly round Al's waist as they tottered an unsteady path down Main Street. Which was all rather odd, because Al's flat was one floor up, above the Chronicle's offices. Hetty had plans ...

Meanwhile, Dorothy was already in the print room preparing the plates. By 4:30, she was almost done, having proofed every word three times over. There just remained the banner. She was quite proud of the graphics she'd put together for the bugle – she'd managed to shadow the horn so that it looked as if sunlight were gleaming off its upper surface. Yep, that looks the bee's knees, she said to herself. Now for the new name.

As she walked through to Al's office, she looked back over the evening. He wasn't such a bad old stick, she thought. A pang of guilt pricked her conscience for her suspicious frame of mind earlier. She picked up the slate tablet from where Al had left it on his desk. She stared at it in disbelief. Then unadulterated outrage.

'You bastard!' she swore, reading out the words written in Al's hand above her sketch: THE TRUMPET.

So she was right after all. The bastard knew all the

time what he was going to call his bloody paper! And Trumpet wasn't even on any of the lists. It wasn't even on his own fucking list! You bastard, Al Faraday, you absolute bastard!

Incensed, she stomped back into the print room and set to work on the banner, cursing all the while under her breath. She was sorely tempted to restore the Stonyville Bugle to its rightful place. After all, that's what they'd agreed, hadn't they? And how would Hetty feel? Dorothy could picture her now, devastated. It had meant so, so much to the girl that Al had chosen her name. But, in spite of her anger, Dorothy knew in her heart of hearts that she would be stepping beyond the point of no-return if she went against Al's written authority. So, The Stonyville Trumpet it had to be. The bastard!

(The truth of the matter was that Dorothy was being just a little harsh on her boss. Al, being pissed as a newt's fart, had fallen into a deep sleep at his desk and dreamt a vivid dream from his childhood days. He was five years old, back in his infant school, and his class were sitting cross-legged on the floor, slates and chalk at the ready for Miss Gibbons' spelling game. She held up a card with a picture on it and they had just ten seconds to write down the word on their slates, correctly spelt, of course. The countdown was both exciting and scary. 10 - 9 - 8 …

When Al was woken by Dorothy, he had no idea where he was. He certainly had no recollection of the newspaper name discussion, still hovering in that surreal territory of half-dream, half-reality. So when he was given a stick of chalk and commanded to write the correct name above the picture, he scratched down the first thing that came into his mind. And he had only seconds to do it. The picture looked for all the world

like a trumpet, although everything was a bit on the fuzzy side.
    So Trumpet it was ...)

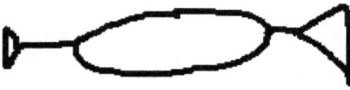

15

Dorothy finished pinning the morning's edition on the Wall at precisely 5:45 am, walked straight back to her flat on 2nd Street, boiled up a cup of strong coffee and went for a crap.

At around 6:30, Al tiptoed out of Hetty's apartment, put his boots on and swayed down to Main Street. He felt totally wrecked. The worst hangover he'd ever had in his life compounded by the pounding he'd taken under Hetty all night. The woman was insatiable. He winced as he felt the chafemarks on his wrists. Where the hell had she got those handcuffs from?

Things were about to go from bad to worse for Al Faraday. He turned the corner to see a buzzing crowd gathered at the Wall, and a large crowd at that, growing bigger by the minute. Ever the optimistic soul, Al's first instinct was to take the hubbub of excitement as acclaim for his new newspaper. With each step closer, however, the hoots of laughter, screams of derision and cruel catcalls cast doubts in his already confused mind.

Someone spotted him approaching. 'Hey! It's none other than the man himself. Make way for Mr Newspaper Man!' The crowd parted to allow Al to come face to face with the new banner of his paper.

A trumpet.

The Stonyville Trumpet.

The Stonyville Trumpet, with a bugle beneath.

Trumpet? His heart hurdled eight beats as he desperately tried to claw back memories of the night before. Hadn't they agreed Bugle?

The crowd were clearly revelling in his state of bewilderment. 'Hey Al, is that what's known as "ironic"?' shouted one reader.

'Nope,' said another. 'That's what's known as plain ... wrooong!'

'That's no trumpet, it's a friggin' bugle. Any idiot can see that.'

The crowd's mockery rained down on poor Al without mercy, who was trying to explain. 'Let me explain,' he stuttered. 'It's all a terrible mistake,' and went to tear down the offending banner from the Wall.

'No, no,' said Judd Scoter, placing a strong hand on his arm. 'No, Al, leave it be. We like it just the way it is.' The crowd bayed its agreement and Al beat a hasty retreat back to his office where he downed the remainder of the Spatchcock in next to no time.

An hour later, Dorothy and Hetty stood in Al's office, summoned to explain their actions.

'Do you realise what you've put me through!' he screamed at Dorothy, banging both fists on his desk. 'I am the laughing stock of the whole town. Who the hell gave you authority to change Bugle to Trumpet?'

'Yes, who?' piped up Hetty, in floods of tears.

'He did!' retorted the incandescent Dorothy, pointing at Al.

'Me? How the hell do you work that one out?'

Dorothy turned on her heels and stamped out of the office.

'Come back here, Dorothy Spigot! Who the hell gave you permission to leave? Come back this instant!'

Dorothy Spigot did come back this instant, slate tablet in hand. She showed it to Hetty, who mouthed

'Whaaaaaat!' She then smacked it down on Al's desk, without saying a word.

Al stared at the drawing of the bugle with a word written above it in his hand.

Trumpet.

And beneath it, his signature.

Gradually, page by page, the horrible truth unfolded. But he sure as hell wasn't going to admit it. He quickly wiped the slate clean and stood up, hands pressed flat so hard on his desk top that his knuckles went white.

'From now on in, no more Mr Nice Guy, do you hear? From now on in, it's either the highway, or my way!'

Hetty opened her mouth to correct him, but a touch from Dorothy on her sleeve stopped her.

'NOW GET OUT!' he bellowed.

Dorothy stood her ground. 'Don't you think we are owed an apology, Al?'

'AN APOLOGY? NO! NOW GET OUT!'

The two left, Hetty slamming the door behind her.

'COME BACK!' screamed Al. 'COME BACK THIS INSTANT!'

They came back, thinking Al had seen sense.

'AND ANOTHER THING! WHO SAID YOU CAN CALL ME AL?'

'Paul Simon?' offered Dorothy unhelpfully.

'You did,' sniffed Hetty. 'When you gave me the job, you shook my hand, gave me a smile and said, "Welcome, Hetty. You can call me Al."'

'And we've always called you Al,' added Dorothy

'Well, I don't want you to call me Al no more,' he said, head buried in his hands.

Dorothy now saw that the whole thing, somehow, had been a genuine mess-up and gestured to Hetty that they should go.

'This has been the worst day of my life,' he sobbed

to himself. 'This has been the darkest hour in the proud history of our blessed newspaper ...'

But for Al things were about to get even worse. At that very moment, Judd Scoter, egged on by the crowd, was adding a single letter to the new name of the town's newspaper. From that day on, Al's newspaper was known by all as ... The Strumpet.

16

It was a fine morning, a thin wisp of cloud high up in the stratosphere, no more. Pumped up from his swim, Rib stopped by at Bettina's Buns and filled a bag with pastries. He was starving and he knew Sunset couldn't say no to a croissant.

'Oh no, Master Rib, I couldn't possibly,' he would say, 'I've got my figure to watch, you know. Someone has to.' And then, when pressed, 'Oh, all right then, if you insist,' and then get stuck into them as if there were no tomorrow. Rib bought five, just to be on the safe side.

Rib arrived back at the Waterloo to find the breakfast table groaning with pots of homemade jam – strawberry, raspberry, blackberry and damson – as well as a jar of honey from the hives out on the Friedlander farm. Sunset was clearly anticipating a treat.

'Good morning,' said Rib, poking his head into the galley where he found Sunset cooking coffee. Another giveaway: tea meant Full English, coffee meant Continental. 'How are you doing?'

'I'm doing good, real good,' the big man said, pouring the strong black stimulant into two mugs. 'I feel good from the moment I open my peep-holes. Mostly...'

They went over to the table and sat down. 'How was your swim? Looks like a nice morning out there.'

'Yeah, this morning was good. Just a short session, a

thousand metres or so, so it was pretty easy going. Once you get over the initial cold shock.'

'Can't say I understand what you see in it,' winked Sunset, casting a surreptitious glance at the bakery bag from the corner of his eye.

'Well, it keeps me in some sort of shape. I popped into Bettina's on the way back and bought us some croissants.'

Sunset's eyes lit up. 'Croissants! Oh, I couldn't possibly, Master Rib, I've got my figure to watch. Someone has to ...' he tailed off in a wheezing cough. Within twenty seconds, croissant number one was being smothered in a thick layer of raspberry jam. 'Really pleased with these. New canes only two years ago.' He closed his eyes to savour the first taste. 'Mmm, damn good jam. Try some!'

'No thanks,' said Rib, toying with a wholemeal roll, his mind elsewhere. He looked across the table at his landlord making light work of his croissant, traces of jam already decorating the fringe of his grey moustache. Sunset Todd had received him with open arms. The Waterloo was like a home from home. And, yes, he liked helping the old guy out in the bar and on the allotment. Thinking about it, he'd learned one hell of a lot in the short time he'd been there: he could now tell the difference between a double Bock 5.7° and a 6.2° with his eyes closed; he knew which side-shoots to pinch out on the tomato plants; and he could trim the wick on a paraffin lamp. Things he'd never done before. But he hadn't travelled half way across the universe to master the basics of vegetable growing by the age of 16. No, he'd come to make his mark, set himself up – maybe start a business of his own. Being a permanent resident of the Waterloo Brewing Co. was certainly not in the plan. He auto-piloted butter onto the brown roll. Plan? What plan? he asked himself. His thoughts were broken by Sunset, who was now back in the world of conversation having demolished the first croissant.

'Now, Master Rib, you've set me a fine example this morning. I think I'll take a dip myself.'

'Eh?' was all the boy could say, the thought of Sunset stripping off and belly-flopping his mass into an unsuspecting Little Ouse being too much to contemplate. He had no cause for alarm. The owner of the Waterloo took croissant number two from the bag and dunked it into his mug of coffee, just long enough to keep it intact, before transferring the dripping pastry into his mouth. A coffee trickle dribbled down his chin. Not a pretty sight. 'Mmm,' he leaned back on the bench and closed his eyes. 'Vive la France ...' He burped, which made him open his eyes. 'Oops, pardon me. Better out than in. I must say, Bettina really does know her stuff. You've just got to have one,' he said, pushing the muslin bag towards Rib.

'No thanks, I'm fine with this.'

'Oh well, maybe I'll just have one more, just to say that I've tried the strawberry,' he said, removing the lid on the jar. Rib watched him deftly cut the croissant lengthwise, fill it with the sweet-smelling conserve, before closing the two halves in a sandwich and popping the whole lot in his mouth. 'Perfect, perfect,' he purred. 'Planted this new strain last year. So sweet, so sweet ...'

Rib decided not to interrupt Sunset's state of ecstasy. Instead, he allowed memories of home to surface. His Mum, the refuge ... God, how he missed them both. What he wouldn't have given for one of his Mum's home-baked blueberry muffins right now.

'Are you OK?' Sunset suddenly asked.

'Yeah, sure,'

'You look as if something's on your mind. Here have a croissant, that will cheer you up. Always works with me.'

'No thanks, I don't feel like one just now.'

An uneasy silence fell between the two. Rib broke first by changing the subject.

'Sunset, there's something I've been meaning to ask you.'

'What's that?'

'How come there's a railway, but people have to travel by horse or stagecoach?'

Sunset wiped his mouth on the corner of the checked tablecloth, giving him time to think. 'It's all a question of natural resources. You know about the Fearance of course.'

'Well, sort of ...' Uzuri had tried to explain to him something about a magnetic pulse coming from the core of the planet which jammed just about any technology devised by man: it chopped choppers from the sky; it sent cars into crash-dummy mode; it hurled hovercraft spinning through the air like a discus; and as far as hydrogen or laser technology was concerned, that was also a no-no. Which was why they had stopped trying to land spacecraft on the planet. The Protectorate's term for the phenomenon was Electro-Sonar Pulse Interference. People called it the Fearance.

'Folks say there's only a 1 in 5 chance of anything working as it should. In the early days, people got it into their heads that gunfights might be a good thing, this being a cowboy town and all. When 4 out of 5 gun-toters had their hands blown clean off, that put an end to that.'

Rib thought back to the scrapyard of wrecked shuttles. 'I guess we're lucky to be here at all, then.'

'Sure are. Now, back to your question. Steam trains are the only form of transport that seem to function anywhere near normal.'

'Why doesn't the Fearance scramble them then?'

'Well, even locomotives aren't totally immune. Every

now and then, you hear tales from down the line of boilers exploding, piston rods shearing, that sort of thing. Derailments are quite commonplace. But what it boils down to – and I'm not a scientist – is that steam engines are the only feasible and sustainable way to move heavy goods like timber, iron and such around the country.'

Rib chewed on a fingernail, reflecting on Sunset's words. Steam engines. Powered by ... coal? 'You said "sustainable", didn't you?'

'I did.'

'I don't see how steam trains can be sustainable. They're run on coal.'

'Ah, I see no-one's told you about the ... er ... Fuel Farms, then?

Rib shook his head.

'Right, this might take a lot of explaining. Let's get the coffee topped up first. Sure you're not going to have one of these croissants?'

Rib relented, 'Oh, all right then.'

'Excellent!' said Sunset, tipping the last one onto his plate. Between mouthfuls of pastry and slurps of coffee, Mr Todd delivered a brief lecture on alternative energy solutions, Tycho-style.

His student, of course was absolutely right. Coal was out of the question as a fuel source to power the giant locomotives. Protectorate Decree 147 clearly stated:

"There shall be no despoliation or mining of the natural resource of the New Planet, unless that resource is restored to constitute at least an equivalent quantum within eighteen calendar months."

In plainspeak, it was OK to chop down a few trees as long as you replaced them with more. So mining was a definite non-starter. Nor would Decree 147 permit whole forests to be flattened to stoke the boilers of trains. So, the Protectorate moved quickly to invent, design and establish a sustainable method of production which would enable the railroads to operate without adverse impact on the environment. Fuel Farms.

Fuel Farms were an important strand in the Protectorate's strategies to keep Tycho free of environmental exploitation and pollution. Under this strictly enforced policy, they created:

- Sustainable public transport spines (people called these "roads")
- Bio-diversity veins (people called these "fields and hedgerows and ditches")
- New infrastructure realms for:

  - housing
  - food production
  - health
  - education
  - waste management
  - energy exchange

(people called these "towns")

The fuel farms were located in Tycho's "holding camps", institutions where new arrivals to the planet were detained until they were able to prove themselves to be law-abiding citizens. People ended up there if they'd failed to satisfy the immigration checks, or if they'd kicked off in the long queue out of sheer frustration. They found themselves sharing cells with petty criminals and political subversants who had been arrested and removed from society. All were obliged to engage in purposeful activity. The work could take a variety of forms, from making mail bags to producing windmill blades, but most of the detainees were employed in the Compression Plant, a large building located in the centre of the compound. Here, the collected faeces of all the inmates was mixed with animal and human poo carted in from the outside world and compressed into blocks by a huge machine, not dissimilar to a cider press, then laid out on slatted wooden trays to dry on shelves over ember beds. The process was repeated with each batch forty-eight hours later, this time squeezing the blocks further into rock-hard cakes, similar in size to barbecue briquettes and perfect for stoking into the boiler of a steam locomotive.

Due to its proximity to Gatwick, the largest fuel farm in the country was located just outside Crawley. The phrase "Carrying coals to Newcastle" was duly superseded by "Carrying crapcakes to Crawley." The Protectorate called the production centres Fuel Farms. People called them Shitsheds.

17

So it was quite fitting that Old Smokey Arkwright was like a pig in shit, as he watched Boilerman Spinks shovel compressed crapcakes into the glowing boiler. It was a bright, sunny day. The sky was a powder blue, with not a trace of a cloud. From his footplate, he could see all the way to the horizon across a patchwork of golden cornfields. It was one of those hot summer days you thought would never end.

The journey from Euston had been as smooth as silk, a pure pleasure, thought Smokey as he eased the locomotive through poppy-filled meadows. It had been love at first sight – she was a willing worker, responsive to the touch and no trouble to maintain. In a previous life, she'd worked the Montana silver mines back in the 1890's. Now, she was pulling ten cars with a single caboose on the end, where three VIP passengers of unknown identity were sat. His was not to ask questions.

On approaching the Henriksson Ranch stockyards, Smokey brought the engine to a halt so they could watch the cowboys tie and brand cattle. After waving goodbye to the men, he eased the locomotive slowly forward to the ranch itself, where the farmer's wife had come out to greet him.

'Good morning, Engineer Arkwright.'

'Good morning, Mrs Henriksson,' he replied, removing his cap. 'And a fine morning it is, too.'

'Makes you pleased to be alive, doesn't it?' she beamed up at him. 'I thought you might like a little something for your breakfast tomorrow,' she said, handing up a muslin bag to him, carefully cradled in her strong, tanned hands.

She was a fine-looking woman. Smokey wished those strong, tanned hands would cradle him.

'Why, thank you Mrs Henriksson.' He knew what was inside the bag, but feigned surprise as he peered in. 'Why, duck eggs! And fine looking ones, too! Thank you, Mrs Henriksson, thank you. I'll have these fried in butter with a side of field mushrooms.'

'My pleasure, Engineer Arkwright, my pleasure,' she said as she turned towards the ranch house with a wave.

Smokey carefully placed the eggs in a straw-lined box in which lay the still-warm body of a pheasant, brought down by Boilerman Spinks with a well-aimed pebble from his catapult a few miles back down the track. Smokey had slowed the locomotive to walking pace to allow the boilerman to jump down from the cabin, run into the field to fetch his bird and sprint back to heave himself one-handed back up onto the footplate.

Smokey sounded the whistle, the engine exploded into life, sending a brown-tinged plume of steam billowing into the sky, and he leant out of the cabin to give the farmer's wife a final wave. As the train accelerated past the ranch's outbuildings, he noticed a slim figure busy tying up some dead starlings to a length of twine stretched out across a vegetable patch. The birds must have been bothersome, probably pulling out the onion sets. It was the rancher's daughter. She was wearing a thin, blue-checked cotton dress, which fluttered in the soft breeze, giving him a glimpse of her long, bronzed legs. Fine young filly she was turning out to be, he thought. Smokey leant out of the cabin, partly to get a better look and partly to hail good morning to her. She gave him a sulky stare, before returning to the task of winding a length of wire round the feet of a stiff starling. Old Smokey's one-track mind immediately made the connection with the night ahead and he opened up the throttle, his thought train now firmly intent on steaming into Stonyville, where it would be all aboard the ever-willing Frontier Fanny.

18

He'd made the switch to Old Smokey because it sounded a real engine driver's name – Arthur John Arkwright sounded more like a cotton-mill owner. On Earth, Arthur had led a mundane working life as an Administrative Assistant in the Pensions Section of the Finance Division of Buckinghamshire County Council. Each morning he would drive his orange Kia Picanto from his one-bedroom flat in Newport Pagnell to the County Hall car park in time to hear the 8:30 news on the radio and eat a low-cholesterol fruit and fibre bar. At precisely 8:59 he would walk up the steps of the main entrance and clock on for work. It is fair to say that the 62-year old bachelor from Newport Pagnell was a bit of a loner. Until the weekend, that was.

Because every Saturday and Sunday, Arthur John Arkwright took on a new persona. He would get up bright and early, polish off a hearty breakfast of bacon, two eggs, mushrooms, beans, tomatoes and fried bread, then hum a happy tune as he donned his uniform. For on the weekend, the caterpillar became a butterfly, the college kid morphed into a Power Ranger, Clark Kent changed his kecks in a phone box, the recluse pensions clerk became a superhero – Casey Jones, the Fat Controller and Ivor the Engine Driver all rolled into one. Arthur John Arkwright was the man who drove steam locomotives up and down a two mile length of track at the Buckinghamshire Railway Centre, which also went by the catchy name of BRC. He was without a shadow of a doubt The Main Man at BRC. Not only was he the godfather train-driver, he also put in herculean six hour shifts at the engineering sheds, working with a team of enthusiasts on rebuilding the Class 4-6-OMT 6989 'Wightwich Hall,' the largest locomotive in the BRC's collection. And, of course, no visit to a steam railway could be complete without a ride on Thomas the Tank Engine, which had become a real money spinner. So much so that BRC invested in a large Thomas the Tank hoarding placed out by the road to attract passing trade.

But from being the weekend King of the Castle, Arthur's life was turned upside down by Watershed. The Buckinghamshire Railway Centre was flattened in the third wave of tsunamis to hit the British shoreline. The Thomas the Tank hoarding was swept eighteen miles to the north-east where it became impaled on the end of a lamp post in the Asda/Wallmart Superstore car park in Bletchley. Thomas hung there for a further twenty two years, grinning inanely in an act of stoic proportion through the greatest natural disaster to hit the planet.

Arthur was one of the lucky few to escape Earth and ended up on a windy hill without highway or watercourse in a far flung corner of the universe. And there, Arthur found himself elevated to the status of demi-god, because he possessed a skill-set held by only a handful of men and women on the planet. Not his ability to calculate annuity yields. Not his ability to change the spark plugs on a Kia Picanto in his garage without the light on, impressive though these attributes were.

No.

Arthur John Arkwright was an engine driver. He was pure gold dust.

Protectorate outriders tracked him down within days and made him an offer he couldn't refuse. Maybe he could have driven a harder bargain, even a $2^1/_2\%$ enhanced employer's pension contribution, but he didn't. He accepted on the spot.

And now, Old Smokey was living his dream. A pig in shit.

19

The Protectorate liked to manage communication so that it was easily absorbed and understood by the population. Censorship, in other words. Any report of an accident on the railroad would first have to pass the desk of Stationmaster Mole and then the keen scrutiny of Marshall Amps before being released to the Strumpet for publication. In spite of this, a surprising number hit the headlines through another channel. On the second and fourth Tuesday of every month, Old Smokey Arkwright held court at the Florence, where he stopped for an overnight stay.

The Florence was quintessentially Cowboy, a place where an L-plate cowpoke could unwind after a hard day breaking in fences and mending horses. The saloon doors swung open into a cavernous, dimly-lit room. On the left loomed the dark oak bar stocked with various bottles of whisky and rye, gin and rum. In the far recesses of the saloon stood four round six-seater card tables. To the right, a stage for the twice weekly line dancing and, of course, Cowgirl Karaoke on a Saturday nite. A hotel inspector would have been far-pushed to give the spit-and-sawdust dive a single horseshoe.

It hadn't always been called the Florence. In the early days, an entrepreneur by the name of Sheldon Lillicrap had opened a new type of hostelry as a radical alternative to the traditional business model presented by the Grand Hotel. He launched Boutique Trampolino as a venue where couples, normally on the rebound, could hire rooms by the hour for a quick squeaking of the bedsprings. But customer reviews were very up and down, a few too many cheques bounced and the venture folded after six months.

Old Smokey was firmly installed on a stool at the far end of the Florence bar, surrounded by a crowd of cowhands, who were plying the grizzly old geezer with Wild Spatchcock to lubricate his tongue. They didn't have to wait long before he had built up a head of steam and was into his first story. Hetty sat a couple of stools away, within easy eavesdropping range. She slipped her notebook from her handbag onto the sticky bar and licked her pencil in eager anticipation.

Old Smokey Arkwright was a native of Newport Pagnell. So it was quite odd that he spoke like Deputy Dawg. But it has to be said that he carried off the Tennessee drawl with aplomb, especially the wheezy, stretched-out laugh. His expectant audience were not, however, gathered to hear tales of henhouse raids. No sirreee. They wanted high-octane action. And Old Smokey seldom failed to deliver.

'Oooh-wee,' he began. 'Dagnabbit, boys, I never see anything like it in all my cotton-pickin' days. It sure is a miracle I'm sitting here at all.' He paused to throw back a slug of Spatchcock, slamming his shotglass down on the bar. It was refilled immediately by a young freckled cowpoke sitting next to him. 'Well, are you sitting comfortably, boys?' The boys murmured yes. 'Then we'll begin.'

'We were chugging over the Nene Bridge without a care in the world when all of a sudden it collapsed beneath us, causing the engine to derail. The bridge piers must have been damaged by the recent floods, I reckon. At first, I thought we'd hit something on the track. It all happened so quickly, I didn't even have time to reach for the brake. The engine smashed through the side rails of the bridge before plunging down into the river. We dang near carried the whole bridge down with us. It's hard to fathom how any of us got out of that wreck alive ...' Smokey paused for effect, taking the opportunity to dispatch another Spatchcock.

'We were pulling five box-cars and a caboose, and they all followed us into the river, crashing down on top of us. The men riding on the loco with me were Lake, Palmer and Emerson. I was in the cab when we went under.'

'What happened? What happened?' lisped a bespectacled young rancher named Vincent.

'Hold on there a cotton-pickin' minute,' said Smokey, clearly annoyed. 'I'm coming to that.' He downed another shot. 'I'd taken a blow to the head, which scrambled my senses. I do recollect somehow pulling myself out of the cabin. One of the sleepers had ended up wedged on top of the engine, which was lying on its side with the cold waters rushing all over it. I straddled the sleeper, holding on for dear life. I could see Palmer was trapped in the cab. I reached down and managed to haul him out. Scarcely able to breathe himself, he pointed to Lake, who was trapped with one of his legs pinned under the fire box. The poor critter couldn't shift an inch. He was trying to keep his head above the water rushing over his back and shoulders. By this time, we were joined by three lumbermen, who had worked their way up from the caboose. Heroes, cotton pickin' heroes, every man jack of them. They stood for two hours in that freezing water, up to their armpits forming a human shield against the force of the river, trying to keep Lake from going under. All in vain ...' he sighed, wiping a tear from his eye. 'We lost him.'

'What happened to Emerson?' asked a wide-eyed Vincent.

'Somehow made it to the bank downriver. Ooh-wee, what a lucky man he was. But poor old Lake ...'

In a collective sigh of sorrow, the cowboys slowly shook their heads.

Old Smokey heaved himself off the stool. 'Just going to dangle the old water hose,' he said over his shoulder as he ambled towards the latrine.

Hetty could hardly contain her excitement. 'What a scoop!' she whispered to herself, before glugging back her gin and hot-footing lickety-spit back to the Strumpet, where she started banging out the headline feature for the morning edition on her trusty Gestetner. It was a pity Hetty left when she did, because Old Smokey returned to tell a second story. She had bought a single can of beans from the buy-one-get-one-free bucket.

'Oooh-wee, that feels better,' resumed the gnarled old engine driver, wiping his piss-splashed hands on the back of his trousers. 'Do you wanna hear one more, boys?'

'Sure do!'

'Well, hold on to your cotton-pickin' cowboy hats for this one, 'cos you ain't gonna believe it.'

'Yeth, Mithter Thmokey,' said Vincent, obediently holding on to his hat.

'Some of you may have heard about the main trestle bridge out at Settle being blocked?'

A couple of cowboys nodded.

'But I bet you's don't know what really happened.'

'No, Mithter Thmokey,' said Vincent.

'The biggest boiler explosion ever to have happened on Tycho, that's what happened. Bang-slap in the middle of the bridge. God knows how the whole bridge didn't burn down.'

'What happened? What happened?' asked Vincent.

'Fireman McCartney's body was hurled four hundred feet in the air, that's what happened!'

'Did he die?' asked Vincent.

'Of course he died, you cotton pickin' dickhead!' snapped Smokey.

'But how the hell did the explosion happen?' asked a ranch hand in the act of refilling Smokey's empty glass.

'The investigator found the cause to be low water. Engineer Starr emphatically denied this to be the case, claiming they'd taken on water at Manchester. But they never found any evidence to prove what really happened. You wanna know why? Because someone had removed all the gauges after the accident. And we all know who that someone is don't we?' he nodded knowingly.

'Who ith it, Mithter Thmokey, who ith it?'

'Dagnabbit Vincent! Does your brain have any gear apart from idle?' A wide yawn revealed a row of tobacco stained teeth. 'Anyway, boys, that's all from me tonight, I'm ready to hit the hay.'

The boys gave him a round of applause and watched his unsteady progress up the stairs towards Room 12, where he would partake of a nightcap with Frontier Fanny before playing a round of his favourite game of Steamtrains & Tunnels, whistles-a-blowin' and pistons-a-pumpin'.

20

It was a Sunday, so the Waterloo was closed. The summer was coming to an end, thought Rib, as he caught the first trace of autumnal chill in the breeze blowing from the west. He walked back to the flat to unpack the two boxes of provisions he'd just bought from the Market Hall, the only place open. Two chorizo pizzas, two loaves of wholemeal bread, a kilo of apples, a slab of red cheese, two bottles of full cream milk, coffee, two bacon pies, a jar of lime pickle and half a kilo of garden peas. He eased the vent on the cast-iron range open and watched the embers smoulder before he opened the door to throw in two silver-birch logs. They quickly caught and he closed the door, put a pan of water on the front plate and a tray with one of the pies onto the middle shelf of the oven. Twenty minutes, he reckoned. He took the bag of peas back out onto the balcony, sat down in the rocking chair borrowed from Sunset, and started to shell them into a chipped enamel bowl. One for the pot, one for me, he murmured as he crunched into the fresh sweetness. When he'd prised every pea from its pod, he took the bowl back into the flat and carefully emptied the contents into the pan just as it came to the boil on the hotplate. As if unsure what to do next, he paused before striding over to the Welsh dresser on the wall to take out a silver teaspoon from the top drawer. Grabbing one of the bottles of milk, he stepped onto the balcony, the evening sun forcing him to squint as it shone sharply through the treetops on the ridge above town. The old rocking chair was positioned to give a good view of Main Street. He sat down, unpeeled the cap from the bottle of milk and dipped the spoon into the thick layer of cream on the top. He put the spoon in his mouth and left it there, allowing the cream to melt slowly on his tongue. It tasted good.

Suddenly, he saw something from the corner of his eye. It looked like two enormous black birds perched on a telegraph pole just down from the butcher's. They were too big for crows. They were massive. Just as he stood up to get a better look, a hissing sound came from inside the flat. The peas were boiling over! He rushed in and moved the pan to the side of the hotplate, then dashed back onto the balcony to check out the birds. They were gone.

21

Ravens are big black birds, commonly known as the vultures of sheep country. They patrol in pairs in search of carrion. Maybe a sickly sheep or a wounded deer, waiting to die. Mostly ponderous and tank-like in their flight pattern, ravens can surprise with a sudden display of stunning aerobatics. In spring, particularly, pairs tumble high in the sky, half-closing their wings to roll over sideways and nose-dive. They also have a trick of flying upside down for short distances. Such antics are said to be part of the raven's courtship display, though sometimes they seem to be performed from sheer high spirits.

There was nothing high-spirited about the pair of ravens perched silently on a telegraph pole on the shadowed side of Main Street. And certainly no signs of courtship. They sat still as statues, observing the humans going about their late business below. No tricks, no aerobatics, no antics. For these were no ordinary ravens. They were giant black birds, measuring some forty inches from bill to tail, larger than a golden eagle.

They were Huginn and Muninn, their names meaning Thought and Memory. Messengers of Odin. Or, at least, they used to be ...

'Tell me how it goes again.'

'What?'

'The article about our Master. You know, the one in the Strumpet.'

'It wasn't in the Strumpet, you fool, it was in the Heimskringla.'

'Whatever. How does it go again?'

'OK, OK. Now, are you sitting comfortably?'

'Wait a minute. Do you mind if I nestle up?'

Muninn paused. 'If you absolutely must.' Huginn shuffled along and laid his head on his brother's shoulder.

'OK? Ready?'

'Yes, thanks. Now, how does it go again?'

'Odin was a great and very far-travelled warrior who conquered many kingdoms. So successful was he that in every battle, victory was on his side.'

'Mmm,' went Huginn nestling further into Muninn's feathers.

'It was the belief of his people that victory belonged only to him. It was his custom, when he sent his men into battle, for him to lay his hands upon their heads and bless them with his powers.'

'Do you remember when he used to do that to us?' Huginn asked, wide-eyed.

'Yes, of course I remember,' said Memory. 'And then they knew in their hearts that they would win. Odin had two brothers – '

Huginn stiffened. 'I don't like this bit,' he said.

'Listen, do you want me to tell the story or not?'

'OK, but try to scoot through this part,' he implored.

'Two brothers, one named Ve, the other Vilje – '

'Ugly bastards!'

'Listen, I'm not going to carry on if you keep interrupting!'

'Sorry.'

'... and they governed the kingdom in Odin's

absence. It happened once when our Master had travelled a great distance away – '

'Shit! I know what's going to happen next.'

'Listen, am I telling this story or aren't I?'

'Sorry.'

'... and had been away so long that his people doubted if he would ever return home, that his two brothers took it upon themselves to divide his estate. And both of them – '

'Aaargh! Oh shit! I know what happens next!'

'Huginn, we both do! We were there, remember?'

Huginn calmed down and nuzzled up to the giant raven on his right.

'Ready?'

'Yep'

'And both of them took his wife, Frigg, to themselves.'

Huginn squawked, lost his balance, emptied his bowels on Muninn's left foot and fell off his perch, flapping out of control towards a birch tree on the other side of the street. This sudden manoeuvre set all the blackbirds, starlings, sparrows and finches who had settled down to roost for the night flapping skyward in a mad panic. Forty minutes later, peace was restored, the birds were back in their nests and Huginn's head was back nestling into the warmth of his brother's shoulder.

'If you ask me, she knew exactly what she was doing,' he mumbled into his feathers, before the storyteller had time to take up the tale again.

'Listen. I'm not going to tell you again. Are you going to let me tell this bloody saga or not! You were there. I was there. We both bloody know what happened!' He took a deep breath. 'It is true that she didn't reckon on him coming back. It is true that the boys saw an opening and went for it. But to say that in any way ...'

Huginn opened his beak to disagree.

'Shut it! I am the storyteller! And the story is as told! No discussion! End of saga!'

Huginn conceded defeat, trying to put to the back of his mind the time the two brothers took their frothing horns to Frigg's chamber to claim their bed prize. The episode brought back distant, confused memories of the moans and groans echoing across the frozen lake from the sauna in the forest. Every night. From half past nine until three in the morning. For three months.

'But remember, my friend, the most important line in the story.'

The big bird nodded.

Muninn took a deep breath. 'OK, here we go. "Odin soon after returned home and took his wife back."'

The two giant ravens went quiet for a good twenty minutes in awe of that simple, ten-word statement. They, and only they, knew what had been involved. Nobody would ever mess with Odin's wife again, kith or kin. And Frigg would never, ever, ever look elsewhere again.

'Shall I continue?' asked Muninn.

'Yes, please.'

'Odin was the cleverest of them all. And from him all the others learned their arts and accomplishments. But now, to tell why he is held in such high respect, we must mention various causes that contributed.'

'I think I can remember these,' chirped Huginn.

'Either I tell the saga or it's straight to beddie-byes,' threatened Muninn.

'Sorry.'

'Thank you. Ahem ... When amongst friends, his countenance was so beautiful and dignified, that the spirits of all were lifted by it. But when at war, his appearance terrified his foe. For he could change his form and skin in any way he wished. Also, he conversed so cleverly and smoothly, that all who heard believed his every word. He spoke everything in rhyme, such as we now call Scald-craft.'

Huginn raised his head to nod, then settled back into the feathered shoulder.

'Odin could make his enemies in battle blind, deaf or terror-struck, and their weapons so blunt that they could no more cut than a willow wand. On the other hand, his men would rush forward without armour, were as mad as dogs or wolves, bit their shields, were as strong as bears or wild bulls, and killed people with a single blow. Yet neither fire nor iron told upon themselves. This was called the Berserk fury.'

'Sorry to butt in, me old cock-sparrow, but what's your take on the berserks? Bear-shirts? Wolf-skin cloaks? Demons? Epileptics?'

'Drugs,' said Muninn, for the hundredth time.

'Oh, yeah. You've told me that before, haven't you?'

'May I continue? It gets dark at nine.'

'Sorry.'

'Odin could transform his shape. His body would lie as if asleep or dead, but then he could take on the shape of a fish, or worm or bird or beast and be off in a twinkling to different places.'

'Those were the days,' sighed Huginn.

'With words alone he could quench fire, still an ocean in tempest and turn a wild wind to any quarter. Odin had a ship called – '

'Skidbladnir!' squawked Huginn.

'Bravo, you remembered,' muttered Muninn, heavy on the sarcasm. 'A ship called Skidbladnir, in which he would sail to any place he wished, and which he could roll up like a cloth.'

At this point, the two ravens chose to reflect in silence at the amazing qualities of the craft in question. A ship you could roll up like a cloth! It would have been the perfect moment for a Gauloise, but it might have looked somewhat conspicuous and attracted unwanted attention.

'Sometimes he even called the dead out of the earth,' continued Muninn, 'or set himself beside the hanged men, whence he was called the ghost-sovereign and Lord of the Hanged. He had two ravens – '

Huginn dug Muninn in the ribs. 'That's us!'

Muninn had to giggle, too, because in spite of everything, he was still proud in an embarrassed sort of way to have been one of Odin's messengers. 'Two ravens, to whom he had taught the shape and speech of man; and they flew far and wide throughout the land and brought him news. Because of all this, he was pre-eminently wise.'

'Mmm, you could say that again,' agreed his brother.

At which point, Muninn excused himself, partly pissed off at the constant interruptions, and partly in need of a quick flap around the block to relieve a build-up of wind that had been troubling him.

'I'm off for a shit,' he explained.

'A blue one?'

'No, not today ...'

22

In the good old days, the job description of Huginn and Muninn was fairly straightforward. Not only were they Odin's messengers, they were his reporters: they gathered news and brought reports back to him every evening, one perched on each of his mighty shoulder blades, where they would take turns to whisper the events of the day in his ear. Odin was not a great one for weather updates, traffic reports or sports headlines. He liked to hear about battles. The bigger and bloodier the better.

So the giant ravens would spend most of their days scouring battlefields, working up a healthy appetite in the process. Battlefields being what they are, there was always a fair amount of readily available carrion for them to feast on. Their ever-presence at scenes of violent conflict explains how they came to be cast in just about every Norse saga and became synonymous with the letting of blood:

"ravens screeching over chopped bodies ..."
"ravens flocked to the reddened sword ..."
"the raven daubed the prow of its beak in waves of red ..."
"he who stains the raven's bill has won ..."

And this went on, day in, day out for hundreds of years. Up with the lark. Chase the lark. Kill and eat the lark – just to raise the blood-sugar level – before flying off to the nearest battlefield for brunch.

Until their lord and master left.

Whilst they knew it was their duty to remain, it has to be said that there followed a dark period in their lives when they flew aimlessly round the world, taking little pleasure in tearing hunks of flesh from corpses slain on the battlefield. Quite simply, they lost their purpose in life. Red bills without a cause.

Until they re-invented themselves.

Until Huginn and Muninn invented Knowledge Transfer.

Now, as everyone knows, knowledge transfer became the in-phrase around the turn of the 21st Century. People would nod their heads knowingly in agreement that knowledge transfer was the key ingredient of a successful, knowledge-based economy.

Ask anybody what it actually meant and the answer would almost certainly begin with 'Er …' Confusing phrases such as enterprise hubs and innovation gateways would be thrown into the mix, leaving 21st Century man and woman not at all comfortable with the concept. But when they Googled it, they found 657,231 definitions, which make them feel better, because they had thought they were the only ones who didn't know the right answer.

Huginn and Muninn became the world's first knowledge-transfer consultants the moment that they discovered their master had left them with a number of very special qualities. They could speak in many tongues. They could change their shape. They could fly faster than the speed of light. But, most remarkable of all, they could transfer knowledge from the brain of one or several human beings directly into the brain of another without use of any electronic or chemical means. No surgical intervention. No hypnotism. Nothing like that. Just direct transfer of knowledge. Giving an already intelligent, creative person that spark of genius which makes them one in a billion. A great inventor, artist, leader, humanitarian. By knowledge transfer, raven-style.

Admittedly, it did take Huginn and Muninn a few centuries to realise that they were blessed with this unique talent. They had, of course, long known that the tastiest delicacy to be had from any soldier slain in battle was his brain. Not always the easiest to access, however, unless the skull had been cloven in two by the blow of an axe. More often than not, the prized morsel was protected by a helmet and only so much could be pecked out through the eye sockets. Hardly enough to see you through to tea-time. Indeed, scarcely worth the effort when there were hearts, livers and lungs piled in copious helpings at the carvery, where you could always go back for more.

But around the middle of the fourteenth century, the two ravens noticed a remarkable change in their bowel movements on the occasions that they were able to feast on the human brain. Their shit turned a pale blue colour.

And when the opportunity presented itself to gorge on the brains of a true hero fallen in battle, they discovered something quite extraordinary. Their creamy-coloured excrement had a bright blue centre. Rather like the yolk of an egg. But instead of yellow, bright blue. This made absolutely no sense at all and it seemed to be of no consequence whatsoever, other than when housewives brought in the washing and cried to their families, 'Have you seen the state of these sheets! Covered in bird shit! And not just bird shit, but fucking blue bird shit!' At which bluebirds would dive, swoop and twitter, 'It wasn't us! It was probably the swallows. We're often mistaken for swallows.'

The light went on in the year 1495. Huginn was happily gliding over the foothills surrounding the city of Rome when he was suddenly caught short. Not that birds have to wait until they find a public convenience before they pass piss or poop. But, believe it or not, they are very particular about where they empty their bowels. When you find the windscreen of your car caked in goose crap, it is no accident. However, Huginn had no option but to jettison his heavy load, and immediately felt the better for it. 'That's a weight off my mind,' he said to himself, not realising how prophetic that statement was to be.

For down below him, on the slopes of an Italian foothill, the young Buonarrotti Michaelangelo was close to orgasm in the arms of his secret lover, Sophia Dolcelatte, whose father owned the olive grove and would definitely not have been amused at his daughter's buttocks being ground into the very soil he had tilled with his own hands.

The giant raven's missile scored a direct, sloppy hit on the bare back of young Michaelangelo, right between the shoulder blades, causing the rutting youth to scream, 'Aaargh! Mother of Jesus!'

'There, there, my little bambino,' soothed Sophia, believing he was in ecstasy.

'Shaddup! Something big and wet and sloppy has just landed on my back! What is it?'

'Er, it's a bit difficult to see from here,' said Sophia, straining to peer over his shoulder.

With a degree of difficulty, he extricated himself from between her legs and stood up, turning his back towards her. 'What in hell's name is it? Can you see?'

'Er, yes. It looks like half a tub of gorgonzola. Runny gorgonzola. Either that or it's blue shit from a very big bird.'

Suddenly, the eyes of the young Michaelangelo glazed over and he spoke, as if in a trance, 'I must go immediately to cover the vast ceiling of the Sistine Chapel with awesome scenes from the Bible.' He then sprinted down the hill, bollock naked, leaving his lover abandoned, legs still wide apart. He stopped and turned to her, shouting something about an erection. She smiled. The boy was still aroused. No man could walk away from the sweet charms of Sophia Dolcelatte. The wind on the dusty hillside then dropped and she heard his cries.

'Get me a scaffold erector, now!'

'Shit!' she said as she gathered up her skirts. 'Shit!'

The ravens followed the fortunes of young Buonarrotti with keen interest and, sure enough, he did turn out be a dab hand at painting. Muninn preferred his statues, especially the ones with no arms. Gave them that certain ... battlefield quality.

For the following couple of hundred years they conducted a series of controlled experiments which proved beyond all reasonable doubt that there existed a direct correlation between the IQ of the consumed brain and the genius-potency of their droppings. As a result they became selective in their choice of prey, sometimes with regrettable consequences for their victims.

Chief Makalele had been fighting a desperate rearguard battle for over five days, driven from the plain by the fierce onslaught of the Soshangene tribe. His villages burned, his women and children slaughtered, Makalele fought his way across the great Limpopo River and up the slopes of Mount Lebombo, towards the summit where his forefathers were buried in the ancestral tomb. His force was now only twenty strong, his loyal band of bodyguards – the finest young men of his tribe – out on their feet. Wave after wave of attacks rained relentlessly down on their shields. In that brave stand on an African mountain top, they fought like demons for two long days and two even longer nights. Over a thousand enemy warriors lay slain on the slopes of Mount Lebombo. And still they came ...

Chief Makalele was the last man to fall, and only

then to a chance arrow loosed from a distance, which embedded itself into the small of his back. As he lay spread-eagled on the rocky outcrop, he stared up into the deep blue sky of the African dusk. Closing his eyes for the last time, he felt his soul being lifted from his body, upwards to heaven to join his ancestors.

Actually, Chief Makalele wasn't quite dead yet. The two giant ravens had begun to grow impatient with the protracted struggle played out beneath them and, as soon as they saw the Chief fall, they cracked on with it. Swooping down, the huge birds each seized one of his feet in their mighty talons, then lifted him up into the air to a height of some ten metres – this was when the Chief thought his soul was being lifted up to heaven.

With Muninn acting as navigator, 'Left a bit. Right a bit. Stop! That's it … no! Back a bit. OK … release!' the birds manoeuvred the father of the Shona tribe until he dangled directly above a huge rock. They then dropped him. His head took the full force, the rock splitting the skull open, from which his still-warm brain spilled out over the rough outcrop, just as a thrush cracks the shell of a snail open on a stone. That was the moment the Chief died.

The ravens argued like two ferrets in a woman's blouse over a name for their invention.

'Let's call it blue-tooth technology,' suggested Huginn.

'Don't be ridiculous. People would laugh their heads off at such a stupid name. They'd think we were idiots. I think we should call it blue-shit technology.'

They finally compromised on blue-poo.

23

Another bright Stonyville morning, another breakfast audience with Mr Sunset Todd. 'It does take some getting used to, I grant you,' said the big man, wiping his mouth on his sleeve. 'I think everyone must find it strange here at first. But to be quite honest with you, I was happy to turn my back on war, starvation, overpopulation. I didn't really feel safe in that world any longer. The only thing we have to worry about here is a plague of locusts destroying our crops.'

'Locusts?'

'Yeah, real cereal killers,' wheezed the old geezer in a fit of laughter. The boy had walked right into that one. 'Nope, I don't miss the skyscrapers, office blocks or queues at the petrol pump at all.'

Rib chewed slowly on his toast. 'I kind of miss the technology, though.'

'Can't say I do. I could never get used to that bleedin' i-shield. Every time I blinked to turn on the tee-vee, the coffee grinder came on and my pile-cream dispenser squirted all over the bathroom floor. I think it was trying to tell me something.'

Rib watched the big man's face crease into a thousand wrinkles and decided to change the subject. 'Did you say something about getting some ham in for breakfast?'

'So I did. Clean forgot to put it on the table. Go and get yourself some – it's in the cellar.'

Rib stood up and walked into the galley. 'Can I cut a slice for you?'

'No, I'm totally stuffed, thanks. Maybe force just one more croissant down. Would be a shame not to finish off old Friedlander's honey ...'

Rib opened the door of the range and lit a spill to fire the paraffin lamp. He then pulled up the hatch door in the floor and fastened it open. As he descended the stairs into the cellar, he could hear the tortured strains of Sunset singing about some woman being as sweet as Tupelo honey.

Rib carefully hung the lamp on a meat hook suspended from the ceiling and waited for a second or two for the light to fill the underground room. The cellar served as the Waterloo's cold store. The floor was bare earth and the walls thick timber pilings, which supported the structure of the building. Along the right hand wall, meats hung from the ceiling to dry – strings of sausages, hocks of ham, a side of venison, a pheasant ready for plucking. Down the left hand side were stored a churn of milk, two large round cheeses, a wooden tub of butter, a second, smaller tub of goose fat. And ahead of him, against the far wall, stood a large rough-hewn trestle table carrying the meat safe and a chopping block. The gauze-mesh door opened easily and there, sure enough, sat a joint of boiled ham on the white marble slab.

Rib carefully removed the meat from the safe and placed it on the block, glancing round for a carving knife as he did so. Something caught his eye on the floor underneath the table. His blood ran cold.

Ever since that fateful evening out on the perimeter platform of his Mum's animal refuge, he had done his best to suppress the chilling memories of that final showdown with Besk. And now it all came flooding back in one numbing flashback shock. The stacked coins, the last walnut, Ainsley the python, the crossbow levelled at him, the pain as the bolt ripped through his side.

The bolt.

With a red feather flight.

Now lying on the cellar floor of the Waterloo Brewing Co.

Instinctively, he ducked and threw himself to one side, coming to rest with his left cheekbone pressed flat against the cool surface of the milk churn. The cellar measured no more than twelve metres square. No cupboards, no alcoves, no hidey-holes. The lamp flickered.

There was no-one there.

Easing himself cautiously to his feet, he moved slowly back to the table, keeping his eyes firmly fixed on the cellar steps. Only when he was a hundred percent sure he was alone, he bent down to take a closer look at the object which had filled him with terror. Sweat trickled from his armpits as he stretched under the table to take hold of the crossbow bolt. He gasped .

It wasn't a crossbow bolt at all, but a sharpening steel which must have fallen off the chopping block. A piece of sacking covered its handle and a couple of red neck-feathers from the pheasant hung on the meat hook above had landed across the shaft of the steel. In the half-light of the cellar, Rib had seen only one thing – the crossbow bolt which had ripped into his body. He stood up and placed both hands on the cold marble, sucking in deep lungfuls of cool cellar air. Once his heartbeat had returned to something like normal, he picked up the meat knife and tried to carve a slice of bacon. His hand was trembling so much that he nearly took the tip of a finger off. After two more tries, he finally managed to carve a couple of presentable slices, put the joint back into the safe, took the lamp down from the ceiling and climbed unsteadily up the stairs into the galley.

'You took your time, matey. Everything OK?'

'Yes, fine,' lied Rib.

Sunset saw the boy's hand shake as he lay the bacon slices on the plate, but said nothing.

'Would you like a slice?' asked Rib. 'I cut two just in case you wanted one.'

'Oooh, no thanks. Very nice of you, but I was just thinking of trying the plum jam on another of these lovely croissants. Victoria never lets me down.'

The boy watched his landlord spoon a generous portion from the jar onto his plate and spread the dark red jam thickly onto the pastry.

Sunset looked up. 'Tuck in, me old mate.'

Rib went through the motions of eating the boiled bacon roll, tasteless in his dry mouth.

He chewed mechanically, gazing over Sunset's shoulder through the window at the kitchen garden: canes of runner beans, rows of soft fruit, the rickety hen-house; and beyond, a stand of silver birch, leaves shimmering in the soft morning breeze like a swirl of starlings at roosting time. His fixed stare took in all these things, yet nothing registered. His mind was elsewhere. On another world.

A world where a girl tickled him in the ribs, cooked him snowgrouse stew, and taught him how to drink Koskenkorva.

A world where a girl slept beside him in an underpass in the ruins of a city. And then walked out on him. Rika ...

Tears welled up in his eyes. He stood up and left the table without a word. Sunset let him go.

Out on the street, the town was coming to life. He nearly stepped out in front of a horse and wagon piled high with onion sacks. 'Watch your step, sonny!'

shouted the driver. 'You'll do that once too often.' Rib ignored him, striding fiercely along the boardwalk, head down. Past the saddler's, then the butcher's, where a queue was already coming out of the door. Children streamed through the school gates on the other side of the road. He didn't give them a second glance.

Behind him, a cloudburst hit Stonyville, blowing down Main Street on a cool breeze from the North. People dashed for cover under the shelter of the boardwalk. Judd Scoter retreated into the Market Hall. Mud spattered up onto Diamond Dan's street sign.

The solitary figure of a 15 year-old boy, shoulders hunched against the downpour, trudged up the hill and out into the countryside.

It rained in his heart as it rained on the town …

24

Stooped against the driving rain and soaked to the skin, he walked for miles along the road, which ran straight as a die due south. He hardly noticed his sodden clothes clinging cold to his shivering skin. He just kept on walking, deep in thought. Every few minutes, a wagon slowed down to offer a lift. Each time he refused. The Meskitoe boy was walking down a long and lonesome road and that was the way it was.

Conditions underfoot were becoming increasingly treacherous and he nearly slithered into a ditch on more than one occasion. He'd struggled on for what must have been two hours when the road entered dense woodland, which gave welcome respite from the rain. About a hundred metres in, a track veered off to the right, into seemingly impenetrable darkness. Ahead, he could see through the tunnel of trees to where the road broke out into open countryside again. Without knowing why, he took the track.

Only a few steps into the forest, he sensed something odd. At first, he couldn't fathom what had put him on guard, but then realised that the answer lay beneath his feet. The track, some three metres wide, was surfaced – a perfectly constructed, cobbled carriageway. Although it had stopped raining, large droplets still fell randomly from the canopy above, breaking on the smooth cobbles with a splash. Eyes still trying to adjust to the gloom,

Rib recalled the last time he found himself in a dark forest on his own. The trail from the MK Citidome debris strip to the Slingshot Inn. He shuddered at the memory. Thankfully, this place bore little resemblance to the sweltering, menacing rainforest. He pressed on.

After two hundred metres or so, the track suddenly threw a ninety-degree dog-leg to the right. A narrow, overgrown trail continued straight on. Rib slowed, then cautiously took the right-angled bend. As soon as he turned the corner, he stopped dead in his tracks. The cobbled road came to an abrupt end at a large fence with a gate, where the forest opened out into a large clearing. Rib could just make out, over the top of the fence, the roof of a building. A strange building, like nothing he'd seen on Tycho, or anywhere else, for that matter. With a distinct feeling that he was somehow trespassing, he started walking warily towards the gate. His fears appeared to be founded when he reached a sign – metal, not wood – which read:

The Mansion

No Unauthorised Access

The message was clear enough, but he was curious. The cobbled road, the fence, the building, the sign – they were all so untypically Tycho that he just had to take a closer peek. Keeping to the left hand side of the track he edged forward, half hidden in the shadow of the forest. With each step, the view through the barred gate became clearer. First, a lake, with a couple of swans. Sweeping lawns, wooden huts and then … what he saw next took his breath away. An old house. Made of brick. With painted gables. At least three, he counted. And a kind of green dome, faded metal of some sort. A large door with a stone arch. Presumably the entrance. Open-mouthed, he was too busy cataloguing the architectural features of the building – which must be the Mansion – to notice the guard striding across the lawn with a large German Shepherd straining at the leash. Rib nearly pooped himself when the dog started to bark, now rearing up and baring a ferocious set of fangs. In a flash, Rib was legging it back down the cobbled road, not stopping until he reached the dog-leg, where he dared a nervous glance behind to make sure he wasn't being followed. The guard stood inside the gate watching him, the dog thankfully still held on a tight leash.

'Clear off!' shouted the man. Rib had no intention of hanging around and sprinted back through the forest. Once he was certain no-one was after him, he slowed to catch his breath. Soon back on the highway, he let out a huge sigh of relief. What the hell was that place? He certainly wouldn't be going back to find out ...

25

The late morning sun had come out to dry up all the rain. He'd left the Waterloo in such haste he'd forgotten to bring his hat. Although his long hair offered some protection, he was already feeling the heat burning on his neck. At least his clothes would soon dry out, he thought, as he headed back towards Stonyville.

Again, he refused lifts from slowing carriages, but this time with a smile and a wave. Being out in the open countryside had been good for the soul and, apart from the scary episode in the forest, he was feeling a lot better about himself. He decided there and then that he should get out of town more often.

Loud rumblings from his stomach reminded him of the succulent boiled bacon and he wished he'd eaten more than the one slice before rushing out. Now he was really hungry. And thirsty. He quickened his pace, soon passing familiar landmarks, the Friedlander Farm, the Henriksson Ranch, and before long he was back on home territory. First stop, the Market Hall. It just had to be the hog-roast.

The very thought of juicy roast pork with all the trimmings – crisp crackling, apple sauce, sage and onion stuffing – drove all other thoughts from Rib's mind as he sped down the hill into town. He just hoped there wasn't a queue. His saliva glands were in overdrive and there was only so much a boy could dribble.

Down towards the middle of Main Street, he saw Marshall Amps during his morning rounds on Shaft. He was leaning down talking to someone on the boardwalk outside the bank. Rib couldn't quite make out who. He didn't care, as long as it wasn't him. And he had something far more important on his mind. Hog-roast.

Larix LeRoux was widely acknowledged to be the best hog-roaster for miles around. Not bad for a fifteen year-old kid. With one arm. He'd left school the year before with an impressive string of qualifications to his name. Turning a deaf ear to his teachers' advice to stay on, he quit. He was having none of it. He had plans. To be the best hog-roaster in Stonyville County. And he certainly was.

No denying it, thought Rib, as he bit into the warm pork sandwich. 'Mmm, that's just perfect, man,' he said, wiping apple sauce from the corner of his mouth.

'Glad you like it,' said Larix, turning his back on him to rotate the spit. Larix was a boy of few words, keeping himself to himself. Rib had never seen him hanging out with sprogs of his age. Being a regular customer he'd often tried to engage him in conversation, but it was heavy going. Not helped by the fact that Rib couldn't put the How-come-you've-only-got-one-arm? question out of his head. Hardly the best opening line in small talk.

Today was no exception. Once he'd polished off the stellar sandwich, he took leave of Larix, who nodded a farewell. A nod was as good as it got from the introverted boy who, on account of his disability, got more than his fair share of jeers, jibes and general abuse from the less enlightened members of the Stonyville community. Once, when the banker's son, Edward Schilling, called him "Stumpy", Larix responded by calling him a bankerwanker, giving him the appropriate gesture with his good arm as he did so. Edward immediately ran home to tell Daddy, who immediately ran to the Sheriff's office to report the "serious incident". Marshall Amps looked up from his desk, let out a big sigh and said he'd have a word. When challenged by the Sheriff, Larix explained in wide-eyed innocence, 'I was only telling Master Schilling about our latest speciality – hand-pulled pork ...'

The sundial next to the horsetrough told him it was about half eleven. In his heart of hearts, he knew he should be heading back to the Waterloo to explain why he had run out so suddenly. But Rib wasn't up for explanations right now and, anyway, the train was due to arrive in town at noon and he didn't want to miss that.

The warm breeze which wafted down Main Street carried the unmistakeable smell of barbeque smoke accompanied by the unfortunate strains of the Stonyville School Brass Band. Rib walked across to Third Street and hurried towards the station.

It seemed as if the whole town had turned out to watch the Iron Horse steam in, mostly gathered around the railroad depot. The building was quite a large structure, one annexe being two storeys high. The lower part was used as a freight and telegraph office, the upper part of the stationmaster's quarters. Blue and white striped awnings fluttered over the windows. Since the railroad handled little passenger traffic, the platform was a rudimentary wooden structure, no more than twenty metres in length. Farmhands, who'd earlier drawn up their wagons in the yard behind the depot, waited patiently, some playing cards on upturned wooden crates, others watching an increasingly noisy game of Polish Horseshoes, where one team was dishing out a sound thrashing to the other, amid much shouting and spilling of beer. A cowpoke called Turley objected loudly at every point lost, but to no avail. He was getting hammered, every which way. A stone's throw down the tracks stood Stonyville's only French resident, Yves Eau, arms folded, ready to take on all-comers in the tug-of-war contest.

There was a hubbub of excitement as necks were craned and eyes were turned down the line to catch first sight of the train. Suddenly, a whistle blew and a billow of smoke rose over the treetops south of town. This was the cue for the band, conducted by newspaper owner Al, to strike up 'Smoke on the Water.' They kept it simple. They had to. Anything more complex and it would have been totally unrecognisable. A bit like the antique Buzzcocks musical quiz show, where the contestant had to guess the massacred rendering of a famous tune performed by his teammates. So they stuck to the refrain:

'*Da-da-daaa*
Da-da-da-daaa
Da-da-daaa
Da, da-daaa,'
Over and over again.

The crowd cheered, waved and threw their hats in the air as the giant locomotive eased into the station. And not a soul thought for a single moment it the slightest bit strange that there, on a planet billions of miles from Earth, a Northern Pacific Class F locomotive that used to transport silver ore on the Elkhorn branch line in Montana in the 1890's, driven by a 62-year-old ex-pensions administrator who talked like Deputy Dawg, should be played into town by a brass band conducted by the owner of a newspaper called the Strumpet to the tune of a Deep Purple rock anthem.

26

All of a sudden, a wave of exhaustion flooded over Rib. Normally he would have stayed and watched the box cars being unloaded, but not today. Leaving the crowd behind, he set off back towards Main Street. Passing the Sheriff's office, he slowed. The Waterloo would be open by now, yet he still wasn't ready to face Sunset. Maybe he'd be in a better frame of mind if he got his head down for a couple of hours. So, instead of taking the front door, he crossed over the street, went round the back of the Trading Post and entered by the back door, tiptoed up the stairs to his room, where he collapsed into a deep sleep on the unmade bed.

What seemed like only a nano-second later, he was woken by loud hammering at his door.

'Rib, are you there? It's Norm.'

Rib stumbled out of bed and opened the door, his confused brain trying to make sense of the breathless Norm. What was he doing here? At this time of day? Norm was a regular stalwart of the first shift, come rain or shine. So what was he doing here on the top landing mid-afternoon?

'Have you seen Sunset?' he asked. 'The bar's closed.'

'Closed? That can't be right,' said Rib, realising in an instant that if he hadn't snuck around the back, he would have seen for himself over an hour ago.

'Yeah, it's closed all right. I reckon something must

be up. We've looked through the window and there's no sign of him. Cliff's asked up and down Main Street, but no one's seen him anywhere.'

'Hold on,' said Rib going back into his room. 'I've got a back-door key somewhere.' He rummaged about in a drawer. 'Here it is! I'll go round the back and see if I can get in.'

They ran downstairs, the boy a flight ahead of the wheezing Norm, who exited by the front door to update Cliff and Woody, still waiting outside. In less than ten seconds, Rib had raced round and opened the back door. The breakfast table was just as when he had left. Two plates, two cups, a can of coffee, pots of jam and honey, a half-eaten boiled bacon roll. But no sign of Sunset.

A groan came from the galley. 'Oh my God! Sunset!' cried Rib as he sprinted into the kitchen. There was nobody there. A second groan came and Rib froze.

It came from the cellar.

The cellar with the trap door left open.

The cellar with the trap door left open by him.

Rib scrambled down the stairs into the black hole of the basement, feeling his way towards the large shape in the middle of the floor. He stumbled in the dark and his right boot came into contact with something soft and squidgy.

'Ow! That was my nose!'

'Oh my God! Sorry, Sunset! Are you all right?'

'Yeah, I'm absolutely fine. I thought I'd throw myself down the cellar stairs and lie here in the dark for half a day just for the fun of it. No, I'm not fucking all right! And where the hell have you been? You took your bloody time coming back.'

'Er, let's get you out of here,' said Rib. 'I'll go and get the boys. They're waiting outside.'

'Waiting outside? Fucking waiting outside? How long have they been waiting outside? Fucking typical!

Between them they've got as much fucking initiative as a carrot in a coma!'

Struggling with the carrot metaphor, Rib shot back up the stairs, grabbed the front door keys from the hook behind the bar, and let the boys in.

Norm was first through the door. 'Have you found him? Is he all right?'

'No! I'm not fucking all right!' came the muffled scream from the cellar.

'He's fallen down the cellar steps,' said Rib. 'I think he's quite badly hurt. And he's ... not in a very good mood,' he added. He hadn't heard Sunset swear before.

The four of them raced round the bar and into the galley. They stood and peered down into the black hole. Woody broke the silence by asking. 'Sunset, are you all right?' and immediately wished he hadn't.

'How many fucking times do I have to tell you that no, I am not fucking all right! Have you called for the Doc yet? Here I am, lying with a broken back, broken leg, broken arm and broken collar bone and all anyone does is ask whether I'm all-fucking-right!' A short silence reigned, broken by a scream from Sunset. 'Aaaargh!'

'What's up?' asked Norm, wisely leaving out the are-you-all-right question.

'And I think he's broken my fucking nose as well!' came the angry reply.

Unable to take any more, Rib left the scene of the crime. The crime which he had committed. 'I'll go and get the Doc.'

It hadn't been easy getting the big man out of the cellar, the heavy cargo being less than co-operative. Once Doc Stimpson's initial diagnosis had confirmed that there were no broken bones – apart from a rather badly fractured nose – it took them a good ten minutes to carry the complaining patient up into the bar, where they lay him carefully on one of the leather sofas.

'You've been very lucky,' was Doc Stimpson's verdict after a thorough examination. 'Slipped disc, bruised ribs, sprained ankle, torn shoulder muscles, sprained wrist, but nothing broken. Apart from the nose, that is. Could have been a lot worse, Sunset. A lot worse.'

'Woo-hoo! Let's open the fucking party-poppers, shall we?' grizzled the big bear with a sore head, sore back, sore ribs, sore ankle, sore shoulder, sore wrist. And a broken nose.

'Nothing that two weeks' total rest won't cure,' said the Doc as he waved goodbye. 'And I mean total rest,' he added.

'Thanks, Doc,' said Sunset struggling to shift his weight to a comfortable position. 'Drop by for a growler on the house, yeah?'

'Will do,' he smiled as he left the bar.

Woody and Cliff helped prop the patient up into a sitting position with a couple of cushions behind his back. Norm brought a bowl of hot water from the galley and began to daub Sunset's bloodied nose with a flannel.

'Ow! Thanks Norm, but I'll do that,' he grimaced.

Rib stood awkwardly, not knowing what to do or say. Finally, he summoned up the courage. 'Is there anything I can get you Sunset?'

'Yeah, a glass of water wouldn't go amiss. And are there any of those croissants left?'

'I'll go and have a look,' said Rib, knowing full well that the big man had scoffed the lot at breakfast. He came back with a glass of water. 'Sorry, Sunset, I couldn't find any croissants. Tell you what, I'll go and get some from Bettina's.'

'That sounds like an excellent idea, son.'

'And ... Sunset,' Rib began.

'Yes, son?'

'I'm really sorry, I – '

'Forget it. You've got a busy two weeks ahead of you,' he smiled. 'Now look sharp, Bettina closes at four.'

'Sure!' Rib smiled back, starting to feel relieved as he made to leave the room.

'Oh, and there's one more thing I've got to say to you,' said the man on the sofa.

'What's that?' asked Rib nervously.

'You might also like to get a couple of chocolate doughnuts, a box of Danish pastries and half a dozen custard slices.'

'Aye, aye, Cap'n!' saluted Rib.

'Oh, and before you go, you'd better go behind that bar and pour the boys a beer. And I'll have three pints of Dog's Dribble, while you're at it.'

27

It was tea-time at The Mansion. It had been an arduous afternoon for the Protectorate High Command. The weekly ops meeting had been characterised by an uncustomary level of tetchiness and High Commodore Munroe, as chair, had had to call her colleagues – Commodore Dunoon, Brigadier Blanchard and Colonel Carruthers - to order on more than one occasion. What on earth had set them at each others' throats? she asked herself. Granted, the minor insurrection in Luton needed delicate handling, but the committee's decision to draft in Marshall Amps from Stonyville to quell the disturbance seemed to satisfy everyone.

With more than a sense of relief, Munroe declared the first part of the agenda closed and the High Command adjourned to the library for tea. She paused on the landing to allow the fingers of her left hand to caress the polished dark wood of the bannister before proceeding downstairs into the hall where, for a moment, she paused to absorb the special aura of the place – The Mansion, which had once stood in the grounds of Bletchley Park, Britain's famous code-breaking centre in the Second World War. Shipped in its entirety by her predecessor, High Commodore "Loony Willy" Pempwell, to Tycho as part of Operation Exodus. Enigmatic, some called him. Mad as a March

Hare was the majority verdict. When she entered the library, her colleagues were standing by the large coffee table, waiting for her to be seated first.

'Where would you like to be, Angela?' smiled Commodore Dunoon.

'Thank you, Donald, I'll take the Chesterfield.'

The very thought of food and drink already seemed to be lightening the mood, thought Munroe, ringing the brass hand-bell three times. Almost immediately, the rattling sound of a trolley being pushed at speed came from down the corridor. The library door crashed open and a stacked tea trolley swiftly followed by Brenda the Tea Lady came into view.

'Ah tea!' exclaimed Blanchard unnecessarily.

'Good afternoon, Brenda,' greeted Angela.

'Y' areet, hinny?' came the response.

High Commodore Angela Munroe tolerated the Geordie woman's overfamiliarity on two counts. Firstly, she liked her. Secondly, nobody could put on afternoon tea and beverages like Brenda. The tea lady swiftly went to work – plates, cutlery and napkins distributed in a trice. Then came the masterpiece. A cake-stand laden with home baked delights.

'Cupcakes, Chelsea buns, meringues and Battenborg,' she announced proudly.

The Committee attacked the cake-stand as if they had been on rations for weeks.

'Battenburg,' salivated Blanchard, emphasising the third syllable. 'I haven't had that since I was a child.'

'Give o'wer, y'a kiddin'?' came Brenda's shocked comment. 'Will ya's be havin' tea and coffee, or will ya's be need'n summat more fortifyin'?' she asked.

The Chair responded on behalf of the Committee. 'Something more fortifying is an excellent suggestion. Thank you, Brenda.'

Clearly pleased at the compliment, the Tyneside tea

lady reached down to the bottom shelf of the trolley and carefully placed three wine coolers on the coffee table.

'Brenda,' said Blanchard. 'I don't suppose you could lay your hands on a bottle of port?'

Angela groaned inwardly, knowing that Brenda would not take kindly to this request.

Indeed she didn't. 'Hadaway, man! Ya canna drink port with Battenborg!'

Blanchard beat a hasty retreat and allowed Brenda to introduce the fine dessert wines, selected from the Mansion's cellar.

'We have the Muscat de Rivesaltes, Domaine Cazes 1982. Will gann reet neece with the Chelsea buns. Then there's the Chateau d'Yquem 1998 Sauternes Premiere Cru Superieur. Should teest greet with the meringue. And then, finally, there is Tokaji Aszu Puttonyos 1957. Betta and betta with age. Rich and toffee-leek, leek. And that, Brigadier Blanchard, I would recommend with the BattenBORG!'

'You have chosen well Brenda. I think we'd like you to open all three bottles for us, if you would be so kind,' intervened Angela.

Brenda dutifully obliged, deftly handling her bottle opener like a Harley Street surgeon would his scalpel, removing the sealed wax, inserting the corkscrew, and easing each cork out with just the right amount of pressure.

'You may leave us to pour,' said Angela.

'Thanks, pet. I was thinkin' of gannin' yem noo, if that's alreet?'

'Yes, of course, Brenda. You, er, gann yem noo.'

'Thanks. Tara pet,' she smiled at one of the Protectorate's most powerful representatives on Tycho.

'Tara, pet,' replied Angela. It didn't sound at all right when she said it. She'd been practising in secret, but it still sounded so wrong, so awfully wrong ...

Tea time ran on well into early evening. The Committee took a welcome time-out in the good company of delicious cakes and the finest wines on the planet. And, reflected Angela with a smile, Brenda was absolutely right. The Tokaj did go well with the Battenborg.

At precisely 5:25, High Commodore Angela Munroe reconvened the Ops Committee Meeting to consider the main item on its agenda.

The Expedition.

28

Rib had never worked so hard in all his life. Up at six, quick swim, sweep taproom floor, polish bar, wash glasses, take used arsegrass out to composter (important to do this after washing the glasses, he'd learned on Day 3), help Sunset get out of bed and get dressed, cook breakfast, clean up after breakfast, 15-minute break to read Strumpet, polish bar again, work on kitchen garden for an hour, take produce to Market Hall, change beer barrels, polish bar once more, open bar at 12 on the dot, serve in bar, eat on the hoof, close bar at 9, give whole place spick-and-span clean, glug down pint of Piss Poor, collapse into bed.

All under the close supervision of the proprietor, who surveyed the day's operations from a bath chair installed at the far end of the bar, from where he would bark the occasional instruction to his apprentice, sometimes helpful (You'll pour a perfect head, Rib, just by tipping the glass a couple of degrees more) and sometimes not so helpful (Nooo! Not like that!)

Not surprisingly, things didn't always go to plan. After the second Meskitoe-style breakfast, Sunset pushed away the plate of burnt bacon, undercooked sausage, cold beans and fried egg with more eggshell than yolk, saying 'I think we'll go for a Continental tomorrow.' And the time when Rib had forgotten to issue tabs with each beer, realising only when Norm fell backwards off his chair to knock himself unconscious after the sixth snifter of Brickhill Barley Wine. Sunset barred him for 24 hours for "taking advantage", as he put it. Not that Norm was in any state to be doing much drinking for the next 24 hours, anyway.

Exhausted as he was, Rib enjoyed every minute of it, on a number of counts. Firstly, it helped wipe the guilt-slate clean on the trapdoor episode. Secondly, being responsible for the day-to-day operation of the Waterloo Brewing Co. gave him status, gave him stature, not only in the eyes of the Stonyville community but also, more importantly, in his own mind's eye. He was happy. He felt good about himself. And another secondly, he was earning money. In spite of Rib's protests, Sunset insisted on paying him an hourly rate of twenty five dollars, which was great. He was working hard and earning a real wage. This was what he had come to Tycho for. Thirdly, through working at the bar, he got to know Larix better.

The one-armed hog-roaster helped Sunset cultivate fruit and vegetables on the sizeable plot behind the pub and he would take basketfuls of salads, potatoes, greens and soft fruit to the Market Hall to sell to the traders. Being on first name terms with all of them, he knew how to cut a good deal, and a succulent pork sandwich laced with sweet apple sauce often formed a persuasive part of the negotiations. Given that the allotment was no more than the width of Diamond Dan's Liquor Store away from the market, its fresh produce could hardly have been more locally sourced. In eco-footprint terms, no more than a bunion shaving's distance away.

Larix grew his apples in the orchard at the bottom of the kitchen garden. It was mostly down to apple and pear trees, with two Victoria plum trees standing guard at the back gate. Larix knew how to get the best from his trees – when to prune, how to graft, when to feed.

The result was the tastiest apple juice in the County, with just the right sweet-tart balance. Even the farmers' wives acknowledged its perfection.

Although the land belonged to Sunset, no rent was paid or asked for. Larix helped him at peak periods: when it was time to dig in the heap of well-rotted manure; when there was an end-of-season glut of runner beans to pick and sell; or when, for some reason or other, Sunset couldn't get out into the plot. And now was such a time. It was mid-September and the experimental crop of second early potatoes needed lifting. The two boys worked from opposite ends of each row, lifting each plant with care with flat-tined forks to avoid splitting the tubers. Rib was staggered how quickly his partner worked and had trouble keeping pace. When four rows were cleared, they took a break under the shade of an apple tree. Rib had cooked some coffee and they sat surveying the fruits of their hard labour – six wicker baskets full to the brim with sweet earlies.

'I reckon Sunset will be really pleased with those,' said Rib, taking a first sip of the strong brew.

'Yep,' said Larix, studying the dirt under his fingernails.

The two drank their coffee in silence. A brightly-coloured dragonfly hovered overhead before darting off towards the river. Something strange then happened. Larix began to talk.

'New potatoes were my father's favourite,' he said, without looking up. 'He used to say that you couldn't beat Jersey Royals. Just plain boiled, no salt, with a knob of butter … '

Rib said nothing. Silence fell over the two boys again like a thick cloak. Not an awkward silence. More of a pregnant pause. As though Larix were deciding whether to go on.

'Mum used to cook them as a special treat for him.

If the weather was good, she'd lay the table out in the garden. White tablecloth, blue napkins, cut flowers in a vase, a bottle of red wine. As soon as Father came home from work and saw the table out on the lawn, he'd know. "Jersey Royals," he'd say with a smile, and give Mother a big hug.'

At that very moment, the one thing Rib wanted more than anything else in the world was a big hug from his Dad. He looked into the far distance and dared the dangerous question. 'Are they both still alive?' He regretted his words immediately.

Larix turned away, picked up a blade of rye grass and started to chew on it. He then looked Rib straight in the eye. 'Nope, I lost them both when I lost this,' he said, waving his stump.

'God, I'm sorry ... '

'Stagecoach overturned. It was getting near dark and we were on our way back from Oxford. We were behind schedule. They'd had to re-shoe one of the horses. It was probably too dark to be on the road. The driver was pushing the horses hard to make up for lost time. Inside the carriage, we could hear him cracking his whip.' He paused to spit out the chewed grass. 'Something ran out into the highway and spooked the horses. Someone later said it might have been a fox. The front team reared up and the whole stagecoach overturned. We were all crushed underneath. All I could remember was the awful sound of the trapped horses whinnying in pain. Then I passed out. I was the only one to make it ...'

'I'm sorry, so sorry,' said Rib, his insides aching for the boy.

'No worries. It just doesn't seem fair though does it? They'd done the hardest part. Survived Watershed, survived Exodus and then ... a stupid accident at less than thirty kilometres an hour. Doesn't make sense, does it?'

Rib shook his head, unable to speak.

'Anyway,' Larix said, jumping up to throw the cold coffee grounds into the long grass. 'We've got work to do. See those broad beans over there? Next job is to pinch out the tops of every single plant, otherwise the blackfly will be all over them.'

Rib followed him over to the rows of waist-high beans and watched how he tackled the first plant. But all he could do was fumble at the fleshy foliage, his eyes misted over with tears.

After that, the two boys met up most days, even if just to have an ice cream at the Big Licker Parlour, where you could either sit inside or take away. Either way, you placed your order at a hatch on the street front, where a sign said 'Strictly No Horses at the Window.' A skinny, freckled girl by the name of Amy served them. Rib noticed her blushing when she took Larix's order and wondered whether she was keen on him. His suspicions were soon confirmed by the extra dollop scooped out for his friend every time they paid a visit.

You could get ice creams in almost every flavour under the sun. In addition to the traditional vanilla, chocolate, rum and raisin varieties, you could choose oak leaf, curried leek or dried chipmunk. Salt liquorice was Rib's favourite, mainly because of its colour. He just loved pressing the soft black ice cream down into the cone with his tongue before finishing it off in three noisy crunches.

'Bye, Amy,' Larix waved as they left the parlour. Amy returned the wave with a bright blush thrown in for good measure.

29

'Here's your reward for working so hard,' said Sunset, pressing a fold of recycled dollar bills into Rib's palm.

'But ... no, Sunset, you've already paid me,' he protested.

'I know, I know. But you've done an excellent job. The punters like you, the whole place shines like a new pin, you've kept on top of the allotment at the height of the cropping season, and I like the way you've taken Larix under your wing. I've never known that lad to say more than one word to anybody.'

'Yeah, we get on really well.'

Sunset's recovery had taken a week longer than expected. Doc Stimpson had given a clean bill of health the day before. All shipshape and ready to go. All shipshape apart from a nasty kink on the bridge of his nose, that is.

'I've been thinking,' he said, spreading a thick layer of yeast extract on a doorstep of wholemeal toast. 'The last three weeks have given me plenty of time to think. About the future.'

'Oh yeah?' said Rib, uneasy as to what was coming next. A niggling gurgle churned in his stomach. Was Sunset about to tell him that he'd decided to chuck it all in? Sell the Waterloo? Retire? Shit, he hoped not. Just when he was settling down, starting to feel good about things.

'So I thought I'd like to make a proposition.'

'A proposition?'

'Yes, that's what I said. A proposition.' He bit on the slab of toast and chewed slowly. 'Now, I know that you've probably got plans. Buy a place of your own, raise a family. So let's get one thing clear, a "No" will not offend, OK?'

Rib nodded. Raise a family? Had Sunset not noticed the important missing ingredient in the raise-a-family mix?

'So, Rib, I'd like to offer you a job.'

Rib's jaw dropped.

'As Deputy Manager of the Waterloo Brewing Company.'

'Deputy Manager...' Rib repeated to himself in disbelief. Him, manage? It was all he could do to manage his bowel movements. Deputy Manager ...

'Now, I'm not expecting you to give your answer straight away.'

'Yes! I'll take it!' blurted Rib. 'That would be brilliant! Thanks, Sunset, thanks!'

'Well, that's that, then,' said Sunset, clearing his throat. 'Must be getting on. There's barrels to be changed, the bar to be polished. We'll talk terms over breakfast tomorrow.' He made to stand up.

'No, leave that to me!' said Rib jumping to his feet.

Sunset eased himself back into the bath chair and studied the boy as he busied himself firstly behind the bar, polishing the glasses, and then at the far end of the taproom, buffing the ironmongery on the door. The boy had learned quickly. The old man allowed himself a smile. It felt good, it felt somehow right having the lad about the place. Of course, he told himself, it wouldn't last forever. Nothing ever does. One day the boy would move on. But for now, it felt just fine ...

30

Alcohol is a depressant.

Any physician, doctor, community health worker or alcoholic will tell you that. This fact is at times difficult to square. Like chucking-out time every night at the Florence when the young cowboys of Stonyville competed to see who could pee the highest up the shop window of Bettina's Buns. Absolutely hilarious. Funniest thing on earth. Did these boys feel depressed? Hell, no.

In the case of Cliff Heathcote, however, alcohol definitely was a depressant. 'It's time for you to stop sobbing, Cliff,' said Sunset. 'She's gone and, me old mate, I'm afraid she ain't coming back. And more to the point, every little tear that falls from your eyes is leaving a salty sediment on my bar, and I've got better things to be doing than be wiping away your stains of sorrow all afternoon. So stop it, right?'

'Sorry, Sunset,' blubbed the inconsolable Cliff, blowing his nose rather unsuccessfully on a dock leaf, most of the mucus shooting up his left sleeve. Cliff was bewailing the loss of his fiancée Jennifer, also known as Jenny, also known as Jen. This had all happened two years previously, but still came back to haunt him every Thursday afternoon at the Waterloo after two pints of Peaches Amber and a bag of pork scratchings.

The lost love was a young woman whose real full

name was Jennifer Beccles. Having been orphaned by Watershed, she found herself on arrival in Stonyville placed in the care of the Widow Hansworth, under whom she suffered a repressed, overbearingly strict upbringing. The one thing that kept Jennifer going through her times of darkness was the thought that, one day, she would be sixteen and be a free person. Not allowed pictures or posters of any description on her bedroom walls, her five-bar-gate countdown to independence calendar was kept carefully concealed under a floorboard. Every fibre of her body yearned for that day to come. The day she would become a woman.

She had planned for the arrival of her sixteenth birthday with military precision. In secret, she had packed her bag, ready to close Widow Hansworth's front door behind her, never to return. Where she would spend her first night of freedom was as yet undetermined. With whom she would spend that first night was an irrelevance. There were only two things that mattered. One, that she find a new roof over her head. And two, that she get laid. For Jennifer Eccles was a girl whose body had the characteristics of a shaken bottle of champagne about to pop its cork. She was ready to blow.

And blow she did on the night of her liberation. By happy coincidence, the Annual Young Cattle Ranchers' Dinner Dance was being held at the Florence. Young Cliff Heathcote had cause to celebrate, having earlier in the day nailed down the deal on a thousand acre plot of fine cattle-grazing land the other side of the Brickhills. This would enable him to bring his head of cattle and horses to over five hundred and make him the most successful rancher in the County. It had been a long, punishing year. A seemingly never-ending story of mending fences, breaking in broncos, branding steers, digging new waterholes, chasing off wolves. So tonight, he could look back over what he had achieved in the past twelve months with a sense of pride: a two-storey, 10,000 sq. ft ranch with twin-deck veranda, built-in-barbeque and charcoal-fired hot tub; a state-of-the-art galley with a replica Aga; the finest buggy in town, with gold-painted wheels. Everything a man of twenty-five could dream of. Except one thing.

A good woman.

Cliff had been looking forward to the Dinner Dance, the highlight of the year. Considering himself something of a gourmet, he let his eye play down the menu, which offered a tantalising array of sauces and dips to go with the obligatory Surf n' Turf combo of a 20oz Ribeye and Half-lobster. For the steak, which he would naturally order blue, he had his eye on the Worcestershire Piri-Piri.

And, indeed, the evening lived up to his every expectation. All agreed that the meal was the best yet. The womenfolk left the tables to powder their noses and the menfolk sidled into the saloon area to partake of a furtive cee-gar, smoking being strictly verboten in public places.

Then came the dance, for many the highlight of the evening. Cliff, however, was happy to watch the increasingly frenetic reels and hoe-downs from the safety of the large, red leather sofa in the main bar, a quadruple Wild Spatchcock on ice cupped in his left hand. And then he saw her. A vision of beauty. Their eyes met across the crowded room and she floated like an angel over to him.

'May I have the honour of joining you, Mr Heathcote? Please allow me to introduce myself. My name is Jenny Beccles.' Jennifer's metamorphosis had already begun. Jenny, as she was now called, had gained entry to the Young Cattle Ranchers' Annual Dinner Dance by giving one of the waiters a quick back-alley snog and grope with a promise of more to follow.

She managed to coax the awestruck Heathcote onto the dance floor, where he felt the pressing proximity of her pelvis within seconds. One-and-a-half hoe-downs later, he was whipping his horses into a frenzied gallop down Main Street. The buggy hurtled through the fine clear night out of town towards the Lucky Horseshoe Ranch. Jenny was not a great one for stargazing, so she busied herself with unpopping Cliff's trouser buttons instead. It was touch and go whether they would make it to the ranch, where they consummated their new-found love in a forty-six second explosion of unadulterated lust.

Jenny lay back in the four-poster bed beside the snoring Cliff and reviewed the night's events with a satisfied smile on her red lips:

Objective Number One: Find a new place to live. This will do nicely, she thought. Very nicely indeed. She toyed with the idea of walking back to the Florence to search out her young waiter, but maybe she could keep him for later. After all she had also achieved Objective Number Two: To get laid.

The very next day, Cliff proposed to Jenny and she accepted. They agreed to be married in the spring of the following year and, until then, to maintain an aura of respectability in the eyes of the outside world, the young fiancée would reside in a separate annexe. The arrangement worked very well. Kind of ...

While Cliff Heathcote considered himself to be a gourmet, Jenny's more-than-healthy appetite for rumpy-pumpy put her in the classification of sexual gourmand. She didn't mind what it tasted like or how it was presented, as long as the plate was piled high and she was served at least four generous portions a day.

Unfortunately, Cliff did not make the earth move for Jenny. In fact, it's fair to say that he didn't even manage to scratch her fertile loam into anything approaching a fine tilth. So it came as no surprise that, when Cliff was away on business, Jenny's annexe became a regular bolthole for a queue of cowpokes, happy to swap a hard day in the saddle out on the plain for a hard night in the saddle in Jenny's plush boudoir. So things didn't turn out too badly for her at all. Cliff was a very happy man, too, blissfully unaware of the goings-on behind his back. He strutted around the town like a dog with two dicks, even though he hardly ever used either of them. Of course, he was the only person in Stonyville not to know of his fiancée's infidelity.

The next phase of Jenny Eccles' coming-of-age was to live out her girlhood dream, all based on a fictional tee-vee character called Joy. Her Dad had bought her a "golden oldie" i-shield collection for her tenth birthday. Her favourite was the series 'My Name is Earl' and her heroine was Joy. She worshipped her. She could now admit to herself that she'd had a real thing about Joy. The way she spoke, the way she dressed, the way she treated her men. There was only one thing she wanted to be when she grew up. She wanted to live like Joy. And now, as the female in residence at the Lucky Horseshoe Ranch, she could live out her every fantasy. She changed her dress, her hairstyle and the way she spoke. Jenny became Joy. In all but name which she shortened to Jen. At first, Cliff didn't go along with his fiancée looking and sounding like a piece of white trash from a trailer park on the other side of the tracks, but Jen's powers of persuasion between the sheets soon put a stop to any objections.

31

One day when Jen was shopping in town, she was accosted by Scoter. 'Sharpen your knife for fifty cents, Missy? Or are you too high-and-mighty for household chores now?'

Affronted by the coarseness of the vile man, she replied sharply, 'No I certainly don't want my knives sharpened. And if I did, you'd be the last person I'd go to.' And with that, she turned on her heels and set off down the street in the direction of the bank.

By amazing coincidence, Scoter was also a secret aficionado of 'My Name is Earl.' In fact, he regarded Earl as a role model. On seeing a real-life replica of Joy wiggling her way past in a pair of white high-heeled shoes, cut-off denims, her hair tied back in two bobs, red-checked shirt open four buttons at the front, there was only one thing he could do. Play the Earl theme on his harmonica.

Jen stopped dead in her tracks. The effect on her was as dramatic as it was instantaneous, the atmospheric tones of the mouth-organ churning her loins to chili-jelly. She walked back to the knife-sharpener with a seductive sway and placed the red-nailed forefinger of her right hand on his abrasive wheel. 'Well,' she said, tracing her finger over the rough surface. 'I guess a girl can always find time for a slow afternoon grind.'

Scoter didn't even pause to pack his stand away, he

just nodded to her and headed off nonchalantly toward the Grand Hotel, where he rented a room on the top floor. Jen pretended to take an interest in something in Diamond Dan's shop window before following him into the hotel lobby.

Judd Scoter's room wasn't really a room. Little more than a broom closet in size, the hotel were happy to let him have it at knock-down rate. Not only was it small, it was at the back of the hotel over the stables where it ponged a bit and, being on the top floor, became unbearably hot in the summer.

There was barely enough space in the room for a bed, but that was all Judd needed. And certainly all that Jen needed. She attacked him like a sex-crazed vixen, ripping off his clothes in seconds. 'Play the harmonica,' she gasped as she undressed. 'Play it, you bastard!' Judd did as he was told, and now astride her, played the first thing that came into his head, quite aptly, "She'll be coming round the mountain when she comes." The strains of Judd Scoter's mouth harp acted as an aphrodisiac of atomic proportions for Jen. She didn't only come round the mountains, she came river deep mountain high and over the hills and far away.

Because it was so stiflingly hot and smelly in the small attic room, the window was nailed permanently open. Jen's cries of ecstasy, accompanied by Judd's increasingly frantic harmonica playing, could be heard all over town, and indeed beyond. A ranch hand named Hank paused to look up from his fence-mending duties in a field next to the Brickhill Woods, some seven miles south. 'That sounds like Jen Beccles,' he said to his horse, Silver. 'You should know,' snorted Silver in disgust.

That night, truly fulfilled for the first time in her life, Jen rode back to the Lucky Horseshoe Ranch, broke off the engagement and packed her bags, leaving Cliff in a state of utter shock and despair. From that day on, she lived a happy life, experiencing joy on multiple levels four times a day in the sweltering heat of Scoter's long-term let.

Quite naturally, the more prudish members of the Stonyville community were quick to complain at the volume levels of her orgasms. Marshall Amps, however took no action. Judd Scoter was the nearest the town had to a criminal element. If eggs had been stolen from a hen-house, Judd was the man. If a coil of fencing wire had gone missing from the Trading Post, more likely than not it was stashed under Judd's bed. Nothing of a serious nature, but Booker T figured that he would rather know the exact whereabouts of Mr Scoter rutting his butt off four times a day than have to go looking for him. So he let sleeping dogs lie.

32

Jen had broken Cliff's heart. Into a thousand crazy-paving pieces. Two years on, he sat at the far end of the Waterloo bar, sobbing till his shoulders shook. Just when Sunset's mild words of admonishment seemed to have stemmed the flow, Norm asked a question he really shouldn't have.

'And what in high heaven's name does she see in him anyway?'

The question was intended as rhetorical, but Woody felt obliged to answer. 'Well, he gives her a good seeing-to four times a day. That's a good reason, for a start.'

Cliff opened his mouth to protest, but it was too late.

'And how many men can screw a woman and play a mouth-harp at the same time?' asked Norm.

'Yeah, how the hell does he do that?' said Woody. 'Sometimes he starts all wooing-like, with the Moonlight Sonata or suchlike, just to get her in the mood.'

'But sure as hell he always finishes on "She'll be coming round the mountain when she comes".'

'Shut up, both of you!' snapped Cliff and tried to get off his bar stool. It fell over, nearly taking him with it. Sunset calmly made his way round to the other side of the bar.

Norm pressed on regardless. 'Maybe he's not

playing it with his mouth at all. Maybe he's got the dang thing clenched between his buttocks.'

'Now that would be impressive,' said Woody.

Sunset, now holding the struggling Cliff in a headlock, had to agree. 'OK, boys, that's enough now,' he said. 'OK?'

'OK,' mumbled Woody and Norm, returning to their beers.

'OK, Cliff?'

'OK,' came the muffled answer.

He let Cliff go, who righted his stool, climbed up on it and took a deep draft of Peaches Amber.

'Hey, man, I'm sorry ...' offered Norm.

'That's OK, guys. It's just ... it's just that it still really hurts,' sobbed Cliff.

Sunset returned to polishing glasses behind the bar. Calm prevailed.

Until Woody said, 'But I bet she's got the sharpest set of kitchen knives in the County!'

This time Sunset had to heave his heavy frame over the bar to restrain the raging bull that was Cliff. Finally, he managed to wrestle him over to one of the worn sofas, where he sat on his chest. 'Now listen, me old mate, you really have to let go.' Cliff was having none of this and started shouting. Sunset promptly smacked him on the kisser. Cliff then stopped shouting. He was finally persuaded to take himself home with a growler of Dog's Dribble on the house.

'And as for you two,' said Sunset, once Cliff had left, 'you are bang out of order. Any more of that and I could become highly displeased with you. And, as you know, once I get started I'll go to town on you both. Now, that will be thirty-two dollars for the growler.' Woody and Norm handed over the money without a word.

Stonyville had two resident hobos, Dave and Nick.

They slept in the livery stables behind the Grand and spent most of the day sat on the boardwalk of the Florence, begging pissed punters to spare them a dime. Taking its corporate social responsibility very seriously, the saloon's management scrawled a notice on the door which read "Please do not spit on the hobos".

Dave and Nick's social calendar revolved around the carnal union of Judd and Jen, up in the attic of the Grand Hotel. They looked forward to it through their wood-spirit-soaked fog with eager anticipation. For them, it was the Last Night of the Proms, the X-Factor final and the Eurovision Song Contest all rolled into one. And four times a day! Life didn't get any better than this, they would say to each other.

'I never promised you a rose garden,' Dave would say to Nick, 'but things could be a lot worse couldn't they?'

As soon as they heard the first squeaks of Scoter's bedsprings, swiftly followed by the strains of his harmonica, the two hobos staggered across Main Street, skirted round the Sheriff's office with exaggerated tippy-toe caution, before taking up their front-row position in the side alley directly below Judd's open window. And as soon as Scoter's mouth harp announced to the world that his partner would shortly be coming round the mountain, Dave and Nick would link arms and dance around with gay abandon, wheezing the refrain:

'Singing aye-aye yippee-ippee-aye
Singing aye-aye yippee-ippee-aye
Singing aye-aye yippee
Aye-aye yippee
Aye-aye yippee-ippee-aye!'

With the occasional unrehearsed 'Yeee-ha!' thrown in for good measure.

Up on the third floor, the first act was over. Sated for the time being, Jen would disengage herself from her lover, pull the chamber pot from under the bed and relieve herself into the enamel receptacle. Not the dainty tinkle of a maiden. More the power-jet of a horse. She would then take the pot over to the open window and hurl its contents down onto the hobo hoe-down below.

Now, it is fair to say that Dave and Nick would have preferred an ice-cool shower from waters of a mountain stream, rather than a piss-pot full of lukewarm pee. But beggars can't be choosers.

So, on being soaked by the cascade from above, Nick and Dave would launch with gusto into their signature tune:

'It's raining Jen,
Sock it to yah,
It's raining Jen,
Yeah!'

33

A rather impressive piece of antique furniture dominated the end wall of the Waterloo taproom. At first, Rib had thought it to be some kind of a drinks cabinet, with distinctive grains and swirls in its dark, shiny wood. The crank-handle sticking out from the side should have told him that this was no ordinary cabinet.

It was a gramophone. An HMV Table Grand, Circa 1933. Sunset's pride and joy. He was the only person allowed to touch it. A double door at the front opened to reveal seven horizontal slots, where seven vinyl long-playing records – or LPs, as Sunset called them – were stored, still in their original sleeves. The doors were fitted with a tiny brass lock, the key to which Sunset kept in his wallet.

On Earth, music had literally been available at the blink of an eye. Three rapid eye movements would enable the wearer of an i-shield to download from an infinite stream of songs, anthems or instruments, any time, any place. On Tycho, that had all changed. Music was live. It had to be, which, in many ways, was for the good, because people came together to play, sing and dance. Children learned to pick out chords on a guitar at an early age. A musical instrument was to be found in most households. Dorothy occasionally scratched her way through a passage of Mozart on her old violin, the School Band slaughtered

Deep Purple at every opportunity and Judd Scoter played "She'll be coming round the mountain" four times a day.

Not surprisingly, Country & Western was King. Bluegrass, to be more specific. Every Saturday night, the Florence was filled to the rafters with Stonyville citizens all dressed up to the nines in cowboy/cowgirl gear. And with it, of course, came the music. Purebred Country.

Sunset Todd had a strong aversion to the strains of Wee Willy Harris, Dolly Parton, Johnny Cash and their ilk. Once, Norm had entered the bar whistling "Stand by your Man" and was promptly banned for forty-eight hours.

So, the only music to be heard on the premises of the Waterloo Brewing Company came from the seven vinyl LPs housed in the cabinet of the HMV Table Grand. And, of course, the only person allowed to play them was the owner himself. Normally once a week, about an hour before last orders, he would open up the phonogram and put a request on. The bar would go quiet, the punters would put their glasses down and the scratchy sounds of a golden oldie dating back to the 1960's or 70's would fill the room. No tapping of the feet. No joining in the chorus. It was almost spiritual, a slow lonesome stroll down memory lane as the last faint rays from the Old Planet filtered across their minds like the final breeze of a summer's day across the roof tops.

The collection consisted of seven records salvaged by Sunset in the mad dash of Exodus:

The Kinks	*by*	*The Kinks*
The Court of the		
Crimson King	*by*	*King Crimson*
Tea and the Tillerman	*by*	*Cat Stevens*
Wish You Were Here	*by*	*Pink Floyd*
Five Bridges	*by*	*The Nice*

Who's Next?	*by*	*The Who*
Are you Experienced?	*by*	*The Jimi Hendrix Experience*

Unfortunately, the Listen with Sunset slots were brought to a sudden end by the accident in the basement – the only thing on the owner's mind during his convalescence was to keep the bar open. His apprentice proved to be willing, able and a quick learner. Sunset was more than pleased with how things were working out. His customers seemed happy enough with the new arrangement and the boy was certainly taking everything in his stride.

Then, totally out of the blue one Thursday night, Norm shouted over, 'How about some music, Sunset?'

The few other occupants of the bar murmured their support for the proposal. Sunset was in no fit state to move, let alone be able to apply the delicate touch required to operate his gramophone. He ignored the request.

But it didn't go away. 'Let Rib work the turntable,' shouted Woody.

'Yeah, how about a track from King Crimson?' said Abe, a ranch hand from Henriksson's.

'No,' chipped in the stable-boy Sam, 'we had that last week. Let's do Floyd.'

'Hold on, hold on!' said Sunset, not liking the way the conversation was going one little bit. Letting the boy loose on his prize possession was not on the agenda. Gawd knows what damage he could do. 'Maybe later on in the week,' he grunted.

'Aw, come on,' persisted Abe, 'let the boy have a go.'

'I said, later on in the week!' Sunset snapped.

The bar went silent without anyone being brave enough to voice what they were thinking. An uneasy atmosphere reigned for some five minutes before Norm downed the dregs of his Big Blonde Bear, climbed off his stool and declared loudly in the direction of the big man on the sofa. 'I don't know about you, boys, but I'm going over to the Florence to hear some music.' And, swiftly followed by Abe and Sam, he left. Woody hesitated, casting a nervous glance at Sunset, who was staring out of the window at some non-existent object of interest across the street.

'What are you waiting for, Woody?' he said.

'Er, well, yeah, I guess I'd better be going. Good night, Rib. Night, Sunset.'

'Good night, Woody,' said Rib. Sunset said nothing, his stare still fixed elsewhere. Woody scuttled out of the bar without looking back.

'Time to shut up for the night,' said Sunset through gritted teeth.

'Shall I give you a hand upstairs?'

'No. You go up. Turn down the lamps and lock the door behind you.'

'OK. Good night, Sunset.' He waited for a reply but none came.

34

'Sunset, I really don't want to be doing this,' said the boy, beads of sweat forming on his brow.

'It'll be fine. Just do as I tell you and it will be fine,' soothed the old man.

'No, I'm not feeling comfortable with this at all. I shouldn't be doing this ...'

The day had started off fine enough. The usual morning constitutional down to the river, a bracing swim – three sets of 100m crawl against the current, coupled with easy breaststroke with the stream. Back at the Waterloo by eight, bakery bag in hand, the aroma of fresh-cooked coffee hitting him as he came through the back door.

The conflict of the previous night seemed to have been slept off. 'You OK?' Rib checked.

'Yep, couldn't be better,' came the answer from a mouthful of croissant slabbed with strawberry jam.

Little conversation passed between the two over breakfast. Rib cleared the dishes and was about to move into the bar to prime the pumps when he was called back.

'Leave that till later, Rib. There's something I want you to do.' Avoiding the boy's eyes, he paused and drew a deep breath. 'I never thought I'd be asking you to do this. Never ...' he tailed off. Sunset's hand shook as he raised his cup to his lips to down the last of the coffee.

Wiping his mouth on his sleeve, he looked the boy straight in the eye.

'Rib ...'

'Yes, Sunset?'

'I'm going to have to ask you to do something that's going to be really ... difficult for you.'

'Erm, OK ...'

'But I want you to know that it's going to be every bit as hard for me as it is for you.' He stood up, took him by the hand and led him through to the bar. The old man slumped into the sofa. He seemed troubled, in two minds. The morning sun streaming through the window highlighted the grey stubble shadow on his cheeks. He patted the sofa cushion beside him. 'Come sit down.' Reluctantly, Rib obeyed. The old man, breaths now coming quick and fast, said to the young boy sat beside him words he thought he'd never say. 'Rib?'

'Yes?'

'Today I'm going to teach you how to play an HMV Table Grand gramophone.'

Thank fuck for that, thought Rib, wiping the sweat from his brow.

* * *

First came the theory part.

'Records have a spiral groove that goes from near the outer rim to near the middle of the record. See?'

'Yes, Sunset.'

'The groove isn't completely straight. This you can't see.' Rib shook his head in no-I-can't-see agreement. 'It has tiny ripples in it that store the music. Do you hear me, Rib? Store the music! Isn't that wonderful?' Rib nodded, having lost the plot already. How could ripples possibly store sound?

'The needle reads the sound. It is attached to what's

known as a diaphragm,' he pointed. 'And a sound horn,' he pointed again. 'As the record spins, the tiny ripples cause the needle to vibrate to and fro. These vibrations ... Rib! Are you listening to me?'

Within a time-gap spanning no more than seven seconds, Rib had dived into a deep but vivid daydream in which he was walking at night in the dark depths of a Swedish forest, chased by a werewolf which had jumped out from behind a tree. 'Aaargh! Silver bullet!' he blurted out.

Sunset side-stepped the werewolf and pressed on regardless. 'These vibrations are amplified by the diaphragm and broadcast out of the horn. And there, my son, you have the sweet, matchless music of the long playing record.'

'Now,' he continued, 'the first thing to learn is how to get the RPM right.'

'RPM?' said Rib, wishing he was back with the werewolf.

'Revolutions per minute. RPM. The number of times the record goes round on the turntable in sixty seconds.'

'Oh, I see.'

'Do you know how many times that is for an LP?'

'No idea.' How the hell could he possibly know that?

'It's thirty-three and a third.'

'Thirty-three and a third,' repeated Rib mechanically. Of course. Silly me.

'No more, no less, otherwise it sounds all wrong.'

No pressure there, then.

'So, let's have a trial run. We'll do it without the record first. Safer that way...' he tailed off, looking for a moment as if he wanted to abort the whole operation. But he pressed on. 'See that small handle on the right?'

Rib stepped over to the gramophone and stood poised for the next instruction.

'OK, now open the lid, take the handle and gently

turn it clockwise. That's good … easy does it … a little slower and you're just about there. Try to keep a nice and steady rhythm.'

This was easy. There must be more to it than this.

There was.

You would think it a simple task to remove a vinyl disc from its sleeve, then its dust cover, and then place it flat on the turntable without once touching the playing surface with your fingers, wouldn't you? Well, it isn't. And having a large shape looming over you, screaming 'AND IF YOU SCRATCH THAT RECORD, I'LL HAVE YOUR GUTS FOR GARTERS!' doesn't help one little bit.

Sunset's direct tutorial style served only to heighten Rib's anxiety. 33⅓ rpm suddenly became 78½ rpm and made 'Morning has Broken' sound as if Cat Stevens had inhaled a baloonful of helium. It was funny, though Sunset didn't think so. 'Whoa! Stop! Too bloody fast!' he shrieked. And so it went on.

35

Now that the music was back on stream, normal service was resumed. Well, almost normal. Sunset noticed a change in Rib. The lad seemed distraught, distracted, spending every free moment up in his room. The boy walked around with a frown on his face, as if he had the troubles of the whole world on his shoulders. He wasn't like himself at all. Ever since the gramophone lessons. Maybe he had been a bit too hard on him. After this had gone on for over a week, he decided he'd have to say something. Best to get it out in the open. A problem shared is a problem halved, that sort of thing. Maybe tomorrow. Over breakfast.

After a sleepless night, Sunset rose at four and busied himself in the galley – swept the floor, cleaned the stove, scoured the pans, turning over in his mind what he was going to say. At six on the dot he heard Rib's footsteps on the stairs. The front door slammed and he caught a glimpse of the boy through the front window. After his swim and his visit to Bettina's Buns, he'd be back for breakfast. Sunset laid the table, then sat down, cleared his throat and took a deep breath. How was he going to broach the subject? He needed a script. He needed to rehearse his lines. Role play, that's what he'd do. Role play.

He leaned back on the bench so that his body rested up against the wall. This was what known in the counselling trade as open, relaxed body language. It was so relaxed that he promptly nodded off for a couple of seconds, to be woken with a start by a spoon jumping off the table at the vibrations of his snoring. Sunset sat up, passed wind, and started the role play.

'Hiya, Rib, how was the swim?'

'It was great, thanks,' replied Sunset in a high falsetto voice.

Back to deep pitch mode. 'Now, Rib, you and me, we get on fine, don't we?'

'Yes,' squeaked the eunuch voice.

'Well, I was wondering if there was anything you'd like to talk to me about?'

Rib didn't reply. What would his next move be if the boy said nothing? Maybe use the pregnant pause strategy. Sit back in open body posture, nod a couple of times, and wait for the lad to tell all. But what if that didn't work? How long could he sit like that without his tummy rumbling?

Sunset decided to rehearse a more directive approach as a fall-back option to the pregnant pause. He cleared his throat.

'Hiya, Rib, how was the swim?'

'It was great thanks,' came the high-pitched reply.

'Rib, there's something I just have to say. You've been walking around like a fart in a trance these past few days. Now what the fuck is up with you?'

The back door burst open. Sunset jumped out of his skin. The contents of his cup redecorated the wall in a matt-caffeine emulsion.

'Oh! Sorry to startle you! Let me wipe that up,' said Rib, disappearing into the galley to fetch a cloth. Sunset quickly rehearsed his lines in his head. Rib came back and did his best to daub the splash from the wall.

'Hiya Rib.' That didn't sound right for a start. Too false. 'How was the swim?'

'It was great thanks,' came the reply in a normal voice.

Sunset paused. Which to choose? Good cop or bad cop?

'Yeah, it looks like it's going to be a nice day, too,' Rib continued while stacking the selection of buns, muffins and pastries onto the large, oval plate in the middle of the table. 'The river was running faster than normal. Did we have rain last night?'

'Er, no, yes, I'm not sure,' Sunset stuttered. 'Now Rib ... '

'Yes?'

'We get along just fine, don't we?'

'Of course we do. Here, try one of these muffins while they're still warm – they're the best.'

The boy sounded totally different today. Perky. Chipper. More like his old self. Sunset took a bite of the muffin. The boy was right. It was delicious. But even better mixed with a sip of coffee and swilled around the inside of the mouth until the cake melted. One of Sunset's less endearing habits. The boy's buoyant mood had caught him off guard. In the horns of a dilemma, he didn't know what to say next.

Rib filled the vacuum. 'What's the plan for the barrels today? We're running low on the Piss Poor and you said you might want to replace it with something new, remember?'

Sunset nodded. 'No, I think we'll brew another batch. Keeps the Marshall happy, if nothing else.'

Rib jumped up from the table and nipped back to the galley. All Sunset could hear was the opening and closing of cupboard doors. 'Have we got any more of that Victoria plum jam left?'

'Er, I don't think so,' said Sunset, knowing full well that he'd scraped the last bit from the bottom of the jar in the middle of the night.

'How about the honey, then?'

'Er, yes, there should be some on the top shelf of the right hand cupboard.'

More closing and opening of cupboard doors. 'Yep, got it!'

Rib marched back in holding the pot of Friedlander's finest aloft in triumph with a broad smile on his face. 'Been looking forward to it all morning. As soon as I got out of the water, I couldn't get honey on toast out of my head.' He spread a slab of butter onto a slice of wholemeal, dipped the wooden dipper into the pot, twirled it until the last thread of runny honey was captured, then drizzled it carefully over the surface of the toast in a criss-cross pattern. 'Mmm, perfect,' he mumbled at the first mouthful of golden sweetness.

The big man watched all this with an air of bemusement. He didn't quite know what to make of it all. Days on end without so much as a bleedin' word, and now suddenly back to being the chatty little sunbeam. He just didn't get it.

Suddenly Rib jumped up from his seat. 'I've got something for you,' he laughed.

'For me?' said Sunset, making to get to his feet.

'No, you stay there. I'll go and fetch it. And, by the way, there's a couple of pain au raisins with your name on the bag.'

Sunset watched the boy leave the bar and heard him sprinting hell for leather up the stairs. Pain au raisins, eh? Haven't had one of those for weeks. Would be a shame to see them go to waste ...

The two pastries became recent history in the ninety seconds it took Rib to return, carrying a wooden box about the size of a crate of apples, which he placed carefully on the floor beside the gramophone. Sunset had left the table and now stood beside him, staring at the box.

'Go ahead. Open it.'

Sunset bent down, for once not complaining about his knees, and opened the hinged top. Inside was a jumbled mass of metal rods, levers, chains, cogs and balls.

'Er, thanks. What is it?'

'It is a Meskitoe Mark 1 invention, patent pending.

'Eh?'

'Why don't you pour yourself another coffee, make yourself comfortable on the sofa and watch a master at work.' Feeling rather full after his breakfast treat, the old man didn't need persuading. And his knees were giving him gip, too. He watched the boy take the gleaming metal parts out of the box and start to piece them together, whistling while he worked. He couldn't help but marvel at the lightning speed with which he handled the components and deftly locked, screwed or bolted them in place. The contraption was taking place before his eyes, but what it was he had no idea.

'Exactly what is it, Rib?'

Without looking up, he replied. 'It's a quasi-perpetual motion machine.'

'Eh?'

'Let me explain. Are you sitting comfortably? Any perpetual motion machine has to disobey one of the three laws of thermodynamics ... '

Sunset's eyes began to glaze over.

' ... and the secret is to invent a machine that simply draws energy from its initial state ... '

Sunset's eyes closed. He started to dribble.

'... and it is termed a perpetual motion machine of the first, second or third kind, depending on which law it violates. Are you following?'

Sunset had slipped into a deep dream where he was hiding on the top floor of a pain au raisin round house and an enormous killer whale was trying to squeeze through one of the windows. 'Fuck off!' he screamed, awaking with a start. He blinked and stared wide-eyed at Rib, then looked out of the window to check Main Street for cruising orcas.

'Have you been asleep?'

'No, of course not!' came Sunset's indignant response. 'I was just studying the insides of my eyelids. I concentrate best that way.'

'Good, I'm nearly finished.'

Sunset leaned forward to take a closer look. Beside his prized gramophone was now erected an intricate stack of wheels, pulleys, cogs, rods and levers. Hanging from the body of the machine was a single pendulum with a brass orb the size of a tennis ball suspended from its end.

'That's incredible, Rib. How the hell did you do that?'

'Easy, I used to do this sort of thing all the time back on Earth,' he said, smiling at the memory of the yellow motion simulator he'd once converted into an all-terrain vehicle.

'Well, blow me down. I have to say that I'm seriously impressed, young man, but you still haven't told me what it does.'

'Let me show you.' Rib unfolded the crank handle from the side of the gramophone and coupled it to the machine by means of a connecting rod fitted with a sleeve. 'There, that should do it.' He then lifted the lid of the gramophone, took out Five Bridges and placed the vinyl disc on the turntable. Very, very carefully, he lowered the needle into the groove. 'OK. See that ball at the end of the pendulum?'

Sunset nodded.

'Just tap it lightly with your toe'.

He stepped up, gingerly prodded the brass ball with the end of his boot and watched as the machine whirred into motion. It took a full twelve seconds for the complex connection of moving parts to translate into the first smooth crank of the handle. The opening bars of the Fantasia track filled the bar. Sunset stood in stunned silence until the classic track finished, lifted the stylus, placed the record back in its sleeve and returned it to the drawer. 'My boy,' he said, turning to Rib, 'you're a genius, a bloody genius.'

'Steady on, now, it's not the finished article, you know. Remember, I said quasi-perpetual. I've had a bit of a problem getting hold of a really low-friction precision bearing. But I reckon you'd lose only about 0.35 of an rpm over the course of six 3-minute tracks. Would that be OK?'

The old man enveloped the young man in a bear hug. The boy was quick to start platonic back-pats,

a) to confirm the status of the manhug.
b) to signal that it was time to let him go now, please.

The old man took no notice and held on, not wanting the young man to see the tears rolling down his cheeks.

36

Dorothy Spigot left her flat on 2nd Street carrying a long black cloth holder and headed purposefully towards Main Street. She had timed her promenade to coincide with the school's afternoon break and stopped to look through the railings at the groups of children huddled together, in floods of tears. They all had shaven heads. Not only that, the skin on their scalps was red raw, in places still bleeding. No jeers, sneers and catcalls today, children, thought Dorothy, permitting a smile to cross her lips.

When putting the previous day's edition of the Strumpet to bed, she had allowed herself a little sub-editorial licence in adding a feature of her own at the bottom of sheet 3:

HEALTH WARNING TO ALL PARENTS OF STONYVILLE SCHOOL PUPILS!

A particularly INFECTIOUS species of HEADLICE is reported to have found its way into the school. Parents, you are advised to shave your child's head tonight and scrub the head with high-strength carbolic soap using a steel-toothed brush. DO NOT LET HEADLICE INFECT YOUR HOME! Challenge any parent whose child has a full head of hair. DO

NOT LET THEM INTRODUCE HEADLICE INTO
YOUR NEIGHBOURHOOD!'
A few days in advance, Dorothy had given the nod
to Hank at the Trading Post, and he had stocked up.
Sure enough, a thirty-strong queue stood at his door at
opening time.

That will serve the little bastards right, Dorothy
muttered as she set off down Main Street, noting that
Judd Scoter stood at his usual pitch outside the Market
Hall. Their eyes met as Dorothy neared to a distance of
some twenty metres. Judd instinctively rehearsed in his
mind the chords for Purple Rain.

'Good afternoon, Miss Spigot. Can I sharpen your
knives, scissors?'

'No thank you,' replied Dorothy, cucumber-cool.

Judd was leaning forward to blow his first note
when she stopped in her tracks, turned to him and said,
'Well, actually, I do have something which might need
sharpening.' This totally threw Scoter, who was still
struggling to get over the shock when she walked right
up to him and produced a long black case from the
cloth bag.

It was a sheath.

Of a Samurai sword.

Which she drew with effortless ease and held
horizontally with both hands clasped around the
hilt, the tip of the blade two inches from the knife-
sharpener's nose.

'I said "might" need sharpening. But first I need to
test just how sharp the blade is. I wouldn't want to be
wasting my money now, would I, Mr Scoter?'

A warm sensation trickled down the inside of Judd's
left thigh.

'Would I, Mr Scoter! ' she shrieked.

'No, Ma'am, certainly not,' he stuttered.

Dorothy took a step forward and angled the

gleaming blade so that its cutting edge brushed against Scoter's stubbled jaw. 'Now, Mr Scoter, I wouldn't move if I were you. My eyes ain't what they used to be and, round about this time of the day, I sometimes get the shakes.' She then started to dry-shave the three-day growth from the side of his face with the tip of the sword. The warm trickle had now turned to a flood and filled his left boot. Bristles of hair cascaded down the front of his shirt. Then, things went from bad to worse. One of the bristles pinged up his right nostril. He wanted to sneeze but knew he risked losing an ear at the very least if he did. Every muscle straining in his body to stop the sneeze, he was about to explode when the old woman lowered the Samurai and leaned forward to stroke his shaven jaw with the back of her warty hand.

'Smooth as a baby's bottom,' she remarked, proudly. 'Maybe the old girl doesn't need sharpening after all. What's your ... expert view, Mr Scoter?'

'Yes, I mean, no, it seems fine as it is. Just fine,' he said, feeling his cheek. It was, indeed, as smooth as a baby's bottom.

Dorothy calmly returned the sword to its sheath, which she placed carefully back into the black cloth bag. She turned to leave, but then stopped. 'And one other thing, Mr Scoter. From now on, it will be "Good morning, Miss Spigot, hope you're having a nice day". No more of that Purple Stain shit. Do I make myself clear?'

'Absolutely!' said Scoter, 'And I hope you're having a nice day, Miss Spigot.'

She certainly was. 'And a good day to you too, Mr Scoter,' the little old lady smiled as she walked off in the direction of the Strumpet offices.

An hour later, Jen Beccles found Judd Scoter stretched out semi-conscious on a bench in the Florence, an empty bottle of Wild Spatchcock rolling on the floor beside him. There would be no aye-aye-yippee-ippee-aye that night. She was not amused.

37

'My pet hedgehog died yesterday,' said Larix, with a lump in his throat.

Rib didn't know what to say. 'I'm really sorry to hear that, mate,' came his lame effort. He couldn't remember Larix saying anything about having a pet, but this must be terrible for the boy. 'If you don't mind my asking, how did he die?'

'He ran out into Main Street right in front of the stagecoach. Squashed flat, he was. Looked like a bristle doormat.'

'Jeez, that really is terrible,' Rib paused, not knowing what to say next. 'What was his name?'

'Invincible Harry!' said Larix, with a peal of laughter.

Larix certainly was coming out of his shell. How could he have fallen for a hedgehog story? What a prick. The two were heading back down Main Street from the Big Licker, where the usual flushed glances had been exchanged between Larix and Amy. Rib wished he wouldn't keep on staring at her while licking his cornet – it fair put him right off his black salt liquorice. But on the other hand, it was good to see his friend coming out of himself. Sick hedgehog jokes aside, he was good company.

They stopped at the Wall to scour the Strumpet for the day's news. Being mid-morning, there wasn't a crowd. A headline near the bottom of the centre sheet caught Rib's attention and he crouched down to read the article.

EXOTIC DANCING CLASS, ran the headline. *'Students at Our Lady of Lourdes Institute in Woburn say that exotic dancing was part of a professor's after-hours seminar, writes reporter Hetty Huxtable. Officials at the private Roman Catholic college confirm that an investigation into the events of the night 15th July is now underway. The seminar is said to have ended abruptly when the Dean walked through the door. Students say that the dancers kept most of their clothes on. Final-year student, Max Bunge, told the Trumpet that one of the girls was giving a lap-dance to the Head of School, Professor Walter Werther. "She was grinding her rump in his groin like a pestle cracking peppercorns in a mortar," he alleged.*

Aged 61, Professor Werther, originally from East Grinstead, was not available for comment when our reporter visited his house at 51, 4th Street, Stonyville (the red-painted clapboard house with the white picket fence out the front). His wife, Enid, aged 64, said that he was "currently indisposed," but that he would be available for comment "after she'd finished with him." Students say they now have a new teacher.

Rib laughed, stretched his back, and joined Larix reading a feature further down the Wall:

FINE CROP OF PICKERS – *Stonyville Bluegrass Festival Invests in Youth*

Caleb Cowshed watched his beloved bluegrass music nearly die. Bluegrass was almost dead and buried back on the Old Planet, but now there's a real resurgence amongst the younger folk here in town. This Saturday, the 28-strong membership of the Stonyville Bluegrass Association will parade down Main Street to launch its annual festival. "*There's some youngsters here who would hold their own with any professional bluegrass band in the land,*" *says Caleb, a man who certainly knows pickers when he sees 'em!*

The boys slowly shook their heads in a show of studied disgust. 'I hope Sunset doesn't read that,' said Rib.

'Why's that?'

'His favourite joke goes something like this: "What happens if you play a bluegrass record backwards? Answer: your crop doesn't fail, your dog doesn't die, and your woman doesn't take her love to town."'

Larix didn't seem to hear. He was pointing at a poster which someone had defaced. The Stonyville Community Health Trust had been running an anti-smoking campaign for a couple of weeks. It was a bit like pissing in the Pacific, for all the good it did. Undeterred, their latest offering was a course of counselling aimed specifically to support young men in the early stages of smoking cessation.

GIVING UP *SMOKING?*
THE FIRST SIX MONTHS ARE THE HARDEST BUT BOYS, HELP IS AT HAND!

Someone had crossed out the word 'smoking' and scrawled the word 'masturbation' above it. It bore all the hallmarks of Judd Scoter. Rib burst out laughing, then caught Larix's eye. An impish grin spread across the boy's face.

'No! You didn't! You didn't!'

He was still laughing when he pulled up a chair at Larix's Hog-roast stand in the Market Hall. The slight figure of a boy with one arm looked even smaller standing beside the enormous carcass impaled upon the spit. The charcoal embers had begun to glow and the first drips of hot fat from the pig sizzled as they burned and turned to smoke on the coals.

'Time to give it a turn,' said Larix, taking hold of the handle with his only hand and pushing it a quarter-turn away from him. It seemed to take an awful amount of effort. Beads of sweat appeared on his brow.

'How often do you have to turn that thing?'

'Well it depends on the stage of the roast. In the very early stages, like now, you can turn it once every fifteen minutes or so. But once the crackling starts to crisp up, its best to keep it turning all the time, otherwise it will get burnt.'

'How long does it take to cook from start to finish?'

'Seven hours. And I don't cook it, I roast it.'

'Sorry.' Then without thinking, Rib asked a third question. 'Surely there must be a better way of doing it? How about I put together a mechanical spit for you?'

Larix went silent, then turned on Rib with venom in his voice. 'And why the hell would I need that? Just because I've only got one arm doesn't mean I can't do my job!'

'But – '

'And who are you to tell me how to roast a hog? Just because you're a … Deputy Manager,' he scoffed, 'doesn't mean you know diddly-squat about roasting hogs.'

'Look, I was only trying to help … '

'Yeah, well I don't need your help. Butt out!' His eyes flashed with rage as he turned his back on Rib and took hold of the handle again.

'Fine!' said Rib, storming out of the Market Hall. If that's the way you want it, you ungrateful little turd …

38

'Well, you have to understand, Rib, that Larix isn't like everybody else,' said Sunset between mouthfuls of muffin.

'I know that, but I was only trying to help. There was no need for him to fly off the handle like that.'

'Try and look at it from his side. His world revolves around routine, order, his way of doing things. I once made the mistake of telling him the best way to prune an apple tree. Didn't speak to me for a week. And you have to hand it to the lad, his way works for him. Whatever he turns his hand to, he's bloody good at it.'

'I know, I know ...'

'It seems to me like a case of two best buddies having a bit of a barney, that's all. Bet your bottom dollar he'll be as upset as you are. You've both had a chance to sleep on it. I suggest you get over there this morning and take him out for an ice cream. He'll never say no to that. Now, pass me the coffee.'

Reassured by Sunset's counsel, he helped clear away the breakfast dishes before heading over to the Market. At this time of day, he should find Larix raking out the coals from yesterday's roast before lighting up the fresh charcoal. Rib rehearsed his lines as he walked into the hall. 'Hiya, mate, sorry about yesterday. All a bit of a misunderstanding. How's about you and me strolling down to Lickers for a couple of cornets? My shout.'

He fixed a smile on his face and strode through the Market Hall, where queues were already forming at some of the stalls. He craned his neck to get an early glimpse of Larix to gauge what sort of mood he was in, but couldn't pick him out through the crowd. He couldn't pick him out because he wasn't there. No charcoal, no pig, no Larix. Just a sign propped up against the spit: HOGROAST CLOSED UNTIL FURTHER NOTICE. Rib stood in front of the empty stand scratching his head. Surely this couldn't be because of their argument? Or could it? With Larix, there was no way of knowing. None of the neighbouring stall holders could shed any light on the mystery. Rib decided to try the Big Licker. Maybe Amy would know ...

The look on her face told him at once that something had happened. She was busy serving a customer and Rib had to hop impatiently from foot to foot until the cowboy had paid up and left. As soon as he was through the door, Amy rushed around the counter and threw herself in Rib's arms. 'Oh, Rib, thank God you've come. It's Larix. He's had a terrible accident.' Her slender frame trembled against him. She started to sob.

'It's OK, it's OK,' he said, not knowing what to do with his hands. He led her over to the dining area, sat her down at a table and took the chair opposite. 'OK, Amy, tell me all about it.'

She took a handkerchief from her apron pocket and blew hard on her nose. 'He's been thrown from his horse and he's broken his arm and cracked three ribs.'

'Jeez! How the hell did that happen?'

'The Benjamin brothers saw it all. They said he came riding up the hill like a bat out of hell. Then, some small critter ran across the street and spooked Champion. Jamie reckoned it was a big rat. The horse veered to the left and smashed through the railings outside the undertakers.'

'That's terrible, really terrible. Was Champion hurt?'

'Champion!' the girl screamed. 'Do you think I give a friggin' fig about the friggin' horse?'

'No, no, I meant Larix. Was Larix hurt?'

'Did I not just tell you that he's got three broken ribs and a fractured arm! Is that not hurt enough?'

'Yeah, sorry, of course. How is he now?'

'He's doing OK. Doc Stimpson patched him up last night and he's at home in bed.' She paused and fiddled with her apron strings. 'I sat by his bed through the night ...' An awkward silence followed.

'Was it you who put the sign on his stall?'

'Yes, first thing this morning before I opened up.' Another pause. Longer this time.

'Well, I suppose I'd better get over there and see how he is,' he said, rising from the table.

She put her hand on his. 'I'm not, er, sure that's a good idea.'

'What?'

'He doesn't want to see you.'

'Oh ... er, OK, then. Um, just let me know if there's anything I can do and, er, say hello to him from me, will you?'

'Yeah, of course.'

'Bye, then.'

'Bye.'

Rib left the parlour with a heavy heart.

Riding like a bat out of hell, they'd said. Just after their argument. It was his fault. If he hadn't made Larix see red, then all this would never have happened. A broken arm! Bad enough for an able-bodied person, but when you only had the one ... How was he going to manage? How long would it take for his arm to mend? A month? Maybe two? And would it ever be strong enough to turn that heavy spit again? The salvo of questions battered his brain unanswered. It all came down to one truth. First

Sunset and now Larix. Both nearly killed, because of him. It was his fault. He ran back to the Waterloo, went straight to his room, locked the door behind him and sat on the bed, head in hands.

The next morning , Rib skipped his daybreak dip to seek out a bleary-eyed Sunset pottering about in the galley. 'I'd like to ask if I could take a week off?'

'I guess this is about Larix – I heard last night. Sure, no bad idea to get out of town for a while. Clear your head. But listen, you can't blame yourself for this. It was an accident.'

'I'm not going anywhere. I just need a week off. That's all I'm asking.'

'Of course, of course.' That would mean he'd have to go and get his own pastries in the morning, but he'd manage. The exercise might even do him good.

'Thanks,' said Rib, hurrying out of the bar. He raced down the street and skidded to a halt outside Sam the Blacksmith's, who was just opening up. 'Morning, Sam.'

'Morning young man. And what can I do for you?'

'I need another favour.'

The sinewy man clad in a brown leather apron smiled through his bushy ginger beard. 'Aha, let me guess. That contraption of yours didn't work and now you want me to take the metal back.'

'No, no. It's working fine, just fine.'

'Glad to hear it. So what can I do for you?'

'I need to build another machine. A bigger one this time. A much bigger one.'

Sam scratched his chin. 'Well, I ain't a charity you know.'

'Of course not, I'll pay for everything. I've got cash.' He then told Sam what he needed the metal for. To build a perpetual motion rotary spit for Larix.

'Mmm, great shame about the accident. He's a good kid.' Sam paused to stroke his beard. 'Tell you what, you give me a list of what you need and I'll supply and cut the materials for ... let's say, four growlers of Dog's Dribble. Is that a deal?' He spat in his palm and held it out.

Rib followed suit by spitting in Sam's palm. He sensed he'd got it wrong somehow. 'It's a deal,' he faltered.

'Fine, you'd better get working on that spec then,' said the blacksmith, wiping his hand on the front of his smock.

Rib laboured feverishly on the machine from dawn till dusk, making frequent site visits to check and double check the mechanics of the spit. By comparison, the gramophone project was a piece of piss – the amount of sustained force to turn a carcass weighing over two hundred kilos was going to take some doing.

It was difficult, but he made a conscious decision not to visit Larix. Amy kept him fed with regular updates and he was mightily relieved to hear that Doc Stimpson saw no reason why Larix shouldn't, in the long term, regain full use of his arm. She reckoned he'd be coming back into town in three or four days.

As if this weren't pressure enough, the town's fast-food vendors immediately sensed an opportunity. Entrepreneurial spirit being the very essence of Stonyville, Larix's competitors circled his wounded business like vultures slavering over a dying steer in the desert. But unlike vultures, they were showing no intention of waiting for their victim to die. They were moving in for the kill.

Within two days, George Christadoulou moved his doner kebab stall into the Market Hall from behind the Freight Depot, Storm Holm was doing a brisk trade in grilled hot-dogs with fried onions right opposite the hog-roast pitch and, most alarmingly, the Hernandez Brothers had dug a pit on the plot at the back of the

Market and were serving Cuban hog-roast at twenty cents less a sandwich. Time was not on Rib's side.

39

It was the night before Larix's estimated time of arrival back into town. By the light of four kerosene lamps, Rib was working flat-out to install the shoulder-high machine. The Jones boys had contributed to the cause by preparing a pig carcass, now firmly fixed on the spit. The stuck pig observed his feverish activity with an air of contemptuous challenge.

'It's never gonna work. I ain't gonna budge an inch,' it seemed to say.

Rib needed a break. He'd assembled and re-assembled the machine and tried to start it three times. It hadn't worked, even though he was sure he'd fitted everything correctly. Maybe some fresh air would help. Stepping out from the dark interior of the Market Hall, he surprised Dorothy, who was pinning the day's edition of The Strumpet on to the Wall.

'Jesus Christ, boy! What the hell do you think you're doing, sneaking up on me like that?'

'Sorry! I didn't mean to. Er, good morning ... '

She ignored his greeting. 'And what the hell do you think you're doing in the Market Hall at this time of the night?'

'We're preparing a sort of surprise welcome for Larix – he's due back in town today.'

'Oh, I see,' she softened. 'How's the boy doing?'

'Doc Stimpson says he should make a full recovery.'

'That's good, that's good. He's a nice, polite lad. Now, if you'll excuse me … '

'Of course, have a nice day.'

Dorothy wasn't planning on having anything of the sort and turned her back on him.

Taking a final lungful of the cold morning air, he went back into the hall. He stood before the machine and took a deep breath. It was now or never. Ten minutes later and he was still no further forward. The worst possible scenario was looming as a real possibility: Larix arriving to be presented with an automatic rotary spit that didn't rotate, a heap of scrap metal dumped on his pitch. Maybe he should give it up as a bad job. Maybe he'd somehow got the sums wrong. Maybe the pig was just too damned heavy. To put the last hypothesis to the test, he disconnected the machine from the spit and pushed against the handle. It certainly was damned heavy and took some effort to turn. But turn it did. This unexpected turn of events caught the pig off guard, causing the apple to drop from its mouth, bouncing once, then striking Rib's left boot before rolling under the machine.

'Shit, it'll be all covered in sawdust now,' he swore under his breath, kneeling down to reach for the apple. His fingers came into contact with something cold and smooth. He grasped the object, stood up and took it over to one of the kerosene lamps. It was a locking pin! He rushed round the rear of the machine and soon found where it had fallen from. The brass pin was supposed to lock a male rod into a female sleeve. Without the pin, the rod would just slide in and out of the sleeve just like … well, er … a rod sliding in and out of a sleeve. Rib deftly inserted the pin into place, retrieved the apple from the floor, wiped off the sawdust on the back of his trousers, and popped it back into the pig's mouth. Now for the moment of truth.

He prodded the ball fixed to the end of the pendulum and stepped back to watch his creation come to life. Like a brightly-coloured fairground merry-go-round slowly picking up speed against the black backdrop of a midsummer night, whirring cogs shone, brass rods gleamed, polished levers glinted. After a twenty-second eternity, the spit handle started to crank and the carcass slowly rotated in a macabre, horizontal pirouette. Rib felt a sudden urge to run out of the hall, grab Dorothy by the waist and plant a juicy kiss on her purple-painted lips. Fortunately for him, his brain kicked into gear and quashed the impulse, the Meskitoe frontal lobe having quickly computated the two most likely consequences of such an action:

Likely consequence Number One – a painful boot in the nadgers. Or even worse,

Likely consequence Number Two – being dragged off to the bedroom of her flat on 2nd Street.

The boy shuddered a picking-up-a-slug-mistaking-it-for-a-stick-of-liquorice shudder. Instead, he turned his attention back to the Meskitoe Rotary Spit Hog-roast Machine, which was now dancing a slow waltz of engineered elegance before him, evoking bitter-sweet memories of a big frog in another time, another place.

The first sliver of morning light had now slipped unnoticed into the Market Hall. Larix was due in about four hours' time. Just enough to get back to the flat and catch some zeds. He stopped the machine, roped off the area and blew out the lamps. Out on Main Street, he was relieved to find Dorothy gone. In less than a minute he was lying on his bed, too tired to take off his clothes. He was absolutely shattered.

But he couldn't sleep. A single thought kept gnawing away at him. What would Larix's reaction be?

40

Larix looked terrible, leaning heavily against Amy, his left arm in a sling, his right arm now even more conspicuous by its absence. The Doc had fitted him with a bandage corset to knit his ribs back together. Bruising still seeped out from his right cheekbone, an autumn-yellow hue. Rib was about to say that he looked like shit warmed up, but stopped himself just in time. Instead, he said, 'How's it going, Larix?' Amy flashed him a menacing stare.

Larix appeared not to hear his well-chosen words of comfort, staring at the machine. 'Get that thing away from my hog-roast,' he hissed through gritted teeth.

'Look, Larix,' said Amy, gently stroking his arm. 'Rib was only trying to help, weren't you Rib?'

'I don't give a toss what he was trying to do. He had no right to go near my roaster. Now get that thing taken down and shipped out!'

Rib was rapidly reverting to ungrateful little turd mode. 'OK, Larix, you have it your way. I'll start taking it down. While I'm getting my tools out, do just one thing for me, huh?'

'What's that?' the boy said, addressing him for the first time.

'Take a look around you. What do you see? What are folks eating?' Larix turned to survey the busy throng of market-goers. 'I'll tell you what you see. You see people eating kebabs, you see people eating hot-dogs. You even, and you're not going to like this, you even see people eating Cuban hog-roast.'

'What!' exploded the boy.

'Yes, Cuban hog-roast, cooked in a pit with banana leaves.'

'Shit,' Larix swore.

Now warming to his theme, Rib pressed on. 'And what don't you see, my friend?'

Silence.

'You don't see anyone eating a hog-roast sandwich cooked – sorry, roasted – by the best damn hog-roaster in the County.'

Larix looked down at his feet.

'And that's why I've built the machine. To make sure your customers don't leave you and never come back. The best of butchers has the worst of holidays,' he added sagely.

Larix had to admit to himself that Rib was talking sense. He knew only too well how fickle trade could be.

'And the second reason I built this thing was to ... was to ... say sorry.'

Larix looked up. 'What for?'

'I reckon it was down to me that you had the accident. I was out of line. Way out of line.'

Larix turned to Amy, who smiled and nodded. 'I don't know ... ' he wavered. 'Look Rib, I'm not blaming you for me falling off a horse. That had nothing to do with you. But I don't take kindly to you, or anyone else, telling me what's best for me. I've done fine doing things my way up to now and that's the way I want it to stay.'

'And that's exactly how it should be. All I want is to help you over the next few weeks until your arm mends, that's all. Why don't you come over and have a closer look, huh? Let me give you a demonstration of how this wonderful machine of yours works.'

'Mine?'

'Yes, yours. Now, are you going to stand there all day?'

Amy prodded Larix in the small of the back and he relented. Within minutes, the two were engaged in animated conversation, huddled close over the machine. A broad smile spread across her face. The two friends were back together again.

'But as soon as I'm fit again, I'm gonna be turning that handle. There's no substitute for the real thing,' she heard Larix say.

'Sure, sure. But don't judge too soon, matey. You haven't even seen it work yet. Which reminds me – it must be time for the opening ceremony.'

'Opening ceremony?'

'Yep, I've arranged a VIP to come along and start the machine.'

Larix looked around nervously. 'Who?'

'You, you dipstick.' Rib laughed and guided his friend to the front of the stall before he had time to protest. 'See that brass ball on the end of the pendulum? Just give it a tap with the end of your foot.'

Larix paused, looked over to Amy, suddenly every bit the little boy lost.

'Go on,' she said gently.

He managed to stem a tidal wave of tears and gave the ball a tap with his foot.

'I declare the Larix Le Roux Quasi-Perpetual Motion Rotary Hog-roaster well and truly open,' announced Rib. Amy jumped up and down, clapping her hands. A couple of onlookers joined her.

Larix heard none of this, held spellbound by the magic of the machine unfurling itself before his eyes. Transfixed, he followed every motion, counter motion, push, pull and turn until reaching the rod connecting to the spit handle. There it stopped. For a second, the whole universe held its breath. Then, with a slight judder, the handle started to move and the spit started to turn. The whole universe breathed a sigh of relief. Amy wiped a tear from her eye, Rib cheered and Larix turned to his friend. 'Thanks, Rib. It's ... it's ... it's brilliant. Just brilliant.'

'Right, let's get this fire lit then, shall we?'

'Hold on a minute. I won't be able to baste. I won't be able to carve.'

'No worries, we've got that sorted. Sunset's closing the Waterloo early and coming over with a dozen growlers. He's been practising carving all week. Got his chef's hat and apron all ready. You should see him.'

'Sunset's doing that? For me?'

'Sure is. Now, are we going to stand here blubbing or are we going to get this show on the road?' On cue, one of the Jones boys stepped forward with a lighted spill to ignite the kindling under the coals.

The evening went down as one of the most memorable in Stonyville's short history. Word had got around and folk flocked into the Market Hall. Sunset got the music going with a gravelly rendition of the Coney Island Washboard Blues swiftly followed by another rendition of the same. Fearing a third, Pat and Sookie Flanagan took over with fiddle and bodhran, which got everyone up and dancing. Even Marshall Amps turned up to pose for a photograph with Larix in front of the hog-roast. 'Cheese!' came the muffled cry from Al beneath the black cowling as the magnesium flash made everybody jump, even though they knew it was coming. Mr T then parked himself on an upturned orange crate to watch the revelry. It was said that he consumed six hog-roast sandwiches in the hour that he sat there. Hetty danced the night away with Al. Dorothy drank the night away with abandon. Judd Scoter played peace songs from the 1960's on his harmonica. Jen bought Dave and Nick each a roast pork sandwich, smothered with apple sauce, washed down by a growler of Big Bear Blonde, by way of apology for pouring a potful of piss over them every afternoon. The two hobos linked arms and danced a reel in the middle of Main Street, casting only the occasional nervous glance skyward.

It had been an emotional day for Larix and he signed off at eleven. Everyone went out onto the street to wave and cheer him and Amy goodbye as they left in the Jones boys' waggon. The party finally wound down in the early hours of the morning, within touching distance of dawn. It took Rib and Sunset, both extremely rat-arsed, a full twenty minutes to stagger the twenty metres from the Market Hall to the Waterloo's front door. Mainly because Sunset insisted on staging a none-too-accurate re-enactment of Ricky Villa's goal in the 1981 FA Cup Final. The old man scuttled from one side to another, like a giant crab on LSD.

'He went round one, then another, then another, then aaarghh!' he screamed, as he went crashing arse-over-head off the edge of the boardwalk for the umpteenth time. When he finally made it to bed, the last thing Rib could remember before he closed his eyes were the melancholic strains of Judd Scoter's mouth harp wafting upwards in the warm night air.

'*For the times, they are a changing ...* '

41

Happily, Doc Stimpson's prognosis had been spot on and he signed off Larix as fit for active duty again three weeks later. The machine, however, stayed connected to the spit. It had become the town's first tourist attraction, folks flocking in from miles around to witness the whirring wonder. And, while they were there, what better way to pass their time than to bite into a succulent pork sandwich? Takings increased by forty percent and Larix got closer to his customers. One Friday morning, as if in mass surrender, the competition vanished: the pitta-patter of tiny Greek feet could be heard as George Christadoulou trundled his stall out of the Market Hall; the Dane Storm Holm stormed home with a cart of half-cooked hot-dogs; the Cubans turned on their heels to return to the other side of the tracks, leaving a trail of banana leaves behind them. The Larix LeRoux Hog-roast reigned supreme again.

It was two weeks later, over a cup of coffee on the allotment, that Larix first mentioned The Mansion. 'Have I ever told you where I go on Monday evenings?'

'Nope, I don't think so. '

'I go to a school. A special school.'

'Oh, I see.' A pause.

'No, not that kind of a special school. It's a school for gifted and talented people.'

Another pause. Maybe a tad too long. Rib might

as well have said, 'Then how come you're there?' He recovered just in time to say, 'I've never heard of the place. What kind of things do they do there?'

'Well you know how it is with the Fearance?'

Rib nodded.

'It's like a school for inventors. All sorts of bright sparks trying to come up with alternative sources of energy. It's called the Research & Innovation Centre.'

'The RIC?' laughed Rib. 'What sort of name is that?'

Larix joined in his laughter. 'You think that's funny? When they first opened, they named it the Primary Research & Innovation Centre.'

Rib spat out his mouthful of coffee, splashing Larix's boot. 'Sorry,' he choked.

'No worries. Everybody just calls it The Mansion now.'

The Mansion! Wasn't that the place he'd stumbled across, deep in the woods?

Larix bent down to wipe the coffee from his boot with his handkerchief. He seemed to be waiting to say something. 'I was wondering,' he said without looking up, 'whether you might be interested in joining up? I mean, what you did with the spit machine was ... amazing.' Their eyes met.

'Thanks, mate. I suppose I've always had a knack for that sort of thing. Sounds interesting. How would I go about applying? I've never seen anything advertised in The Strumpet.'

'No, you won't have. It's a kind of secret.'

'A secret? Then how come you're telling me all about it?'

Larix busied himself with his boot again, which was now so shiny he could see his face in it. 'Because I trust you.'

Now it was Rib's turn to concentrate on peeling a Granny Smith with his pocket knife. The two boys immersed themselves in boot-polishing and apple-peeling activity for a full minute until Rib came up for air. 'So how do I get into this place, then?'

'It's by personal recommendation only. I was put forward by my Uncle Dave. I could have a word, if you wanted?'

'Yeah, thanks. Why not? I'd have to see Sunset about changing my shifts, but I'm sure that'd be OK.'

Weeks went by without further mention of The Mansion. Rib assumed that either Larix had forgotten about it or his enquiry had drawn a blank. Then, on a Thursday night, Larix strolled into the Waterloo, tried not to look at the sobbing Cliff and signalled Rib to join him.

'What's up?' he asked.

'Nothing,' whispered Larix, holding a finger to his lips.

'Then why are we whispering?'

'You've got an interview at The Mansion tomorrow.'

42

'And you were under whom at College?'

'I beg your pardon?'

'Who was your professor?'

'Oh, I see. Riley, Professor Riley,' said Rib.

'Ah, a sound old egg, if ever there was one. Followed the wrong code though, if I recall.'

'I beg your pardon?'

'Soccer. The bally idiot followed soccer. Ghastly! Absolutely ghastly!'

The interview with Major Claude 'Bonkers' Bonkerstone was not going at all well. Larix had accompanied him to the Mansion and left him waiting in the hall outside the library, where he sat for ages feeling like the naughty boy outside the Head's study. When Bonkerstone appeared, he was wearing white cricket flannels, a straw boater and a monacle, of all things.

Greeting Rib with a 'What-ho!' he then ushered him into the library. 'Yes, now remind me, Meskitoe. Who referred you to us?'

'Larix, Sir'

'Ah yes. Dashed bright boy. An absolute topper. Pity about the one arm, though. Must have been a pretty frightful ordeal for the chappie.'

'Er, yes. I suppose it was.'

'Well Meskitoe, when can you start?'

'Start, Sir? So I've got a place?'

'Yes of course, my dear boy. LeRoux is a sound sort and his word is good enough for me. No sense in beating about the bush. Shall we say next Monday, eleven hundred hours?

'Yes. Thank you, Sir.'

'Excellent! LeRoux will show you the ropes.' He shook Rib's hand, then held onto it. 'And remember, Meskitoe, not a whisper to anyone. Our work here is all very hush-hush. Mum's the word, Meskitoe, Mum's the word ... '

* * *

They worked in huts.

Some sat side by side, the occasional whisper shared, no more. Most sat as solitary souls at deliberate distance from the others. Each immersed in a world of calculations, measures and equations. Academics and artisans, scientists and hairstylists, engineers and eco-techs – with the odd trading standards officer thrown in for good measure. Each seeking, under the strict supervision and intellectual copyright of the Protectorate, to come up with the answer. To crack the Fearance.

Rib's first day at the RIC was not the best. Because it coincided with Larix's monthly check-up with Doc Stimpson, he had to report for duty on his own. He was issued with two sheets of paper, one pencil, one strange instrument (which he later learned to be a slide rule) and an incomprehensible set of tables. He was shown to a seat in Hut 8, where he sat for half an hour at a loss what to do. When he finally summoned the courage to talk to his neighbour to ask, he was met with a loud "Shhh!" from the inhabitants of the hut.

It was hopeless. He couldn't even begin to come up

with anything sensible. Out of pure frustration, he went out for some fresh air and walked around the lake in front of the Mansion. Two swans swam over to him in the hope of being fed. He promised them that he would bring some bread next time.

On his return to Hut 8, he found his seat gone. Not taken, but gone. Disappeared. OK, he thought, message received. Loud and clear. This had been one bad idea from the beginning. How did he check out of this place? Because that was exactly what he was going to do. He slammed the door shut and set off back towards the Mansion.

'Cloaca!' came the cry from an open window a couple of buildings down. At least, that's what he thought he'd heard. Rib peered inside to see a little old man with a shock of frizzy grey hair jumping up and down. He caught sight of Rib through the window. 'Come take a look at this,' he shouted in an American accent. Rib opened the door to Hut 10 and stepped in. A large table dominated the room, its surface completely covered with paper, each sheet in turn covered with sketches, diagrams, equations, all in the same scratchy italic script.

The old man was painfully thin. His skinny legs stuck out of a pair of canvas yacht-shoes, two sizes too big. Faded blue shorts, an off-white T-shirt hung from his spare frame. With no attempt at introductions he flashed a welcome from sunken, hollow eyes.

'You're new, huh?' The thin, rasping voice came as little more than a whisper.

'Yes. Started this morning.'

'I guess they will have put you in Hut 8?'

'Er, well, yes they did, actually.'

'Assholes every one.'

Rib smiled. 'Yeah, not sure I'm cut out for this place.'

The old man cleared a corner of the table.

'Why don't you pull up a chair and work here a while?' he said, without looking at him for a response.

'OK, er, thanks,' said Rib

And not a word more was exchanged between the two over the course of the next three hours: the old man looking and acting every bit the mad professor – scribbling feverishly, mopping at his brow, sometimes tearing at his hair – as if in a race against time; the young man playing the serious student, head down, concentrating on the task in hand. No doubt about it, the sparky energy in the room was contagious and he soon found himself putting pencil to paper. Firstly, a sketch. Of an air balloon, shaped like a cigar. Then a couple of quick equations to calculate the pedal-power needed to propel the thing. Then a list of musings as to who would be best suited to crew the airship. Maybe shitshed inmates? On second thoughts, no. "How the hell did they escape?" "Well, Governor, they flew right over the wall in a pedal-powered air balloon …"

The sudden presence of the old man at his right shoulder startled him. He leaned forward to touch Rib's design with a gnarled forefinger, tracing the shape of the Zeppelin. A couple of nods, a murmur and he was gone again, back at his end of the big table. Was that a gesture of approval? He lost all sense of time and only realised that it was late when he took a pee-break and checked the sundial in front of the Mansion. Rib raced back to Hut 10.

'Hi, er, excuse me, but I've got to go. I'm supposed to be back here again next week. Would it, would it be OK if I joined you?'

The old man said nothing, but looked away through the far window into a distance only he could see …

43

It had become part of their regular routine to meet up at the Big Licker of a Thursday morning. Rib found Larix ensconced in the company of a cone with no fewer than four scoops of rum and raisin.

'How did it go?' came Larix's immediate question.

'More importantly, how did you get on with Doc Stimpson?'

'Fine. Last time I have to see him.'

'That's great. Really good news, mate. Hiya Amy, two scoops of salt liquorice, please.'

'So tell me, how did it go?'

'Well, OK, in the end.'

'In the end?'

'Yeah. They put me in with a bunch of twats who didn't go out of their way to make me feel welcome.'

'Hut 8?'

'That's the one.'

'Twats is a good description.'

'Then I went and worked in Hut 10.'

Larix dropped the ice-cream cone into his lap. Amy rushed forward with a cloth to wipe the front of his trousers just that little too eagerly. When she'd deftly removed the dollop, Larix hissed.

'You were allowed into Hut 10?'

'Well, yes.'

'But that's not allowed. No-one's allowed into Hut 10!'

'Nobody told me.'

'But how did you get in there?'

'An old guy invited me in.'

'Whaaat!' Larix exploded, so loud that a couple of queuing customers turned to see what the commotion was all about. 'Don't you know who that is?'

'No, he didn't introduce himself.'

Larix looked around furtively, then gestured Rib to lean forward. He whispered in his ear. 'It's The Buzz. Professor Clayton E. Buzzard.'

'Whaaaat!' Now it was Rib's turn to explode. The queue turned again, now fully expecting to see fists flying. 'Clayton E. Buzzard?'

'Shhh!' Larix clapped his hand over Rib's mouth. 'Shhh! It's a secret. No one's supposed to know he's here.'

'Then how do you know?'

'Once I overheard a conversation between two guards, arguing whose turn it was to take his meal over.'

'So what's he doing here, in Stonyville?'

'I don't think he ever leaves the Centre. I've never seen him in town, anyway.' Larix paused before going on. 'I think he's in some kind of custody.'

'You mean he's a prisoner?'

'No, I wouldn't go as far as that. There's talk of him leading a team of scientists on some sort of expedition. Although maybe you're right. Those two guards are never far away. But remember, not a word to anyone, hear me?'

'Yeah, of course.' For once, Rib let his tongue run over the black ice-cream without tasting its sharp saltiness. Larix had changed subject and was now telling him about an article he'd read on the Wall earlier. Something about a wildfire somewheres. Rib wasn't listening.

Clayton E. Buzzard, he kept saying to himself. He had been working with Clayton E. Buzzard! One of the greatest scientists in the whole history of mankind. The man responsible for Exodus. The man who discovered and named Planet Tycho after his only son. Wow! He couldn't believe it …

In a half-daze he took his leave of Larix and walked out onto Main Street. It was already turning into another scorching, late summer's day and he had to shield his eyes as he stepped out into the dusty road. Two huge shadows crossed his path. A split second later, something wet and sloppy slapped against his raised forearm. He stood and stared in disbelief at what looked like a runny fried egg with a blue yolk sticking to his skin. Narrowly avoiding an oncoming waggon, he immediately started to run down Main Street. Something told him he had to get to the Trading Post. And fast! There was no time to lose!

44

Luckily, there was no queue. 'Morning, son,' said Hank. 'What the hell's that on your arm, boy? Looks like a flock of geese been using you for target practice.'

'Hank, I need a fishing lure, a pair of narrow-head pliers, a solder iron, a small vice, a bulldog clip, and some fuse wire, thinnest you've got.'

'Fuse wire? What the hell you gonna use fuse wire for? Just in case you haven't noticed, there's no call for fuse wire round here.'

'But I need some!' said Rib, raising his voice.

'Take it easy, boy, take it easy. I'll go check out the back. Got a few tins of old stuff in the storeroom. Give me five minutes. In the meantime, go pick the fishing lure you want. They're over there on the wall.'

The selection was surprisingly wide – Slender Eels, Funk Bugs, Spoon Lures, Fatso cranks - but Rib went straight for the Savoy Shad, snatching it from the wall. Hank was already back at the counter holding a card of fuse wire. 'Looks like it might be your lucky day, boy.' He took a bulldog-clip from one of the pigeon holes behind him. 'This size do for you?'

'Yes, that's perfect thanks. Now, how much will that be?'

'Let's say forty dollars all in.'

'Thanks,' said Rib, handing over the money.

'Out of curiosity, what the hell do you want the fuse wire for, boy?'

The little bell tinkled loudly above the Trading Post door. The boy was gone.

Dashing into the Market Hall, he made a beeline for Abe's Herb & Spice stall, where he waited impatiently for the Widow Hansworth to be served before buying six cinnamon sticks.

'You sure you need six?' asked Abe.

'Yes, I am sure,' he shouted over his shoulder, already rushing to leave. Rib Meskitoe carried his precious cargo of small vice, pair of narrow-head pliers, soldering iron, solder, bulldog clip, Savoy Shad lure and six cinnamon sticks up the stairs to Flat 3 of the Waterloo Brewing Company. He closed, then locked the door behind him. He set to work, driven by a single, persistent thought nagging at his brain. All the intellectual energy and inventive effort he'd seen so far seemed to be aimed at overcoming, or overriding the Fearance. The answer had to lie somewhere else. If the Fearance was a natural phenomenon – and there was nothing to say it wasn't – then surely the challenge was to understand exactly what it was and why it was there. Somehow he had to talk to Tycho. It was going to be a long night …

45

The sun was high in the sky by the time he emerged hollow-eyed from his room. It had taken him the best part of eighteen hours to finish, but now it was done. He cradled the shining casing of the fishing lure in the palm of his hand, admiring his handiwork, before slipping it into his pocket. He was pleased with the outcome of the night's labour. But what to call it? He hadn't even thought of a name. Something simple. Something from nature. The name of a bird, a fish, a plant, maybe, designed to be attached to the human body. How about ... The Leech? That would do for now. The world would have to wait for a better name. The important thing was, would it work? Only one way to find out. The question was, where to try out his new invention? Best to steer clear of the stockyards, he reasoned. And definitely a good idea to give the slaughterhouse a wide berth. Then, bang-slap before his eyes, he saw the perfect guinea-pig, stood loosely tethered to the rail outside the bank. Not a real guinea-pig, but Shaft. No sign of Marshall Amps. He must be inside.

Rib sauntered along the boardwalk, reached into his pocket to fish out the leech, clamped it to his left earlobe and sidled casually up to the big horse. He whinnied good morning softly in his ear.

The giant shire-horse reared up in surprise. 'If you try that one more time, I'll re-arrange your face so even your mother won't recognise you!' he said, pawing the ground with a plate-sized hoof.

The man-mountain that was Booker T Amps rushed out of the bank. 'Mumble hum fooling mumble hum my horse mumble hum little mother mumble!' came the distorted oath.

In panic response, the boy neighed, scooting off round the corner as fast as his trembling legs could carry him. Once he'd put a safe distance between him and the Sheriff, he stopped to catch his breath. Did that really happen? Did Shaft really understand what he said? Of course he did! He offered to re-arrange his face for him. It really did work! It bloody worked! He could talk to the animals. And they could certainly talk back. True, some adjustment was needed if he wanted to receive animals and humans at the same time, but for a trial run, amazing, just amazing!

A bee alighted on the blue buddleia blossom just above his head. As it collected nectar on the hair of its legs, it buzzed out a report:

'Light, south-westerly breeze on Main Street, veering to cool, easterly by mid-afternoon. Warning of heavy midge traffic over Friedlander farm. Advise to seek alternative routes. Pollen count – thirteen million, two hundred and two thousand, four hundred and seventy three. Over and out.'

'Bzz, bzz, buzzy zerp, zib, zub, zoo?' interrupted Rib, asking the worker when he thought his queen would be leaving the hive. The bee promptly dive-bombed and stung him on the nose before flying off angrily.

Rib's initial research was already pointing towards the Natural World's total hatred of Man. Probably with good reason, he thought. But maybe he should try a more domesticated animal next. Perhaps a pet. He knew just where to look.

And sure enough, Invincible Harry was in his cage

on the kitchen floor of the Big Licker. One day at the Market Hall, Larix had made the mistake of sharpening a pencil in front of Harry, who immediately put two and two together and came up with the picture of an impaled rodent rotating on a mini-spit. Ever since then, Amy had taken over hamster care duties while Larix roasted hogs.

'Eeek peep, bpp, pip, beep?' enquired Rib

'Oh, not so bad, mate. Just doing a few sets in the old wheel. Up to 475 so far. Shouldn't do the old cardio-vascular any harm eh?'

'Er,no,' Rib agreed. 'Must keep you pretty fit. So, er, do you prefer the wheel to the plastic ball?'

'Plastic ball? Don't get me started on that! Trapped in that bloody thing for hours on end. Only yesterday, bumped into a cat sleeping under the bed. Scared the living daylights out of both of us, it did. Only went and emptied me bladder, didn't I? Spent the rest of the afternoon body-surfing on a wave of piss!'

Trying his best not to laugh, Rib told Harry he should be proud of the fact that he was probably the world's first surfing hamster. Maybe he should audition for a part in Hawaii-Five-O?

'Proud be buggered! More like Ha-wee-wee-Five-O, if you ask me!' came the immediate retort. This time Rib laughed out loud. Harry certainly shared his owner's sense of humour. Or was it the other way round?

Late that night, a lone dog howled down on Main Street. 'Anyone out there interested in sniffing my bum?'

Rib removed the leech from his earlobe, turned over in bed and dreamed a sticky dream of being kicked around a stable floor in a huge plastic ball half-filled with honey.

46

As soon as he opened his eyes the next morning, he wanted to tell the whole world. Shout it from the rooftops.

The Leech ... he kept saying to himself, over and over again. Surely one of the greatest inventions ever, standing alongside the wheel, electricity and the Corgi Trouser Press. He'd be famous overnight.

The chill waters of the Little Ouse brought him to his senses. As he dried himself, he asked the million-dollar question. What was he going to do with the leech? Go on tour with Invincible Harry in some sort of freak-show? No, of course not. Become an animal-rights campaigner, a champion against abuse and cruelty? The sort of work his Mum devoted her life to? Maybe. But here on Tycho, where there wasn't the wholesale exploitation of animals like there had been on Earth, who'd bother to listen? And anyway, he'd have to give up eating meat. Hold on now, he thought, there are limits.

And how would Stonyville react to the news? He could just picture Hetty Huxtable's exclusive headline scoop. Knowing the Strumpet, instead of reading '*Local boy makes a major scientific breakthrough,*' it would probably say something like:

STONYVILLE'S VERY OWN DOCTOR DOOLITTLE

Local boy Rib Meskitoe has invented a gadget which lets us humans talk to our critters and vice versa. In the future we'll be able to understand why dogs sniff each other's arses, why they wear that tongue-lolling crazed expression when they drag their backsides across the floor, and why they always wait until everybody's sat at the dinner table before they lick their balls. Let's hear a big cheer for Stonyville's very own Doctor Dolittle!'

Wasn't the whole idea behind this invention to explain what the Fearance was and how it worked? Yes, but at the moment, he couldn't begin to figure out exactly how the leech would help him do that. He needed more time to think.

Maybe he should ask Sunset? Or Larix? No, he decided, until he knew exactly what he was going to use the leech for, something told him his secret was better kept to himself. Unless ...

Unless he could seek the advice of the greatest scientist on the Planet. Of course! Professor Buzzard! He'd know what to do. Rib strode down Main Street with a spring in his step. He couldn't wait until Thursday.

47

The atmosphere in the NAAFI cafeteria was somehow different. At first, Rib couldn't put his finger on it. A hubbub of conversation filled the air, just like any normal caff. But the NAAFI was no normal caff. Then it dawned on him. This was the RIC, where people didn't talk.

'Are you sure they'll let you go back to Hut 10?' asked Larix, mouth full of doughnut.

'No harm in trying,' said Rib, trying hard to conceal his anxiety. What would he do if he couldn't get to Buzzard?

A handbell rang to signal the first session. The morning diners returned their trays and spilled out onto the Mansion lawn before heading off to their huts, many still deep in animated conversation.

'Good luck,' said Larix with a wave. 'See you at break.'

'By the lake, yeah? I've brought some bread for the swans.'

'OK. See yah.'

Rib watched Larix merge into the crowd filing its way between the low white buildings. He looked up at the cloudless sky before setting off towards Hut 10. Looked like it was going to be a nice day.

It wasn't.

As he turned the corner, the sight of the rope and

cordon running round Hut 10 and the two guards in the doorway stopped him in his tracks.

'Beat it!' said the bigger of the two before Rib had chance to open his mouth. About to back off, he was then nearly knocked off his feet by the form of Larix flying round the corner.

'What's up?' he asked the breathless, wide-eyed figure.

'It's ... it's ...' Larix gasped, trying to catch his breath. 'It's Buzz ... '

'What? What about him?'

The boy with one arm burst into tears. 'He's dead!'

* * *

The rumour mill went into overdrive. Some said it was an accident. Some said it was murder. Some said it was suicide. But the fact of the matter was that no-one really ever knew why or how Tycho's greatest scientist died. They just found him that morning sitting stiff as a board on the bench overlooking the lake. Some said the man who was responsible for Watershed simply couldn't live with himself any longer. But no-one ever really knew ...

48

'Take a seat, Meskitoe,' motioned Major "Bonkers" Bonkerstone, pouring himself a large scotch into a cut-glass tumbler. 'Care for a quick bracer?'

'Er, no thank you, Major,' said Rib. It was eight thirty in the morning and he was still wondering why he had been summoned to the library – he'd turned up for work at eight with Larix and had been promptly escorted to the Mansion by one of the guards he'd seen at the door of Hut 10 the previous week.

For a few seconds an awkward silence reigned, finally broken by the chunk of ice cubes as Bonkers took a sip of his whisky. 'Dashed rum do,' he said.

'Sorry?'

'Ghastly affair, absolutely ghastly ...' The Major took another sip, this time a longer one. 'Pretty frightful, the whole business.'

There's only one thing he can be talking about, thought Rib, but what did it have to do with him?

Bonkerstone emptied his glass, walked over to the drinks table and poured another. 'Sun's not quite over the yard-arm yet, but probably is in Singapore, eh Meskitoe?' he chuckled.

'Er, yes.'

'Absolutely certain I can't tempt you to a quick sherbert?'

'No thanks, Major.' Sherbert?

The man they called Bonkers sat down on the red leather Chesterfield. 'Dashed fine fellow, he was.'

Rib looked down at his feet, wondering where all this was leading.

'Awfully decent chappie, awfully decent.' The Major took a deep pull on the malt and cleared his throat before carefully placing the glass on the coffee table between them.

'Now, Meskitoe, you're probably wondering why I've asked you here this morning.'

'Well, yes, Major.'

'You may have heard a ... rumour that Professor Buzzard is no longer with us.'

'Well, erm, yes, I have.'

Bonkers cast a furtive glance around the Library. 'Strictly hush-hush, you understand.'

'Of course, Major.' Even though everyone at the RIC was talking about it.

'Well,' Bonkerstone coughed, 'the old egg certainly left his affairs and papers in good order. And it appears that he thought very highly of you.'

'Me? Really?'

'Indeed he did. You must have made an impression on him, Meskitoe.'

'Me?'

'Indeed.' He leaned forward. 'You may have heard that the Professor was due to take part in a scientific expedition?'

Rib shook his head.

'Yes, the Professor was to join fellow scientists – geologists, naturalists, oceanographers and what-not – on a three-month research tour of the Orkney, Shetland and Faroe Isles and, of course, the poor blighter will now sadly ... not be making the trip.'

Rib shook his head again.

'But it is – or rather was – his express wish, clearly

stated in a letter left in his lodgings, that you, Meskitoe, take his place.'

'Me?'

'Yes, Meskitoe, you. You will depart the day after tomorrow by stagecoach to Liverpool, where you will join the rest of the party.'

'Erm, but ... '

'Yes, Meskitoe?'

'Can I ... think about it?'

'Think about it?'

'Er, yes. This has come as a bit of a shock and I'd just like to, erm, maybe think it over.'

'Think it over, man? I'm only glad poor Buzzard isn't here listening to this kind of talk!'

'No, sorry, I mean it's a great honour to be asked, but – '

'Topping! That's settled then. The day after tomorrow. Eight o'clock sharp. Bring some warm clothes. Off you pop now.'

Rib stood up in a daze, shook the Major's outstretched hand and walked to the door. 'Bye, Major.'

'Toodaloo,' came the reply from the drinks table.

49

'But I like it here, Sunset! It's the first real job I've ever had and ... I love it. You've put your trust in me and it doesn't feel right, just walking out on you'

'Well, all I'm saying is– '

'I really like it here. Our little morning routine. Me going off for a swim, bringing back muffins and pastries from Bettina's Buns ... '

'And croissants.'

'Yes, and croissants. And what about Larix? He's a good mate and I feel as if I'd be leaving him in the lurch.'

'He'll be fine.'

'And you said yourself, you'd planned to bring in a few new lines this autumn. You're going to need all the help you can get.'

Sunset spread a thin layer of plum jam onto a slice of wholemeal toast and bit into it.

'And, and ... I love it here. It feels ... ' Rib looked away '... like home.'

'Listen,' said Sunset, wiping his mouth on his sleeve before topping up the two mugs of coffee. 'I can understand how you feel, but all the things you've just talked about – the early morning dip, Bettina's Buns, The Waterloo, Larix, me – we'll be waiting for you when you get back.'

'You mean I could have my job back?'

'Of course.'

Rib stood up, left the table and walked over to the window.

'Now I don't want you going all emotional on me, especially over breakfast, or I might just change my mind.' He cleared his throat. 'How long did you say this expedition was going to last?'

'Three months.'

'No time at all. You'll be back before you know it. And chances like this don't grow on trees, my son. You've got to consider that. If you turned the offer down, would you live to regret it?'

Rib knew Sunset was right. And what he hadn't told him was that he would be stepping into the shoes of Professor Clayton E. Buzzard. What's more, one of the last things the great man had done was to write his name, Rib Meskitoe, on a piece of paper. How could he possibly refuse the last wish of a dying man. How could he possibly live with that? He knew what he had to do. But it was with a heavy heart that he said his goodbyes and packed his things that night.

50

The stagecoach trip did little to allay his sense of unease about the whole undertaking. From the very outset, driving rain lashed down from dark storm clouds and the bad weather stayed with them for the rest of the journey. His fellow passengers – a geologist named Green, a physicist named Evans and a biologist named McNaught – were uncommunicative in the extreme, hardly a word exchanged between them throughout the three days on the road. And whilst they doubtless shared a common interest in matters scientific, each remained locked in his own ivory tower. On the rare occasion they spoke, it was in whispers, and never directly to Rib. The three regarded him with ill-disguised disdain. He would have gladly traded their company for that of the old spinster, Miss Ginsoak. He wondered where she was now, and what she was doing. He also wondered what the hell he was doing. He should have been excited, but he wasn't. Something deep inside told him that he had made a terrible mistake. Something told him that he was moving from one unreality to another. He had learned to live with, indeed enjoy, the unreality of Stonyville. But the new unreality was unknown. And it scared him.

Cold rain continued to fall from the heavy skies as they finally reached Liverpool. Down at the docks, the tired team of horses slithered to an unsteady halt on the cobbled quayside. McNaught had difficulty in forcing the stagecoach door open, so fierce was the wind whipping in from the sea in sharp squalls.

The harbourside was a hive of feverish activity, an army of mercenary souls consumed in their own urgency to the exclusion of all around. It was no place to stand and stare.

'Keep hold of your coffer, or it will go walkabout,' said Evans, his first words to Rib.

The dark shape of a three-masted, single-funnelled ship loomed above them, straining at the four hawsers which groaned and creaked in their struggle to keep the ship captive. Its prow rose and fell to the rhythm of the swell. On the tar-soaked timber was painted a name in gold letters.

Lusitanic.

51

She was still angry with herself for what had happened. Unplanned, unprofessional ... unexpected. She needed to distance herself, both physically and emotionally, from the whole episode. The scars on her legs and the wheals on her arms told their own tale of three months' harsh existence in the unforgiving rainforest. Living the life of a wild animal. A constant cycle of foraging, hunting, hiding, fleeing. Mating was the only basic instinct absent.

Ever on the move, ever in danger. Always careful to stick to the narrow trails trodden by deer, boar, wildcats. The last thing she wanted was a chance encounter with a Slakterghast squad – the band of low-life cannibals whose main leisure pursuit was to hunt, torture, rape and consume any man, woman or child unfortunate enough to cross their path. Whilst she would happily dedicate the rest of her days to eradicating them from the face of the earth, one by one, it would have to wait. Now was not the time.

To begin with, all Jonathan had asked her to do was to keep tabs on the boy, just as she'd done with the other new arrivals to Middlemedes. Check them out, test their compatibility, report back. Nothing more, nothing less. Easy work, for which he paid handsomely. Over the odds, in fact. Then out of the blue, a new instruction had come. The boy was planning to escape.

She was to go with him. To the MK Citidome. She had asked why, only to be told that it was not her place to know. Clearly someone was pulling Jonathan's strings. Jonathan was a weak man, for which she pitied him. But he was, for the moment, her paymaster, and the arrangement suited her well.

All that mattered to Rika Latukartta was her independence, for her to be in absolute control of her thoughts and actions. That way, you couldn't get hurt. Which was why she was now so angry with herself. It had never been in the script to actually like the kid. Though she tried her utmost to put him out of her mind, part of her couldn't help wondering what had happened to the boy named Rib Meskitoe, the boy she'd left in a cold underpass beneath the Citidome. She was troubled, deeply troubled, by her own actions. It was time to return to Middlemedes …

52

Once on board, they were shown to their quarters down in the vessel's deepest bowels by an unsmiling sailor, who left them with a terse instruction to meet in the mess room up on second deck in fifteen minutes.

'Gentlemen, I bid you welcome on board the Lusitanic. I am Captain Zoothorn and it is my privilege to be providing safe and comfortable passage for your expedition.'

Comfortable? thought Rib. From what he'd seen of the cramped bunkbeds down below, comfortable was not the first word that sprang to mind.

Captain Zoothorn had a lean, chiselled look about him. Dressed smartly in navy jacket, dark twill trousers, bright blue shirt and, of course, a peaked cap, he surveyed with an air of detached superiority the team of scientists huddled at the far end of the mess room. The low-ceilinged saloon was dominated by a large wooden table. Presumably, this was where they would all be eating. Sturdy timber shelves ran the length of each wall, bearing boxes, tins and crates of supplies. Biscuits, corned beef, dried fruit, cocoa, more biscuits.

Captain Zoothorn proceeded to introduce his second in command, a naval clone called Rollo, who stepped forward and nodded without expression. Zoothorn then reeled off the names of the crew. All Scandinavian, all wearing white roll-neck sweaters, all bearded and all smoking pipes. After the third Svensson was announced, Rib lost interest, his attention drawn to a discarded packet under the table. MacBaren's Dark Twist, read the label. A tell-tale pall of aromatic tobacco smoke hung from the ceiling. ' ... and last, but not least, the ship's cook, Ibrahimovic,' concluded the roll-call.

'Our first port of call will be Lerwick, on the Shetland Islands. There you will disembark. From there, the Lusitanic shall sail on to more ... ' he hesitated for a moment ' ... northerly climes.' Sensing a few questioning looks on the faces of his passengers, he swiftly brought the briefest of briefings to a close. 'You are to return to your quarters, gentlemen, where you shall remain until instructed to do otherwise. We set sail in fifteen minutes. The barometer is falling. '

53

The secret entrance to the Middlemedes colony was no secret any more. The mob had broken in not by sneaking down the back alley and climbing quietly through the bathroom window. In true Slakterghast style, they'd kicked the front door off its hinges – trees parted, soil trampled to a sea of mud where the brigand army had marched in.

Rika remained in hiding for the best part of twenty-four hours, keeping the scene under keen surveillance for any sign of life. Not a leaf stirred. When she finally considered it safe enough to venture forward, she did so with heavy heart. She knew what she would find.

She found the Village Square violated beyond recognition: its huge geranium-filled terracotta urns overturned and smashed into a thousand shards; the whitewashed walls of Chez Claude, where she had once worked, smeared with blood; the Mede Mart looted and ransacked, not a single item of food left on its now buckled shelves. Moving through to the lake, she found Friggya's Fondue House burnt to the ground, wisps of smoke still rising from the charred timbers. The surface of the lake was littered with half-sunken red and yellow canoes and, closer to shore, she saw a destroyed swans' nest. It was as if an evil whirlwind from the darkest depths of hell had passed through, destroying everything in its path. Without trace of mercy.

Now, in the afterstorm, it was as silent as the grave. No birdsong, no squirrel chatter, no duck quacks. And no Medemates. Those who hadn't escaped to the forest would now be bound and trussed, captives with little life expectancy. With growing confidence that the coast was clear, she crept along the edge of the path beside the driving range, bore right at the Rural Retreat, then entered Conifer Quarter, where the green-numbered lodges stood in surreal stillness, like the ghostly backlot of a movie set.

Once through this silent suburb, she slowed, taking a narrow gravel path which wound its way into thickening forest. She held her breath, listening for the tell-tale snap of a twig, the sudden scurry of a small mammal in flight, her every sense screaming that this was classic ambush country. Edging forward soundlessly, she drew her hunting knife.

Round the next corner, the bird hide came into view and, beyond, a clearing in the wood, populated by tables and feeders, empty of life. Solemn bird-seed tombstones. No finches, tits, tree-creepers. Not even a single, scavenging squirrel. An eerie silence enveloped the scene, as if the whole wood were holding its breath.

The door of the hut was ajar. Was it a trap? An open invitation to enter? There was only one way to find out. She picked up a pine cone and lobbed it through the dark doorway.

'Come out, you fuckers, you're surrounded!' she shouted. 'The next one's a grenade!' Nothing. The second pine cone flew through the narrow slit, bouncing off the wooden walls before coming to rest. Nothing. Without taking her eyes off the hide, she felt for the lumpy object in the side pocket of her back pack. She was hoping she wouldn't have to use it. Her last grenade …

54

With all the innocence of a lifelong landlubber, Rib had been oblivious to the Captain's reference to a falling barometer. He lay back in his bunk, hands clasped behind his head, and closed his eyes, the gentle, rocking motion of the ship starting to soothe away his doubts. True, the stagecoach journey had been uncomfortable, but he could now look forward to a nice cruise for a few days where he could relax, unwind. A good night's sleep, a brisk stroll around the deck in the morning to work up an appetite, followed by a Full English breakfast, Sunset-style. Yeah, things were looking up. He remained blissfully unaware that a falling barometer can mean only one thing.

A rising sea.

A common definition of seasickness is "a form of motion sickness characterised by a feeling of nausea experienced after spending time on a craft on water." Whilst the condition certainly originates from the rocking motion of said craft, the real cause is in the brain, which receives conflicting signals: the eyes see a world that isn't moving, but the equilibrium sensors in the ears tell you loud and clear that it is. The mind, unable to decide, moves into default mode and sends the whole body an evacuation alarm. The first to respond is usually the digestive system.

'Blurrk!' said Rib. Followed by a 'BluuurK!'

On a ship, the toilet is called "the head". Which was really quite fitting, because he spent the next half hour with his head down the toilet bowl. From the moment the Lusitanic left the relatively sheltered waters of the Mersey for the heaving, grey-green seas of Liverpool Bay, he knew something was wrong. Terribly wrong. This was ten times worse – no, a thousand times worse – than the near-death flight on Shuttle 495. He needed to get off the ship. He had to get off the ship. But, of course, he couldn't. He was hostage to the head.

The ship began to roll and pitch, battered by a barrage of waves from every direction. The wind roared and whined a hellish lament in the rigging. Angry squalls of rain rattled against the hull, its timbers creaking and groaning under the onslaught. Worse was to come.

When they entered the Irish Sea, a terrible storm blew up from the north, swiftly rising to gale, then hurricane force. It was a storm of nightmares, hurling all its fury at the ill-matched ship, more suited to sedate coastal passage than open sea exposure, pounding its tortured hull mercilessly. Relentlessly.

Somewhere in the sponge of nausea that used to serve as a brain, he registered cries of panic from above, from the crew-hands on deck frantically pumping and bailing to keep the craft afloat. He was ill again, until there was no more. Then he was ill again.

There are two distinct stages of sea sickness.

Stage 1:   You feel so bad, you think you're going to die.
Stage 2:   You realise, to your horror, that you're not going to die.

Rib was now creating his own version of Stage 3.

The door had been locked for his own safety by one of the crew, the natural reaction for anyone in his condition being to find fresh air. Up on deck, he would have been swept overboard in a moment. Not that he cared one bit whether he was lying on the floor of the head or lying on the bottom of the ocean, so hopelessly, helplessly awful he felt. Curled up and shivering on the stained tiles of the floor, he drifted in and out of consciousness, woken only by the raging of the storm above, half-fearing, half-hoping that the hungry sea would at any second smash down the door and devour him. He finally fell into a deep, dreamless coma as black as pitch, as cold as ice.

Distant voices roused him. Was it his imagination, or had the ship stopped moving? To his surprise, he found he could stand up without being hurled into the bulkhead. He tried the door. It was still locked. Someone had placed a plate of dry toast and a beaker of water on the floor inside the door. He took a bite of the burnt crust, swallowed, then swayed back to yawn into the porcelain again.

The thump of the ship's engines coming to life reverberated against his knees. Had they reached land, and were now leaving? Shouldn't he have got off? Why hadn't anyone come for him? There came no reply from Shanks & Co. Too weak to stand, he remained kneeling, holding onto the bowl as the ship started to wallow from side to side. Rib groaned while the heaving seas welcomed the ship back into their fold. If only, if only he could die ...

55

No ambush awaited in the hide. A quick scan of the hut's interior told her that the coast was clear. With a trained eye, she examined the floorboards in the far right hand corner, looking for any sign of the concealed trapdoor being disturbed. She saw none. The likelihood of a Slakterghast being so meticulous was small. Nonetheless, she took the grenade from its holster and felt for the blast adjust, turning it to the 3-second notch. After a deep breath, she tapped out the code on the hollow floor with her heel.

Seven ... Two ... Seven again.

Silence.

Then, unmistakeably, the slightest of creaks. Rika crouched, grenade at the ready. The trapdoor slowly opened, just wide enough to reveal from the darkness a pair of eyes, wide with fear.

'Suki,' breathed Rika, a flood of relief coursing through her body.

'Rika! Is that you?'

'Yes. Now open the hatch and let me in.'

She'd discovered the bunker some three years before. She remembered how amazed she'd been at its sheer size – it stretched to almost twice the area of the actual hide. It had its own power supply, living area, storage space and sleeping quarters. She'd often wondered why and when it had been built. Clearly not used for a long time, she could only conclude that it came from the last war, over a century before. Over the course of her time at Middlemedes, she'd gradually stocked up with supplies of food and drink smuggled from the restaurants where she'd worked. It became her sanctuary, a bolt-hole for when she needed to be on her own.

Only one other person knew of its existence, Suki Kurosawa, her Japanese co-worker at Ummagumma's, whose diminutive figure now sat cross-legged in front of her, with a broad smile on her lips. She was the closest Rika had to a friend.

'Thank God you came back,' said Suki.

'I said I would. Tell me what happened.'

'They hit us in the middle of the night. All hell broke loose. It was ... it was awful. They took Jonathan.'

'When did this happen?'

'Only last week. They left three days ago.'

'Then we must leave. We are not safe here.'

'But – '

'I assume they took prisoners?'

Suki nodded.

'They will have taken them back to their camp. And then they'll return. They may even decide to make Middlemedes their base. One thing's for sure – they'll be back.' She looked Suki in the eye. 'Are you sure you didn't tell anybody else about this place?'

Suki averted her gaze.

'Suki?'

'Well ... '

A figure slipped from the bunker's shadows to stand beside Suki.

'Shit! Where the hell did she come from? I told you not to tell anyone!'

'Please don't be angry, Rika. I couldn't just leave her. They would have killed her.'

But Rika was angry. Very angry. She'd placed her trust in Suki. The small Japanese girl commanded her respect. She could handle herself. With her own eyes, Rika had seen her take down men more than twice her size at the Taekwondo Club. She was the one person you'd want at your side if the going got tough.

But this other girl, no way. Rika recognised her as the kid who worked in the library. Whilst Suki could put in an hour's session in the weights room without breaking sweat, the nearest this girl came to physical exercise was picking up a book from a trolley and placing it on a shelf. She would be a burden, a total liability.

This was where the quiet girl with the straight brown hair should have fallen to her knees, tears streaming down her cheeks, begging Rika to take her with them. She didn't. She just stood there, staring with unblinking eyes.

'She has … qualities,' said Suki.

'What qualities?' scoffed Rika. 'So, she can catalogue children's fiction. How useful is that going to be up there?'

'No, it's difficult to explain. She kind of appears and disappears without you noticing.'

Rika looked for the girl. She'd vanished. Rika glanced over her left shoulder. A voice whispered from the darkness into her right ear. 'I understand if you do not wish to take me, but I promise to do my best.'

'Shit!' swore Rika as she whipped round. 'Don't creep up on me like that!'

'See what I mean?' said Suki. 'Stealth, that's what she does.'

'Creepy, I call call it. Now go and sit over there where I can see you. And don't move!' The girl obeyed without a word.

'So will you take the two of us?' asked Suki.

'I'll sleep on it. In the meantime, I need a drink. You haven't touched my stash, have you? If I find out you've been sipping my Kossie ... '

'No, of course not.'

Suddenly the girl from the library was there with two iced glasses of Koskenkorva.

'How the hell does she do that?'

Suki smiled. 'I told you she had qualities.'

'Mmm, I'm not sure. As I said, I'll sleep on it. Cheers!'

After a meal of tinned ham, tinned potatoes and tinned marrowfat peas, washed down with copious quantities of vodka, the two found themselves alone again.

'Does she have a name?

'Bethany Heron.'

Rika paused. 'I shall call her The Heron.'

'Thanks,' said Suki, giving her arm a squeeze.

'Don't thank me. I haven't said I'm taking her yet. And don't push your luck. I'm still pissed off with you for bringing her here.'

Suki sensed she should change the subject. 'So what's the plan?'

'We leave first thing in the morning.'

'Then what?'

Rika pushed the last three peas around the plate with her knife. 'We stay clear of trouble. We survive. It's all we can do ...'

56

What seemed like a lifetime later, the sick-making swell disappeared. The storm had blown itself out, leaving the sea eerily calm, as smooth as glass. A cool morning mist shrouded the ship, which steamed slowly through the still waters, sails lowered. After eating two slices of dry toast and drinking three mugs of water at the insistence of the ponytailed Ibrahimovic, Rib ventured up on deck to join the crew. Of his fellow scientists there was no sign. They must have gone ashore without him, the bastards.

'Good morning, Master Meskitoe. Nice of you to grace us with your presence,' came the sarcastic greeting from Captain Zoothorn. 'We could have used an extra pair of hands yesterday.'

'I'm sorry, I – ' Rib was interrupted by a shout from a Svensson.

'Captain! Something ahead!'

To a man, the crew ran to the bow. At some two hundred metres distance, a freakish bank of thick fog spread out before them. It looked strange, for all the world like a solid wall, perfectly uniform in density and height, rising vertically from the surface of the sea to a height of about ten metres.

'We need someone up in the crow's nest. Time to make yourself useful, Meskitoe.'

Rib needed no second bidding, pleased to be doing

something positive after spending the best part of three days on the floor of the head. Endless hours on the Middlemedes climbing wall enabled him to shin up the rigging without too much difficulty and he was soon installed in the crow's nest.

'What do you see?' shouted Zoothorn. 'Can you see over the fog?'

'I can see land on the other side. I'm not sure, but it looks like an island.'

'It is an island,' said Zoothorn quietly to himself.

'There are mountains, massive mountains, all covered in snow. There's a narrow coastal plain, but I can't see buildings or any sign of life.'

This time, the Captain said nothing.

'I can see clear water on the other side. It's amazing! The fog forms a belt which seems to wrap around the whole island, stretching as far as I can see in both directions.'

'Can you see how thick the bank is?'

'Yes, it can't be any more than fifty metres, maybe even less. There's an open stretch of water beyond and then there seems to be a river mouth of some sort.'

'Excellent,' said Zoothorn and barked an instruction up to Jensen on the bridge. 'Proceed ahead at five knots.'

As soon as they entered the dense fog, the crew of the Lusitanic knew that something was wrong. Seriously wrong. An acrid, sulphurous stench attacked the back of their throats, making them cough, then retch. Strands of sticky fibre clung to their faces like a candyfloss web. High above the deck, all Rib could hear were the muffled cries of the crew hands and officers as they stumbled about blindly. All the while, the crow's nest sailed serenely along the surface of the white cloud. The scene was totally surreal. Then a splash.

'Man overboard!' came the instinctive call to action. But there was nothing anyone could do. They were helpless. Zoothorn had a decision to take. Should they turn back or press on? 'How far to the other side?' he shouted.

'We're almost through,' Rib shouted back. 'But Cap'n, there's something else I think you should know.'

'What?'

'We've got company. Two boats. Coming towards us.'

'How many men?'

'Not many. About five, six in each.'

Zoothorn barked a series of orders to his men. Rib couldn't make out all the muffled commands, but he was sure he heard the word "guns". Guns? He thought this was a scientific expedition. And anyway, guns didn't work on Tycho. Rib had heard correctly. Captain Zoothorn instructed Sorensen to break open the weapons magazine as soon as the ship emerged from the fog.

Meanwhile, Rib's eyes were drawn to the two rowboats, approaching fast. Glints of sunlight reflected from the headgear the rowers were wearing. Above the rhythmic thump of the Lusitanic's engines came another noise. It came from one of the boats, a fearsome bellowing, like a bull about to charge. The hairs on Rib's forearms stood on end. He saw a huge man standing upright in the stern, roaring and beating his chest. Two other men struggled to hold him still, his violent behaviour threatening to capsize the craft. At that moment, the Lusitanic sliced its way through the fog bank and steamed into open water.

What Rib then witnessed from on high would remain with him for the rest of his life. He leaned out of the crow's nest to report what he'd seen in the approaching boats. But no word left his lips. All the men on deck were covered in a white, sparkly, coating. They stood frozen, staring at each other in disbelief.

Zoothorn then sprang forward to get sight of the unexpected company. 'Prepare to engage! Take your weapons!' he shouted. The crew jumped to action. Sorenson broke open a chest and handed out rifles and ammunition. Svensson rapidly assembled a large machine gun, fitted it onto a tripod and fed in a magazine of bullets. Zoothorn instructed the crew to take up position to repel boarders. 'When I give the order, fire at will,' he shouted. His hours of toil in the secret munitions bunker at the Mansion would now be put to the test. His jaw set in a grim smile, Captain Zoothorn was looking forward to demonstrating the benefits of scientific research to the natives.

Two bumps announced the arrival of the boats, one on either side. Instinctively, Rib ducked back into the crow's nest and peered down through the slatted woodwork. Grappling hooks bit into the ship's railings and a blood-curdling roar announced that the bellower was about to board.

The huge creature leapt onto the deck. To a man, the crew gasped and took one step back. He was wearing a helmet and, under a shaggy bearskin, chain mail. He carried a wooden shield, which he was smashing against his chest. In his other hand he brandished a double-headed axe. All the time, he rolled his eyes and howled like a demon. Sword-bearing warriors, some ten in number, swiftly climbed on deck and took up position behind the raging giant. There was a moment's pause as the two sides faced each other. Then the bellower bit into his shield. When he'd chewed three big chunks, he spat them out and hurled the shield overboard.

Then he charged ...

57

'Fire!' came the command from Zoothorn. The crew pulled their triggers. The triggers clicked, but there was no bang. Every single firearm jammed. Even the Gattling gun failed to gattle. The giant attacked in a ferocious frenzy. His axe connected first with Svensson, taking his head clean off in one so that it rolled across the deck like a football. He then rushed forward to hack, chop, cut into the rest of the crew like a threshing machine. Jensen was taken off at the knees. Persson tried to jump overboard, but had his torso split in two by a mighty blow of the axe. Rib pressed his hands over his ears to try to drown out the terrible sounds of the slaughter below.

The Captain was the last to fall. The giant struck him so hard that the axe-head went in right up to the hilt, splitting Zoothorn's head down the middle. In a rage, the berserk tugged back on the axe with such force that he swung the Captain up into the air and over the side. There was not a single member of the crew left standing. All had been massacred by one man.

Meanwhile, the rest of the invading party moved along the deck, casually cutting ring fingers from the still-twitching corpses as if picking strawberries from a field. They laughed and joked in an unrecognisable language. Rib threw up and tried to catch his vomit in his jacket. At that very moment, a tremendous shudder shook the ship, knocking the invaders off their feet. Rib only just managed to stop himself being hurled from his hiding place by grasping hold of the rough slats. The Lusitanic had hit a jagged reef. She was sinking fast. The warriors slid down the deck, already listing dangerously at a forty-five degree angle. Two of them started fighting with each other as they tried to scramble over the side. Another two were carrying the giant, who now seemed lifeless and spent. First the deck, then the bridge-house disappeared under water as the gash in the ship's hull surrendered to the sea. The raiding party managed to make it back into their boats and were now circling at a distance, watching the Lusitanic in her death throes. Rib held on tight as one last juddering jolt sent the ship sliding down towards the seabed.

Between the devil and the deep blue sea. If he stayed where he was, he would probably be sucked down with the ship and drown. If he showed himself, he would be at the mercy of the murderous bastards in the boat. He was at the point of choosing the deep blue sea, when the Lusitanic hit the bottom with an almighty shudder. The hull rocked and swayed before settling. All that could be seen of the ship was the top of the main mast and a small barrel-like structure which looked as if it were floating on the surface of the sea.

That was the good news. The bad news was that the boats were now starting to row back towards him. Something in the water distracted him, bumping into the crow's nest. It was an arm, blood still seeping from its severed stump. The tattoo of a mermaid sitting side-saddle on a motorbike told him it was Jensen's. He threw up again.

He was the monkey up the pole. The fish in the barrel. There was no escape. Whatever he tried now, they would kill him. Rib Meskitoe then did something he hadn't done since he was a little boy at nursery.

He closed his eyes and started to pray. He prayed for his Mum, his Dad, his Gran, the Deccaheads, Kaddie, Sunset, Larix and … Rika. He prayed that they would all remember him and … always love him. He opened his eyes and peeked through the slats. One of the boats was almost upon him. In another ten oarstrokes it would all be over. He screwed his eyes tightly shut.

58

'Skrimsl! Skrimsl!' went up the cry from the far boat. Pandemonium broke loose in both vessels. Men fell over each other, struggling to grab hold of the oars. They finally managed to point the boats towards shore and started rowing hard, still shouting their heads off.

Wondering what the word "Skrimsl" meant, Rib raised himself slowly up on his haunches to peer over the rim of the crow's nest. The Lusitanic had come to rest about half way between the fogbank and land. He could now see the island clearly for the first time. Massive snow-capped mountains loomed almost vertically over a narrow shoreline. The two boats were heading towards the mouth of a fjord, its waters spangling in the strong morning sun. A thin wisp of smoke curled skywards from some sort of settlement nestling in the hills at the foot of the black crags. That's where the murderous band must live, he thought. He shaded his eyes, directing his gaze seawards again. The fogbank stretched parallel to the shoreline as far as the eye could see.

Further along the coast, he spotted three small islands. Strange that he hadn't noticed them before. But hardly surprising, considering what he'd just been through. Something else now caught his eye. A body floating in the water. Then another. And another. The school of massacred corpses was slowly drifting back towards the fogbank, more sociable in death than life. The two boats had now reached the shore and the men were joined on the pebbly beach by a small crowd, who were pointing out at sea. Some seemed to be jumping up and down in a state of excitement. Rib ducked down. Were they pointing at him?

He needn't have worried. They were pointing at the islands. It took him a few seconds to find the three mounds of black rock again. Funny, he was sure they'd been further over to the right. The sun's rays reflected fiercely from the surface of the sea. He rubbed his eyes. That can't be right, he heard himself say. The islands were ... moving. A loose feeling in his bowels sounded alarm bells. He fixed his gaze on the three dark shapes. They were definitely moving. And rocky islets don't move ...

As the shapes drew closer, a long slender neck carrying a large head reared from the sea in front of the line of black mounds. He now knew what a Skrimsl was. He was staring at a huge creature with three humps, carving its way through the water. In his direction. The sea-monster must have been half the length of the Lusitanic. Rib's sphincter quivered as the distance between him and the Skrimsl shortened to fifty metres. He now wished he'd gone for the devil option. The monster dived and disappeared from view. Rib braced himself for the attack. He grasped the rough timber slats and hung on for grim life, splinters piercing his skin.

But instead, the sea-monster surfaced further away from the shipwreck, by the flotilla of corpses slowly circling on the strong eddies. Rib looked on, part in horror, part in relief, as the Skrimsl tore into the first body, biting off chunks of flesh with its razor teeth before raising its head to swallow. The bright glare of the sun spared him the full visual detail, but he heard the ripping of flesh and crunching of bone all too clearly.

It took no more than five minutes for the Skrimsl to consume Midshipman Persson. It then turned onto its back, exposing a huge, pale belly to the sun, and lay motionless on the surface, as if to digest its hastily-gulped breakfast. The monster stayed this way for some half an hour, before going back to the buffet for second helpings. Leg of Norwegian, breast of Dane, buttock of Swede. A true smorgasbord.

A single cloud skudded across the sun, casting a shadowpause over the scene of carnage. The Skrimsl was smooth-skinned, like a seal, apart from a row of horny scales on its forehead. In proportion to its slender neck, the head was large, accommodating a gaping maw chock full of needle-sharp teeth. Then, for the first time, Rib caught a glimpse of the Skrimsl's eyes and, in an instant, the marrow in his bones turned to sorbet. A bright orange pupil pierced through the milky green film which covered each dinner-plate eye. The monster stopped eating for a second to stare at the strange object standing on the water. Rib shrank down into the crow's nest and held his breath. The cloud moved out to sea and the Skrimsl moved on to the next course.

By the time the sea-monster had munched its way through the whole of the Lusitanic's crew, the sun was going down behind the white wall of fog. The Skrimsl slowly moved away until it receded to three black spots in the darkening distance. There was no dusk. Night fell almost immediately.

Rib carefully rose to his feet to stretch his aching limbs, kneading and massaging his wire-taut hamstrings and cramped calves. An involuntary shiver took his body. Suddenly, it had become cold. Very cold. The temperature must have dropped twenty degrees in as many minutes. He huddled back down into the well of the crow's nest to take stock of his predicament. After a few moments' deliberation, he reached the conclusion that he was in the shit. Well and truly.

He did a quick mental jog through his options:

Plan A   Stay in crow's nest all night.

Likely outcome = Freeze to death/nearly freeze to death only to be killed by murderous bastards returning in the morning.

Plan B   Swim to the shore.

Likely outcome = Freeze to death/drown/be eaten by a Skrimsl.

Less than likely outcome = Make it to the shore, only to be killed by murderous bastards.

Plan C   There was no plan C

He stood up again and looked towards the land. Although it was night-time, it wasn't really dark, the sky flooded in pale green light. Straggly wisps of cloud shone gold above the purple crags, each ridge etched against the sky in sharp relief. He thought he could see a spit of land jutting out into the sea just to the right of where he had seen smoke rising earlier. Three, four hundred metres at most, he reckoned. Not far at all. An almost perfect stillness reigned. Not a breath of air, the sea as smooth as a millpond. Plan B it is, he sighed, reaching into his breast pocket to remove the leech and clip it to his left earlobe. Having stripped off, Rib Meskitoe slipped into the jet black water under the clear light of an Arctic moon.

59

Not only was he a strong and confident swimmer, but his early morning dips in the Little Ouse had also accustomed him to swimming wild. The plan was to cover the distance to shore using a long, economical freestyle, the stroke with which he'd clocked up length after length on his Middlemedes training stints. It wasn't the swim that worried him. What scared him cackless was the likelihood of the Skrimsl being ultra-sensitive to moving objects in the water. So, he said to himself, strictly no splash.

'Aaaarghh!'

The sea temperature at the mouth of Borgarfjord that night was 3.7° Celsius. Every single cubic centimetre of oxygen was expelled from his lungs by the shockwave which numbed his whole body. All he could do was thrash wildly with his arms and legs, gasping desperately for air. Even when he managed to point himself in the general direction of the shore, he couldn't swim properly. As soon as he put his head under, the icy water drove slivers of pain into the tender top of his skull, forcing him to flip over onto his back. He kicked out with his legs – if he stopped moving, he was dead – no longer caring what splash he generated. He leaned his head back into the water. Gradually, he was acclimatising. Turning back onto his front, he tried to freestyle again.

This time it worked and he was soon setting a smooth stroke, reeling off twenty metres in a matter of seconds.

The unforgiving waters of Borgarfjord then bit back with a vengeance, seizing the young swimmer in a vice of ice. He screamed as cramp threatened to rip his calves in two. He turned onto his back again and tried to stretch out his arms and legs in a starfish. The agony was unbearable. He cried out and took in water. He went under once. He went under twice. With a lung-busting effort, he clawed his way up to the surface, knowing that this had to be the last time, either way. This time, he stayed there. Inch by inch, he dragged himself across the freezing stretch of water between the wreck and land. Luckily, the sea stayed calm. Luckily, the Skrimsl had eaten enough for one day.

But the cramp attacks kept coming, wave after wave, forcing him to revert to starfish mode. In a routine training session at the Subtropical Paradise, it would have taken him a leisurely four minutes to cover the four-hundred metres to shore. That night, it took him over forty minutes, the longest forty minutes in his life, to reach the pebbly beach. Not having the strength to stand, he lay there, shivering uncontrollably. He had to get up. He had to start moving. 'Come on!' a voice in his brain shouted. It sounded like Kaddie. 'Come on, you little turd, you've done the hard bit. Get up!'

He raised himself first onto hands and knees, then to his feet, then fell over. He tried again and staggered like a drunk up the beach, falling headlong every five or six steps. He had no control whatsoever over his body. His teeth chattered like castanets, his shoulders shook in frozen spasm.

He should be pleased, he tried to tell himself, that he had successfully carried out Plan B, against all the odds. But what next? Plan B stopped at reaching the shore. He had to find shelter, somewhere warm, otherwise he would freeze to death – his body hue was already turning a terminal blue. Maybe he should find the house with the rising smoke, knock on the door and risk the consequences. Anything to get warm. Anything …

Somehow, he managed to scramble up the shingle beach and found himself at the edge of a field which sloped up towards a wall running along the brow of a hill. In the lee of the wall, he thought he could make out a dark shape, a low shed of some sort, and he stumbled up the slope towards it. As he neared he saw wisps of steam seep out from the opening. He bent down to look inside. The acrid smell of urine hit the back of his throat. Sheep. About a dozen of them.

'Bloody hell! In the middle of the sodding night, too!' came a voice from the dark interior. Rib jumped out of his skin, forgetting he had clamped the leech to his earlobe.

'And we know what he wants, don't we? Look at him, he's got his bloody kit off already!'

'Winifrid, up you get. It's your turn to take one for the team.'

Ignoring Winifrid, Rib crept into the shed, squeezing in between two wads of steaming warm wool.

60

Bright sunlight streamed into the shed. Rib awoke to find himself lying on a mattress of straw and sheep shit. For a moment, he struggled to remember where he was. Then it all came flooding back. The fogbank, the attack, the shipwreck, the Skrimsl, the swim, the sheep.

He looked round. The sheep were gone. He had the turf-walled animal shed all to himself. Something nipped him on the arm to tell him that he was not alone. Lifting up the coarse blanket, he saw a dozen or so fleas on his skin. Wait a minute! A blanket? Where had that come from? The rough weave of the cloth rubbed like a bristly doormat as he rose on one elbow to take in his surroundings. He didn't remember finding a blanket. Someone must have covered him over in the night. Shouldn't complain, whoever it was probably saved him from dying of hypothermia. Shouldn't complain at all. Snug as a bug in a rug, in fact. Which reminded him of the fleas and he swept them off his body.

Warm as he was, he couldn't stay there all day. He had to find his bearings, and he didn't want to be found by those murderous bastards. More urgently, he needed food and drink. Wrapping the blanket tightly round him, he crawled out into the daylight glare, then froze in a half-crouch. He had company.

A small girl was sitting on a rock a few metres from the shed. Her face was fresh and tanned. Her light brown eyes stared at him intently, with no trace of expression. Her golden hair was swept behind her ears, save a single strand dangling over her cheek. She wore a thick woollen smock and brown leather boots. On the ground in front of her was placed a bowl.

The two held a silent stand-off for a full ten seconds before Rib moved slowly into a sitting position, not wishing to scare the girl. He was worried that she might run off to raise the alarm with the mad axe-men. She was little more than a child, about eight, nine years old, he reckoned. But she was dressed like a woman, and wore a silver bracelet on her right wrist.

The girl felt for something in her pocket and drew out what looked like a piece of grey cardboard. Her eyes lit up as she studied it and then, suddenly, she tore into the dried fish as if she hadn't eaten for days. She held the tail in both hands and bit, chewed and tugged at the fish until she became purple in the face. The dried fish and bone cracked and snapped between her jaws. All the time, she kept her eyes firmly fixed on Rib. The girl's feeding frenzy called his own saliva glands to attention. When did he last eat? All he could remember was a couple of slices of dry toast an hour or so before they reached the fogbank.

The girl devoured the last shred of fish and wiped her mouth on her bare arm. She then picked up the bowl and raised it to her lips, still keeping Rib held fast in her gaze. When she had drunk her fill, she wiped her mouth on her arm again, stood up, walked over to him and held out the bowl. No word, no gesture, not a flicker of expression. Just a bowl, half-full of a thick, creamy liquid with some unappetising green globules floating on the surface. He took the bowl from her and took a sip. It was sour-tasting. A bit like natural yoghourt which had passed its sell-by date. By a year or two. But his hunger took the upper hand and he drank greedily from the bowl until it was empty.

Rib opened his mouth to say thank you. The word 'tak' crackled from his lips. At the same time, a sharp pain shot into his left nadger, causing him to yelp in pain.

The girl jumped up. 'Are you in pain?' she asked. Her voice sounded as if it were strained through a wire sieve. Tinny. Metallic.

He felt for the leech, still clamped to his left earlobe. He took it off. The girl then said something incomprehensible in a foreign tongue. He put the leech back on. 'No, I'm not hurt,' followed by another stab in the goolie. This time, through gritted teeth, he kept the cry in. Then it dawned on him. The leech! Not only did it do animal speak, but foreign languages as well! How bloody awesome was that? Not too happy about the side-effects, though. Will have to do something about the short-circuited testicles as a matter of urgency.

They looked at each other, waiting for the other to speak. 'What is your name?' she finally asked.

'My name is Oooh-Aargh Meskitoe,' he winced.

'Oooh-aaargh Meskitoe,' she repeated. 'That is a strange name. That is not a name of our land.' She frowned.

Oops, thought Rib, not liking the way the conversation was going. 'What is your name?' he asked.

'I am Thorkatla Grimsdottir,' she proudly announced.

'That's a long name. Ouch! But a beautiful, gnnnn, gnnn, name,' he added hastily.

'You may call me Katla the Fair.'

'Thank you, Katla.'

'Katla the Fair!' she retorted angrily.

'OK, OK. Was it you who – Ow! – covered me with this blanket?'

'Yes. A man must have warmth. A man must also

have boots. I have brought you a pair. I came early to take the sheep to the upper pasture. I found you with no clothes on. I led the sheep to graze, went back to the homestead to fetch the blanket, and then returned to cover you. You have been asleep all day.' She was now chatting freely and the awkward question seemed to have gone away.

'Why do you sleep with sheep?' came an even more awkward question.

'Er – aaargh! - it's not like it seems. I was … Jesus Christ! … lost and needed to find a warm place for the nnng, nnng night … ' His left ball felt as if it had been pulled by a tug-of -war team and then let go like a catapult. He couldn't take any more and removed the leech. Without knowing why, he switched it to his right earlobe.

Thorkatla Grimsdottir was biting her bottom lip and staring at him. She didn't seem convinced by his answer. 'You speak my tongue. Yet you do not speak as you should.'

'How so?'

'You speak with the tongue of a concubine who licks the sweat from the fat belly of her master.'

Rib didn't reply, on two counts. Firstly, he was keen to avoid more mutilation of his manhood. And secondly, he couldn't begin to find an answer to the girl's allegation.

'You must make your voice lower,' she helped out. 'You must use only manly words.'

Rib struggled to think of manly words. All he could come up with was a night out with the lads, pistons, and a 20oz rib-eye with two portions of fries and a hot-chili dip, none of which seemed entirely appropriate.

He tried the deep voice. 'Thank you for the blanket.'

'That is better. As I said, a man must have warmth.' She then pointed to the leech. 'I must also say that you should not wear jewellery, for you will be greatly scorned for being unmanly.'

Rib resisted the temptation of demonstrating his manliness to the girl by picking her up and throwing her over the wall. But something told him that he should treat her with care. She was his lifeline.

'And thank you for the ... drink in the bowl.'

'The whey.'

'Yes, the whey. Thank you.'

'We have plenty. A good supply from last year's milk.'

So he was right about the sell-by date. The girl looked as if she were building up for another awkward question, so he decided to get his retaliation in first. 'Katla ... '

'Katla the Fair,' she corrected.

'Yes, sorry. Tell me Katla the Fair. Where do you live?' As the words left his lips, Rib realised that he was conversing without his bollocks feeling like they were caught up in a bike chain. He felt for the leech. The right ear! That must be it. Left earlobe for animals, right earlobe for humans. Wow!

Unaware of his eureka moment, the girl stood up and pointed along the coast. 'I live at Borg, the homestead of the great Chieftain Hoskuld. He is my grandfather.'

'So ... your parents are not alive?'

'My mother is dead. She was thrown off a cliff by my father.'

'What! Your father threw your mother off a cliff?'

'Yes, she dropped his drinking horn on the floor so that it cracked and could no longer hold ale. My father went into a berserk rage and threw her off a cliff.'

'Oh my God, Katla – Katla the Fair – that is terrible!'

She looked away and paused before saying, 'My father's name is Grim Bellower. He is a much-feared man. He now lives on his own at Grimstadir. It is considered better for me to live at Borg, where there are maids to care for me.'

'Yes, I can see why,' said Rib.

Thorkatla Grimsdottir seemed to take offence at his remark and she snapped back at him. 'My father is a brave and courageous warrior. There is no man stronger when the fury takes him. Only yesterday, he fought a fierce battle and slew twelve frostlings who came from the Milk of Ymer in a great ship.'

The words of Katla the Fair sent a shudder down his spine. Swiftly putting two and two together, for once in his life he came up with four. She was the daughter of the mad bastard with the axe. Grim Bellower was the giant who bit his shield before dispensing with the whole crew of the Lusitanic in a five-minute bloodbath. Frostlings? Milk of Ymer? He'd save those for later. 'And where is your father now?' he asked casually.

'His brothers carried him back to Grimstadir last night. He will now sleep for three days and three nights.'

Berserk rage, thought Rib. Pieces of a jigsaw were falling into place. And he was not liking the look of the picture one little bit. 'Tell me, Katla the Fair, do all the people living in the homestead carry axes?'

Her jaw dropped at the most stupid question she had heard in her life. 'Yes, of course!' she laughed. 'A man never walks away from his house ahead of his axe and sword. Bones cannot tell where the next battle lies.' And with that, she reached down to draw a slender dagger from her boot. The handle was made of horn and the gleaming blade bore some kind of inscription. A pretty little girl carrying a lethal weapon. Rather worryingly, the pretty little girl was now advancing on him, tossing the blade deftly from palm to palm. 'I shall now take you to the homestead. My grandfather will sit in judgement over your fate.'

'Whoa, hold on there, Katla– '

'Katla the Fair!'

'Hold on there, Katla the Fair, what makes you think you have the right to take me anywhere?'

'I have a weapon and you have none. Ravens have flocked to my reddened wound-maker. And they shall do so again.'

Rib got the point and decided he didn't want to get the point. However, he still didn't fancy the prospect of being captured and marched into town by a nine-year-old. 'And what if I don't agree to come with you?' He stood up to put weight behind his words.

'It is unwise to refuse Katla the Fair's bidding. I will tell how you have ravaged the sheep and tried likewise with me. If you flee, my kin will hunt you down. Silence you with iron. Feed the eagles flesh.'

Fair enough, Rib reflected. His options seemed few. Sure as hell, he couldn't survive for long in this alien landscape without food and shelter. But how could he be sure that her family wouldn't lop his head off as soon as they set eyes on him? 'How can I be sure your family will not kill me?'

'I will speak to my grandfather. He is a wise and just man. I will say that I found you wandering and lost. You will tell him that you are a shepherd boy whose family have been slain by Unn the Unwashed. He is hated in these parts and my grandfather will take pity on you. If the questioning becomes difficult tell them that you fell while escaping, hit your head on a rock and cannot clearly recall.'

'A shepherd boy? I know nothing at all about sheep.'

She raised her eyebrows. 'It seems strange to me to hear this from a man who is found lying naked with sheep.'

'Look ... '

'We must make our way to the homestead now.' She

set off purposefully across the field, clearly expecting him to follow. She stopped and turned to shout. 'And I must give you a new name which will not sound strange. You shall be known as Odd the Pale.'

Much as he disliked his new persona, he was too tired and hungry to argue. But he had one more question to ask. A question to which he feared he already knew the answer. 'Katla the Fair,' he called after her.

'Yes?'

'I think you are right. I think I might have lost my memory. Tell me, what is the name of your ... our people?'

She tossed her hair and laughed. 'We are Vikings, Odd the Pale. We are Vikings.'

61

He had difficulty keeping up with the tiny figure skipping ahead of him up the hill, the spongy grass treacherous underfoot. They had been climbing steadily for some ten minutes when Rib's footing gave way beneath him and he lost his left boot in the boggy ground. Sitting on a tussock to tie it back on, it was amazing to see how high they had climbed.

There was only one word for the landscape. Wild. Quite clearly he could make out below him the narrow spit which had been his landfall. Along the shoreline, a pebbled beach skirted the waters of the fjord. Sand-flats shimmered offshore. Of the Lusitanic mast there was no sign. It must have listed further in the night, or rolled over on its keel. Rib also scanned for the three rocky islets, but again no sign. He was still trying to come to terms with what the girl had said. Vikings? How could that possibly be? His thoughts were broken by a shout from Katla, who was pointing up at the mountains ahead, where a black cloud had already covered the peaks and was moving down the steep sides of the fjord towards them.

'Quick!' she shouted. 'We must run!' The menacing blackness was swiftly upon them, transforming a still, sunny day into a raging storm in seconds. Horizontal sleet stung Rib's face as he stumbled over the uneven terrain, now snags of grey-green turf, now splinters of coal-black rock. The sleet turned to snow and visibility quickly reduced to whiteout. All he could see ahead were glimpses of Katla's bobbing locks, like a miniature mobile lighthouse. Suddenly the ground gave way beneath him and he fell heavily. Momentarily stunned, he lay spread-eagled on his back, trying to blink away the snowflakes crowding into his eyes. A dull throb in his left cheekbone told him how hard the rock was. Out of the white flurry appeared the face of a small girl to peer down at him. She had come back for him. He felt her tiny cold hand take his and she helped him to his feet. 'Come!' she shouted in his ear. 'You cannot stay here!'

The two battled their way forward in the teeth of the storm in a crouching run, hand in hand. The ground levelled out and they came to a stone wall, where she motioned him to huddle down and shelter. She put her mouth to his ear again. 'We have reached the home field. Do as I say. Do not speak unless spoken to. If my grandfather addresses you, you must call him "My Lord" as a sign of respect. Rib nodded, wondering whether a sign of respect would be enough to prevent an axe from separating his head from his body. He put his hand up to his cheek. It was still bleeding from the fall. He was in the process of making his mind up whether to faint or not when the girl tugged at his arm. 'Follow me,' she said, clambering through a gap in the wall.

The stinging snow relented just enough for Rib to look up. They were now in some kind of enclosure, surrounded by low walls. Katla the Fair was striding towards a hillock in the middle of the field. He walked right up to the hillock, where she stood waiting for him. The hillock had a door.

'Welcome to the Great Hall of the Chieftain Hoskuld!' She pushed against the heavy door timbers and disappeared inside.

Although Rib was inwardly resisting with all his might the hypothesis that he had somehow strayed into the land of the Vikings, the very mention of the words Great Hall brought back memories of tutorials at MK College under the tutelage of Professor Riley, who liberally laced his lectures with the heroic myths and deeds of Old Norse legend. So he already had a clear view of what to expect: the Great Hall swept clean and decorated festively in preparation for the feast; ale and mead in plentiful supply; a sacrificed goat turning slowly over the glowing embers of a log fire; diners eating and drinking at a long table by the light of flaming torches; at the far end of the hall, a fire blazing in the hearth; folk gathered around a storyteller, recounting the epic sagas of heroes and gods; in the High Seat the Great Chieftain dressed in fine robes, his arms heavy with amulets of gold; against the far wall, perhaps a flat pack shelving unit housing hollow books and a blue candle tastefully set in a square glass vase quarter-filled with pebbles ...

He was jolted from his solo flight of fancy by a small face re-appearing from the shadow of the doorway. 'Come!' it hissed. 'Now!' He followed her into a dark entrance hall, dimly lit by a solitary lamp perched on a slab of rock. It was not as he had expected. A foul stench – a pungent mix of human faeces and rotten fish – filled the small room. He started to choke. Katla put her hand over his mouth. 'Shh!' she said and guided him over towards a door opening, where light flickered through a thin partition. Something crunched under his feet as he shuffled forward. He looked down to see that he was walking on a carpet of fish bones. The whole floor was covered in a thick layer of fish skin, scales and bone. Muffled voices seeped through from the other side of the partition. Katla opened the flimsy door, beckoning him to follow her in.

The Great Hall fell silent, broken only by Rib's

coughing fit caused by the pall of acrid smoke hanging at head height. Through smarting eyes, he tried to focus on the gloomy interior. They had entered a huge, long chamber, which seemed to widen in the middle before narrowing again at the murky far end. Smoke rose from a long hearth in the middle of the floor. No flames, just vile-smelling smoke drifting up into the vaulted roof. The hall was lit by rows of lamps on benches along each wall, throwing a flickering light on figures, some sitting, some standing at the far end of the chamber. In the half-gloom, it was impossible to say how many. Rib's coughing continued as the only sound in the menacing silence.

The girl stepped forward to stand before a line of four people seated against the right hand wall. Rib joined her, still spluttering. On a large chair with a high carved backrest sat the shrunken figure of a frail old man, his rheumy, red-veined eyes staring at Rib. Surely this couldn't be the Great Chieftain Hoskuld? To his right sat a woman with blond hair intricately arranged in a bun. High cheekbones and clear blue eyes gave the impression that she had once been a beautiful woman. She deigned to give Rib a brief glance before returning to her knitting.

But it was the two large shapes flanking the old couple which grabbed his attention, immediately recognising them as two of the warriors who had attacked the ship. The one sitting next to the old woman stood up and placed his hand on the hilt of his sword.

'Thorkatla Grimsdottir. You bring a stranger to our house without warning. You must know that this is not right.'

The small girl ignored him. 'Chieftain Hoskuld, I bring before you a poor shepherd boy in need of shelter. I found him without food and clothing in the sheep shed.'

Rib became conscious that the angry-looking

hulk was staring intently at the side of his head. Shit, the leech. What had she said about unmanliness? He quickly unclipped it from his ear and drew it inside the fold of his blanket.

This was not a wise move. The warrior drew his sword. 'Beware, my lord, I fear he hides a weapon.' With a deft flick, he whipped off the blanket with the point of his sword, leaving Rib totally naked, apart from a pair of boots a couple of sizes too big.

The woman raised her eyes from her knitting again and looked him up and down. 'I see neither prodder nor thunder-iron,' she remarked, before returning to needles and yarn. A ripple of laughter spread from the back of the chamber. Katla picked up the blanket and handed it to Rib, but not before taking a peek herself.

The old man spoke. 'Tell me, what is your name?'

'My name is Aaaargh! Fucking hell!' Rib screamed as the electric shock scorched his right gonad. He swiftly moved the leech to the flap of skin on the inside of his right arm.

'What does the R stand for?' asked the Chieftain.

Katla gave Rib a piercing look before kicking him on the shin.

'Er, no, my lord. My name is indeed not, er, Aaaargh Fucking Hell. It is, er, Odd the Pale.' The giggle of a girl came from somewhere in the dark recesses of the hall.

'What brings you here?' continued the Chieftain.

'Er ... my father was killed by ... er ... Unn the Unwashed and I ... er ... ran away and ended up .... here.'

The four absorbed his words in silence, before the warrior on the right nodded his head slowly. 'People in these parts care little for Unn the Unwashed. He is always causing trouble.'

'Unn the Unwashed commits misdeeds for which he

refuses to pay the compensation,' added the Chieftain. 'What is the name of your father?'

Bollocks! That wasn't in the script. 'I took a mighty blow to the head, my lord, and can recall nothing,' he said, pointing to the cut on his cheek.

The angry warrior, still standing, did not seem convinced. 'This boy speaks a strange tongue. I do not believe his story. Where did you find him, Katla Grimsdottir?'

'In the sheep shed on the lower pasture near Digranes,' she said without looking at him.

'Hah! That is near to where we fought the great battle against the frostling horde!'

Great battle? thought Rib. I didn't see any great battle. Massacre, more like.

Katla the Fair now looked directly at the man. 'Skeggi Cod-biter,' she said. 'My memory has it that you reported to my lord that every man on the vessel had been slain.'

Her uncle was clearly irked at being addressed in this manner and turned to Hoskuld the Great. 'I consider the boy to be a frostling spy, my lord. They have magic powers and he is sure to bring ill upon our family. Let me part his head from his body and make blood-waves for ravens,' he said, drawing his sword again.

Katla stepped between Rib and the huge man, acting as a human shield. 'He is no frostling, my lord. He is a poor shepherd boy.' She then caught Rib totally unawares by spinning on her heels and whipping off his blanket, leaving his privates on parade for a second time. He quickly covered himself with his cupped hands, but not before the old woman had stolen a second look. 'See, my lord, he does not shine and glitter. Before it dies, a frostling glistens white like a silver moth. This body is weak and pale.'

Rib didn't care much for the less-than-complimentary

plea from the defence counsel, but he was in no position to protest. The old man stroked his beard, deep in thought. Rib's knees began to knock, partly because he was cold, partly because he was petrified poopless.

The chieftain's wife spoke for a second time. 'The newcomer has numb knees. He is in need of warmth. He who has walked over mountains needs food and fresh linen.'

'But my lord!' spluttered Cod-biter.

'Enough!' snapped the woman. 'Hoskuld the Great has spoken. He will consider the matter overnight. In the morning, he will pass judgement on the stranger. Give him broth, night clothes and our friendship. For this night, he is our guest.'

Rib bent down and retrieved his blanket, which he wrapped tightly round him. Was that a pardon or merely a reprieve from the death penalty? He was too tired to think, too drained to care. All that mattered was that his head was still on his shoulders. Skeggi Cod-biter sat down in disgust and drained his ale horn in one gulp before smacking it down on the table beside him. The old woman took no notice.

Katla the Fair led Odd the Pale through the hall to a place where wide benches lined each wall. She disappeared into a closet and was soon back with neatly folded night linen. With what seemed like a thousand eyes on him, Rib managed to put on the night shirt without exposing himself for a third time. While he had been performing his contortion act before a rapt audience, Katla brought him a bowl of lamb broth, which he slurped down in no time. It was lukewarm and tasteless, but it was food.

'Thank you,' he said, wiping his greasy mouth on the clean sleeve of his nightshirt.

'You will sleep here,' she said, pointing behind him to the wide bed on which he sat. She took the bowl away and returned with a pillow and a rough blanket-case filled with straw. Rib took them and lay down on the prickly mattress. He pulled the blanket right up to his eyes and peeked over the top at the girl, who gave him a broad smile.

'Nighty-night, Odd the Pale.'

'Nighty-night, Katla the Fair.'

She left and he snuggled down in the warmth of the straw. Still alive, belly full, King-size bed. Could be worse. The low hum of the hall faded into the distance as he drifted off into a deep sleep.

62

He dreamed the sweet dream of a child without a care in the world. He rode over hill and dale on the back of a black sheep named Charger, holding on tight by gripping the ruff of wool on the back of his brave steed's neck and by pressing into the sheep's warm flanks with his knees. The sun burned high in the sky. They stopped to drink the ice-cold water from a mountain tarn as swallows swooped under a cascading waterfall high above them on the fell. Their thirst quenched, they rode down to the coast where they met up with their chum, Skrimsl the Sea-monster. Rib rode out to sea on Skrimsl's back, the mercury ocean swaying beneath them. Instead of burning, the silver metal soothed his senses, cleansing all disquiet from the corners of his mind. They were escorted by a school of acrobatic dolphins and a killer whale, bringing up the rear. Mandy the Dolphin Queen twisted and spiralled high into the air, making Rib squeal with laughter each time she soaked him with her splash. Ahead, he saw sleeping peaks and blue-green canyons. He wanted to be there. In the background, the orca played Brown-Eyed Girl on his waterproof harmonica. Round a headland their destination loomed into view.

Gorgonzola Island...

A welcoming party of seven mermaids windsurfing on seven blue-flecked cheeseboards sailed towards them and piloted them into a pretty little harbour. One of the mermaids cut in front of them and alighted at a stone jetty with steps leading up to the quayside. She held out her hand to help Rib clamber off Skrimsl's back.

'Welcome to Gorgonzola Island,' she murmured in a silky, seductive tone.

Mesmerised by the rhythmic movement of her silvery body, he followed her up the steps along an empty street of brightly painted houses, until they reached a large, cobbled square. There was not a soul to be seen. Closed blue shutters on every window underscored the silence. Large black and white birds with long legs and long beaks looked down at him from huge nests perched precariously on top of each roof. One of them clearly took exception to his presence and dive-bombed him. Arms flailing in the air, Rib sprinted across the square after the mermaid, who had disappeared into an alleyway, a dark narrow passage where the buildings were so close their roofs almost touched overhead.

Having successfully survived the stork challenge, he paused for breath, his heart pumping. The mermaid took him by the hand and guided him through a door into one of the houses. It was totally dark inside. He thought he could hear singing. She led him down a corridor. The noise above them grew in volume. A solitary light bulb lit a sign above a tunnel at the end of the corridor. It read 'THIS IS ANFIELD'.

A tumultuous roar greeted Rib as he stepped out onto the pitch. The mermaid had slithered across the lush green sward and was waiting for him in the centre circle. Subtle scouse wit cascaded down from the terraces:

'Frying tonight!'

'I'll have salt and vinegar with mine, love.'

'Batter late than never!'

'Come over here if you think you're lard enough.'

The mermaid climbed onto a large trestle table where she lounged like a model on top of a car bonnet at a motor show. In her hand was a microphone. Her first attempt at addressing the crowd resulted in ear-piercing feedback.

'Can you hear the mermaid sing?

No-o, No-o ...' came the chant.

Undeterred, the mermaid tried again. 'Ladies and gentlemen, welcome to tonight's round of – '

'You're not swimming,

'You're not swimming,

'You're not swimming anymore!'

'Please put your hands together and welcome tonight's contestant, Mr Rib Meskitoe!'

The Kop politely enquired who he was.

'And, as usual, to win the first prize, our contestant has to taste each of our Island's three cheeses: mild, mature and mouldy.'

'You're fish,

And you know you are ...'

'What is the first prize?' asked Rib, trying very hard not to look at the mermaid's pendulous breasts and failing miserably.

'You will be crowned King of Gorgonzola, the big cheese. You will have seven mermaids as seven brides, one for each night of the week.'

'Which night of the week will, er, you be?'

'Saturday, of course,' she smiled a smile which turned his legs to jelly. 'I shall be your something very special for the weekend, sir.'

Fair enough, can't say no to that, he thought. 'What exactly do I have to do again?'

'You taste each cheese in turn. First a lick, then a bite.' She licked her lips and Rib couldn't stop himself from licking his. He sat down at the table and studied the three pieces of cheese. Seemed pretty straight forward. A hush fell over the packed stadium as he leaned forward.

Tension mounted. 'Get off, yer little bastard!' screamed a spectator, knocking Little Tommy Tension, a dwarf from Dingle, off his back.

The first cheese was marbled green. Rib ventured a lick. It had a creamy texture, quite sweet on the palate. He took a bite of the soft, creamy cheese and swallowed.

The crowd erupted. '*One-nil, one-nil, one-nil, one-nil* ... '

He raised his arm in acknowledgement before focussing on cheese number two. The neatly, hand-written label said "mature" and it certainly was. The bluish-green tinge looked innocent enough, but it packed a tangy punch which nearly made him choke. But he managed to keep it down and milked the cheers of the crowd by sprinting over to the corner flag and diving onto his chest. He was promptly summoned back to the table by the unimpressed mermaid, who told him that his mother would be livid when she saw the grass stain down his front.

Rib now fixed his eye on the remaining chunk of cheese. Just one more to go, then he would be king. Roll on Saturday night.

The stadium held its breath. You could hear a pin drop. 'Ey, has anyone seen my friggin' pin? I've just dropped it,' said Little Tommy Tension.

As soon as his nose neared the crumbly slab, Rib knew that he had a fight on his hands. It smelled rotten, rank and rancid. Just as he stuck out his tongue, a maggot wriggled out from one of the blue penicillin-mould veins. Rib retracted his tongue.

A murmur ran round the crowd. It was Billy Murmur, the peanut seller. 'Peanuts! Luverly peanuts!'

'Shut yer gob, yer soft shite. E's about to lick the cheese!'

Carefully avoiding the wriggling maggot, Rib's tongue approached the crumbly mould. The stench was overpowering. The putrid fumes brought tears to his eyes. The mermaid commenced a countdown. Fifty thousand fans joined in.

'*Five – four – three – two – one ...* '

He closed his eyes and licked the rancid surface.

63

He opened his eyes mid-lick. The stench was overpowering. The putrid fumes brought tears to his eyes. He slowly withdrew his tongue from the big toe he was licking.

Rib stared at the broken black toenail. The tuft of coarse, brown hair sprouting from the joint, the puss oozing from the open sore on the unwashed skin. Having breakfasted on the crumble of grey crud built up between the toes, a small millipede scuttled down the scabby slope of the filthy foot before disappearing under the blanket.

There was no mermaid, no Anfield, no cheese.

Rib blinked rapidly in the hope that it would change his new-found reality. It didn't. He was the end-sardine in a bed shared by four other occupants, sleeping head to toe. The good news was that the body lying beside him had not been woken by its big toe being licked. The bad news was that a single, unblinking eye belonging to the next body along the row was staring at him, having clearly witnessed Rib's act of unintentional intimacy. On the furrowed brow was registered a mixture of disbelief and disgust.

Rib quickly turned over, disturbing the sleep of a cockroach, which beetled from the pillow into a crack in the turf wall. It was all he could do not to cry out. Instead, he screwed his eyes shut tight in the hope that this wasn't really happening to him: that he hadn't been the sole survivor of the Lusitanic massacre; that he hadn't found himself in some throwback Viking colony; that he hadn't been licking a man's filthy big toe. At least, he assumed it was a man. Actually, he reasoned, it might not be as bad if it was a woman's. On second thoughts, would he really want to get so close to a woman who let her feet get into that state? Either way, it was not good. What he needed more than anything else was dental floss and mouthwash, but something told him that wouldn't be happening.

The clinking of pots and pans galvanised a morning chorus of curses, belches and farts from his bedfellows before they untangled themselves from their bed-linen and started to get dressed. Rib stayed put, still facing the wall, clutching his blanket tightly round him. He heard the morning huddle move off down the hall and was about to breathe a sigh of relief when a hand grasped his shoulder and jerked him over onto his back.

'Good morning, Odd the Pale,' said Katla the Fair. 'Did you sleep well?'

He decided not to tell her about the mermaid with the beautiful boobies. 'Yes thank you, Katla the Fair.'

'Good, it is well, for today will be a day of fate for you. Here are some clothes. Put them on.' She watched Rib get dressed in the woollen trousers and the long shirt, careful to use the blanket as a modesty-screen. His lungs must be getting used to the stifling foulness of the atmosphere, he thought, because he found he could breathe without coughing. He saw that smoke was still drifting up in a thin spiral from the long hearth where he'd stood before the Chieftain the previous night. Of him and his family there was no sign. He noticed on the opposite wall a closet with closed doors and wondered whether they slept there. In fact, he and the small girl were the only occupants of the Great Hall. Voices were coming from an opening at the far end of the chamber.

'Come. We must take breakfast in the fire-hall,' she said, tugging on his arm. 'Today you will need strength.'

Rib didn't like the sound of this, but followed her down the hall, his hunger overriding the nagging fear in his mind. A hush fell over the fire-hall as they entered. About twenty pairs of eyes looked up from their bowls and stared at them. A quick scan told him that they were standing in a much smaller room than the Great Hall. It, too, had benches running along the side walls, but much narrower. The main difference was the fire, which crackled and sprickled from a sunken stone box, beside which was stacked a pile of dried brushwood. Pots and pans of varying size stood heating on the stone lip of the fire. Bright flames cast a dancing light which flickered on the faces of the room's occupants, all still staring intently at him.

On the bench to his right sat the men, all looking pretty much the same: dark, thick tangled hair; broad, furrowed foreheads; big noses; scratty attempts at facial hair. Rib couldn't remember ever seeing such a collection of butt-ugly specimens of manhood. Which one of them had woken up with a wet toe? he wondered. Forcing the thought from his mind, he turned to the women. Now they were something else. Ranging in age from young teen to forty-something, they all shared attractive features of blonde hair, blue eyes, high cheekbones.

A sharp kick on the shin deflected his attention from the women. Katla the Fair grimaced at him. 'You have no time for gawping at the womenfolk, Odd the Pale, you must eat,' and with that she handed him a bowl and led him to a raised wooden platform against the far wall. 'Both benches are full. We shall sit here.'

Rib had been hoping for something warm in the bowl. Maybe porridge, laced with golden syrup. Or honey. His heart sank. It was the same sour yoghourt she had brought him the day before.

'No Viking sets out in the morning without a nice bowl of skyr inside him,' she said between slurps. Reluctantly, Rib followed suit. He had to eat something, but this thick gloop – it was awful! Something ran over his foot. It was a shiny-cased beetle, with long stag horns. Instinctively, Rib made to kick it away, but was stopped by the girl's hand on his thigh. In a flash, she drew her dagger from its sheath and pierced the scurrying insect clean through its armoured shell. To Rib's horror, she held the skewered beetle, still struggling on the knife tip, up for inspection before popping it into her mouth. He turned away as she crunched hard like a dog cracking a marrow-bone. It was all he could do to keep the sour curds in his stomach.

'Mmm, fresh meat,' she said, wiping her mouth on her sleeve, before picking her teeth with the point of the blade. And then she was up and off. 'Follow me,' she ordered and they joined the file traipsing back into the Great Hall. Rib automatically looked for the Chieftain and his wife, but there was still no sign. Something strange caught his eye. At first, it didn't click, but then when they came to the long, smouldering hearth, he noticed that the high seat had disappeared. He was still pondering why the Chieftain's chair would no longer be there as they walked through the dark entrance hall, dried fish bones cracking underfoot, and out into the bright daylight. It took a few seconds to shield his eyes from the glare, but the first thing he saw was Chieftain Hoskuld in his high seat. For some reason, the massive timber chair had been carried outside, which couldn't have been easy. Beside him, as before, sat his wife. The two were, again, flanked by the two warriors. All the other members of the household had formed a straight line a couple of paces behind the chairs. They looked as if they were waiting to have their photo taken, all smiling at him. But he wasn't the camera man ...

He turned to the girl. 'What's going on?'

'Odd the Pale. Things have not fared well. My uncle, Skeggi Cod-biter, does not believe you are a shepherd. He believes you to be a frostling and has counselled strongly for your death.'

Deep down, Rib felt a bad bowl on the rise. 'So is this some sort of execution squad?'

'No,' she paused, 'at least, not yet. I have pressed your claim again this morning that you are indeed a shepherd and the great Chieftain Hoskuld has judged that you be put to the test.'

'Put to the test?'

'Yes. If you can show that you can herd a flock of sheep with mastery, then your life will be spared.'

'But ... but ... Katla!'

'Katla the Fair!'

'Katla the fucking Fair! YOU made the story up about me being a shepherd yourself! I know nothing about sheep!'

She gave him a sardonic look. 'A man who chooses sheep as his bedfellows must know something about their ways.'

'Look. I already told you–' He was interrupted mid-bleat. Something had excited the crowd. They began to point and cheer. A flock of twenty or so sheep was being driven down the hill by a couple of boys.

'I have been told to give you your instructions. You must follow them exactly, otherwise you will be deemed to have failed the test.'

Further protest being of little use, he decided to listen and take notice.

'You will herd the sheep once around the homefield towards the sun.'

'Towards the sun?'

She sighed. 'That way,' she pointed above the longhouse. 'You will then drive them through the gate, and up to the large black rock over there, on the lower pasture. You will then herd them round the rock, over the pasture, where you will allow them to graze. You will then drive them back down the hill and, finally, herd them into the pen in the corner of the homefield and close the gate. If one sheep strays from the flock, you will be judged to have failed the test.'

Is that all? thought Rib. 'Do I get a dog?' he asked.

'These are not the words of a wise man, Odd the Pale. The task will be testing enough for a skilled shepherd as it is. A dog would be sure to scare the sheep and make them flee in fear. Come, you must now hear the words of Hoskuld the Great. You will do well to address him with respect.'

I'll do well to kick him in the nuts and leg it, thought Rib. They walked over to the spectator gallery to stand before the old man. The little girl bowed and the boy followed suit.

'Odd the Pale, you have been made welcome as a guest in my house. Yet your story is not proven to us. I am a fair and honourable man and I shall not pass judgement on you until I witness your prowess as a shepherd with my own eyes. My grand-daughter has explained the task to you. If you pass the test, you will be accepted into my household. If you fail, the penalty will be death by the sword. Give the boy a crook.'

Skeggi Cod-biter hurled a long wooden pole at Rib. It bounced off the top of his head, nearly knocking him senseless. The crowd roared with laughter. Dazed, Rib picked up the staff and started to walk slowly towards the sheep, who were now huddled nervously against the stone wall just inside the gate.

He needed a plan, and he needed it fast. How easy

would it be to make a dash for the gap in the wall and keep on running? While his chances of survival out there were slim, the likelihood of him being able to herd a flock of sheep around a mountainside obstacle course without error was absolutely zero. A plan started to formulate in his mind. Sprint through the gate, up and over the hill, then inland towards higher ground, where he'd have a better chance of holing up. He'd be easy pickings for a posse down by the shore. Holing up, easy pickings, posse … how strangely foreign those Stonyville phrases sounded now. How he wished were back there. With a final look over his shoulder, he drew a deep breath and started walking. All or nothing. Shit or bust. He scanned the hill to double-check his escape route. He stopped in his tracks. Sitting on a boulder high up on the ridge was the shape of a giant man. Even from this distance, Rib recognised him at once. Katla's father, the berserk on the boat. Shit! Back to one man without his dog …

He could already see that his approach was spooking the flock. If he wasn't careful, he could mess it up and feel a sword up his jacksie before he'd even started. Somehow, he had to work his way behind them and gently shoo them along the wall and hope for the best.

'Baaa – baa – baaaah.' The sheep were becoming more agitated the closer he got. If only I knew what they were saying, he thought, then I might have a chance. Shit! The leech. The leech! He felt beneath his shirt and transferred it from the inside of his right arm to his left earlobe.

'Good morning,' he bleated.

The sheep stared at him in astonishment.

'Good morning,' he tried again.

Silence.

Then, 'Oooh, isn't it that nice young man who slept with us the other night?' This set them all off. 'Yeah, but the other night he didn't have his big stick with him.' One of the ewes giggled.

Now safely out of earshot of the Vikings, Rib felt confident enough to start up a conversation. 'Hello, it's nice to see you all again – '

A fierce looking ram interrupted him. 'You're like all the rest of them. You're going to hit us with that stick.'

'No, no, I won't! I promise. Look, I'll lay it down in the grass. See?'

This action drew a murmur from the Vikings.

'I, er, wondered whether you might like to play a game?'

'A game?' asked the suspicious ram. 'What's a game?'

'Well, er, do you remember when you were little lambs and you frolicked and gambolled in the meadows all day, leaping over babbling brooks?'

'Frankly, no. I can't even remember when I last had a crap. So piss off!'

'Get on with it!' shouted Cod-biter. 'My blood-iron becomes impatient.'

Rib was in desperate need of a crash-course in sheep psychology. What would sound a ram's horn? What would make a ewe turn? 'If you let me be your shepherd, I will lead you to the sweetest pastures, I will bring you fresh straw for your bedding and – '

'Would you read us bedtime stories, like they do in the longhouse?' asked a sheep named Gunhilda.

'Yes! Yes, of course I will! All you have to do is let me herd you around for a while.'

'Will you sleep with us, too?' asked a ewe named Agnes.

'Er, yes, all right,' replied Rib with a note of hesitancy.

'And you won't hit any of us with that big stick?'

'No, I promise.'

The ram pawed the ground, clearly unconvinced.

'What is your name, good sir?' asked Rib.

'I am Ragnar the Ram,' said Ragnar the Ram.

'That is a fine, proud name. You are clearly a born leader, Ragnar the Ram. I shall teach you how to master your flock like no other ram has done before. Your reputation for, er, ramliness will be the talk of ewes across the whole land.'

'Well, if you put it like that,' bleated Ragnar, 'we'll give it a go, won't we girls?'

'Whatever,' said Agnes.

'Great! Now, listen carefully, Ragnar. I would like you to walk slowly to the far corner of the field, staying this side of the longhouse.'

Ragnar dutifully trotted off.

'Whoa! Stop! I need you to tell the flock to follow you.'

'Come on, girls.'

The apprentice shepherd held his breath as the sheep moved off slowly behind the ram. 'That's great, that's perfect,' bleated Rib, taking up position behind the flock. A swift glance over to the line of Vikings was met with a wave from Katla. He didn't wave back, his every fibre focussed on the flock before him. So far so good, but just one mistake and, like a spring lamb, he would be ready for the chop.

Once they disappeared from the crowd's view behind the longhouse, he let out a sigh of relief. For the first time, he looked at the Great Hall from the outside. It was covered in turf and looked like a long grassy mound, bulging slightly in the middle. Smoke spiralled up from the two chimney holes at either end. It was hard to believe so many people lived and slept in there.

'What do we do now?' asked Ragnar, having reached the corner of the field.

'OK, now I want you to walk slowly round the

other side of the house, behind the row of people and out of the gate.'

'Okey dokey,' replied Ragnar. 'Follow me, girls.' And off they trotted, happy as Larry. The sheep swept smoothly in perfect flock formation past the impressed onlookers and through the gate into open country.

'OK, team, well done! Let's just pause here for a moment.'

'Here is not a good place to stop,' said Ragnar, sensing his ewes becoming agitated at the presence of the giant on the ridge above them. 'We must go now or the girls will panic.'

'Fine. Walk on,' said Rib, casting a furtive look at the menacing silhouette on the skyline. They traversed the hill, heading for the black rock some fifty metres to their right. Rib asked, 'Exactly why are the sheep so afraid of the giant?'

Without slowing, Ragnar answered, 'When the berserk rage takes him, he throws sheep over the cliff. He also threw our last shepherd over the cliff. After he'd bitten his head off.' Rib wished he hadn't asked.

Within a couple of minutes, they reached the outcrop jutting from the field like a blackened tooth. 'OK, let's just rest here for a bit. But make sure we all stay together,' he added.

'Take five, girls.' The sheep immediately began to munch the coarse, wiry grass. They were noisy eaters. Rib clambered up onto the rock and looked down at the farmstead, amazed at the changed perspective given by such a short climb. Much of the previous night's snow had melted under the morning sun, making the hill look like it were covered by a patchwork quilt of dull green and brilliant white. The line of men and women was still standing behind their chieftain. One of the Viking warriors was pacing up and down in front of the longhouse, swishing his axe in the air. Surrounding the house, the enclosure was almost perfectly square, containing two sheds, presumably for livestock. Along the length of the far wall ran a cultivated plot where a few stunted vegetables poked through the snow. The bright sunlight glittered on the waters of the fjord, which narrowed to a river some thousand metres past the longhouse, before cutting into a steep valley between the towering, ice-capped crags. Then, to his left, Rib's attention was drawn to more traces of smoke coming from a raised, flat piece of land on the slope above homefield. More houses, he wondered?

The sheep had stopped grazing and were again looking nervously at the lone figure on the ridge. Maybe time to move on. But there was just one more thing Rib wanted to try. 'Ragnar, do you think the girls might like a little geometry lesson?' The ram passed the question onto his flock, unable to field it himself.

'Oooh, yes please,' said Gunhilda

'Whatever ...' said Agnes.

Rib sat on the rock and the flock gathered round. After a mini-tutorial in degrees and angles, with a hypotenuse thrown in for good measure, he took them over to a patch of hillside where all of the snow had melted. He wanted to make quite sure that the practical part of the lesson would be clearly visible from the farmstead.

'Now, let's imagine there's a line running straight up and down the hill.'

'It's easier if you explain it in our words,' advised Ragnar. 'Tell them it's a sheep track.'

'OK. Thanks. Imagine there's a sheep track running straight up and down the hill – '

'Sheep tracks don't run straight up and down the hill. They run across,' interrupted Ragnar.

'For goodness sake! You were the one who told me to say sheep track!' After a frustrating dip into the shallow but muddy puddle of the sheep psyche, Rib finally managed to get the flock to form two perfectly straight lines each fanning out at 45° from Ragnar, standing proudly at the apex. Rib stood back and smiled. 'Well done, team, that's perfect. Absolutely perfect.'

Down in the homefield, the Vikings stared up at the hill, mystified at the massive woollen V-sign meant just for them.

Rib was still giggling when he herded the sheep with consummate ease back into the enclosure. Now for the final part of the test, to drive the sheep into the pen and close the gate. 'Ragnar, do you think the girls might like to walk backwards for a change?'

'Oooh, yes, that sounds fun,' piped up Gunhilda on behalf of her sisters.

And so it came to pass, that the assembled Vikings became the first humans, either on Tycho or Planet Earth, to witness a flock of sheep reversing into a parking space, always the trickiest part of a driving test. With a broad smile on his lips, Rib closed the gate. Ragnar bleated five times. It was a 5-baaa gate ...

64

'Odd the Pale, 'said Katla, running up to him. 'You have deceived me.' Rib quickly switched the leech back under his shirt. 'You are indeed a shepherd of great standing. And now you must stand before Hoskuld the Great to hear his judgement.'

The excited chatter of the line subsided as the boy and small girl approached the high seat of the Chieftain. The old man stroked the straggly wisps of his grey beard. 'Odd the Pale, you have performed well. You have completed the task to my satisfaction and I accept you into the Hoskuld household as a thrall.'

Skeggi Cod-biter jumped to his feet. 'But my lord! The boy has deceived you with his cunning. He is no shepherd. He is a frostling with magic powers.'

'Silence!' snapped the chieftain's wife. 'You should think twice before challenging the judgement of your father. Hoskuld the Great has spoken and no more will be said on the matter.'

Cod-biter stomped off back into the longhouse. Hoskuld and his wife stood and four of the women moved quickly to carry their seats back into the hall. The rest of the gathering dispersed to start the day's work in the field, leaving Odd the Pale and Thorkatla Grimsdottir standing on their own.

'That turned out rather well,' said Rib.

'Yes, it is fortunate that your life has been saved.'

'So, I am now a thrall of the Hoskuld household,' he said proudly. He had no real idea what a thrall was, but it sounded quite important in a Knights-of-the-Round-Table sort of way. Maybe a couple down the pecking order from a prince?

'What's the job description, then?'

'Katla the Fair does not understand.'

'What's the job? How much will I get paid? How will people address me?'

She laughed. 'A thrall will work as his chieftain commands. In reward, he will receive food, drink, clothing, shelter and protection. He will be called sheep's arse, goat's prick or just plain slave.'

'Slave! What do you mean, slave? The Chieftain said that he'd accepted me into his household!'

'Yes, as a thrall, which means slave.'

'Jesus Christ!'

'Who?'

'Never mind. Are you telling me that you brought me here to go on trial under the threat of death, only to be told that I'm a slave? Thank you very much, Katla.'

'Katla the Fair! And you would do well to consider your position, Odd the Pale,'

'Rib Meskitoe!' he corrected.

'I repeat. You will have food and drink, clothing, shelter and protection. You had none of these when I found you yesterday.'

'Protection? From a family with a berserk who throws shepherds off a cliff?'

The girl flashed her eyes at him in anger. Did he detect a tear? Maybe there was something in what she was saying. Until he could come up with a better plan, maybe he'd have to make the best of it. And getting on the wrong side of the Chieftain's grand-daughter maybe wasn't the best start.

'OK, I'm sorry. Thank you for helping me. But you need to tell me what I have to do, how I have to behave.'

'Your words are accepted. And, yes. I shall be your guide. But these things must wait.' She looked up at the sun's elevation. 'Come, it is now toilet time.'

'Toilet time?'

65

Bemused, he followed her back into the longhouse, where the atmosphere assaulted his senses anew. Smoke stung his eyes, bones crunched underfoot. Chieftain Hoskuld, his wife and their two sons were just emerging from the small doorway directly opposite the main entrance. A queue waited respectfully for them to pass before filing through the door.

'Where are we going?' hissed Rib.

'The latrine.'

'What? All together?'

'Yes, of course. As a Viking, this should come as no surprise to you, Odd the Pale.'

Ask any woman or man on the street to name as many aspects of Viking life as they can, and they'd probably come up with rape and pillage, dragon-headed long ships, saga-telling, burning down monasteries, and struggle from there on. It is a little-known fact that an important part of everyday Viking life was to go to the toilet together.

It is fair to say that Rib Meskitoe was not expecting this. In his world, there were certain things which you did in private. And going to the toilet was on the medal podium every time. He was not prepared for this at all. As he sat, trousers around his ankles, facing a blue-eyed, flaxen-haired maid with her skirts gathered up, to say that he was out of his comfort zone was the understatement of the millennium. His buttocks shifted uncomfortably over one of the six holes carved in a wooden bench running the length of one side of the latrine, where six boys sat. Six girls sat opposite. Beneath them, a deep stone-lined gutter filled with faeces. The gloomy interior was lit by two flickering oil lamps, one at each end. The stench from the trench was unbearable.

The six males and six females sat in silence, as if waiting for a signal. All eyes seemed to be fixed on Rib, especially those of the girl opposite. To avoid her stare, he averted his gaze down to her bare knees. They were nice knees. Really nice knees. Noo-oo, this was neither the time nor place to be thinking about nice knees. So he looked further down to her shins. They were nice shins. Really, really nice shins. Shapely, and covered with a fine down of golden hair. He wondered how it would feel to stroke the hairs so that they lay flat against her skin. Stop it!

One of the girls whispered to another, who giggled. She then raised her right hand and pointed at the skinny runt of a kid sitting opposite, who returned her gesture with a toothy grin. The silence suddenly went more silent. Something was about to happen …

The boy emitted a high-pitched squeak of a fart, which he held for a full five seconds before tailing off in four staccato bursts. The strain showed clearly on his face, cheeks blown out and eyes bulging.

'The peep-peep of the sandpiper scouring the shoreline for food,' the girl said. Everybody nodded and murmured approval. She leaned forward and touched the boy's hand. He smiled, shyly.

Then, at the other end of the row, a more ample young woman pointed at the Neanderthal squatting opposite, who, without further prompting, let rip a flappy fart which reverberated like the exhaust of a

Harley. A real hum-dinger. And boy, did it hum as well. The flame of the oil lamp flickered in its draught. It was a miracle the whole place didn't explode.

'The voice of thunder rolls down the valley from Troll Mountain,' said the plump girl. Again, the seated gathering nodded its approval and the pair touched hands.

What the hell was going on here? Rib felt as though he were bearing unwilling witness to a primitive courtship ritual, a latrine love scene – a theatrical piece of foreplay enacted not on the stage of a playhouse, but on the slats of a shithouse. With musical accompaniment, too. Not from the orchestra pit, but from the cess pit. The most bizarre wind-recital he'd ever been privy to …

Now the flaxen-haired girl with the beautiful blue eyes, the nice knees and shapely shins was signalling to him that it was his turn. Oh shit! Which, unfortunately, was exactly what he did, his bowels having last moved three days before onboard the Lusitanic. So the three slices of toast, the dried fish, the bowl of curds, the lamb broth made from overwintered pickled meat, topped off by the bowl of sour whey, all joined forces in a bubbling battering ram to surge their way down through his helpless bumhole into the trench below.

'AVALANCHE!' the latrine screamed, holding its nose. All except the girl with nice knees, who was giving him a livid scowl. Rib sat with his head in his hands, trying to shut out the sounds of everyone now doing what you're supposed to be doing in a toilet. He didn't look up until he'd heard them all leave. When he thought it was safe, he looked up. One person remained, and it wasn't the blonde with the shapely shins.

'Odd the Pale,' the little figure said sternly. 'You have not acted in a manly way. You have shown disrespect to Melkorka.' She handed him a handful of grass – about the only thing Vikingland and Stonyville had in common. God, how he wished he were back there.

Actually, he didn't give a toss if he'd upset Melkorka. He felt tired and dirty. 'Where do I get a wash?' he snapped.

66

Neither the warmth of the sun nor the freshness of the breeze drifting down from the mountains failed to lighten his mood. Still smarting from the latrine humiliation, he trudged several paces behind the girl, head down, studiously ignoring her attempts at conversation. Every now and then, she stopped to pick star-shaped flowers to twine them into the rough weave of her cloak.

They had climbed quite steeply, into the foothills, where the spongy moss gave way to a crumbly surface of red and black cinder, which crunched underfoot. A smell of rotten eggs made him look up. 'Was that you?' he shouted at the slim figure skipping ahead. It was her turn to ignore him.

'Take care to keep to the path,' she said after a while. The dramatic shift in landscape advised him to heed her words. The slope now flattened out onto a plateau, where clouds of sulphurous steam rose from both sides of the narrow, but well-trodden track. Small boiling mud-pots spluttered an unfriendly welcome. A plume of steam shot up high into the air with a crump some hundred metres ahead.

'Be very careful here,' she turned to say. They came to a cauldron in which red mud seethed and boiled. 'This one is ill-tempered and will not be slow to do you harm. We call him "The Slob". Wait! It is not yet safe to cross.' On cue, the crater squirted a spray of scalding mud into the air, fanning right across the path at waist-height. The whole field around them was leaking acrid vapour, making Rib cough.

'How the hell do we know when it is safe to cross?' he asked.

'You count the bubbles. I will show you on the way back.'

The mention of bubbles flashed him back to the Big Frog. But not for long ...

'Come, now, quickly!' With care, they skirted the Slob and continued along the path. She led him to the top of the smoking field, where she made him stand a few metres behind a huge bowl scooped out of the rock – a perfectly round crater, filled with perfectly still water. 'Watch!' she said. The surface began to agitate, swirling slowly in powerful eddies before suddenly sinking by a good half metre, as if it were being sucked down. A huge bubble-dome of air rose, then sank, then rose again to explode in a jet of boiling water rocketing high into the air with a roar. The ground thumped under their feet.

'Wow!!!' he screamed. 'That was incredible. Absolutely incredible!' The plume of steam drifted down over the lavafield and the water in the bowl was still again, as if nothing had happened. 'That was amazing. How often does it do that?'

'Oh, many times a day. Geysir will spout for any man who cares to wait.'

'Can we see it again?'

'Yes, if you wish.' They watched the spectacular show repeat itself three times over. It was of another world. The boy could have stayed there all day. 'Come. You asked me to lead you to the wash-tubs.'

'Did I?'

'Yes, and I have towels for us,' she shouted over her shoulder as she set off again. Some fifty metres upwind of the geysir, the path ended on a raised platform of rock at two circular ponds of still, milky-blue water. They were just like outdoor spa tubs, very similar to the ones at the Aqua Sana. But these were made of rock. 'This one's for washing clothes,' she said, pointing to the nearest. 'It is too hot to sit in. It will take your skin off. That one is where we bathe,' she said and, before Rib could look away, she stripped off, threw her clothes onto a rock and stepped into the water, where she sat waiting for him to so the same. 'Do not be shy. There is no shame in baring your body.'

This just wasn't right. Not right at all, he said to himself, while trying to undress with his back turned towards the girl. He had more than half a mind to set off back down the track, but in the end his need for a bath was the greater and he was soon sitting in the warm waters. On the opposite side of the tub to Katla the Fair. As opposite as he could possibly get.

The gentle waters soothed and caressed his bruised body. He hadn't realised how much his ordeal had taken out of him. He leaned his head back onto the warm rock and looked up into the deep-blue sky, where a large eagle circled high above the crags. He closed his eyes in a state of utter relaxation. The hissing sounds of the hot springs faded into the distance as he drifted off.

'Soon you will die,' came the bucket of ice-cold water from the girl sitting on the other side of the tub.

'Eh?'

'You are a frostling. All frostlings who come from Ymir's Milk perish within four days. First, their hair falls out. Then, their white body is covered with boils. Then, their tongue swells up and a great fever comes upon them. Then, they die. A horrible death.'

Now wide awake, his hand went to his scalp. Then he examined his skin and waggled his tongue. How long had he been there? This was his third day, wasn't it? 'If you think I am a frostling, why haven't you handed me over to what's-his-name, Shaggy Cod-pieces?'

'Skeggi Cod-biter.'

'Whatever. Why are you protecting me?'

A blush came to her cheeks. 'You are pleasing to me. You will be my pet. My poor, sick pet. I have always wanted a pet. I will care for you. As long as you live, that is.'

Oh, whoopee-do! thought Rib, trying to push from his mind the picture of being pulled along on a collar and chain by a nine-year-old.

Katla Grimsdottir then slipped out of the tub, took something from her bag and slid back into the water right next to him, before he had time to move away. 'And now,' she said, brandishing a wire scrubbing brush, 'I am going to clean my little pet all over.'

'No you're fucking not!' he screamed, snatching the brush from her grasp and hurling it as far away as he could. The little girl burst into tears. 'Listen, Katla ...'

'Katla the Fair,' she sobbed.

He drew a deep breath. 'Listen, Katla the Fair. Let's play a game instead, shall we? I'll ask you some questions and you see if you can give me the right answers. Yes?'

At first, she looked doubtful. Suspicious. Then, wiping the tears from her eyes, she relented. 'Yes, I will do as you suggest. Katla the Fair likes playing games.' She rested her chin on his shoulder and looked up into his eyes. 'Ask the first question.'

'Right. Question number one. What is, erm, Ymir's Milk?'

'That is an easy question. Everybody knows the answer to that one. Ymir was the great frost giant who created our island out of his body. His blood became the sea and rivers, his flesh the earth and his bones the mountains. He left a trail of semen all around the island to protect us.' She pointed out to sea at the band of dense fog. 'We call it Ymir's Milk.'

'Erm, yes, of course. Well done, Katla the Fair, that is the correct answer.' She clapped her hands, clearly pleased. So, it definitely is an island, then. Surrounded by the wank-juice of a giant. Silly me for not knowing that. It brought a whole new meaning to The Circle of Life. Rib wondered what Disney would have made of it. 'OK, next question. How big is the island?'

She paused. 'It takes ten days to ride to the other side.'

'And how many people live on the island?'

'That I know not. All I can tell you is that there are twelve chieftains, each with his great hall, his family, his farmhands and his thralls.'

'Like me,' he muttered.

'And then each chieftain also has a number of farmers in thing with him, each with their own homestead.'

'In thing?'

'Yes, they pay allegiance to him. There are many blood feuds and disputes on the island.'

A picture was forming in his mind of a primitive community, or collection of communities, inhabiting a sparsely populated island cut off from the world by a trail of troll spunk. A violent society, where people carried weapons, ate disgusting food and for some god-unknown reason chose to shit together. He had to get out of there. But this Ymir's Milk thing worried him. He checked the back of his hand. No sign of pustules. Yet ...

The little girl pressed up against his side. 'Next question!'

'Right,' he said, easing himself away. 'Tell me, Katla the Fair, exactly how many people there are in Chieftain Hoskuld's family.'

'Ah, that's easy for me to tell. Hoskuld the Great is married to Helga, a proud and strong woman, and they have seven sons. Two remain at the farmstead. Leif Tanglehair - he is the youngest and knows yet not the ways of women – and Skeggi Cod-biter, he is the eldest and knows the ways of women, tries to have his way with women but women take care to keep out of his way.'

Serves him right, the ugly twat ...

She started to count on her wet fingers. 'Ulf the Fart lives at Stangarholt, Eysteinn Shaggy-breeches lives at Grisatunga, Thorkel Twig-belly at Jardlangstadir and Finn Flat-nose has a farmstead at Munnadsnes.' She then fell silent.

'That makes six. You said there were seven brothers.'

'Yes. There remains my father, Grim Bellower. Sometimes he lives at Grimolfstadir, other times he lives wild in the mountains.'

Of course, the berserk. How could he forget? 'You have answered well. I have just one more question. How many boats does Hoskuld the Great have, and where are they moored?'

'Each chieftain owns only one boat and I am not permitted to tell you where it is moored.'

'I find that strange,' Rib thought aloud. 'I thought that Vikings were a proud, seafaring race.'

A puzzled look came over the girl's brow. 'No, that is not so. Firstly, we no longer have the timber to keep more than one ship – most of the trees were chopped down many years ago. All that remain are a few stands of birch trees. We have two and defend them fiercely. They are the family's most prized asset. We need them for the charcoal.'

'Charcoal?'

'Yes, for the forge where our swords are made.'

295

'Ah, yes, of course. Silly me ...'

'Yes, Odd the Pale, you are indeed silly. And secondly, Vikings cannot sail off the island. I have told you already. Any man that enters Ymir's Milk will perish. By the way, has any of your hair fallen out yet?'

Rib tugged on a handful of hair which, to his relief, didn't come away at the roots. But boy, did it need a wash. He closed his eyes and let his body slide beneath the warm waters of the pool, causing sixteen bugs to abandon ship and struggle to the surface. Another seventy three perished at sea, enmeshed in the wiry tangle of pubes down below in the engine room. Rib allowed the gentle thermal currents to caress and cleanse his body.

The soothing sensation was, however, short-lived. Katla was yanking on his arm, pulling him up to the surface. 'It is not wise to go under. The water of the hot spring will be harsh to your hair.'

Never being one to bother overly about split ends, he ignored her. He felt refreshed. He felt relaxed. He felt good. But things don't stay good for long. This he should have known by now.

'Come, we must leave. Bad weather is on its way,' she said, tugging at his arm again. The air had become ominously still. They quickly dried, dressed and set off back down the track through the steaming field and bubbling mud-pots. Rib stopped in awe when Geysir sent a plume of boiling spray high into the sky with a thump that made the earth tremble.

'Come on! We must not let the weather catch us here or we will lose sight of the track.' She pointed up to a cleft in the black crags spewing forth a dark cloud which was now rolling down the foothills at alarming speed. They started to run, past deep fissures seeping sulphurous steam, through the field of angry mud-pots until they reached the Slob. Katla stopped. Rib turned to see the bank of black cloud engulf the hot pools. A cutting wind was now upon them, whipping the acrid vapours into erratic swirls. Geysir thumped again, now hardly visible in the gloom of the gathering storm.

'Why are we stopping? You said we had to get off the lava field.'

'Yes, but there is something important I must show you first.' She pointed at the seething Slob. 'Look, you see the bubbles which form at the edge? There! Now you count – one skrimsl, two skrimsl, three skrimsl, four skrimsl. Now!' On cue, a vertical jet of scalding red mud spurted skywards with a whoosh. She carried on counting, ' ... five skrimsl, six skrimsl, seven skrimsl ... Now!' Again, the Slob came to life, spraying a fan of sulphurous steam across the path. 'Now we can go. Remember, four skrimsl and seven skrimsl. Now, come on, run!'

The blizzard bullied the two fragile figures down the hill, buffeting them from side to side as they struggled to stay on their feet. The stone wall of the homefield was a welcome sight and they huddled behind its moss-covered rock while the storm raged over them.

'Wow!' said Rib. 'One moment it was clear blue skies and then ... this!'

Katla's perfect pearl-white teeth shone up at him. 'On Iceland, we have four seasons in one hour.'

'You can say that again.'

She hesitated. 'On Iceland, we have four seasons in one hour.'

On Iceland, he thought. They call it Iceland, too. Interesting ...

His thought train was interrupted by a giggle from the girl.

'What's up?'

'Your hair. Touch your hair.'

His heart missed a beat. Ymir's Milk must have taken its toll. The beginning of the end. And she found it funny! He slowly reached up to feel for the bald patches on his scalp, only to touch a straw-like substance covering his whole head. A piece snapped off in his hand. 'What the hell's happened to my hair?'

'As I said, the waters of the hot spring are harsh. You now have a bird's nest for hair.'

Rib examined the brittle piece of straw which he'd snapped off. She was right, it was like a bird's nest. But he didn't find it funny. 'Will it stay like this?'

'No,' she smirked. 'If you wash your head for five days under an ice-cold waterfall, your hair will be as before.'

'Can't wait,' he muttered, as the two ran over the homefield to the longhouse.

67

Helga, wife of Chieftain Hoskuld, was riding across the heath with her son, Eysteinn. 'It has come to my ears that Ketil Uggason is spreading a bad rumour about your wife,' she said.

'I have heard no such rumour,' he answered.

'Is it true that your wife, Gudrun, is often dressed in breeches and wears a cod-piece?'

'Not that I've noticed.'

'Not that you've noticed! You can't be paying her much attention, then! If you haven't noticed this strange behaviour, how do you account for folk calling her "Gudrun Great-cock"?

'She can't have been called that for long.'

Helga pressed him. 'If women go about dressed as men, they invite the very same treatment as men who wear their shirts cut low so that their nipples can be seen. Both are shameful grounds for divorce!'

'I am not going to divorce Gudrun,' said Eysteinn and spurred his horse on so that he rode ahead of his mother. No more was spoken on the matter that day.

* * *

The following morning, Helga served her son breakfast.

'What is this on my plate, Mother?'

'It is the limp, shrivelled penis of a ram. It matches

your manhood, Eysteinn. It is a sad thing to have such a coward for a son. It would have been better if you had been a daughter, then at least we could have married you off. Remember my words from yesterday. If you do not divorce Gudrun, you must kill Ketil to avenge the dishonour brought upon our family.' She picked up the penis from the plate and dangled it in front of his face.

At this, Eysteinn became enraged. 'I wished for whey for breakfast and instead you serve me a dish of cold insults.' He then got up and left the table without a further word.

That afternoon, Eysteinn summoned his brothers and they gathered up their weapons. They were six in number: Skeggi, Ulf, Finn, Thorkel, Leif and Eysteinn himself. They rode quickly, following the shoreline. When they stopped to feed and water the horses, Eysteinn told his brothers of his plan. He had been told that Ketil was staying up at a shieling with only a few farmhands there, making the hay, and they would surprise him there. They all agreed to his plan and rode hard through the night, arriving shortly after dawn.

Ketil was, indeed, at the shieling, in quarters down by the river. His farmhands were making the hay in the meadows further up towards the foothills. The brothers dismounted and waited behind an outcrop of rock until they were sure that all of Ketil's men had gone up to the meadows to work. Earlier that morning, Ketil's shepherd had gone out to tend to the flocks on the upper pastures. He caught sight of the men and their tethered horses behind the rock. Suspecting that they could hardly be there on a peaceful errand, he set off back to the shieling to warn Ketil.

Finn, who was a man of sharp sight, spotted him running down the hill. 'We'll have to cut him off before he is able to raise the alarm,' he said. They quickly mounted their horses and galloped after the boy. Thorkel Twig-belly was the first to catch up with him and drove his spear through the shepherd boy's shoulder blade, lifted him up into the air and hurled him to the ground, breaking his back with a snap.

They then rode down to the cabin. Ketil had been up early that morning to give instructions for the day's work and had then, after the farmhands had set off, gone back to join his wife, Ingiborg, in bed. They awoke at the noise of the men dismounting and heard them discussing in loud whispers who should be the first to enter the building to attack him.

Ketil recognised the voices of Eysteinn and his brothers and told Ingiborg to get dressed and leave the cabin. She said she wanted to stay by his side, but he insisted, and she left by the back door and walked down the slope to the river, where she began to wash some linen. Now alone in the cabin, Ketil collected his weapons, placed his helmet upon his head and picked up his shield and his sword, Leg-biter. He cursed himself for leaving his coat of mail back at the homestead.

In the meantime, Eysteinn and his brothers were still discussing how to go about the attack. None of them was eager to be the first to enter the cabin.

Skeggi Cod-biter then spoke. 'Eysteinn, this feud is between you and Ketil. You should lead the attack.'

'My brother,' Eysteinn replied, 'this man has heaped dishonour and shame upon our whole family. You, as eldest son, should bear the mantle of this man's abuse and strike the first blow.'

'Bollocks!' retorted Skeggi. 'It is your wife who wears the cod-piece. We shall be right behind you.'

The youngest of the brothers, Leif Tanglehair, had never been in a swordfight and this weighed as a heavy burden upon the heart of the virgin Viking. While his brothers were still arguing, he rushed into the cabin, holding his shield over his head. Ketil struck him a mighty blow with Leg-biter, severing the tail of the shield and splitting the boy's head right down to the shoulders, killing him instantly.

Skeggi followed on Leif's heels, sword drawn and shield up. Ketil, still trying to pull Leg-biter loose from the boy's head, let his shield slip to one side. Skeggi saw this and took the chance to deal him a deep wound to his left thigh with a slash of his sword. Ketil responded with a blow to Skeggi's shoulder, causing him to drop his weapon. At that very moment, Finn Flat-nose burst into the room bearing a spear, whose blade was a full ell in length. On seeing this, Ketil threw down his sword, took his shield in both hands and charged at Finn in the doorway. Finn lunged and the spear pierced both shield and man.

Ketil leaned back against the wall, gulping deep breaths. Now Eysteinn and the others brothers came rushing in. Ketil spoke in mocking tone, 'Now's the time to join us, boys, now the fighting's done.'

'Now's the time, horsehole, to put some space between your trunk and your head,' said Eysteinn.

Ketil was still leaning against the wall of the cabin, holding his cloak tightly wrapped round him to contain his entrails. Eysteinn rushed at him and struck him a mighty blow, severing his head cleanly.

He then picked up the head and carried it down to the river, where Ingiborg was still washing her linen. She was wearing a long tunic, a close-fitting bodice and a mantle over her head. Around her shoulders she wore a fine shawl decorated in silver and black stitching. Eysteinn tossed Ketil's head into her basket and laughed, 'Make sure you wash and comb all the blood out of these fair locks, woman.' He took the end of her shawl and wiped the blood from his spear. Ingiborg looked up and, without a word, returned to her washing.

Ulf, who had joined Eysteinn, said, 'That was a vile thing to do, brother, and most merciless of you.'

Eysteinn shrugged. 'She is known to be an ambitious woman. She always wanted to get ahead. Now she has one.'

Ingiborg followed them and talked to the brothers while they untied their horses. She smiled and gave them a wave before turning back. Skeggi Cod-biter remarked that she seemed to care little that her man had been slain.

Eysteinn answered him, 'I suspect that it was not because Ketil's killing meant nothing to her that she saw us off, but rather that she was intent on finding out exactly who had taken part in the attack. She is a strong woman and I am sure we have not heard the last of this.' They carefully lifted Leif's corpse out of the cabin and tied him to his steed. They then rode back to the homestead, this time not even stopping to water their horses.

When they reached Borg, Hoskuld the Great came out of the house to meet them. On seeing the body of his youngest son, he began to wail and beat his chest. The family averted their gaze from this show of unmanliness. 'I have lost my youngest son and am sorely grieved. No good will come of this. There will surely follow bad blood between the families and a claim for compensation at the Assembly.' He ordered the manservants to take Leif's body down from his horse and make preparations for his burial.

Eysteinn strode into the Great Hall to look for his mother. He found her spinning yarn and told her of the deaths of Ketil and her son. She asked him how late in the day it was. He said that it was around noon. Without looking up, she said, 'I have had the busier morning. It has taken six of you to kill Ketil and I have spun seven ells of cloth without help from anybody.'

68

The very next day, Helga was out riding with her son, Skeggi Cod-biter. 'It is reported to me that one of the farmhands of Thorvald the Thin is grazing his cattle on our land.'

'Where is this, Mother?'

'South of the Hafslaek Brook.'

Skeggi knew exactly where she meant. There was a marsh which lay submerged in the winter, but in spring, once the ice had thawed, it was such rich pasture for cows that it was considered to be worth a whole haystack. The Hafslaek Brook had marked the boundary between the two families from early times. 'I know of the situation and can tell you that the matter is in hand, Mother.'

'How is it in hand? It was reported to me only yesterday that the cattle were grazing on our land. So how can it be in hand?'

'I have already spoken to Thorvald's farmhand and told him that he can graze his cattle there this season, but next year we shall be reclaiming it.'

'You are a spineless child!' snapped Helga.

Not wishing to discuss the matter further, Cod-biter spurred his horse on to ride ahead of his mother. No more was spoken of the matter for the rest of the day.

The following morning, Helga served breakfast to her son.

'What is this on my plate, Mother?'

She answered with a snort. 'I have cooked you two ox testicles. It appears you are lacking in this respect. Never, never would your proud grandfather Eirik have acted in this way and it grieves me sorely to have such a coward for a son.'

'Do we have any gravy, Mother?

Helga gave her son a swipe round the back of the head and stormed out of the hall in a rage. As Skeggi chewed on the sinewy testicle, he considered his predicament. He knew only too well that she would goad him at every turn and never leave him in peace. On the other hand, he was in no hurry to confront Thorvald's farmhand.

The man's name was Jokul. He was an exceedingly large and strong man, ugly, stooping, with long legs but a short trunk. Even with his stoop, he stood five hands taller than Skeggi. Jokul was a great troublemaker, overbearing, difficult to deal with, ruthless and excessively quarrelsome. He was also a berserk.

Skeggi finished eating the ox balls and pushed his plate away. He saw that there was only one road to take. He left the chamber, gathered his weapons and rode off towards the Hafslaek Brook. Better to face a berserk than suffer the wrath of a mother, he reasoned.

Cod-biter rode hard and came to the marshes just before noon. He found Jokul sitting barefoot on an outcrop of rock. When the giant saw Skeggi dismount and approach, he began to put his boots on. Noting that the arrival was carrying an axe, he drew his own, Slicer, from his belt.

'What do you want?' he asked gruffly.

'I am here to tell you again that this is my family's land and your pasture is on the other side of the brook.'

'I don't care whose land it is. I will let the cattle be where they want to be.'

'And I say to you once more that you must move the herd over the stream to the other pasture.'

'You can kiss my axe,' said Jokul. 'I have twice your strength, three times your courage and Slicer is four times keener than your weapon.'

'You will do well to mark my words, for you will answer not only to me, but the whole of the Hoskuld family.'

The giant exploded in a roar of laughter. 'Hah! You speak of your dung-beardling brothers.'

Skeggi bristled at the insult. While he knew only too well that rubbing dung on their faces was the only way his younger brothers would ever grow a beard, hearing this from the giant was not to his liking.

Jokul bared his blackened teeth in a wide grin. 'And the old man, Chieftain Hoskuld, is sure to die a straw death.'

To imply that his father would die not the death of a warrior, but the unmanly death of a coward in his bed was too much for Skeggi Cod-biter. The hairs on his neck stood on end. His blood boiled.

The giant, still laughing, stood up and advanced towards Skeggi, axe raised.

'Take care you do not trip on your loose shoelace, Jokul.'

Jokul sat down on the rock again and bent over to tie his shoe. In one bound, Skeggi leapt forward, raised his axe high in the air and struck him on the back of his neck so hard that his huge head fell down onto his chest. Skeggi piled some rocks over the body and rode back to Borg.

There he strode into the Great Hall to find his mother spinning yarn. He told her that he had slain the giant Jokul. She asked him how late in the day it was. He said that it was mid-afternoon.

Without looking up, she said, 'I have had the busier day. You have killed one man and I have spun yarn for three ells of cloth.'

69

It's not often you rejoice at the news that you have to sleep in a sheepshed. But when Rib learned over a bowl of sour whey that he, as the household's shepherd, would not only be permitted but expected to snuggle up beside Gunhilda, Agnes and their sisters, his joy was boundless. The prospect of waking up in the morning to a mouthful of big toe – or something even worse – made his stomach churn.

Ragnar and his flock were pleased, too. They made him stick to his word and each night he told them a fairy tale at bedtime. And what's more, having Katla teach him *The Tale of the Raven, The Hired Hand and the Lake Dwellers*, and other riveting Norse classics was giving his Old Icelandic a much-needed boost. While the leech allowed him to communicate at a certain level – 'No, thank you, I couldn't possibly manage another bowl of curds' ... 'After you with the arsegrass' – it was becoming increasingly clear to him that the Viking tongue was intricate and complex. Not the language of a primitive race at all, in fact. And when a two-year-old ewe tells you that your syntax is shot to bollocks, then it's probably time to do something about it.

Rib surprised himself how quickly he picked up the art of shepherding. Actually, it shouldn't have really come as a surprise. All he had to do was take the lead from Ragnar the Ram – 'I think it's time we went to the upper pasture now' ... 'Looks like we're in for some rain, how about us heading back to the shed?' Nonetheless, it made Rib feel good to think he was in control.

But it wasn't all smooth going. Thrall status meant that he could and would be assigned duties that no-one else wanted. Like watching fish dry. "To watch paint dry" means being bored out of your skull. Which was nothing compared to how he felt sat on an exposed hillside keeping guard over seventy-two cod being wind-dried on a large wooden rack.

Why the hell the fish had to be dried in the first place was beyond him. But here on Iceland, cod was never eaten fresh. Goodness, no! Not until it was dried to the consistency of weathered leather was it deemed fit for consumption, and then only with a liberal dollop of rancid butter. In fact, his brief experience of Viking life had taught him that nothing was eaten fresh. The rivers teemed with salmon – only a couple of days before he'd seen one of the boys return with a basketful. And what did they do with this beautiful fresh fish? Cut it into flakes and hang it in the smokehouse. OK, what's wrong with smoked salmon, you could argue? Well, that depends entirely on the smoke. Only recently had Rib finally cottoned on to the source of fuel which kept the hearth smouldering in the Great Hall. Dried sheep dung ...

Which partly explained the overpowering stench in the longhouse. And there was only one way salmon smoked in sheep dung was going to taste, wasn't there? Nor did it take him long to discover that "Collection of sheep dung for the purpose of smoking fish" was a principal duty on the job description of a thrall-cum-shepherd. To make things easier, he issued immediate instructions to the flock to crap only in designated areas. Much to his annoyance, they didn't take a blind bit of notice and continued to defecate all over the hillside.

Much as he hated to think of his sheep as food on the table, that's what they were. In Rib's view, however, the very least they deserved was the respect of being served with all the trimmings – roast spuds, Yorkshire pud, sprouts and mint sauce. And what did the Vikings do? Cut the mutton into chunks, boil it, squeeze the liquid off, store it between boards for nine months, then serve it all covered in dirt and hair, probably with a dollop of rancid butter. (At this point, Rib felt himself going into a full-on mental rant, but he couldn't help it. He just had to get it off his chest.)

And what's more, sheep's heads, udders, ram's testicles and bone jelly were all cooked and preserved in huge vats of sour whey, stored in the side room to the fire-hall, a dark hell-hole which also housed large tubs of curd and whey, half-sunk into the ground. From this was made the yoghourty skyr, which Vikings seemed to eat morning, noon and night. For a special treat, they chopped up lichen and sprinkled it on the surface, would you believe?

But! But these were nothing compared to the chamber of horrors which Katla the frigging Fair had insisted on showing him the previous week. Every now and then, a poor whale found itself beached on the Borgarfjord shore. It would take two men three whole days to hack the dead creature into manageable chunks. Surely time to bring out the barbecue, crack open a few beers and feast on whale steaks down on the beach? Or maybe cook up a cauldron of whale, potato and leek broth?

No, no, and no.

Instead, they dig a huge hole in the ground – the whale pit - line it with moss and throw the meat in. There, the meat and blubber is covered with turves and left to rot and ferment for a year. Then, and only then, will the Vikings eat it. Raw ...

He'd tried to rationalise why every piece of fresh food had to be preserved to death. No doubt the winter was long and harsh – he could imagine the whole community being holed up for weeks, maybe even months on end. Which would explain why they always needed a plentiful supply of food in storage. But why, on days like this, why not enjoy the pleasure of fresh meat and fish?

Katla the Fair had the answer, of course. 'It has no taste. It is without tang.'

Rib was so reluctant to eat anything put before him that there were times when he was tempted to go down on his hands and knees and munch grass with the flock. To date, he'd resisted the urge, mainly due to the glint in Ragnar's eye. Of all the potential threats to his life – axes, spears, daggers, mudpots, berserks – it was the food he feared the most. Just one melting mouthful of Mum's blueberry muffins ... Just one bite of Sunset's Victoria plum jam on a thick slice of buttered toast. Mmmmm ...

He vent his frustration by chucking a stone at a crowd of crows who had been heckling him all morning. 'Look at the state of its hair,' 'Shagged any sheep lately?' and so on.

'Piss off!' he shouted in crowspeak, which came out as 'Kraaaak!'

'I'll chase them away for you, sunbeam,' came a voice from right behind him, making him jump out of his skin. He spun round to find a small dog with a wiry grey-blue coat staring up at him.

'Who are you?' Rib growled.

'No need to get all shirty, sunbeam. My name's Alf. Alf the Arctic Fox. Now, as I was saying, why don't you just run off and get your hair seen to? There's a stream just the other side of the hill. I'll keep watch and make sure none of those bandits get hold of your fish.'

An Arctic fox called Alf? Certainly a cocky little sod. True, his crackling bird's nest did need to be washed right out of his hair. But leave this chancer in charge of his seventy-two wind-drying cod? Not on his nelly. Foxes, Arctic or otherwise, are known for one thing. Their cunning. 'Thanks, but no thanks,' he barked.

Alf seemed genuinely hurt. 'Look,' he whined, 'you can trust me, sunbeam. Why don't you go and get your hair fixed? What do you think you look like?'

These were the exact words, the exact words his Mum had used whenever he came home with a radical hairstyle or a discreet application of eyeliner, usually at the instigation of the Deccaheads. "Rib Meskitoe, what do you think you look like!"

'The answer is no!' he snapped.

'OK, OK, keep your bird's nest on. Listen, give me just one piece of fish and I'll leave you in peace. You think those crows are bad? I can be really annoying if I put my mind to it.'

'No! Now go away!'

'Oh you really are a bad-tempered little sunbeam, aren't you? Refusing a simple request for one piece of cod in exchange for information about the other frostling ...'

'What? What other frostling?'

'Why should I tell you? You're not even prepared to let a poor old Arctic fox have a – '

'OK, OK, just one.' Rib pulled a near-brittle piece of cod from one of the wooden spikes and held it by the tail in front of the fox's nose. 'Now, what other frostling?'

Alf started to salivate, having eaten nothing but berries for two days. 'Food first,' he barked.

'No, information first,' insisted bird-nest boy.

The fox growled his annoyance, baring his sharp white teeth, before relenting. He was so, so hungry. 'The night you splashed ashore – and what a bloody commotion you made, enough to wake the dead – another frostling had already landed, earlier that night.'

'Where?'

'Just there, near the point,' Alf pointed with his nose.

'What did he look like?'

'White Caucasian, slight limp, brown hair, mole on left cheek, about 1.85 tall and a tattoo on his neck which read Cindy.'

'Really?'

'How the fuck would I know what he looked like! He was two fields away and it was the middle of the bloody night! And anyway ...'

'Yes?'

'Don't take this the wrong way, but you all look the same to us.'

Deep in thought, Rib tossed him the fish. A fully-grown Atlantic cod is a large fish. Alf the Arctic fox attacked his bounty in a systematic feeding frenzy, ripping huge chunks of flesh, first from the sides, followed by the tail, then the head, and finally the bones. The boy observed the cod's disappearing act without emotion. His head was elsewhere, trying to absorb what the fox had told him. How could anyone else have come ashore? He was the sole survivor, wasn't he? Or could it have been someone who hadn't been on board the Lusitanic? Surely not ...

The little fox lipped his lips. Of the huge fish there was not a trace. Not a flake of flesh, not a sliver of skin. 'Thanks, sunbeam, see you around,' he said, making to leave.

'Wait! Where is the other frostling now?'

'Ah, now there's a question. A question worth, oooh, at least two cod, wouldn't you say?'

'Possibly ...'

'Well, I'm fit to burst, sunbeam. So, if you will excuse me, we'll save that conversation for another day. When are you next on drying-duty?'

'Er ... I'm not sure.'

'Don't worry, I'll look out for you. See you later, sunbeam.' And with that, Alf trotted off, belly dragging along the ground.

'Wait! There's one more thing.'

'Yeah?'

'There's been some incidents over the last couple of days. Reports of sheep being chased by a wild animal. That's not you, by any chance?'

'No, not guilty. That'll be Ulf the Wolf.'

'Ulf the Wolf?'

'You're a quick learner, sunbeam. Now, if that's all, I'll be off.'

Rib hadn't heard anything about there being wolves on Iceland. 'You promise me you're telling the truth,' he shouted after him. 'It's not you harassing the sheep, is it?'

Alf the Arctic fox barked over his shoulder, 'I promise! No worries!'

70

Leif Tanglehair was lain to rest in the ship grave of his ancestors, in a sand dune along the shore some ten minutes' walk from the Borg homestead. The young Viking body, swathed in white linen, was carefully placed in the grave dug beside the bones of his forefathers. The boat had been built centuries before, when larch and spruce were in plentiful supply. A length of white whalebone adorned each side of the stern. Leif took with him a collection of precious artefacts: a pendant of gilt bronze; a fashioned piece of lead inlaid with green-coloured glass; two bronze bracelets; sixteen sparkling beads and a silver Thor's hammer, placed on the middle of his chest. In the hope that Leif Tanglehair would pay more attention to his personal grooming in the afterlife, a walrus-bone comb rested in each of his upturned palms.

From their vantage point high on the upper pastures, Odd the Pale and Ragnar the Ram watched the solemn procession file back to the farmstead. After a few moments' respectful silence, Ragnar said, 'That boat won't be going anywhere, you know. The tide doesn't come in that far. They should have put it in the water. I've been watching it every day and it hasn't moved an inch.' He chewed on a stem of wiry grass. 'How do they think it's going to float when it's filled with sand? And then they pile stones on top of it! Fools!' Odd decided to leave undisturbed the universe according to Ragnar and said nothing.

Later that afternoon, Katla came to find Rib up on the meadows. 'Come, Odd the Pale, you are to join the family in the festivities.'

'Festivities?'

'Yes, today we shall celebrate the life of my brave uncle Leif and the heroic act of Skeggi in slaying the giant, Jokul.'

If only the giant had won, dreamed Rib. Split Skeggi Cod-biter in two with a blow from his axe, cut his flesh into fish-finger-size pieces and then sizzled them in a pan, liberally doused with blood-red tomato sauce. He stopped short the fantasy there and then – he'd only been there a few weeks and was already thinking like a Viking ...

'Food and drink will be plentiful,' said Katla.

Yeah, right, like a bowl of curds to eat and a bowl of sour whey to drink. No, wait, maybe they'll bring out the pickled cockroach.

'And there will be ale.'

Now this puts a different complexion on things, he thought, as he left Ragnar with instructions and followed the slight figure of Thorkatla Grimsdottir back down the hillside. When had he last had a drink? Memories of sharing an after-hours growler of Dog's Dribble with Sunset listening to Pink Floyd came flooding back. Sunset Todd, you'd get me out of this mess. How I wish you were here ...

71

A truly remarkable scene awaited them at Borg. The flat area immediately in front of the longhouse had been transformed into a scene half-way between a street party and a school sports day: a square of the field roped off with brightly coloured rag bunting; two long trestle tables groaning under the weight of food and drink; Hoskuld and Helga sitting very king-and-queen-like in their high seats; and music, albeit strangely off-beat – a stringed instrument playing a dirge to a repeated single drumbeat. The whole community was gathered and seemed to be in high spirits. In the crowd were many faces Rib didn't recognise, presumably from the brothers' households.

Katla was quick to point out her family members. 'Be careful of them,' she warned. 'When they drink, they can become crazed.' On the topic of crazed, Rib was keeping a watchful eye on the towering figure of Grim Bellower, standing at the far end of the table, ale horn in hand. He hoped Katla's Dad wasn't going to drink too much, having seen the carnage he could create when sober.

There was no queue for the food, just a mad scramble. When he finally managed to push himself to the front, Rib's jaw dropped. Before him on a circular wooden platter was a large stone-baked flatbread, covered in melted cheese and topped with thyme. He tore off a slice and bit into it. Pizza! Delicious, four-cheese pizza! He couldn't believe it! As he gobbled the slice down, his eyes greedily scanned the rest of the table and nearly popped out of their sockets. He saw filo prawns, he saw spring rolls, he saw cheese and bacon quiche, sausage rolls, garlic bread, onion rings, potato wedges. And, at the far end, Black Forest gateau, sugared doughnuts and custard slices. Absolutely unbelievable! He thought he'd died and gone to heaven, and hurried to pile as much as he could onto his board, before joining Katla, who was dipping a celery stick into a bowl of skyr.

'This is brilliant,' he said between mouthfuls.

'It is not to my taste,' she replied, rather snootily. 'It is good fortune that we eat such food only on the occasion of births, deaths and marriages.'

'Well, I think it's bloody fantastic. Do you have a name for this type of feast?'

'We call it Iceland Party Food.'

'It's great! It must have taken loads of people hours to prepare.'

'No, the food is prepared by one woman.' She pointed at a dumpy, suntanned maid flirting with Thorkel Twig-belly by the entrance to the house.

'What? You're telling me she did all this on her own?'

'Yes.'

'Wow! She must be a good cook.'

'That is not all for which she is renowned,' scoffed Katla, again staring fiercely in the direction of the maid, who now seemed to have her hand down the front of Twig-belly's breeches. 'She is a frilla.'

The leech crackled at the last word, unable to find an exact translation. But Rib got the drift. 'What's her name?'

'Kerrika Toenail.'

A loud trumpet blast signalled the start of the games.

The first contest involved hurling a ball-shaped boulder encased in an animal skin. A knock-kneed thrall named Arvid stood nervously in the outfield holding a marker pole. The first contestant, Eysteinn Shaggy-breeches, strode into the field and gathered up the two lengths of rope attached to the skin. He then swung the boulder in a circular motion, slowly at first, spinning his body round faster and faster until he released the boulder with a shout, sending it high into the air. With a shrill shriek, even louder than Eysteinn's, Knock-kneed Arvid flung himself to his right as the rock embedded itself into the turf on the very spot where he'd been standing. The crowd cheered and everyone thought that it was an excellent throw which would be hard to beat.

Other throws followed, but none as far as Eysteinn's effort. Up stepped Grim Bellower, the final contestant. A hush fell over the spectators. A ptarmigan rattled somewhere on the fell. The huge man spat on the palms of his hands, grasped the two ropes and started to spin. Accelerating until he was no more than a blur, he let out a blood-curdling howl as he released the ball. In the wrong direction. It was a lottery where it would land. Screams rang out from the crowd – the rock was flying towards the longhouse.

The turf on the roof of a Viking building is especially lush, mainly due to it being untrampled and seldom waterlogged. The sure-footed Gisli the Goat had climbed up and was happily chewing the succulent grass. He liked to eat on the roof at this time of day, midway between morning meal and lunch. He called it Munch. Mid-afternoon, he also liked to partake of a light meal up on the roof, from where he could look down on all the humans and animals in the field below. He called it High Tea.

Gisli the Goat was just ruminating how perfect life was – mouthful of sweet grass, sun on his back, both

eyes pointing in the same direction at once, for a change
– when his bliss was shattered, as was his skull, by the
meteoric arrival of the skin-clad boulder. If Rib had
been wearing his leech on the other earlobe, he would
have heard the poor creature's last word. 'Oooff!'

The goat's lifeless form fell to earth with a thud
on the other side of the longhouse. No amulets, beads
or rings were to adorn his deceased body. No place
was found for him in a boat grave in the dunes. Gisli
the Goat was lain to rest in a vat of curdled milk to
marinate over the winter. As a token gesture, a handful
of juniper berries was scattered over the surface.

Melkorka of the shapely shins was serving ale
from a massive cauldron. Rib overheard the whispered
conversation of two farmhands in front of him in the
queue, catching the word "brisk". They were clearly
talking about her. If "brisk" meant what he thought it
did, he was inclined to agree. When it came to his turn,
Rib took one of the ale-horns from the table and held it
out.

'No-ooo!' she hissed and snatched it from his grasp.
'Cannot you see that this belongs to Skeggi Cod-biter?
Cannot you read the runes?' She pointed at the angular
inscription which ran round the lip of the finely carved
horn.

Well, actually, no, he couldn't read the bloody
runes. He was having enough trouble keeping up with
the everyday language to have time to decode stupid
stick symbols.

'It appears to me that you are a muchly foolish
boy. Do you not realise what would befall you if he
had discovered the theft? Take one of those,' she said,
pointing to a stack of wooden bowls.

First the latrine scene, and now this. Somehow, he
wasn't quite hitting it off with Melkorka. 'Thanks,' he
muttered, avoiding her stern gaze as she ladled ale into

his bowl. Having beaten a hasty retreat to the far side of the field, he inspected and sniffed the cloudy brew in the bowl. Definitely not an IPA, yet too light to be a porter. He took a cautious sip. Mmm, interesting ... Something of a barley wine about it, without the sweetness. One swallow told him that the ale was strong. Very, very strong. Journey into space strong. The type of brew confined to a small snifter glass in the Waterloo. Not having had a drink for ages, however, he necked it down in three. My God! Twenty percent proof, it had to be! Wiping the froth from his lips, he went back for more.

Katla the Fair found him an hour later sitting on the ground, slouched against the homefield wall, snoring his head off. She woke him with a kick to his side. He opened his eyes, blinked twice, then began bleating at her. 'You have not heeded my words, Odd the Pale. Nothing good will come of drinking ale in the afternoon. Thor's Hammer will wreak its revenge on you.'

Thor's Hammer was the name given to the super-potent ale brewed for special occasions:

- After one bowl, you were rat-arsed
- After two bowls, you had the gait of a goat with three legs
- After three bowls, you were away with the Valkyries
- After four bowls, you were struggling with your serpent
- After five bowls, you were hammered out of sight.

'How many bowls have you drunk, Odd the Pale?'
'Shicks ...'

'That is not good. Come, I shall pour cold water over your head.'

Attractive as this sounded, Rib refused to budge. He couldn't. She left him to slip back into a deep slumber for the rest of the afternoon.

Katla returned two hours later to rouse him by inserting the point of a carrot into his right ear and twiddling it like a pencil in a pencil-sharpener. It could have been worse – she could easily have selected an alternative orifice.

'Ow! What the hell are you doing?'

'It is time for you to wake. The final games are now taking place. Come!'

His stupor having receded to goat-gait level, he managed to stagger in the girl's footsteps to where the crowd were cheering the contestants in the games square. The wrestling match was nearing its conclusion. Thorkel Twigbelly was now regretting his energy-sapping exertions with Kerrika Toenail behind the cattle byre. Ulf the Fart clearly had the upper hand, lifting him high above his head and whirling him round, before throwing him to the ground in a body smash which shook the earth.

'Do you yield?' asked Ulf for the umpteenth time.

'Rather I would yield to the curved prick of a mountain troll than yield to you!' came the answer.

The crowd gasped as Ulf lowered his trousers and sat on the face of his brother. They knew what was coming next and held their noses. Ulf the Fart then did what he did best and was declared the winner by knockout. It took four men to carry the limp figure of Thorkel Twigbelly from the field.

A thrall named Gylfi said, 'It is an ill wind when a match is decided so.'

'An ill wind it certainly was,' replied a fellow-thrall named Skum.

The final event was a ball game in which large men

knocked seven bells out of each other with wooden bats. The ball had little to do with the proceedings, often taking on a passive spectator role as tackles flew, shins barked and noses bled. The bone-crunching championship decider was being played out between Skeggi Cod-biter and Finn Flat-nose. As far as Rib could make out, the score was three apiece and Finn was pressing for the winner. Having manoeuvred himself into a strong field position, he tossed the ball in the air and was about to thwack it goalwards when Skeggi flattened him with a flying body check that wouldn't have looked out of place in the wrestling bout. Standing over his prone opponent, he picked up Finn's bat and broke it in two. Less than amused at this, Finn struggled to his feet and pushed Skeggi roughly to the floor.

Helga brought the ensuing scrap to an abrupt halt by striding across the field of play, grabbing both sons by their hair and cracking their skulls together. The sickening thud of bone on bone echoed off the rock face on the far side of the fjord. 'Enough! Let no more blood be spilt between brothers. Let the homefields of others play host to our battles. The Great Chieftain Hoskuld declares the games to be over!' (Which was rather odd, because at that very moment, the Great Chieftain Hoskuld was sitting on the latrine, his mind elsewhere, with a strained look on his face). A muted cheer greeted her announcement, the crowd disappointed that play had been stopped just when things were starting to get lively. But no-one argued …

Katla joined Rib. 'How is your head now?'

'It's, er, OK, I think. What happens now?' People were clearing away the tables and chairs and filing back into the longhouse.

'There will be a rest-pause before the festivities begin.'

Oh, good, thought Rib. Would be nice to grab a couple of dozen zeds.

'But not for you, Odd the Pale. Your flock awaits you on the high pasture and they must be safely returned to their shed by nightfall.'

Odd the Pale has not a happy bunny as he trudged up the hill.

72

Still nursing the mother-and-father of all hangovers, it was late in the evening by the time he'd finally found the flock up near the shieling, driven them home and settled them down with a bedtime story – *The Wizard of the Westman Isles*, one of Ragnar's favourites. In two minds whether to go back down to the hall or not, the call of the ale prevailed and he headed off down the hill again.

The noise of a party in full swing drifted up onto the fells. Two flaming torches either side of the longhouse door guided him in like beacons in the half-light. A group of farmhands standing at the entrance stopped talking as soon as he approached and made no move to step aside. Rib sidled round them, avoiding eye contact with their sullen stares.

Once inside, he immediately sensed that something was different. Or rather, everything was different: the fish-bone floor was covered with a carpet of dried reeds; a brightly-coloured tapestry hung on the ante-chamber's previously bare wall; a posy of delicate white flowers adorned the latrine door. Stepping into the Great Hall, it was hard to believe that this was the same place. The wall of sound which met him was like last orders at the New Pitz, when you had to press your mouth to a mate's ear to make yourself heard. Everybody seemed to be shouting. Music from a number of stringed instruments struggled against the raucous hubbub. Flaming brands in metal holders lit up more red and gold tapestries. A roaring fire replaced the smouldering sheep dung in the hearth, a thrall feeding the blaze with dried willow root and brushwood. A carcass roasted on a spit, fillets of oily fish sizzled on a griddle, a concoction of something smelling strongly alcoholic simmered away in a pot. Hoskuld and Helga sat in serene silence, surveying the scene from their high seats. Both wore fine robes, their arms heavy with amulets.

Rib gave them a wide berth, edging his way through the throng to the back of the hall. The wide bench where he had once licked another man's toe had been pulled out to form a large table, where hot and cold meats were piled high on wooden platters beside trays of freshly baked bread and dishes of salmon and other small fish which he didn't recognise. Rib folded a thin bread round a slice of warm lamb and bit into the wrap. It was delicious, the meat juicy and tender, the bread soft and fresh. Why couldn't they eat like this all the time?

Now that his stomach was lined, he headed for the drinks table. And who should be standing there, ladle in hand, but the beautiful Melkorka. He wondered what he would call her if they were on more intimate terms. Mel? Or Korka? That was a no-brainer ...

'So, Odd the Pale returns for more punishment. Is that a wise thing to do?' came her words of welcome. Ignoring her comment, he ordered a Thor's Hammer. She smiled as she ladled the brew into a bowl. 'Take heed of my words, for I have a feeling that you may be called upon to show your manliness before the night is out.'

Ten out of ten for directness, he thought, returning her smile. 'Fear not, Melkorka, I will be ready and more than able.'

Her sky-blue eyes captured his. She held out the

bowl of ale. He reached to take it and their fingers touched. She did not withdraw her hand, but held it there, her forefinger slowly caressing his thumb ...

'So here you are, Odd the Pale,' came the shrill voice of Little Miss Piss-on-My-Parade. 'Come quickly, it is time for the skaldic verse.' Thorkatla Grimsdottir tugged at his arm to pull him away. Melkorka let go of his hand. He tried to catch her eyes, but she was already serving someone else. The moment was gone.

Through gritted teeth he snarled, 'Thank you, Katla, thank you so very much.'

'Katla the Fair!' she squeaked up at him. Should he pour the ale over her head and smash the bowl down on her tiny skull now? He was sorely tempted. Instead, he took a deep breath, then an even deeper draught of his ale and followed her back into the main body of the longhouse.

Chieftain Hoskuld slowly rose to his feet and the hubbub in the room subsided. 'Welcome, family, friends and household to the Great Hall of Borg. We gather here to hail the heroic deeds of Eysteinn and Skeggi and ...' he paused to wipe away a tear, '... and to mourn the loss of their brave brother, Leif. I call upon my son, Eysteinn, to speak a verse.'

The man called Shaggy-breeches rose to his feet, ale horn in hand, bowed once to his father, once to his mother, then recited:

'Home to Ketil we rode
To draw our war twigs
On that foul bearer of lies.
Brave son of Hoskuld,
That valiant Leif,
Was dealt death there.

My wound-sickle was stained
With the braggart's gore.
His Leg-biter lost its gleam.
Ravens gorged upon his blood
When Ketil ran out of steam.'

The gathered assembly murmured its approval.
'You have spoken well, my son. I now call upon your brother, Finn, to speak a verse telling of his brother's slaying of the giant.'

The man called Flat-nose rose to his feet, bowed once to his father, once to his mother, then recited:

'Skeggi's breeches filled with fear
When Jokul raised his axe.
Life hung but by a shoestring
As the giant made to attack.

Skeggi's chopper, quick to rise,
Won warm blood for the raven.
The berserk mountain now lies slain
Beneath a mound of stone.

Let us leave no drop undrunk,
Bring brimful horns 'til morn!'

The whole hall cheered and raised their drinking vessels. Unable to locate Melkorka anywhere, Rib decided to spend the evening in the company of Thor's Hammer and nestled in a seat in the far corner of the chamber, getting quietly pissed while observing the increasingly boisterous behaviour of the increasingly drunken Hoskuld household from a safe distance. At one stage, the shouting and cursing became so loud that he switched leech to hold a perfectly civilised conversation with a cockroach called Kormak. Once his little friend had scuttled back into a crack in the wall, Rib settled back to soak up the atmosphere, which was getting lively, to say the least. As the ale flowed, the tempers flared, particularly between Thorkel and Ulf. Hardly surprising, given that the former had had his face smothered by the hairy arse of the latter earlier on in the day. Without warning, Thorkel strode over to where Ulf was sitting, seized him by the shoulders and violently thrust him up against a pillar, lifting him off his feet. He followed this up by spewing a torrent of sick all over Ulf's face, into his eyes and down his beard. Near to choking, Ulf reached for his sword and had to be restrained before he had the chance to cut at his brother. In an instant, the hall had fallen silent, save Ulf's grunting and cursing in his attempts to break free. Everybody present who had witnessed the act knew that Thorkel had committed a base and despicable deed by vomiting in his brother's face in the Great Hall. He should have done it outside ...

That is to say, all in the hall fell silent apart from Little Rib Horner, sat in the corner, for once not eating his curds and whey, but instead well into his fourth bowl of Viking brew. Finding the whole episode hilarious beyond words, he was now laughing his head off at the globules of spew trickling down Ulf's beard. 'Carrots!' he gurgled. 'And sweetcorn! Where the fuck did the sweetcorn come from?' The next thing he knew, he was being picked up in the air and thrown down onto the floor like a rag doll.

Skeggi Cod-biter stood over him, hand on sword. 'So, the frostling chooses to pour scorn on our family. I think it is time to put him to the test again. This one he will not find so easy.' As he spoke, he deftly grabbed a length of cord from a table and tied Rib's hands tight behind his back.

Finn piped in, 'And let him have company. The useless idiot Arvid deserves punishment for dropping the skin of milk yesterday. Let them both be put to the test!' The hapless Knock-kneed Arvid and Rib were bundled out of the longhouse into the cold night air. The two were led, stumbling, out of the homefield and up the hill, guided by regular slaps on their calves from the flat of Cod-biter's blade.

Behind them, Rib thought he could make out the chant from the crowd:

'Thrall-scald!
Thrall-scald!
Thrall-scald!'

73

Six thralls ran ahead with flaming brands, their enthusiasm doubtless fired by the fact that they would not be starring in the evening's performance. They were heading towards the hot springs.

Thrall-scald. That could mean only one thing ...

Arvid had clearly been there before and was struggling to break free from the walking headlock applied by Finn Flat-nose. What were they going to do? Throw them into a pool of boiling mud? Was this how it all was going to end? Would he be spending the rest of eternity lying in a burial ship covered in sand? No, stupid, he wouldn't be that lucky. More likely, his body would be thrown off a cliff to splatter on the rocks below.

The advance party had now reached the smoking field and formed two lines of blazing torches, like runway lights on an airstrip at night. Why had they stopped? They seemed to be forming a pathway, but to where? The answer came in the shape of a gush of seething mud, which spurted into the air with an angry hiss at the far end of the guard of honour.

The Slob! They were going to throw him into the Slob! He turned to run but came face to face with the grinning Cod-biter, fingering the blade of his sword. The crowd had now gathered round and set up the

chant again, those who bore weapons beating their shields in a frenzy:
'*Thrall-scald!*
Thrall-scald!
Thrall-scald!'
'The rules of the thrall-scald are thus,' said Finn Flat-nose. 'The thrall must leap over the Slob within the count of ten. He who fails to complete the leap will be thrown in and boiled alive.'

My God! They had to jump over the bloody thing! Was this why Katla had been so insistent on stopping to explain to him the Slob's eruptions? Addled by the ale, his recollection of the detail was unclear. All he could remember was some sort of counting rhyme. In a state of panic, he desperately scanned the faces in the crowd, but she was nowhere to be seen. Where the hell was she when he needed her?

The skinny little runt named Arvid was first to go. Flat-nose untied his hands, manoeuvred the boy into position with a boot up the backside, then raised his sword as a starting signal. 'The thrall-scald commences … now!'

'One – two – three …' screamed the crowd. The clock was counting down, but the boy didn't move a muscle. He had clearly done this before. The Slob exploded into life on the count of four and shot a jet of boiling mud into the air. At this, Arvid sprang to life and sprinted towards the seething pot. 'Five – six – seven …' His take-off foot hit the rim of the crater and he soared over the bubbling pot in classic long-jump style, pelvis thrust forward, torso arched backward, arms high above his head, legs whirring in a bicycle kick. It was an awesome jump. 'Eight – nine …'

The Slob spat an angry jet skyward. The only problem with the classic long jump style is that the hindmost part of the athlete to land in the pit is the bum. Arvid screamed as his backside was blistered by a spray of sulphurous steam and he landed in a crumpled heap in the black lavadirt, writhing in agony. The crowd fell still.

'Ten ...' said someone from the back.

Two maids ran forward to carry the poor wretch away. His screams could still be heard from up on the plateau as they gently lowered him into the soothing waters of the pool.

Rib felt his knees knocking. What had the girl said? One potato, two potatoes, three potatoes, four? No, that wasn't it. He was still racking his brain for the rhyme when he felt his hands cut loose and Finn raised and lowered his sword again. The count began: 'One ... two ...'

Rib Meskitoe didn't check for bubbles on the surface. Rib Meskitoe disregarded the significance of four skrimsls and eight skrimsls. He just ran full-pelt towards the crater with a full-blooded scream: 'Aaaaaaarghhhhhh!'

As is often the case when the human body and mind experience extreme trauma, everything goes into slow-motion – the flickering of the torches, the crunch of the loose lava underfoot, the contorted faces of the baying crowd, the overpowering fumes of the acrid pool – as he launched himself, eyes closed, into the air. The gathered assembly groaned its disappointment to see the flying thrall crash-land on the other side unscathed. The Slob sputtered its utter disgust, its scalding spurt having missed the flailing form by a whisker, cursing in rage as its lethal spray had come within a hair's breadth of stripping the skin off the human daring to violate its airspace.

'Ten ...' said someone from the back.

Rib opened his eyes and saw the tiny face of Katla,

who was lying beside him with her cheek pressed to the ground, their noses nearly touching.

'You failed to heed my advice, Odd the Pale. You are fortunate indeed to have survived the Ordeal of the Slob.'

'No thanks to you! Where were you when I needed you?'

Before she could reply, a large boot moved her aside. It belonged to a large right foot, which belonged to the large body of Skeggi Cod-biter, stood towering above them. The Viking, clearly vexed at the thrall's escape, placed this large boot on the side of Rib's head and proceeded to grind his cheek into the brittle lava cinder. Immediately, Rib could feel not only pain but also the heat rising through the thin crust of rock from the boiling matter beneath. 'You are mistaken if you believe your trials are over. I will haunt you like an unwelcome spirit. I will be your death shadow.'

The grinding of soft cheekbone into hard cinder was cut short by the plaintive bleating of a sheep. Two farmhands carrying a struggling ewe, shorn of her shaggy coat, stepped over Rib and continued up the path. Skeggi's attention was drawn to the other side of the steaming field, where a large shambling shape was pacing up and down.

'Look yonder, Thorkatla Grimsdottir. Your father is ready to rumble.'

He then turned to join the throng, jostling and elbowing its way up the narrow track. Rib sat up and put his hand to his cheek. It was bleeding and hurt like hell.

'You will live,' said Katla, taking his hand. 'Come, or we will miss the sheephurl.'

Live and kicking, the ewe was suspended over the crater of the geyser by ropes attached to each limb, pulled taut to position her exactly above the centre. It was Gunhilda ...

'Noo-oh! Stop!' Rib rushed forward.

A small leg stretched out to trip him, sending him sprawling face first into the lavagrit for a second time. 'Do nothing, Odd the Pale. My uncle will need little persuasion to do likewise with you, to see you boiled alive.'

Boiled alive ...

Gunhilda's eyes met his as the men started to lower her toward the simmering surface. Rib Meskitoe then made the mistake of a lifetime. He switched the leech.

'Oh, Rib, please help me. It hurts so much,' she bleated. 'Help me, Rib, please help me.' Then came a scream of agony.

He turned away, staggering back a few paces before being violently ill. Geysir now became still, swirling eddies sinewed across its surface as if savouring its latest sacrifice. Then, from nowhere, the huge bell-dome of water rose in the centre of the basin, carrying with it the body of the ewe, still bleating a tortured cry. The men shouted excitedly and held the ropes taut. As quickly as it had risen, the dome fell.

'Ready!' shouted the crowd. At this signal, the giant figure of Grim Bellower started to foam at the mouth and beat his chest, before setting off on a shambling run across the smouldering crust of the lavafield. Then the second bell rose and on it the now lifeless form of the sheep.

'Steady!' everyone screamed. The berserk now started to sprint, looking back over his left shoulder. 'Blow!' cried the crowd. The men released the ropes, the geysir sucked its dome inward in one last deep breath before erupting. The earth trembled at the mighty thump of the jet which catapulted Gunhilda fifty metres up into the night sky. Her body wore a death-shroud of vapour, which drifted down the field to fall as scalding drizzle. Now running at full pelt, the massive hulk of the berserk dived full length to catch the steamed carcass in his outstretched arms. The flank of the ewe and Grim's right shoulder sizzled as they hit the red-hot grit. 'Touchdown!' screamed the crowd.

With a roar, the giant rose to his feet and carried his feast off the field to a raised slab of rock, where he ripped and tore into the flesh of his catch with the feeding frenzy of a great white shark. Their entertainment now at an end, the crowd started to drift back down the path towards the longhouse. The traumatised boy stood rooted to the spot, unable to move. He had witnessed it all. Every nightmarish clip of this reality horror-movie, frame by frame. How his friend had been brutally tortured, then slaughtered in a depraved act of cruelty. All for the sake of ... what would they call it? Sport? And what had he done to stop it?

Nothing.

The very thought of the atrocity made him retch again, his whole body quivering with grief. Now thoroughly chilled by the combination of cold night air and shock, he finally wandered back down the path, oblivious to a disdainful spit from the Slob. Approaching the longhouse, he could hear the party back in full swing again: music, singing, raised voices – some in laughter, some in anger. He didn't join them. He had no place with these people.

Instead, he walked aimlessly around the homefield in the pale light of the Arctic night, until he came to the pen in the far corner. The pen into which Gunhilda had reversed with such glee. The forlorn figure of Odd the Pale opened the five-bar gate, entered the enclosure and sat down on the wet turf, hands clasped around his shins, rocking to and fro. There, he sang softly to himself a doleful Hendrix ballad about a girl with a wheelchair on the shore, who watched her golden-winged ship sail on by.

The gate squeaked open. 'What are you doing here?' asked Katla. 'It is too cold for you to be here. Come into the Great Hall and be with us.'

'Go away, little girl.'

She turned and disappeared without a word. A few minutes later, she came back to place a heavy cloak carefully over his shoulders. She left him, again without a word.

The first orange glow of the morning sun had begun to appear over the high mountain crags when he set off back up the hill to the sheep-shed. A sleepless night of turmoil had resulted in two decisions:

Decision Number One: He would never, ever allow a morsel of meat to pass his lips again.

Decision Number Two: He had to get out of this place.

Ragnar was up, waiting for him. 'Rib!' he bleated. 'Thank Thor you have returned! Two men came and took Gunhilda and she has been gone all night. Have you seen her?'

'No,' he lied, pushing his way past the ram to crawl into his bed, where he tried to get to sleep. But however much he screwed his eyes tight shut, he couldn't stop the tears from pouring down his cheeks.

74

Twenty days after Ketil's burial, Ingiborg summoned her sons to her leek garden. When they arrived, they saw spread out on the ground garments of linen, a shirt and breeches greatly stained with blood. Ingiborg then spoke, 'What you see here reproaches you for not seeking revenge for your father. I have few words to add to these clothes as a reminder.'

The sons were much shaken by their mother's words and could only answer that they felt too young to seek revenge and lacked someone strong to lead them. Ingiborg said that she suspected they gave more thought to horse fights and looking at themselves in mirrors than planning retribution. The sons were hurt at these remarks and could not sleep that night. They spoke of their grief and their mother's reproaching tones. Together, they agreed that they should tell her that they now wished to seek revenge, which they did over morning meal the following day. Ingiborg immediately saddled her horse and rode out alone to where a man called Hallvard the Log lived.

He greeted her: 'It is five years past that we last met, Ingiborg. I suspect you do not come to engage in little talk.'

She paused, then said, 'It seems to me, Hallvard, as if my sons have now had their fill of doing nothing and are in the mood to avenge their father. Things have had to wait until now because I felt they were too young to be picking up their swords straight away to slay their father's killer, Eysteinn Shaggy-breeches.'

Hallvard answered, 'I know not of what interest that is to me. You will remember, I am certain, that you refused to marry me. I have not changed my mind. The question is, whether you are prepared to consider a change in yours.'

Ingiborg then spoke: 'It appears that no-one is more suited to lead such a difficult undertaking than you, Hallvard.'

'I do not feel it beyond me to take Eysteinn, or anyone else for that matter, if you are the prize. There, I've said my last word on it. If you promise before witnesses to marry me, I will help your sons get revenge.' Ingiborg replied that she would keep any promise she made and asked Hallvard to ride back with her to her homestead.

On their return, she summoned her sons, who came at once. Their mother explained the situation to them. 'Hallvard has promised to offer his leadership for a journey to avenge your father. Hallvard has made it a condition for the journey that I agree to marry him. I wish now to declare, before you all as my witnesses, that I promise to marry Hallvard and no other man if Ketil's death is avenged.' Hallvard nodded, satisfied that the promise was binding enough and looked to the sons for their response.

'Mother,' said Hunbogi the Bald. 'It is true that we do indeed now wish to avenge our good father's death and Hallvard the Log has the reputation of being first to draw his sword, but –'

'Yes?' snapped Ingiborg, clearly angered at her son's hesitancy.

'His previous marriage was the source of dishonour and public humiliation throughout the land.'

Ingiborg sucked in a deep breath, upset by her son moving against her plan. Before she could reply, Hallvard spoke:

'Let me now tell, in my own words, of this injustice. My wife, Unn, went to her father, Hrapp, to tell him that I was unable to consummate the marriage and give her satisfaction. So much is true. Those were her very words.'

The brothers sneaked grins at each other.

Ingiborg then spoke: 'I do not see what business this is of ours!'

'Allow me to speak further,' said Hallvar. 'The exact words of Unn to her father were as follows: "Whenever he touches me, he becomes so enlarged that we cannot have enjoyment ... (here, Hallvard paused to form a circle between thumb and second finger, at which Solvi the Squint rubbed his eyes, Auðun Noisy-arse let go a flapper, and Ingiborg swallowed hard) ... although we both passionately desire to reach consummation. But we have never succeeded. And yet, before we draw apart, he always proves to me that by nature he is as virile as other men."

Thorvald the Thin whispered to Skallagrim the Vain what everybody present was thinking: 'So that's why they call him Hallvard the Log.'

'Mother, I do not feel that this union will be a satisfactory one,' said Solvi the Squint.

'On the contrary,' she answered back. 'It is clear to me that Hallvard is an upstanding man and I believe that I will be wholly satisfied with the arrangement and the sooner it happens the better.' Thus, Ingiborg brought the conversation to a close and it was settled that Hallvard would lead the attack.

75

Early the following morn, Hallvard rode off with Ingiborg's sons – Hunbogi the Bald, Thorvald the Thin, Hakon Neck, Solvi the Squint, Skallagrim the Vain and, bringing up the rear, Auðun Noisy-arse. They rode hard without stopping and reached the outlying fields of Grisatunga early in the evening. They noted that a shieling stood a short distance from the water's edge on the west side of the river.

Hallvard told them that they would make camp and spend the night there. 'I shall go up and look around, to find out whether Eysteinn is at home. I am told that he often has a servant or two with him and is ever on guard, sleeping in a sturdily-built closet.' The brothers, being tired and eager to rest, said that he should do what he thought best.

In the morning, Eysteinn awoke, told his shepherd boy to leave his bed and go outside to look around to see if there were any men gathering there. 'I had a dream last night which greatly troubled me.'

The boy, although eighteen years of age, was of slight build and bore the countenance of a maiden. His name was Gurli. He did as asked and was gone for quite some time. When he returned, his master asked him what he had seen. 'I have seen something worthy of telling,' he said. Eysteinn asked what this was and the shepherd boy replied that he had seen no small number of men gathering, 'And they do not look like they come from these parts.'

Eysteinn asked, 'Where were they when you saw them and what were they doing? Did you notice their appearance, how they were dressed?'

'I crept up quite close to them, master, but was so stricken with fear that I rushed straight back. They are but a short distance away from the shieling and are eating their morning-meal.'

Eysteinn asked whether they were sitting in a circle or a row. The boy answered that they sat in a circle, already mounted in their saddles, with one man a distance away.

'Try and remember what these men looked like. I want to see if I can guess from your description who they are.'

Gurli said, 'One of them sat on a saddle of coloured leather and wore a black cloak. He was a good-looking man, but with little hair.'

Eysteinn said, 'I recognise this man clearly from your words. You have seen Hunbogi the Bald. I suspect I know what he is doing here.'

'Next to him sat a man on a purple saddle. He was wearing a tunic of scarlet and wore a large bright ring on his hand. About his head was fastened a gold-embroidered band.'

Eysteinn sat down next to the shepherd boy and held his hand while he continued. 'This man had fair hair, falling in waves down to his shoulders. He was of fair complexion, with handsome blue eyes and clipped eyebrows. He was well-built at the shoulders and broad across the chest. His smooth hands were well formed,' … Eysteinn clasped the boy's hand a little tighter … 'and his arms were strong and muscular. I must say that he looked a valiant man. Yet he was also youthful, with hardly a hair on his face. It seemed to me that his face was burdened with sorrow.'

'Yes, it is a shame to see such grief on such a pretty face,' said Eysteinn. 'You have observed this man well and, from your description, I will imagine this man to be the first man's brother, Skallagrim the Vain. He is, indeed, said to be a good-looking young man.' He gently began to stroke the shepherd boy's arm.

'Another man sat on an enamelled saddle, wearing a yellow-green tunic. He was also a thick-set, handsome youth, with curly brown hair that suited him well.'

'I think I know who this man is, too. You have described Hakon Neck. You are indeed a clever lad with a keen eye. And such soft skin,' he added, as he stroked the boy's cheek.

'Next to him sat a young man wearing black breeches and a black tunic girded at the waist ...'

'Most fetching.'

'... who had a thin, slender face and pleasing features.'

'He is one of the younger brothers and goes by the name of Thorvald the Thin. We have indeed a nice group of well-mannered young men come to pay us a visit.' Eysteinn loosened the top tie of the shepherd boy's tunic.

'Shall I continue, master?'

'Yes, please do. Take no notice of my actions.'

'Next was a man of mighty build. He was sitting on a stand-up saddle. He wore no jewellery. A warrior, by the look of him. No longer young, he bore a scar across one cheek.'

Eysteinn jumped to his feet and adjusted his breeches. 'Your tale takes a turn for the worse. This man you have seen must be none other than Hallvard the Log. He has not come to borrow a bowl of skyr, of that I am sure. Were there others?'

'Two young men of similar appearance, with red and freckled faces. One of them looked two ways at once and the other sat apart from the group.'

'I know well who these men are. Solvi the Squint and Auðun Noisy-arse. That completes the pack. You have given me a thorough report. We must now prepare ourselves for a visit, for it is my guess that these men will be knocking on our door before they leave the district. And remember ...'

'Yes, master?'

'Whatever happens, do not speak of our actions to anyone. We do not wish to be outlawed for unmanly behaviour, do we?'

'No, master,' said the shepherd boy. But he thought, yes, master, I would follow you to the ends of the lavafield ...

'Now go and tell the women in the shieling to throw on some men's clothes, take the horses and ride as fast as they can down to the farmstead. Our visitors may think it is men riding off and give chase. We need only gain a little time to seek help and then we shall see who has the upper hand.' The shepherd boy did as he was told and four women rode off together at speed.

Hallvard was just giving orders to mount and advance on the shieling, when they were startled by four riders spurring on their horses. Solvi said that they should give chase at once and all of his brothers agreed. Hallvard halted them. 'I think these riders are hardly likely to be Eysteinn and his companions. They look to me to be women.' Solvi opposed but Hallvar, being leader of the group, had his way. 'I will give you every opportunity, Solvi, to show me whether Eysteinn is in the house or not.' They approached the shieling and dismounted.

Hallvard then sent Solvi the Squint forward to see whether Eysteinn was at home. He knocked on the door, but there came no answer. He then looked through a window and shouted in. At that moment, Eysteinn shot an arrow through the window right into Solvi's eye socket. Solvi walked back to Hallvard and his brothers with the arrow sticking out of his eye.

Hallvard asked, 'Tell me, Solvi, is Eysteinn at home?'

'I know not,' he replied. 'All I can say is that his bow certainly is.' And with that, he retreated behind a rock to try to wrench the arrow from his eye socket. From that day forth, Solvi the Squint squinted no more and was known as Solvi the Socket.

Hallvard told his men to approach with caution and be careful to protect themselves from injury.

'It's a bit fucking late for that!' complained Solvi from behind the rock, still tugging at the arrow.

'We should have more than enough strength to take the shieling, as I think he can have no more than one or two men in there with him,' said Hallvard.

The shieling was built with a single roof beam reaching from one end to the other and which stuck out through each gable end, with a thatch of young turf which had not yet taken root. Hallvard told Auðun and Skallagrim to take one end of the roof beam and Hunbogi and Thorvald the other. He sent Hakon around to the back of the house to watch the rear doors. Hallvard then stood outside the front door and shouted the command for the brothers to push the roof beam upwards with all their might. When they did so, it split in the middle, causing the whole roof to fall in on itself. Hallvard smiled at the success of his plan. It never failed to bring the house down.

Eysteinn rushed out of the front door and Hallvard struck him with such a mighty blow with his sword that he took his left leg off just above the knee. Yet Eysteinn did not collapse, but hopped over to a tree stump where he stood, resting his own stump on it.

'Now that you are past fighting,' said Hallvard, returning his sword to its sheath, 'I shall not fight with you, a wounded man, any longer.'

'It is true that things are not going my way,' said Eysteinn, 'but I can still give you a run for your money if only I could have something to drink first.'

'I shall do as you ask and bring you water in my helmet. But I warn you – do not trick me!'

'I won't trick you,' Eysteinn said.

Hallvard went to a nearby brook, scooped up some water in his helmet and brought it to the wounded man. But as Eysteinn reached out to take it with his left hand, he stabbed at Hallvard with a dagger which he had hidden in his cloak, opening up a wound in Hallvard's side.

'Now you have cruelly deceived me and you have acted in an unmanly way, since I placed my trust in you.' He then drew his sword and dealt Eysteinn a death-blow, driving the weapon's blade through his heart. The brothers, who had all been hiding behind the cabin, now ran to join Hallvard and, seeing his wound, quickly bound linen tightly round his body.

Suddenly, the shepherd boy, who had been hiding under the bed throughout the whole attack, ran out of the front door and made a break for it. Skallagrim tripped him up and pointed his sword at the fallen boy's throat.

Hallvard raised his hand. 'No base deeds are to be done here on our part. The shepherd boy is to be spared.' The boy was released and the brothers thought this was a generous and noble act. After all, he did seem a nice boy.

Following these events, Hallvard the Log and the brothers rode over the ridge to the nearest farmstead to declare responsibility for the killing. They then returned home by the same route they had come, not slowing their pace until they arrived. Ingiborg was waiting for them at the front door and declared herself relieved to see them all return alive.

'We shall hold a great feast tonight in honour of our victory,' said Skallagrim.

'I shall skald a verse to celebrate the killing of Eysteinn,' said Hakon.

'And I shall drink ale from the horn 'til it flows from my eyeballs,' said Thorvald.

'Thank you, brother, for your sensitive choice of words,' said Solvi. 'As for me, I shall pour brennivin into my socket until I see double again.'

'And mother, will you join us in our great moment of triumph?' asked Hunbogi.

'I think not. I see that poor Hallvard the Log is in urgent need of succour. I shall administer to him personally in my bed-chamber ...'

Hallvard the Log must, indeed, have been in much pain, for he could be heard groaning and crying out all through the night, long after the festivities were over. What the brothers found difficult to understand, was why their mother chose to moan and cry out loud, too ...

76

'Just run that past me one more time,' said Alf. 'How's this plan of yours going to work? This vegit-something. What did you call it again?'

'Vegetarian,' said Rib to the fox.

'Mmm, let's see if I've got this right. You are going to stop eating meat at the very time you are going to flee from the farm and live out in the wild?'

'Correct.'

'You do understand, don't you, that such an act will make you an outlaw?'

'Becoming a vegetarian?'

'No, although people will think of it as unmanly and worthy of outlawry. It will mean that no family will give shelter or food to you, a thrall who has run away from his household. And have you not considered the possibility that the men will hunt you down?'

'That's a chance I'll take. There's nothing you can teach me about being hunted.'

Alf the Arctic fox took another bite from the strip of dried cod while he struggled with the concept of a human knowing more about being hunted than a fox. 'Let us return to the food plan,' he said, giving up. 'How will you survive without meat?'

'Well, let's see,' thought Rib out loud, going through the list of vegetarian options he could take with him from the Hoskuld house. 'There's the skyr, then there's the leeks,' he paused, '... and bread ... there's the bread.'

'Hm,' came the unconvinced response. 'So you plan to run away with a large skin of whey on your back, a bundle of leeks under one arm and a loaf of bread under the other. Is that it?'

'Well, no, maybe not. But I'm sure the countryside is rich in edible plants and fruits and berries and things.'

Alf the Arctic fox found this highly amusing. 'Look around you, sunbeam. What do you see? Let me tell you. Grass, rocks, moss, lava, rock, more moss.' A sandpiper peeped from the shore, giving Alf and idea. 'Unless! Unless you are a fisher. There are many fish to be caught here. In the rivers, in the sea. With nets and sticks with string on. I've seen men do it with my own eyes. Can you do that?'

'Well, er, no, Alf. Fisher I am not. Anyway, a true vegetarian does not eat fish.'

'Who says?'

'Er, my Mum.'

'This I don't understand. A sheep is meat, yes. A horse is meat, yes. A crow, even. But a fish? How can that be the same?'

'Of course it can! They have eyes, ears, and a heart. A beating heart. Fish have feelings, Alf, just like you and me.'

Alf stopped chewing. Fish? Feelings? There was no hope for the boy. No hope at all ...

The two sat in silence at the cod-drying station. Rib had been quite relieved to have been given fish protection duties out on the windy hillside – the news of a second family death had hit the household hard. Chieftain Hoskuld had taken it really badly and the Great Hall was not a good place to be. He changed the subject: 'Well, you don't need to worry about me, I'll be fine. And that's where you come in, my little friend.'

'Me?'

'Yes, you. Why do you think I'm allowing you to sit here beside me eating dried cod? Out of the goodness of my heart? Hardly. In exchange for a full belly, you're going to show me an escape route.'

'No problemo, sunbeam,' said Alf. 'Just tell me which way you want to go. Down the coast? Up the coast? Along the fjord? Over the mountains?'

'Er ...'

'And when do you want to go? Hour of rising? Morning-meal time? Midday? Mid-evening? Night-meal?'

Rib flinched at the onslaught of options. He hadn't given much thought to the exact detail of his departure. 'What would you reckon, Alf?'

The Arctic fox answered without hesitation. 'I'd take the mountain pass above the shieling. It will be hardest for them to follow you by horse there. That is where the other frostling is hiding.' The fox turned and trotted off across the field, a dried cod dragging from his jaws.

'Tomorrow!' shouted Rib. 'At hour of rising, by the Black Rock!' The other frostling ... he'd clean forgotten about the other arrival to the island. Another frostling, here, on Iceland. That had to be a good thing, didn't it?

77

The python which had threatened to crush the life out of Hesperus Besk proved to be his saviour. As soon as they crashed through the refuge's barrier to plunge into a 400-metre plummet to the rainforest floor, the huge snake uncoiled its tail from the human's body, instinctively snatching at branches to break its fall. It worked, but only partially, their descent through the upper canopy slowed, but not halted.

Seconds before impact, the python's tail grappled onto a lateral branch of a cedar palm and curled round it in a vice-like grip. The coil held for a moment, then started to slip. The prey was too heavy. There was only one thing to do. Let go.

Ainsley pulled his great length up onto the branch before slithering towards the safety of the tree's massive girth, where he could find refuge and lick his wounds. The human fell the final twenty metres to the forest floor, enough to snap his spine in two like a brittle stick.

How long did he lie there? Difficult to be certain. Three days and three nights, possibly more. Long enough for the resident rodents and insects of the Underdome to devour his toes, his fingers, then both feet and one hand, the other bent beneath his body where he lay. As a third party, the cold grey eyes observed the extended feast impassively – the body was no longer his. The man lying on the forest floor felt nothing. From the neck down, he was completely paralysed. No feeling, no pain. No emotion.

If Ainsley the amethystine python had been the torn parachute which saved the man from being smashed to death, then Olass and Maliss were the search-and-rescue team which saved him from being totally consumed by the creatures of the rainforest. The two hardened thugs cried in anguish when they first found their mutilated master. With the good sense not to move him, they sent for assistance in the form of a captive consultant surgeon by the name of Draper, who administered life-saving drugs before overseeing the transportation of the barely-breathing body back to camp. Once his condition was stabilised, they then began the painstakingly slow stretcher journey back to the Wigan Citidome, where their master's metamorphosis began.

Hesperus Besk was a man who left nothing to chance. A man who planned for every eventuality. A man who left precise and detailed instruction for the rebuilding of his body should it no longer be fit for purpose.

Hesperus Besk was a survivor. But as he lay, unanaesthetised, hour after hour, day after day beneath the surgeon's saw and the technician's drill, his thoughts were not of survival. His thoughts were of revenge ...

78

There is nothing like a fine Icelandic dawn. It can be a thing of beauty – clear sky shifting from pale green to bright blue, light breezes blowing crisp and fresh down from the mountains, sea still and smooth as a mirror.

This was nothing like a fine Icelandic dawn. Rib pulled up his collar, thankful for his sheepskin cloak protecting him against the elements as he climbed the slippery slope up from the Black Rock. The cutting wind blew in from the sea in gale-force gusts, heavy with thick clouds of vapour which clung to the high ground before falling as chill rain. Alf trotted on ahead, oblivious to the storm's onslaught. After half an hour's hard slog in the open, they entered a narrow ravine, which gave welcome respite from the howling wind, and pressed on, clambering up a treacherous path which switched between slippery rock and loose scree.

On his fourth fall, Rib shouted for Alf to stop. 'Wait, I've got to have a rest.'

'No, not yet. We must go on!'

Ignoring him, Rib sat down on a moss-covered slab of basalt. From the folds of his cloak he produced a bag containing food smuggled from the fire-hall the previous night.

Scenting breakfast, the fox scurried back down the scree to sit in front of Rib with his tongue hanging out. 'OK, if you insist, sunbeam.' He quickly wolfed down a slice of dark bread topped with a slice of hard cheese before asking, 'What, no fish?'

'No!' snapped Rib. 'If you remember, I don't eat fish!'

'Me, me, me,' muttered Alf. 'Come on, we must carry on now. I've got something to show you.'

It was more a narrow recess in the rock than a cave. 'This is where he stayed.' There was little evidence of anyone having been there, save traces of ash where a fire had been kicked out. 'He used to walk down to the upper pasture first thing in the morning and look at the longhouse with his long-eye.'

A telescope, figured Rib. So someone was keeping surveillance. Was he the one being watched? 'Where is he now?'

'Don't know. Haven't seen him for a couple of days. Now come on, we really must move.'

The going got tougher by the minute, the ravine narrowing to barely a man's width as the path steepened dramatically to a thirty-percent incline. The black ridge towered above them, a waterfall spilled forth from a dark crag. Without warning, the mist suddenly came down. They were in cloud. Wet, freezing cloud. Rib could hardly see his hand in front of his face. He struggled on, sometimes clambering on all fours, often sliding back two steps for every one taken.

Alf kept tracking back to check on him. 'Come on, we're nearly at the top. Not far now.'

Then, in an instant, the cloud lifted and a shaft of bright sunlight flooded the gorge. Rib stood upright, shielding his eyes. He blinked twice, rubbed his eyes, then blinked again, not wanting to believe what he saw. Standing before him on the path, at no more than twenty paces, stood the figure of a man. A massive man. Massive as the sheer granite walls which seemed to hang from his shoulders like a black cloak of rock. Grim Bellower.

The berserk.

The man responsible for acts of inhuman brutality: the murder of his wife for dropping his ale-horn; the hurling of decapitated shepherds from cliff-tops; the massacre of the Lusitanic crew; the frenzied devouring of Gunhilda. Now standing in front of him ...

But there was no beating of the chest, rolling of the eyes, foaming at the mouth, or biting of the shield. The berserk just stood there, arms folded across his chest, in menacing silence. Time stood still. Waterfalls froze mid-fall. Alf, crouched flat to the ground between them, broke the silence by emptying his bladder.

Something told Rib that he had to make the next move. 'Good morning! And is it not a fine morning to be out for a walk, my noble lord?' Unfortunately, having neglected to switch the leech, 'Roff, roff, grrr, grrr, rup, raff, roff, roff, yelp?' was what the berserk heard. At this, Alf the Arctic fox took the executive decision to dart between Rib's legs and bolt back down the track. Taking his lead, Rib turned and hurtled after him at breakneck speed, his shoulders scraping against the sides of the ravine as he half-slid, half-jumped down the loose scree. His ankle gave way and he fell, struggling to his feet in blind panic to continue his headlong flight, not once daring look back to see if the berserk were chasing. Not until he emerged from the gorge onto the open pasture did he cast a hurried glance over his shoulder. There was no sign of pursuit. There was no sign of Alf.

* * *

Much to his surprise and relief, he was able to slip back unnoticed into the day's routine, as if nothing had happened. Even Ragnar kept his unending stream of questions to himself for once. Having left the flock to feed on the pastures, Rib resumed his watch at the cod-drying station, where he took up position on a rock overlooking the bay, the noonday sun warm on his back.

He stared unseeing at the glistening waters, deep in thought, rewinding and replaying over and over again the events of the morning. Who was the mysterious man in the cave? And where was he now? How did the berserk come to be waiting for them in the pass? And why hadn't he ripped them to pieces? Too many imponderables in one go for him to handle, he turned his attention to a small flock of sea-fowl grazing on the shoreline, some thirty or so metres below him.

Something moving amongst the rocks, just to the right of the birds, caught his eye. A small animal of some sort. It was … a fox! Alf, the cowardly little git! He had half a mind to run down and give the dirty little deserter a kick up the arse, but instead, the fox's antics made him stop and stare. Alf had broken cover from the rocks and was now edging slowly towards the seabirds. Backwards.

Not only backwards, but belly flat on the ground with his brush straight up in the air. Rib watched open-mouthed. What on earth was he up to? The fox was now almost upon the flock, who didn't seem to be paying the slightest notice to him – Alf's blue-grey coat matched the plumage of the fowl perfectly. Still crawling backwards, his erect brush nodded at them. Rib gasped, suddenly realising what was going on – the birds were clearly mistaking the dancing tail for one of their kind! In a flash, Alf turned and leapt at the nearest fowl, seizing it by the neck. The flock took off in a flurry of wing-beats, their too-late alarm calls sounding across the bay. Alf began to tear into the bird's plump breast.

The sly fox was not the only one enjoying a feast. Two

hooded crows were making the most of the diversion by tearing beakfuls of flesh from one of the fish.

'Oy!' screamed Rib, jumping to his feet. The birds lazily flapped away to alight further up the field, just out of stone-throwing distance. They were true professionals. Meanwhile, Alf had joined him and was now lying on his back, exposing his full belly to the warmth of the sun. He licked his lips, closed his eyes and sighed the sigh of an utterly contented Arctic fox.

'I'm surprised you dare show your face round here so soon, after running out on me this morning.'

'I was merely leading from the front, sunbeam,' the fox replied, without opening his eyes. 'And,' he continued, 'I had assumed that you still wanted my help in leaving the farm. In exchange for a few fish, of course.'

'A fat lot of bloody good your help was this morning!'

'The berserk's appearance was rather unfortunate.'

'I should say so!'

'But, we now know what to expect. Next time we shall not take to the mountains. Tomorrow, we shall follow the shore.'

'Tomorrow?' Rib wasn't at all sure whether he was up to another escapade so soon. Then he thought of Gunhilda. 'OK, you're on. Same time, same place.'

79

The new day dawned in dramatic style, the dull orange glow over the mountains transforming in moments into a bright turquoise sky. It was a truly beautiful Icelandic morn. Boy and fox set off at a brisk pace, slowing only to skirt the longhouse by keeping low around the homefield wall. Once at the top of the ridge, Alf decided it was already time for a comfort break and ran around in circles, sniffing at the ground as if he were trying to pick up a scent. Rib took a final look back down at the settlement, where smoke now spiralled from the longhouse roof, signalling morning-meal time in the fire-hall. Thank God he wouldn't ever be going through that again. Up to his right, steam rose from the hot springs, from where the smell of rotten eggs drifted on the light breeze. The scene of the atrocity still fresh in his mind, he felt a pang of guilt for not sharing his plans with the flock. But, on the other hand, would they miss him anyway?

A clod of turf hit him on the back of the head. Alf was the culprit, scratting into the earth with his hindquarters, sending clumps of grass flying everywhere. 'Hey! Do you have to do that?'

'Certainly do, sunbeam. Can't have everyone sticking their nose in my business, can I now?'

For the next hour, they made good progress, traversing the undulating strip between the shore and the foothills, slowed only by the occasional boggy tract.

A clump of bright orange mushrooms stood out from the grey grass.

'Whatever you do, do not go near those,' said Alf. 'I remember the time I was so hungry I ate a mouthful and spent the whole morning trying to fly. Thought I was a goose. I could do the noise, all right, but I just couldn't get off the ground. Must have looked a right sight, running up and down the field, honking me head off. And if that wasn't bad enough, I then spent the whole night sitting on a cold pebble – a very cold pebble – waiting for it to hatch. Fair froze me arse off! No, don't go anywhere near those ...'

Before them now stretched a field of black rock. Up to their left, they could see where the lava had streamed down the mountain before solidifying on the flat. It made for treacherous walking – the black cinder crust gave way easily and, if you weren't careful, you could lose your footing down a jagged hole. The two tip-toed gingerly through snags of sharp rock, at times forced to take wide detours around deep chasms. By the time they'd negotiated the lavafield, the sun was high in the sky.

'When should we stop to eat?' asked Rib.

'There runs a river, just over the top of the next hill. It is a good place for fresh water. We can stop there.'

Now with a fresh spring in his step, the boy followed the fox up the grassy incline. Then he stopped dead. A deep, rumbling noise came from the other side of the hill. Spray hit their faces as they reached the crest. A waterfall! Torrents of raging water roared down in a sheer drop from a high black ravine in a foaming mass. The ground shook underfoot. Rib could only stand and stare at the powerful force screaming its fury before him. Slabs of ice, dislodged from somewhere up in the frozen mountains, bobbed up from the boiling plunge pool like white life-rafts, before floating down the swollen river out into the deep waters of the fjord.

With a sense of unease, Rib shouted above the roar. 'Alf! The escape route was to follow the shore, right?'

'Yes ...'

'Then how are we supposed to get to the other side of ... this?'

The Arctic fox scratched behind his ear before answering, 'Mmm, good question, sunbeam. I've only been as far as here before.'

'Whaaat! So you're telling me there's no way round?'

'Get down!' the fox barked, crouching low onto his belly and creeping towards a large rock to their right. 'Follow me!'

'What is it?' asked Rib, once they were safely behind cover.

'Humans. Down there, by the river.'

Shit! This was all he needed. 'How many?'

'Three.'

A search party, was his first thought. Probably led by that Cod-biter bastard. No doubt armed to the teeth with axes and swords, ready to slice him into little pieces. He ventured a peep over the outcrop. No more than thirty metres below them were three figures by a pool, playing some sort of chase-game. They were girls. And he recognised them immediately.

'It's Katla, Melkorka and Kerikka Toenail,' he shouted to Alf. 'What the hell are they doing here? They can't have come here this morning.'

'Maybe they stayed at the house over there,' said Alf, pointing with a paw in the direction of the shore. 'Where the berserk lives.'

Time stood still as Rib struggled to absorb this latest piece of information. Then he exploded. 'So you not only bring me to a river we can't cross, you deliver me

right back into the arms of the mad axe-man I'm trying
to escape from!' He should have known better than to
trust fox news.

The fox gave no reply, instead turning his attention
to a particularly troublesome colony of fleas which had
set up camp in his brush.

Not wishing to give Alf another second of his time,
Rib stretched his neck over the rock again for a second
look. The girls were playing by a sheltered inlet of the
river which formed, quite strangely, a still pool, its clear
waters moving in gentle eddies in stark contrast to the
seething torrent only metres away.

Something then happened which caused him to
pay closer attention. The girls were taking their clothes
off. His eyes were fixed on Melkorka. If only things
had gone better in the toilet, he thought, as she lifted
her tunic over her head to reveal her breasts. If only I
could have been your closet Casanova, if only I could
have been your latrino latino, if only I had a pair of
binoculars ...

The girls, now naked, were still playing tig.
Melkorka was It. She certainly was, as far as he was
concerned, too. Kerikka jumped into the water. Katla
squealed with laughter and ran round to the far rim of
the pool. The bronzed beauty chased after the skinny
little figure who, shrieking in mock fear, leapt up onto a
slab of rock.

'Careful, Katla,' he said to himself. 'That looks
dangerous ...' Rib knew exactly what was going to
happen next, but was powerless to prevent it. Thorkatla
Grimsdottir lost her footing on the spray-soaked slab
and slid slowly off its edge into the raging torrent.
Above the roar of the falls, the cries of the girls reached
his ears. 'Katla!' he screamed.

80

The girl disappeared from view for what seemed an eternity, before her head broke surface some twenty metres downstream. Rib raced towards the river, trying to tear off his clothes. He lost sight of her again, then she re-appeared even further downriver, an arm raised in the air. He was being outrun by the current.

Ahead of him, he spotted a raised overhang. He stopped to rip off his boots, then hurtled towards the steep bank. Even as he threw himself into a dive as far out into the foaming waters as he could, he knew the odds were stacked against him. The chances of his brains being smashed to pieces on the rocks were high. But he had to gamble.

The ice-cold shock to his system told him he was still alive. Swept along like a twig, he struck out away from the shore, snatching a gulp of air above the boiling surface every four strokes. In a matter of seconds, the maelstrom sucked him out to midstream. He had absolutely no control and was now fighting for his own life. Where was Katla? He caught a glimpse of her head over to his left and he struck out again, his muscles straining to breaking point against the will of the river. In an instant, she was sucked under and it was all he could do to fight against the strong undertow which was trying to pull him down, too. Something bumped into his side. At first, he thought it was a large branch, then realised it was the limp form of the girl. He grabbed at her and turned over onto his back, gripping her tightly to his chest, at the same time trying to keep her head above water. There was no sign of life in the frail body. He had to get her to the shore, if it wasn't already too late. Locking her to him one-handed, he flailed with his free arm and kicked hard, edging stroke by stroke away from the middle of the river. Was it his imagination, or was the torrent weakening? As if to serve him a sharp reminder of who was boss, the current pulled them both under. Gasping for air, he surfaced, now holding the girl tightly with both arms.

Craning his neck backwards, he looked over his left shoulder to try to get a fix on where they were. The river seemed to be broadening out into an estuary. They were being swept out away from land into the fjord! Memories of a close encounter of a skrimsl kind came flooding back. He had to make it to the shore and started to flail and kick again. Then, his knuckle hit pebbles. He found the bottom with his feet and stood up unsteadily, lifting the girl above the swirling waters. Although now only thigh-high, the river was reluctant to release him and dragged at his legs, threatening to take him down. Step by stumbling step, he waded towards the shore, knowing that they would both be sucked back into the torrent if he lost his footing. Her body hung in his arms like a limp rag doll. He looked down at her little face, drained of all colour, and feared the worst.

They made land on a narrow shingle spit which curved out from the shoreline into the black waters of Borgarfjord. He staggered up the pebble ridge and carefully set her down. She lay there motionless, lifeless. In a panic, he racked his brain for the life-saving drills he'd learned at the Sub-Tropical Paradise. What was he supposed to do first? The cold had now taken hold, freezing him to the core. He started to shiver. He couldn't think straight.

Out of nothing but instinct, he took her by the ankles and held her upside down. A gush of water poured from her lips. He lay her carefully down again. Her face was turning blue. He slapped her cheek.

'Katla, don't give up on me! Katla!'

Nothing came back. Not a flicker. He took her cold little hand in his. She'd stopped breathing. Desperately, he looked round for help, but there was no sign of the girls, no sign of Alf. He could make out the shape of a wooden shack just above the shoreline, but there was no-one to be seen. His own hands were now turning blue and he began to tremble violently. 'Come on!' he cursed. 'You can do this!'

Somewhere deep inside him, the kiss-of-life autopilot kicked in – tilt head back, pinch nose, take deep breath, form seal round mouth with lips, give four breaths, look for chest to rise and fall. The roar of the falls and the pounding in his head shut out the sound of someone approaching. It was not until he heard the crunch of pebbles underfoot that he looked up and saw he had company. A giant hulk loomed over him in silhouette against the bright blue sky. It was the berserk. Before he lost consciousness, he wondered how he could possibly begin to explain to Grim Bellower how he came to be kissing his naked nine-year-old daughter on a beach.

81

Before he opened his eyes, Rib heard the sound of water cascading somewhere in the distance. Not too far away. Somewhere to his left.

Before he opened his eyes, he felt the pain. His arms felt as if they'd been wrenched from their sockets, his knees and elbows cut and bruised. And the top of his head was so sore he could hardly bear touch it.

Before he opened his eyes, he smelt the pungent aroma of rotten fish. Shark, he reckoned. He felt the heavy weight of a bearskin covering his body.

He opened his eyes. He was lying on a rough-hewn bed in a small hut without windows, dimly lit by the flickering embers of a fire in a stone hearth. He tried to call out but all he could do was groan. Before drifting back into unconsciousness, he heard a distant scratching sound ...

Over the next hour, he slipped in and out of sleep, gradually absorbing the sensory clues: the smell of putrid fish; the itch of a hundred flea-bites; the acrid fumes of smouldering sheep dung. So when he finally came to, he felt almost acclimatised with his surroundings. He knew exactly where he was. He was back in a Viking house. He was back in Hell.

The scratching became more persistent. Rib climbed gingerly out of bed, wrapping the bearskin round him.

Nearly collapsing under its weight, he staggered over to the door.

'Rib! Are you there?' came a rasping voice. It was Alf.

Rib automatically felt for the leech. It was still, God knows how, clamped to his earlobe. If he'd lost that, he would have been up shit creek without a lilo, without a doubt. 'Yes, I'm here,' he whispered through a crack in the door.

'You're still alive, then?' came Alf's surprised tone.

'Yeah, no thanks to you. How come you always do a runner when the going gets tough?' There followed a pause which clearly was not going to be filled by the fox. 'I think this hut belongs to Grim Bellower,' said Rib.

'Yes, that is correct. He is the berserk who bit the last shepherd boy's head off before throwing him over the cliff. It was some show!'

'Yes, I know all about that, thank you very much! How the hell did I end up in here? Where is he now?'

'The berserk brought you both here, you and the little girl. He carried her in one arm and dragged you along by the hair with the other. It looked really painful.'

That explained the excruciating scalp agony ...

'The next day, he took the little girl back to the big house – '

'The next day? Day?'

'Yes, when the bright orange thingy comes out of the sea and climbs high in the sky ...'

'I know what a bloody day is!'

'Oh well, that's it, really. Well, maybe one more thing you should know.'

'What's that?'

'He placed a big round stone in front of the door so that no-one can get in or out.'

'Great!'

There was a pause, before the fox said, 'Can I ask you something?'

'What?'

'You promise you won't get angry?'

'I promise I won't get angry.'

Another pause, then, 'Are there any dried fish in there?'

'No!'

'OK, sunbeam, keep your hair on. Oh, and there's one more thing you might want to know.'

'Which is?'

'The berserk, he's coming down the hill right now. I'm off!'

The grating sound of a millstone being rolled to one side was quickly followed by the heavy door being thrown open. Rib could only cower in terror as the huge frame squeezed through the narrow doorway. Rib cried out for mercy. A searing stab of pain shot through his left nadger.

'Ah-woooh!' he howled. 'Ah-woooooh!'

82

Not a single word was exchanged between Grim Bellower and Odd the Pale on the return journey to Borg. Just relieved to be alive, Rib sat on the back of a sullen pony, aching to know how Katla was, but not daring to ask in case he didn't like the answer. A wet sea-mist rolled in, the grey morning gloom matching his mood. What were they going to do to him?

A reception party awaited them as they came over the brow of the hill – a couple of farmhands jumped up and ran down the slope towards the farmstead, shouting at the top of their voices. People came pouring out of the longhouse to form a line behind the high seats carried out by four thralls. Chieftain Hoskuld, his wife Helga and their sons were the last to emerge, walking in solemn procession before taking their seats. The berserk motioned Rib to dismount and led him by the arm to stand before the old man. On the ground between them was a large block of granite, hewn into a perfect cube.

'Kneel before the mighty Chieftain Hoskuld,' commanded Grim. Rib obeyed. 'Now place your head on the block.' Rib did not obey at once, so the berserk cupped his enormous palm round the back of the boy's head and pushed it firmly downwards so that his forehead pressed flat against the cold surface of the stone. At that moment, Rib knew that he was going to die. They were about to execute him for trying

369

to escape. His last breath would be taken here, in the company of primitive, flea-ridden throwbacks. Too tired to care anymore, he just wanted it to be over ...

The assembled gathering hushed as the old man rose unsteadily to his feet and stepped forward. Rib heard him draw his sword from its sheath. Slowly. Deliberately. Not like a warrior preparing to do battle. More like a high priest about to perform a sacrificial ritual. Sensing the cold blade poised above his neck, ready to strike, he screwed his eyes shut. He only hoped Hoskuld wouldn't mess it up ...

'Odd the Pale, news has been brought to me that you left my household without my permission. I have also received news of your deeds committed with my grand-daughter. It is, therefore, my duty, as chieftain of this district, to pass judgement on your actions ...'

The reservoir of wee in Rib's bladder couldn't take any more and chose that moment to make a splash for it.

' ... by declaring you to be a freed man.' Chieftain Hoskuld touched him lightly on each shoulder with the tip of his blade. 'Odd the Pale, you have acted bravely in saving the life of Thorkatla Grimsdottir. In return, I intend to give you freedom and grant you the right to live as a freedman in my district.'

***

Katla was sitting up in bed, chewing on a stick of dried stockfish. So pleased to see her alive, he threw his arms around her. 'Katla!'

'Katla the Fair,' she corrected, clearly well on the road to recovery. They were in a small bed closet, partitioned off from the main sleeping quarters. An oil lamp burned on a low table. 'Look!' she said, ferreting under the blanket to produce a whalebone on which were carved strange inscriptions. 'My father cut these runes and placed them under my pillow. They made me whole again.'

'Can I see?'

'No, they are magic. Many a man becomes lost in these dark letters.'

Fair enough, then. 'Can you remember what happened to you?'

'I can recount the game I played with the two maids by the great river. Then all became blackness.'

'You fell into the river and I, er, saved you.'

She paused before looking him straight in the eye. 'Then I am in your debt.' She paused again. 'It is told that you lay me on the ground and put your lips to mine.'

'Well, no, it wasn't like that. I gave you the kiss of life.'

Her eyes lit up. 'That is good. You are now my kiss-gulper.'

Rib didn't like the way the conversation was going. 'Kiss-gulper?'

'Did you not poke your tongue into my mouth?'

'No! I certainly did not! Certainly not, Katla!'

'Katla the Fair.'

'Listen, I want you to get this straight, for once and for all. I was trying to save your life. Make you breathe again.'

'Can you show me exactly how you did it?'

'No!' He wondered how loud she would scream if he poured the hot oil from the lamp down her back. Instead, he tried to change the subject. 'Katla the Fair, Chieftain Hoskuld said that I was a freedman. What does that mean? Am I no longer a slave?'

'Not quite yet. A feast will be held tomorrow in your honour. In a ceremony to confirm your freedom, my father will craft a verse and you shall reply.'

'Me? Reply? What shall I say?'

'You must compose and recite a verse.'

'What! I can't do that!'

'You must. To refuse would be both unmanly and an insult to my father.'

Rib's throat suddenly went very dry.

'And I give you wise counsel not to pour scorn on my father.'

'No, I'm sure you're right,' he murmured to himself.

'But do not be solemn, Odd the Pale. As a freedman, you will be able to own your own farm, on condition that you pledge your allegiance to Hoskuld the Great.'

A Viking farmer, with a place of his own? That certainly hadn't been in the career plan.

A huge cockroach scampered across Katla's bed. Quick as a flash, she grabbed it and popped it into her mouth. Rib had to look away as the girl crunched into the hard shell.

'Yes, it will be a good thing for you,' she said after swallowing the still-struggling insect with a degree of difficulty. 'You will be able to carry weapons, keep sheep, play in the summer games ...'

The summer games. Oh joy ...

' ... but the best thing of all is that your children – our children – will be free at birth and be able to inherit our lands.'

Rib choked as if he had been the one chewing on a cockroach. 'Whoa! Hold on there just a minute. Did you say ... our children?'

'Yes, our children. For you will be free to marry me.' She leaned forward. 'Now, Odd the Pale, are you sure you do not want to do the kiss of life on me again?' she said, closing her eyes and puckering up, her lips stained black by the blood of the beetle.

Time for a sharp exit! Rib jumped to his feet and rushed out of the closet, slamming the flimsy door behind him. He stumbled through the hot, smoky hall in a cold, clammy sweat. He needed fresh air. Once outside, he wished he could recreate the Sword and the Stone scene, but this time have Chieftain Hoskuld chop off his head in one, clean swipe. What was the Old Norse for "Out of the frying pan, into the fire", he wondered?

83

'But that's brilliant news, sunbeam!' said the fox. 'A pad to yourself, a flock of sheep, a few cattle. Maybe even some chickens ...' he said, licking his lips at the prospect. 'What's not to like about it?'

'What's not to like about it? Everything! I do not want to spend the rest of my days sitting by a fire of dried sheep shit, drinking bowls of curdled milk, picking lice from my every orifice. And, strange though this may sound, I HAVE NO DESIRE TO GET MARRIED TO A BLOODY NINE YEAR-OLD! That's what's not to like about it!'

Alf paused to digest the baffling trail of logic laid by the boy. 'And just think, you could even have your own rack of dried cod,' he argued, 'where we could carry on having our little chats.'

Rib stood up from the springy turf and strode over to pull a three-pound Atlantic cod from the wooden forks and hurl it at the fox, who had to take swift evasive action. Oblivious to the crunching of bone that soon followed, Rib gazed out over the smooth, calm waters of the fjord. A skein of grey geese flew straight across his sightline, but he didn't see them. In spite of the early morning sun on his back, he felt chilled to the bone. How the hell was he going to get out of this mess? Would he not rather be a freedman than a thrall? Yes, he would, he surely would. If he only could without getting married to the little girl who made him want to strangle her every time she opened her mouth. And then there was the small matter of the ceremony. That very evening. As far as he could gather, he had to write and recite a poem. How was he going to be able to do that? They seemed to take their sagas and verses very seriously round here. He sat on a rock and held his head in his hands. He didn't even know where to begin.

'Why the glum face, sunbeam?'

'I've got to go through some sort of swearing-in ceremony tonight and I haven't got a clue what I'm supposed to do. And I've got to read out a poem I've written!'

'Oh, that's easy,' said the fox, settling down beside the boy in saga-telling mode. 'Let me tell you how it works. Are you sitting comfortably? Then we'll begin. Firstly, the chieftain will call everyone to order, then invite the big hairy one –'

'Grim Bellower?'

'Yes, him. Invite the big hairy one to speak his verse. He will probably say something nice about you saving his daughter. Then the chieftain will ask you to respond.'

'But what shall I say?'

'Erm, well, I would suggest you speak four verses. Nothing too complex. Choose a simple metre and go easy on the alliteration, otherwise they'll think you're trying to show off.'

'Eh?' Go easy on the what?'

Alf looked up to the heavens. This was going to be harder than he thought. 'Alliteration. Where a vowel or consonant of a stressed syllable is echoed by repeating the same vowel or consonant.'

'Oh, yeah, I remember. A bit like "The red fox ran over the rugged rock."'

'Are you taking the piss? And who's ever heard of

a red fox? If you dish up that sort of nonsense in your verse, they'll have your guts for starters.'

'Don't you mean garters?'

'No ... Anyway, do you want me to tell you what to say or not?'

'Sorry. Yes, please.'

'OK, as I said, I would suggest no more than four stanzas. In the first verse, you can tell them how the girl fell in the river. In stanza two, you might want to say how you rescued her and saved her by sticking your tongue down her throat–'

'Listen, I'm not going to tell you again, I did not stick my tongue down her throat!'

'As you wish,' he continued. 'The third stanza could tell how the big hairy one felt about seeing his daughter saved. And the fourth ... let me see ... this is probably going to be the trickiest ... ah, yes, I know. You could tell of your feelings about becoming a Viking freedman. Got that?'

'Er, yes, I think so. Let me just run through it again. Katla falls in river, erm ...'

'You stick tongue down throat.'

'I resuscitate her! Erm, third verse, Grim is a happy chappy and then, finally, something about me embracing the Viking way of life. Yes, I can already see that's going to be the hard bit.'

'Good! Now all you've got to do is go somewhere quiet and compose the poem. Don't worry, I'll take care of the fish.'

'OK, thanks,' said the boy, already deep in concentration. He started walking down to the shore, where he could create his masterpiece in peace and quiet. Mid-stride, he turned back to the fox, whose paw was in mid-air on its way to dislodging a cod from the rack. 'How come you know so much about stanzas and verses and alliteration?'

'Because we foxes use them all the time.'

'You tell poems to each other?'

'Yes, of course. On Iceland, all the animals and birds tell stories to each other. It's in our blood. But us foxes, we're best at telling funny stories. When we get together, we're a right pack of jokers.'

'Now why does that come as no surprise?'

'Try this one for size, sunbeam. You look as if you might be in need of inspiration.'

Why not? thought Rib and sat down beside the fox.

'You'll like this one – it's a true story. Yesterday, I was going about my business when I saw a dog down on the lavafield. He was running backwards and forwards, yelping and whining. I watched him do this for over an hour. I felt sorry for the poor thing, so I finally went down and spoke to him. 'What's up, sunbeam?' I asked him. 'If I don't find a tree soon,' said the dog, 'I'm gonna piss myself!''

'Yes, very funny,' said Rib, ignoring the fox's raucous laughter. 'Now, if you'll excuse me, I've got work to do.' He made to leave.

'Just one more! Please, just one …'

'Oh, all right, then.'

'It is told that Iceland once had a great explorer, whose name was Eiriksson. One day, he set off from his homestead to walk round the whole island. When he returned many, many moons later, he was met at the door by his wife in a distressed state. 'My husband,' she cried, 'I have bad news for you. In your absence, our chieftain has removed your name from the district register.' Greatly angered, the explorer rode his horse straight to the chieftain's house and hammered on his door. 'What's all this I hear about you removing my name from the district register?' he demanded. 'Oh, I'm really sorry,' said the chieftain. 'I must have taken Leif off my census.' Alf rolled over and over in a giggle-fit.

Rib didn't get it. 'Well, Alf, much as I'd like to stand here all day chewing the fat with you, I really must get cracking on this poem. So, if you'll excuse me ...'

84

By the time evening came, the young poet was in confident mood. At Katla's suggestion, he had enjoyed a relaxing soak in the hot-pool – this time careful not to wash his hair – and had put a fresh tunic on. Alf's parting words of advice had been to craft a piece containing noble sentiment, terse humour and a well-placed pearl of wisdom. Rib felt sure that the Ode of Odd the Pale would accomplish all three.

There was a buzz of anticipation in the Great Hall. Torches burned brightly from the walls, sounds from a stringed instrument came from the fire-hall. Chieftain Hoskuld and his wife were already seated and nodded to Rib as he entered. Returning their greeting with a body motion more akin to curtsy than bow, he pushed his way through to join the throng at the ale-trestle. His face lit up when he saw the unmistakable form of the maid Melkorka serving the beer. She was wearing a low-cut bodice which left nothing to the imagination when she leaned over the tub.

His turn in the queue came. He took a wooden bowl and held it out to her. She flashed him a smile which made him go all gooey inside. She then placed one hand on his, taking the bowl with the other. His knees started to tremble.

'Hello,' she said.

'Croak,' came his reply. He tried again. 'Hello.'

'It pleases me to give you the horn.'

'I beg your pardon?'

From beneath the table, she produced an ale-horn made of whalebone, with a rune-embossed rim. Its tip was encased in an intricate piece of soft, dull metal in the shape of a bird's head. 'It's a raven,' she explained, handing it to him. 'Especially made by Smiðr the Black for you.'

'It's ... it's beautiful. Thank you, I shall treasure it forever.'

She took it back from him, her fingers again touching his. 'Let me be the first to pour for you.'

He watched, mesmerised, as she ladled the creamy ale into the horn. He couldn't help licking his lips. 'Bottoms up!' he said.

She gave him a quizzical look. Clearly something had been lost in translation. Or maybe gained? Scarcely had the froth of the brew touched his lips than a huge hand clasped his shoulder and spun him round.

'Come, it is time,' said Grim Bellower. The crowd parted like the Red Sea to allow them through to where the chieftain and his wife were seated. The berserk and the boy stood before them and bowed, Rib making a better fist of it this time.

Finn Flat-nose then spoke. 'Be silent for the words of Hoskuld the Great!' Already on his third bowl of Thor's Hammer, Knock-Kneed Arvid emitted a squelchy fart which flapped its way round the back of the hall. For his pains, he received a boot in the balls from Skeggi Cod-biter.

Chieftain Hoskuld rose to his feet and spoke: 'Welcome, family, friends and household, to the Great Hall of Borg. We gather here to hail the heroic deeds of the thrall, Odd the Pale. I call upon my son, Grim Bellower, to speak a verse.'

The berserk bowed, took a step forward, then spoke
in a voice so deep the flames in the hearth flickered:

'*Katla on the shore was snatched*
By raging surf of foam.
Strong rode the horses of the sea
To stack rocks upon her.
An unfearing warrior ventured forth
To spare the life of the fair.
Deceiver of ravens, fighter of flesh-eagles,
I laud you!

My near-dead daughter
I did clasp in my arms,
Sword-rain drained
From her death-pale face.

I, Grim Bellower, am proud to present
The path on which my verse treads.
I would be deemed undeserving
If I failed to honour his favour.

The deeds of Odd will outlast most men's.
My poem piles a mound of praise
That will stand after seas have dried
To mark the brave act of my kinsman.'

The reviews from the audience were mixed:
"reasonable melody and rhythm, confident delivery"
"alternations of kennings unpredictable, wilful at
times"
"placement of the beat in each half-line erratic"
"alliterative echoes entertaining but over-decorative
in places"
"fucking good for a berserk, I reckoned"

All in all, however, the gathering agreed that it was an excellent effort.

By now, Rib was sweating profusely. Throughout the recital, he'd only been paying half attention, his mind concentrating on his own lines. One word, however, from Grim's last line, grabbed his attention. Didn't he say something about "kinsman"? No time was granted for him to fathom further – the moment of reckoning had arrived.

'I now call upon the thrall, Odd the Pale, to speak his response,' declared Chieftain Hoskuld.

Rib stepped forward, bowed once and cleared his throat.

'Grim Bellower has a fine daughter,
Who unfortunately fell in the water.
Try as she might,
She vanished from sight,
The girl cannot swim, though she oughta.

The river it roared loud as thunder,
The strong current dragged her right under.
Her only salvation
Was resuscitation
That she didn't die was a wonder.

Grim might have flown into a miff
And knocked me about with a biff.
You have to be wary
When a berserk goes larey
'Cos you're likely to fly off a cliff!

(Here, Rib paused to check audience reaction. To a man, woman and child, they all stood, eyes agog, mouths wide open. It was obviously jaw-droppingly good. Now for the final verse. They'll just love this ...)

The food of a Viking
Is not to my liking,
I can't stand the smell of the whey.
A bowl of sour curd
Tastes just like a turd,
Veggie sausage for me any day!'

A deathly hush hung pall-like over the hall. Grim began to shift uncomfortably from foot to foot. You could have heard a cockroach cough, a flea fart, a wood louse lick between its toes.

The silence was broken by the Chieftain's wife, Helga, who erupted in an explosion of laughter, tears running down her cheeks. Within seconds, the whole hall joined her in an exaggerated show of mirth, slapping each other on the back, punching each other on the shoulder. They had never heard anything quite like it. All except the man they called Cod-biter, who stood glowering at the far end of the room.

Even the frail frame of the wise old chieftain shook with laughter. Wiping the tears from his eyes, he took his ceremonial shield and beat it three times with the flat of his sword. 'I declare Odd the Pale to be a freedman. He shall ride with me to the next meeting of the Althing to swear his allegiance.'

A cheer went up and suddenly Rib was mobbed, mainly by thralls and farmhands wanting to shake his hand. Then, from nowhere, a soft kiss was planted on his left cheek. From the sweet lips of Melkorka ...

'Congratulations, young warrior,' she said.

He flushed. 'Did you like my poem?' was all he could think of saying.

'It was ... not a customary verse. But it made me laugh. So it was good.'

It made her laugh, he repeated to himself. And there lies the way to a woman's heart.

She handed him his drinking horn. Already pumped up by the poetry ordeal, Rib's adrenaline levels were further raised by the presence of Melkorka. He took the ale and downed it in one.

'Ay, ay, ay' she said. 'Take it easy, my young wordsmith. I want you to save your strength for one more brave performance this night.' And with that, she melted back into the crowd. Somebody took his ale-horn and returned it brimful with Thor's Hammer. First taking a deep draught, he pressed the replay button on the maid's words. "One more brave performance this night ..."

From being a scorned slave living off scraps, he was now a hero. A Viking hero. Wow! A Viking hero! How chill was that? And to top it all, there was a beautiful blonde goddess awaiting him. Maybe Alf was right. Maybe things were looking up for him. Maybe the secret of life was to make the best of where you're at? When you're up shit creek without a lilo, invest in sewage shares. And what was it Hoskuld said? Ride with him to the Althing, whatever that was? Sounded good – he deserved a day out. Euphoria had him well and truly in her arms as the second Hammer slipped down. How many fifteen year-olds on Tycho – or back on Earth, for that matter – could put Viking Hero on their C.V.? And how many of them had ever drunk beer from a whalebone ale-horn with a friggin' raven's head on the end, huh? And what wouldn't they give to be performing epic deeds in the sweet embrace of a Viking maiden, huh? Huh? Rib Meskitoe aka Odd the Pale took a deep breath. Life wasn't so bad after all ...

85

The crowd had begun to drift out of the hall. He went to look for Melkorka at the ale table, but she was not there, so he refilled his drinking horn, took a deep draught, then headed unsteadily towards the door. On stepping outside, his senses were jolted by two things. Firstly, the cold night air. Secondly, a wall of sound. Confused, he stood and blinked, trying to take in the scene before him. He was like the Dad on his sixtieth birthday who walks into a bar expecting a quiet celebratory drink with wife and son, only to be met by the cheers and photo-flashes of a hundred surprise-party guests.

He stiffened at what he saw, an avenue of flaming brands stuck in the ground, just like at the thrall-scald. He didn't like the look of this one little bit. But, this time, people were not baying for his blood, they were smiling and cheering. He was really confused. His eyes now accustomed to the light, he could make out something weird at the end of the avenue of fire. It was an arch, of some sort, held up by two farmhands. It was made of turf. It looked like they'd cut out a long strip of grass and raised it in the middle to form an arch.

The ringing of metal on stone made Rib spin round. The giant figure of Grim Bellower was kneeling over the whetstone by the door sharpening a lethal-looking blade. He looked up and bared his blackened teeth in a broad grin.

'It is time, my brave young brother.' He strode over to the boy, put his arm around his shoulder and guided him down Torch Avenue to the cheers of the crowd.

The two stopped in front of the arch. 'Now it is time for Grim Bellower and Odd the Pale to become oath-brothers!' the giant announced. 'Our blood shall be blended to swear our friendship and loyalty. We shall be our brother's defender, out brother's avenger!' he cried.

A chant rose up into the night sky, 'Blood! Blood! Blood!'

Up shit-creek-infested-with-piranhas. And not a sewage share in sight. The berserk drew his knife. Rib couldn't take his eyes from it. A single-edged, gleaming blade, passing into an elaborately decorated hilt. Where the blade joined the handle, it was encrusted in a cake of dried blood, skin and hair. He gulped.

The crowd hushed. Grim took the boy's left hand and opened his palm, cradling it gently in his own huge mitt. Then, carefully placing the blade on the flap of skin between thumb and forefinger, he slowly drew it back, slicing through the soft flesh like a hot knife through butter. Rib stared at his palm in a state of paralysis. Though partially anaesthetised by the Thor's Hammer, he had clearly felt the sting of the cut. But he saw no blood. One second, two seconds, three seconds passed. Still no blood ...

And then it came, a bright crimson flow from the deep, diagonal gash. His knees buckled beneath him. Grim held him firm, while repeating the ritual on his own left palm. He then clasped Rib's hand to his and their blood mingled, warm and sticky. The berserk marched the trembling frame of the boy under the arch, raised his knife in the air and cried, 'It is done! Grim Bellower and Odd the Pale are blood brothers!' The crowd gave one final cheer, before turning to make their way back into the longhouse.

'Come, brother,' said Grim. 'We shall drink 'til morn to honour our friendship.'

'You go on ahead, er, brother. I just need to sit down on this rock for a minute or two. See you later ...'

'Later ...' echoed the berserk.

Head in hands, the boy performed a passable impression of a woman in the early stages of labour. Deep intakes of breath, followed by short, sharp exhalations of air. Trying desperately not to pass out, he sucked in more air. Blood dripped down onto the grey grass. All he could do to stem the flow was clasp his hands tightly together. Eyes closed, he couldn't bear to look.

The fingers of a tiny hand gently unclasped his grip and carefully placed a wad of warm wet moss over the wound. Katla then applied a strip of linen to keep it in place.

He looked up. 'Thanks.'

'It is good. You have been brave. Are you now ready to celebrate with us in the Great Hall?'

'No, not just yet. I think I'll just sit here a while longer.'

'It is good. I shall go.'

He watched the girl skip back to the longhouse, tresses bobbing. He wasn't sure how long he sat there. At one point, he tried to stand up, but couldn't. Waves of nausea returned, threatening to suck him down into a dead faint.

A cough signalled that he was not alone. He looked up to see Melkorka sitting on another rock some ten metres away. How long had she been there? She smiled and came over to sit cross-legged in front of him. The fine down on her shins seemed to soak up every ray of the moonlight with such intensity, he could make out every single, golden hair. She was so, so beautiful ...

'So, Odd the Pale, you have had a day full of happenings. Do you wish it now to be a night full of happenings?'

Rib had to take a deep breath through his nose. The sickening dizziness refused to release him. 'I think I might have to give it a miss tonight, Melkorka, if you don't mind?'

She snorted, stood up and flounced back to the longhouse in a huff. Clearly she did mind.

86

The hunched figure fanned life into the embers. There was no time to lose. Life was too short. Like his father before him, he would die a painful death at an early age, taking himself off into the mountains when he knew his time had come.

Smiðr the Black was a master blacksmith. He lived at his forge by the sea at Raufarnes, a good distance from Borg. The distance was important, as was the nearby stand of birch trees, the last living wood left in the district. This prized asset, their main source of charcoal, was guarded fiercely by the Hoskuld family. The berserk included the forge in his daily rounds, noting the wisps of smoke rising from the smithy without taking closer order. Each an outsider, the two men shunned the company of others.

Smiðr lived with his two surviving sons, Svart and Tosti. Five others had been lost in childbirth, the last taking his poor wife with him. As was the custom, Smiðr would be provided with a new wife from the stock of thralls the following spring.

Every man, woman and child on Iceland knew of the forge at Raufarnes. It was told in the sagas how the smithy was first built by the fierce bald man who went by the name of Skallagrim. Though the site's ready access to wood could not be bettered, it lacked stones large or hard enough to forge iron against – there was nothing but pebbles on the shore. It is told that, one night, after everybody had gone to bed, Skallagrim put out to sea and rowed out to the small island off the coast. Once there, he cast his stone anchor into the deep water, dived overboard and brought up a rock, which he put in the bottom of his boat. It was so heavy that the water washed over the sides, nearly causing it to capsize. The exhausted Skallagrim managed to row ashore and carry the stone to his forge, where he placed it in front of the smithy. To that day, the same rock stood there, now with a heap of slag beside it. It was a stone like no other. Smiðr the Black, descendant of Skallagrim, still worked metal on that self-same anvil.

His elder son, Svart, his assistant for the day, groused loudly at being roused at such an early hour. The scornful Smiðr scalded his son with a verse:

'The maker of metal must wake early
To woo the love of his bellows,
The sweet sack that sucks in
Her brother of the sea, the wind.

My age-hard hammer rings down
On gleaming iron of fire.
The bag gulps, greedy for air
As the anvil spells the runes.

'Now pass me my hammer, you sour-tongued weevil,' he wheezed, wincing at the gnawing pain in his lungs.

'Svarti is a weevil, Svarti is a weevil!' came the mocking taunt from little Tosti, who had been hiding behind the smithy door.

'Seal your lips, you excuse for a maggot! For it will be your turn tomorrow,' said Smiðr. 'Now go and fetch me some wood. And mark, take only old wood from the ground. Touch not the trees!'

There was no need to egg on Tosti – the stunted child needed no encouragement to leave the bad company of his father. He limped up the hill towards the small wood, a short climb but nonetheless steep. A plentiful find of small branches and twigs awaited him, brought to the ground by the previous night's storm. The dark-skinned slip of a boy darted between the pale trunks of the birch in an ungainly run, deftly flicking sticks over his shoulder into the bag on his back until it was full. Despite the dawn chill, he decided to linger up in the wood a little longer. If he returned straight away, his father would be sure to give him some unpleasant task. And tomorrow, he would be worked to the bone.

Tosti sat down on a rock and surveyed the scene below. The bright red pinprick of fire down at the forge told him that Svarti was busy with the bellows. Soon, the rhythmic ring of hammer on metal would echo off the towering black crags out over the waters of the fjord. A large skein of geese emerged from the low-lying mist shrouding the shoreline. The swishing beat of a hundred wings accompanied by an orchestra of honks broke the still of the morning, as the birds fought to find formation. The small boy watched the flock somehow organise itself into a perfect V, keeping low to the surface of the water, before climbing to disappear into the distance over the bank of Ymir's Milk. Where could they possibly be going?

A movement back on land suddenly caught his eye. Two figures, a boy and a small girl, were walking towards the forge. He recognised Katla from Borg, but he had never seen the boy before. Tosti jumped to his feet and hurtled headlong down the hill. More than once, his withered left leg almost gave way beneath him on the slippery dew-sodden turf, but he managed to stay upright and skidded to a halt in front of the forge.

'Father, father!' he gasped. 'Thorkatla Grimsdottir is approaching in the company of a stranger.'

'It is expected,' said Smiðr, without raising his bloodshot eyes from the anvil. 'Fetch the brennivin!'

Today was the day Rib was to receive the most important thing any self-respecting Viking could possibly desire – his weapon. As a shepherd, he was no stranger to being up at the crack of dawn, but Katla was insistent that they left before daybreak. 'It must be so,' was her answer. Knowing full well the futility of further argument, he went along with it.

After all, his newfound life as a freedman was treating him well. And, most critically, he'd managed to speak to Grim about the thorny issue of his daughter. Ever since the word had first left her lips, the nightmarish prospect of marriage to Katla had been gnawing at his insides like the dagger of a Roman centurion teasing out the entrails of a Christian on the cross. The opportunity had presented itself the day before. Chieftain Hoskuld had granted him the small stone hut up at the shieling as his new home, which was great. Fond as he was of Ragnar and his flock, he'd had his fill of sleeping with sheep. However, optimism turned to his dismay on his first visit. In one of the corners, the stone and turf wall had collapsed, leaving a gaping hole. Help was at hand in the form of Grim, who appeared unannounced and started to shift the massive slabs of stone as if they were toy wooden blocks.

Rib grabbed his chance during a mid-morning curd break. 'Now that I'm a freedman, Grim, I like to speak to you about marriage to your daughter, Katla,' was his opening gambit. On reflection, the choice of words could have been better.

The berserk looked up from his bowl and fixed

him with a severe stare. 'It is not seemly to lie with a
girl of nine years. If you wish to prove your manliness,
I counsel you to lie with one of the maids of the
household, or several if you so choose.'

There appeared a milky froth at the corner of his
mouth. Was it a whey-bubble, or was he about to fly
into a rage? If Grim went all berserk on him here, he'd
probably tear the whole house down. And then throw
him off a cliff.

'Yes, no, absolutely. My thoughts entirely ...'
stuttered Rib.

'She is only nine years old, by Thor!' bellowed Grim.

'Yes, no, I know. What I actually meant was –'

'I do not wish to hear you speak of this matter again
or it will be a source of great displeasure to me.' He then
paused, swirling his spoon around in his bowl, before
saying, 'You may seek my permission in two years.'

Two years. Breathing space. Relief. He certainly
wasn't planning to be around that long, anyway. So,
for now, he had every reason to be cheerful. And, if he
could patch things up with Melkorka, who knows? He
might even begin to have some real fun. A fantasy of a
close encounter of the naked kind with Melkorka in the
hot tub was cut short as they startled a flock of geese
into noisy flight.

'Look!' pointed Katla. 'There it is!'

The bright glow of the furnace attracted his gaze to
the cluster of buildings just above the shoreline. A tiny
figure half-ran, half-tumbled down the hillside.

'And that is Tosti,' she laughed. 'Smiðr the Black
looks not like others, but be not afraid. He will offer us
a drink. Take it and drink with haste, for we must not
remain at the forge for long.'

Despite her words of warning, he was totally
unprepared for what he saw. A man, no more than four
feet tall, feverishly worked a length of red-hot iron with

hammer and tongs over a massive anvil. Around him, the smithy was a mess of metal, slag and scrap-iron. Next to the forge, the door of a turf-covered building stood open to reveal a black interior. Rib shuddered to imagine the state of the hovel inside. As they neared the toiling figure, Rib gasped. He now knew why the man before them was called Smiðr the Black. He wore no clothing, save a black leather apron and a pair of black leather boots. Black was also the colour of his charred skin. Pitted and pocked, his arms, shoulders and bald head were populated with dark, drying scabs and fresh, oozing pustules. He was a truly hideous, plague-ridden wretch of a creature.

'Good day, Thorkatla Grimsdottir,' he said.

'Good day, Smiðr the Black.'

'I do not relish the company of men,' he said, throwing a suspicious glance at Rib, 'but we have business to do. Tosti! Bring the brennivin!' he croaked.

Uneasy was the silence as they waited. Not wishing to engage the fierce little man in a staring match, Rib turned his attention to the huge block of stone from which the sparks had been flying. At first, he thought it was covered in lichen, so orange was its colour. But that couldn't possibly be. And it seemed to have a geometric form. A perfect hexagon, in fact. The shrivelled runt of a son limped out of the house carrying a wooden board on which were precariously balanced two small stone goblets filled to the brim with clear spirit.

'Svarti, the blade!' came the second command. In an instant, an older boy emerged from the depths of the hovel, again with a wooden board, this time upon which was placed an object wrapped in coarse sacking. Smiðr the Black took both shots, handing one to Rib, then raised his goblet to speak in a low, crackling voice:

'*Lord of bellows,*
King of tongs,
The hardener of weapons
Makes bad wringer of verse.

His ugly bald head
Gifts the frostling
A wound-dagger to own.

Never will this bright blade
Flame in battle,
Shiver through shield
Nor make blood-waves for ravens.

The smith of spells
Cuts on the steel
Secret letters.
He will dare great deeds
Who reads the runes well!'

The reluctant poet clinked his goblet against Rib's, looked him in the eye, nodded once and threw the firewater down his throat in one. Rib did his best to follow suit, the strong spirit coursing down his gullet like a lick of red-hot lava. The elder boy, his dark skin also covered in evil-looking sores, stepped forward to carefully unfold his cargo from its wrapping. Rib gasped. It was a work of unspeakable beauty. Smiðr the Black held it out to him and he took it from the board in both hands. A slender dagger with gleaming blade, its hilt inlaid with a precious stone of some sort. Along the reverse of the handle ran a line of runes, cut into white whalebone.

'Thank you. Thank you so much.'

'It is yours to own and yours to name,' were the smith's final words, now turning his back on them.

The ceremony was over. All of a sudden, Rib felt totally drained. His head was thumping, he was sweating and his hands starting to shake. Must be the brennivin, he thought.

'Come, we must go now,' said Katla, leading him away by the arm. They walked back up the slope a little way before Rib turned to wave farewell. Of Smiðr the Black and his two sons, there was no sign. Only the orange glow from the anvil.

A wave of nausea flooded through his body. His temples were pounding and the trembling in his hands just wouldn't stop. He fell to his knees on a tussock of coarse grass and threw up. Two enormous black birds wheeled high above the crags overhead.

87

Despite her loud and long protestations, the grand-daughter of Chieftain Hoskuld was not allowed to go to the Althing. This came as an enormous relief to Odd the Pale and the other menfolk. Although freeborn Icelandic women could own their own farm, act as head of a household and were subject to exactly the same outlawry as men for a wounding or a killing, they were not permitted to enter the Law Court of the Annual Assembly. That was the entirely legitimate argument for refusing Katla's pleadings. The other was that they all knew she would be a total pain in the arse and ruin the trip for everybody.

All in all, their party numbered thirty men. Four thralls, including Knock-kneed Arvid and the boy with the fart like a Harley, came along to take care of the horses, set up and break camp, and do the cooking. The journey to Thingvellir, the plain where the Assembly was held, took over three days, through the most amazing landscapes Rib had ever seen – at times stunning, often hostile, always changing: through swamps of grey tussocks clumped above red water; over heaths covered with carpet of brightly-coloured flowers; through dried tracts of stunted birch and willow trees, barely saddle-high.

Crossing rivers was tricky. On the afternoon of the second day, Thorkel's steed lost its footing and took a tumble into the swirling eddies of a ford. Horse and rider became separated, much to the amusement of Skeggi. Both were fortunate to struggle to safety on the far bank further downstream. Wherever they could, the party kept to the low-lying river flats, where they could canter along at a good pace. Elsewhere, the going was tough, the ground covered with broken clumps of turf or, far worse, thin crusts of hardened mud, under which bubbled boiling lava.

The journey would have been impossible without the Icelandic ponies, with their incredible instinct for choosing just the right place to plant their hooves, often pausing to lean forward and sniff at the ground to make sure the footing was safe. Through bogs and marshes, the only way was to give them their head, sometimes leading to long detours as the ponies tracked back on themselves rather than risk one uncertain step. But it was the only way.

Tough as the terrain was, the true enemy was in the air. Midges! The meadows and bogs teemed with them, the loathsome little bastards. Whole clouds would descend upon the party to irritate the hell out of horse and rider alike. In an act of desperation, Rib once switched the leech in an attempt to negotiate a peace settlement with the forty-four flies attacking him and his pony.

'For one moment, for just one moment, will you lot FUCK OFF!' he screamed. Which came over to his fellow travellers as, 'Bzzz, bzz, zbz, zbbz, ZIB-ZIB-ZIB!' Needless to say, it didn't work and the midges attacked with renewed ferocity.

That night, he was awoken from a deep sleep by someone jostling his shoulder. It was Arvid.

'Come quickly, it's the fox!'

The fox? Rib's confused brain turned immediately to Alf. Surely the little git hadn't followed them? All thoughts of Arctic foxes disappeared as he crawled out of the tent. 'This must be a dream,' he thought aloud. He rubbed his eyes and looked up again. It was still there, a shimmering curtain of greens and reds moving slowly across the night sky like a fluorescent concertina. It was simply awesome.

'Look,' whispered Arvid excitedly. The light-show was changing by the second, now moving from a green glow into ripples of deep red tinged with blue. 'Foxfires,' he whispered.

'Eh?'

'The naughty fox has started a big fire and, look, he is spraying snow up into the sky with his tail, trying to put it out,' he explained. Rib said nothing. There was nothing to say. The two stood entranced until the lights faded into the rising dawn.

That morning, they were joined by two other groups of riders from outlying areas, followers of Chieftain Hoskuld. After the briefest exchange of greetings, the band of men, now swollen in numbers to more than sixty, rode hard into the afternoon until they reached Thingvellir.

The Assembly Plain.

88

If only Sunset could see him now, Rib smiled, as they rode six abreast along the flat plain – a shimmering lake to their right, a snow-capped mountain ahead in the distance, steep vertical ridges on either side of the valley. True, his fellow travellers lacked the rugged good looks and designer-stubble of a Clint Eastwood, but in his mind he was heading the band of hand-picked gunslingers into town to liberate its oppressed citizens from the ruthless Mexican banditos. This Law Court, or whatever it was, had better come up with the right verdict or asses were gonna get kicked!

Once his testosterone levels had subsided, Rib started to take notice of where they were heading. Up to their left, nestling into the long ridge of black rock, were tents, horses and men. Many men. Heads turned as the Almost Magnificent Sixty Seven reined in by a clear stream, which flowed down into the lake. The Hoskuld contingent must have been amongst the last to arrive, even though their journey was one of the shortest. Whilst the thralls saw to the horses, Rib stretched his limbs, his eyes soaking in the scene before him. The whole place was buzzing.

An immediate benefit of being promoted to the rank of freedman was brought home by the sight of the thralls staggering up the slope under the weight of tents, pots and pans. No wonder Arvid was knock-kneed. After taking a much-needed pee behind a rock, Rib lost sight of them among the crowd, but finally found them at the bottom of the wide thoroughfare which seemed to run the whole length of the ridge. The street was heaving, lined with all manner of stalls, tents and tables. Such was the status of Chieftain Hoskuld that he had his own permanent booths and Rib found Arvid & Co busy erecting tent frames on top of the waist-high turf walls.

The thralls clearly knew what they were doing, swiftly stretching lengths of stiff cloth over the wooden frames, securing them in place on top of the booth walls with heavy rocks. Rib remembered with a smile the time he'd once watched Sunset struggling to put up a deck chair. By the time he'd managed to overcome the canvas contraption, the sun had moved round to leave the seating area in cool shade. The incensed Sunset had picked the chair up and hurtled it into the nettle bed behind the raspberry canes, telling the deckchair in no uncertain terms that it could fucking well stay there.

Clearly exhausted by the arduous ride, the old chieftain sat observing his site team's labours from a large wooden chair. He caught Rib's eye and waved him over. 'Take these, Odd the Pale,' he said, handing him a fistful of small coins. 'And spend them well,' he added with a wink.

'Thank you, Chieftain Hoskuld, thank you,' said the boy, staring at the shrapnel in his palm. All the time he'd spent at Borg, he'd never seen any money. But then again, why would they need it there?

This private exchange was watched by Knock-kneed Arvid who, much too quickly for Rib's liking, leapt forward to offer his services as a guide. 'I can show you the best stalls, all the best places to go,' he wheedled. Reluctantly, Rib gave in and followed the skinny runt up the path towards the massed crowd. The reason for the bottleneck soon became clear. There was a queue which, for Iceland, was extremely unusual.

'Do we have to pay to get in?'

'No,' Arvid laughed. 'Weapons are not allowed in the area of the Law Court, so all swords, spears and axes must be left.' Rib went to reach for the dagger in his boot. 'You do not need to hand that in. It is not considered to be a weapon. A Viking never slays a man with a dagger.' Nevertheless, they still had to wait in line until they finally reached the check-point, a roped-off funnel manned by two enormous bearded hulks. Berserks both, without any question of doubt. They would have eaten the door supervisors at the New Pitz for breakfast. Behind them stood a dozen or so trestle tables groaning under the weight of various implements of violence. To their relief, the boys passed through without incident.

'So, do we have to go through this every day? Does everyone hand in a little pink ticket at the end of each evening to collect their weapons?'

Again, Arvid looked bemused. 'No, the arms will stay here until the proceedings are over. The weapontake signals the end of the Assembly.'

All of a sudden, it dawned on Rib that he had absolutely no idea how long they were going to be there. 'So how long does the Assembly last, then?'

In his most patient talking-to-an-infant voice, Arvid replied, 'Fourteen days.'

'Bloody hell! We're going to be here for two whole weeks?'

'Yes, but is that not good?'

'Well, er, yes, I suppose it is.'

Arvid grabbed his arm. 'Look! Over there is the Law Rock. Come and see.' An old man with long, flowing grey hair and beard to match was standing on a mound addressing an audience of twenty or so men, sat listening attentively on a semi-circle of stone benches. 'The Speaker is introducing the next case to be heard. I know of this one. It is between Sigurd Swinehead and Ulf the Unwashed,' explained Arvid. 'It is claimed that Ulf raised a scorn-pole against Sigurd and, in an act of vengeance, Sigurd slew the slave of Ulf, an unfortunate named Flosi.'

'A scorn-pole?'

'Do you not know of scorn-poles?'

Rib shook his head.

'And yet you claim to be a Viking?'

'I've led a sheltered life.'

Arvid sighed. 'A scorn-pole is a figure made of wood that is carved so that everybody clearly recognises who the person is. The figure is a public insult and seriously damages the honour of the person in question.'

'But that doesn't seem enough to justify a killing.'

'The carving usually shows the person performing a strange sexual act.'

'Oh.'

'Wait, the Speaker is explaining now.' Arvid then giggled, covering his mouth with his hand.

'What is it? I can't make out what he's saying.'

'The scorn-pole showed Sigurd fornicating with a male goat,' he sniggered.

'Yeah, well, I guess that would make him pretty pissed off. So what happens next?'

'This will continue for many an hour. Each side will present its case to a panel of men, speak their testimonies and then agree on a settlement.'

'So no-one gets punished?'

'It is not likely. Only in a harsh case is a man outlawed. If it is allowed to become a family feud, it could last fifty years or more, and that is never good.' Arvid was warming to his task. 'To be judged a full outlaw is the worst thing. It's even worse than being a thrall,' he paused for effect. 'All his property is taken away and he can be offered neither food nor shelter. Wherever he goes, anyone is allowed to kill him. He is as a dead man.'

'Mmm, very interesting.' Rib was getting bored with all this legal stuff. 'What's up there?'

The Law Rock was sited so that it had a spectacular open aspect right across the Assembly Plain, but to the left, where Rib was pointing, the rock rose on both sides of the path to form a steep-sided chasm. And that was where all the noise was coming from. It really was just like a busy street on market-day, jam-packed with people, all trying to talk above each other.

'Oh yes,' said Arvid, rubbing his hands together. 'This is the real Althing. Where promises are given, promises are broken. Friendships made, alliances forged.'

'It looks like people are having a good time, too.'

'Yes, of course. We look forward to it every year.'

Rib noticed a few women in the crowd. 'Hold on, I thought women weren't allowed here.'

'Women are not allowed to play any part in the dealings of the Law Courts, so they cannot be there. But they do attend to sell wares from a stall or to offer ... tee-hee ... other services.'

A picture was beginning to form in the mind of the young freedman. What historians had faithfully portrayed as the birthplace of modern democracy, a prototype parliament, was really no more than an excuse for a piss-up, the Viking equivalent of the business conference in Las Vegas. ("But darling, it really is important that I go ...") But from what Rib knew of the Icelandic women he'd met so far – Helga, Melkorka, Katla – he was astonished they put up with it.

'Hah! Let me tell you a tale!' said Arvid. 'Two years ago, when I was carrying a skin of sour milk, I tripped over the fire-hall threshold and it went everywhere. All over the floor, the benches, it even put out the fire. As punishment, I was soundly beaten, went without food for three days and was not allowed to go to the Althing. I had to stay behind at Borg with the women. They were the worst two weeks of my life.'

'How do you mean?'

'As soon as the men disappeared over the brow of the hill, all the womenfolk from the brothers' farms appeared as if by magic and stayed there for the duration. It was a fourteen-day feast of singing, dancing, playing and drinking. I can tell you, Odd the Pale, that they drank double the amount of ale and brennivin than their menfolk at the Althing, so seriously did they celebrate their absence. And what is more …' he lowered his voice, '… some of the women folk dressed up in men's clothes and did strange things with leeks.'

Rib swiftly changed the subject. 'I'm hungry. How about grabbing a bite to eat?'

'Good idea.' Arvid immediately made a beeline for one of the food stalls, where he stood excitedly, like the little boy in front of the toyshop window. There were so many hot and cold meats and fish on display, it was difficult to choose. He could have had boiled Arctic char in a mustard marinade, he could have had thick beef stew with potatoes and carrots, he could have had spit-roast lamb with leeks. So what did Knock-kneed Arvid choose?

Pickled ox-penis.

The aroma from the lamb drew dribble to Rib's lips. He could have murdered a Sunday roast with all the trimmings. Instead, sticking to his new moral high ground, he bought a couple of thinbread wraps, one filled with honey and the other with sweet berries. They were delicious.

The two boys walked on in silence, concentrating on their food. The ox must have led a long and active life – Arvid was clearly having trouble getting it down, tugging at the sinewy member with his teeth. When he finally managed to bite off a piece, it must have taken him a good five minutes of chewing before he could swallow, and then only with difficulty, his angular Adam's-apple bobbing with the effort. But, in the eyes of Knock-kneed Arvid, it was well worth it.

'It is said that women will flock to the bed of a man who has the penis of an ox,' he said.

Rib didn't quite know how to go about telling the boy that he hadn't quite understood the nuance of that particular Viking saying. Now was not the time, he decided, to disillusion his companion, chewing with renewed vigour on the vinegary muscle.

All manner of wares were being peddled from the tables lining the street. Tradesmen had come from far and wide to sell pottery, drinking horns, carvings, furs. And, of course, weapons. One stall, however, stood out from the rest, displaying beautifully worked amulets, necklaces and bracelets, rainbow-coloured tunics and capes, jet-black volcanic stones polished and set in ornate rings of silver. Every piece a work of stunning craftsmanship. But what really caught the eye was the man standing beside the table: sun-tanned, not weather-beaten; trimmed stubble, not tangled beard; flashing, white teeth, not decaying stumps. Dressed in black from head to foot. His shirt even looked as if it had been ironed. His hair snow-white, cropped in a perfect brush-cut.

'Who is that?' asked Rib.

'That's Karl Lavafield,' said Arvid. 'He sells guilt-gifts.'

'Guilt-gifts?'

'Yes. His stall sells nothing until the final day of the

Assembly. Then, all the men suddenly feel they should be taking a present back home to their womenfolk. The better the time they've had, the greater the guilt and the more lavish the gift. And they all queue up to buy something from Karl. He is said to be one of the richest men on Iceland.'

Rib wondered what he could buy for the Icelandic women in his life. For Katla, first choice, a leather muzzle. Or maybe a silver toothpick for prising out slivers of cockroach shell from between her teeth. And for Melkorka? Perhaps a bronze amulet that he would fasten round her ankle himself. A sharp tug on his sleeve snapped him out of his intimate dreamings.

'Come, we have looked long enough. Now it is time to drink!'

Arvid clearly knew his way around the Althing. The scratty little figure scurried on ahead through the crowds with the purpose of a homing pigeon and they were soon at the ale tents. Stepping over a couple of bodies out sparko on the ground, they joined the excuse for a queue. Serious quantities of beer were being ladled out from four huge vats by the serving maids. In addition to Thor's Hammer, you could quaff a horn of Cloudless Swill, Foaming Doom or Spurt of Surt. Not too keen on the thought of taking Spurt of Surt down his throat, Rib quickly dispatched a horn of Foaming Doom for starters.

The rest of the day passed by in a fuzzy haze. His decision to stay clear of the Spurt proved wise. After knocking back three horns of the lethal brew, Arvid went behind a rock to throw up. Rib watched, mesmerised, as the thrall knelt down on all fours to regurgitate the ox penis in the style of a cat chucking up, his scrawny shoulders jerking forward and his little knocky knees scraping backwards on the bare rock to the rhythm of each sickspasm. It was not a pretty sight.

'Are you all right?'

'Yes, I'm having the time of my life,' came the answer and the two returned to the ale tent. How on earth they found their way back to the booth that night remains a mystery. All Rib could remember was emptying his bladder into an upturned Viking helmet outside a tent, and Arvid performing another virtuoso cat performance on the sanctified mound of the Law Rock. Rib vaguely remembered hoping the Law Speaker would not be wearing open-toed sandals the next day ...

The cases involving the murders of Ketil and Eysteinn were not to be heard until Day Ten of the Assembly, which gave the whole party plenty of time for a little rest and relaxation. And, for Odd the Pale and Knock-kneed Arvid, recuperation. Down on the Plain, crowds gathered to watch and wager on ball games, wrestling and horse races. On the far side of the river, just beyond the waterfall, lay a cluster of red-canvassed tents nestling into the ridge. Frilla Village ...

89

'On his first visit to the Althing, it is customary for a freedman to gush like the Great Geysir.'

'Eh?'

'To let the soft winds from the sea play gently over the rising crag.'

'I'm sorry?'

'It's time for you to get laid.'

And so it went on, the nagging comments directed at Rib every waking moment. So there was a sense of hopeless inevitability when he finally found himself standing in the queue of Vikings waiting to sow their wild oats at Frilla Village.

He, Rib Meskitoe, pay for sex? he scoffed to himself. When had he ever paid for sex? When had he ever had sex at all? came back the answer in the form of the most unwelcome of questions. That memorable, unforgettable night in the rainforest with Rika, he countered. If only, if only he could remember what really had happened that night, on that bed of dry leaves. Did they make love? The quantities of vodka consumed meant that he couldn't be sure of anything. All he knew was that the next day, things were so different. So different. And then she left him. Without even a word of farewell. A tear of anger rolled down his left cheek.

Seeing this, the man in the queue before him said,

'Fear not, young brother, the pain will soon be at an end.'

Rib turned away. Why should he care? What was the big deal, anyway? In the words of all Tycho incomers, he was here, yeah? First the skrimsl, then the sheep trial, leaping the Slob, the blood-brother ordeal – not to mention the daily nightmare of eating their food. If waving goodbye to his virginity in Frilla Village was just another ritual in a young Viking's passage into manhood, then why fight it? The ginger-bearded guy in front was right. Get it over and done with. Enter the red tent, tick the box, get on with the rest of his life. No amount of rational thought could, however, stop the clamminess in his palms, the dryness in his throat. As a brave young stud, he should have been up for it.

He wasn't.

He was just plain scared.

The line shuffled forward. There were now only three in front of him. Maybe he should come back tomorrow ...

Suddenly, all hell broke loose. A terrible howling rent the air, followed by a woman's scream. The walls of one of the tents billowed out, then the whole structure rose off the ground, pulling the guy ropes out with a ping. The tent careered off down the slope towards the river, its red canvas thrashing in the wind. A scared-looking frilla was left lying on her back, exposed for all to see. She hastily covered her nakedness with a night shirt. Her shift was over.

The ginger Viking shook his head, pointing to a sign which read "Strictly No Berserks". 'There's one every year,' he said. Some of the tents' occupants poked their head through the flaps to see what was going on. A fight kicked off in the queue behind Rib. Two burly Vikings, presumably pimps, set off down the hill in pursuit of the runaway tent.

In the commotion, a woman dressed in black from head to foot appeared from nowhere and took him by the hand. 'Come with me,' she whispered in his ear. Her eyes flashed at him from within the dark folds of the cowl covering her head. She guided him firmly away from the village, through the weapontake area, along the street past the ale tents, from where coarse cries of encouragement were hurled in their direction.

The path now climbed steeply. The woman in black pressed on, still gripping his hand tightly in hers. Had he not downed three Thor's Hammers in quick succession to give him Dutch courage for Frilla Village, he might have resisted. Instead, he allowed himself to be led by the mysterious woman up the track away from the crowds. Who was she? Where was she taking him? And what would happen when they got there? If only he could see her face. Was she young, was she old? All he could see were her eyes. Eyes which somehow seemed strangely familiar ...

'Here will do,' whispered the woman, dragging him off the path. 'Come quickly, we do not have much time,' she said, as she manhandled him up a slight incline towards the towering rock-face. There, she pulled him into a dark fissure, a crack in the rock just wide enough for two people to squeeze in sideways, which they did. Now invisible from the track, the two stood, breathless, pressed tightly face to face against each other. As tight as sardines in a can. Yet no cold fish was she. He felt the warmth of her cheek against his, he felt the heat of her body through her cloak.

His hands fumbled their way through the folds of her mantle until they found her hips. She responded by nestling her head on his chest. 'Let me see your face,' he said, aroused.

'No, not yet,' she murmured silkily.

'Then tell me your name.'

'It is Thjodhuld Veturlidadottir.'

'That's a ... nice name,' he said, his hands now wandering down to her buttocks. 'But it's a bit of a mouthful. Do you not have another name? Maybe a pet name?'

The woman in black deftly unclipped the leech from his earlobe and whispered softly in the Welshest of accents, 'Sometimes they call me the Only Grey in the Spillage ...'

90

Agent 07 aka Kaddie Kadwallader aka The Woman in Black held the cursing, struggling Rib Meskitoe aka The Nutter aka Odd the Pale, his hand clamped firmly over the boy's mouth until the first fires of rage began to subside.

'You bastard! You absolute bastard!' spat Rib

'Quiet! We don't want to attract unwanted attention.'

'Unwanted attention! YOU'RE the fucking unwanted attention! How do you think I feel being seduced by a ... whatever you are?'

'OK, OK, I'm sorry about that, but it seemed a good way of getting you on your own. And, you have to admit, it did work rather well, didn't it?'

This set Rib off into another bout of swearing, all the time straining to break free, relenting only after he'd drawn blood from the back of his head by scraping it against the rock. 'Ow, I think I've cut my head!'

'Listen!' hissed Kaddie. 'That's enough now. We are in great danger.'

'Danger?' Rib stopped struggling.

'Yes, we might have been followed. I'm going to leave first and you follow after a minute or so. We must both behave as if we've just had sex.'

'But –'

'Listen! Do as I say. We meet again tomorrow noon

by the Karl Lavafield booth.' He clipped the leech back onto Rib's earlobe. 'Keep your wits about you,' he continued in perfect Old Norse, 'and try to stay off the beer for just one night, yeah? Remember the Viking saying, "A clear head is good company". With that, the Woman in Black slipped out from the crack in the rock and was gone.

Kaddie had been right. Knock-kneed Arvid had, indeed, followed them to their love haunt, the sneaky little twat, and was not slow in spreading the word of Odd the Pale's sexual exploits to the rest of the party and anyone else who cared to hear. That night, he was welcomed back into the camp as a returning hero and could not refuse the odd beer or seven in celebration of his manly act.

In spite of the heavy session, he was up at ravenfart and spent the whole morning prowling restlessly through the Althing, even sitting in on one of the Law Court sessions to try and take his mind off things. It didn't work.

What the hell was Kaddie doing there, and how had he got there? What kind of danger were they in? And how come he could speak Viking? Part of him felt excited and relieved at seeing his old friend again. And if he'd found a way onto the island, there must be a way off. But part of him still seethed at the act of deception. He wasn't really Kaddie, after all. He was an agent, working for the Protectorate. Working for his grandmother. Hold on! Was this just another elaborate hoax to test him out? He'd fallen hook, line and sinker for the lottery trick. Surely this couldn't be another apprentice challenge? Or could it? Nothing was certain any more. The first thing he'd do when he saw Kaddie would be to have it out with him. The very thought made his blood boil.

Noon finally came. It was the fourth day of the

Assembly and, if anything, the street was busier than ever, parties still arriving from the easternmost reaches of the island. As was usual, the Karl Lavafield stall had a crowd admiring its wares, but of an agent dressed as a woman in black there was no sign.

A blind beggar, almost bent double, stumbled into him. 'Can you spare a coin for a poor, starving old man?' he wheezed.

'Piss off, Kaddie, before I shove that stick where the sun don't shine!' Rib then caught sight of a man gesturing to him from the far end of the table. The poor, starving blind man hobbled away, appalled at the youth of today.

'What were you saying to the old blind man?' asked Kaddie, now looking every bit the regulation Viking.

'Never mind!' snapped Rib. 'And who are you today, then?'

'I can be anyone you want me to be,' came the coy answer.

Rib shook his head, trying to banish the previous day's embarrassment from his mind.

'But you can call me Skafti. Skafti the Sly. Come on, we've got some talking to do. Let's go where nobody can see us.'

'Don't think for one moment you're taking me back to your little love nest again.'

'Don't you mean "our" little love nest?'

'Shut it!'

Two men standing next to them turned to stare. 'Follow me,' said Kaddie. This time they walked down the slope, away from the Law Rock, along the banks of the river until they reached the lake, which spread itself like a liquid mirror across the plain. They found a small inlet, shielded by a stand of tall bullrushes.

'Here will do,' said Kaddie, sitting down on a thick tussock.

'Right, there's a few questions I need answering,' said Rib.

'And there was I thinking we might begin with a few formalities, such as "How are you? Nice to see you again." But have it your own way.'

Rib faltered. 'Yeah, well, everything's come as a bit of a shock, you understand. One minute I'm going on a scientific expedition, the next I'm stranded on an island in some sort of throwback Viking colony. How the hell did they get here?'

'We don't know. But they must be here for a reason,' said Agent 07.

Rib stood up. 'And I've got to get my cards on the table. If this is all part of me being sucked back into a Protectorate recruitment drive, then you are bang out of order. My answer was No then, and No it will always be!'

Agent 07 looked genuinely bemused. 'Are you really suggesting that we brought you here, to Iceland, and … in some way contrived to arrange everything that's happened to you?'

'That's the question I'm asking, yes.'

'So you think we would have deliberately orchestrated the Lusitanic massacre?'

'How do you know about that?'

'I was there. I heard it all.'

'But that's impossible! You can't have been! Every single member of the crew was slaughtered. I saw it with my own eyes!'

'Not quite correct. You remember the Man Overboard cry? Just after we entered the fogbank?'

'Yes …'

'That was me going into the water.'

'You?'

'Yes, I had intelligence that contact with the mist would be dangerous. Of course, at that time I had no idea that the ship would be attacked when it came through the other side.'

'Hold on, hold on! You're saying you knew that Ymir's Milk –'

'Ymir's Milk?'

'Yes, that's what the Vikings call the fog. And you're saying you knew that it would be harmful?'

'Deadly. It contains high levels of radio-active material which normally bring on death within a week.'

So Katla was right about the frostlings. But Rib was still finding it difficult to believe the agent's version of events. 'Then, if what you say is true, how come you dived overboard and left me on the ship? To die?'

'It was I who suggested to Captain Zoothorn that he send you up into the crow's nest. It was a calculated risk, but I estimated there to be an 87.5 percent likelihood of it working.'

'87.5 percent?'

'It was all I had to work with. Anyway, you're here, yeah?'

Rib fell silent, partly trying to absorb what the man sitting before him was saying, partly recalling the horror of the bloodbath. 'But if you knew Ymir's Milk was lethal, why did you let me be on board in the first place, for God's sake?'

Agent 07 sighed. 'For the very simple reason that we had no idea that you were going to be on board. That's the truth, and you've got to believe me. As far as we were concerned, you were leading a nouveau-pioneer life in friendly downtown Stonyville.'

'I bloody wish I still was, that's for sure!' Rib stared into the distance at the perfectly conical, snow-capped mountain keeping guard over the plain. 'So let's believe, just for a moment, that you weren't following me. Why were you on the Lusitanic, then?'

'I was there to keep my eyes on Zoothorn. We

believed he was onto the Fearance. I was his tracking device. It made sense to give him, through the Expedition, free rein and see where he led us.'

'And then I took Buzzard's place ...'

'Exactly.'

'I still find it hard to believe that the Protectorate had no idea I'd joined the Expedition.'

'Listen. The truth of the matter is that we do not exercise the same level of ... control ... as we do on Earth. Communication is an ever-constant challenge. I was flabbergasted when you boarded at Liverpool. You weren't in the plan.'

A seaward flight of geese took off noisily, skimming the surface of the lake before gaining height. 'Let me just get this straight.'

'Fire away.'

'You jumped overboard. What next?'

'I had a metal ring attached to the keel. I clipped onto that and let the ship pull me through the fogbank.'

'But that must have taken four, five minutes.'

'In the service of the Protectorate, we are accustomed to taking deep breaths and keeping our mouths shut,' he laughed. 'No, I had a small supply of oxygen.'

'Then what?'

'I came up just as the Vikings attacked. I heard it all, but there was nothing I could do. I just hoped and prayed you would stay unseen in the crow's nest. When the ship hit the reef, I struck out for shore.'

'What about the skrimsl?'

'The what?'

'You didn't see the sea-monster?'

'No ...'

'I guess we were both lucky, then. I suppose it was you holed up in the cave, huh?'

'Yes.'

'Thank God for that. When Alf the Arctic fox told me –'

'An Arctic fox told you …?'

'Never mind, I'll explain later. When Alf the Arctic fox told me there was a man in a cave, my first thought was that it was Besk,' he laughed nervously.

Agent 07 said nothing.

'I said, I thought that it was Besk …'

'No, it wasn't Besk in the cave.' Agent 07 paused. 'But he is here …'

From the moment he'd heard the "We are in great danger" message, he knew deep down that there was only one thing it could mean. Besk was still alive. And he was here. On Iceland. He put the question he didn't want to ask. 'Has he come for me?'

'We have no reason to believe that he is aware of your presence here.'

'Then why is he here?'

'He, too, is in search of the Holy Grail. The Fearance.'

'And you think the Fearance is definitely here?'

'All the signs point to the pulse being generated from a source on this island.'

'What exactly is it?'

'That we do not know. All we are certain of is that it influences every aspect of our existence on Tycho.'

'But that's not such a bad thing, is it? Life in Stonyville, for example, is a good, clean life. I like it. We messed up Planet Earth, so why make the same mistake twice?'

'That's the very point. We, the Protectorate, wouldn't. But we are not everybody. If the Fearance, or even knowledge of how it worked, fell into the wrong hands, then they would have control of Tycho.'

'How?'

'Work it out for yourself. Anyone who knew how

to harness, or even bypass its jamming force, would have sole technological monopoly of the planet. Communication, production, transport ... armaments. Total power.'

'Which is why Besk is here.'

'Correct.'

Rib looked Agent 07 in the eye. 'And which is why you are here, too.'

'The world would be a safer place if the Protectorate had control of the Fearance. We would use it wisely.'

Rib said nothing. He scratched at the scar on the palm of his hand. It had healed nicely, but still itched like hell.

'How did you get that?'

'You know the mad bastard who single-handedly cut the crew of the Lusitanic to shreds?'

'The berserk? The one built like an ox?'

'Yeah, well he ain't just heavy, he's my brother. My blood-brother.'

Agent 07's jaw dropped. 'Explain.'

'Well, I just happened to save his daughter's life and slitting open someone's hand to mix blood is how they show appreciation round here.'

'Your grandmother would be very proud of you, very proud indeed.' It was the first mention of Zeta Meskitoe between the two, as if both had been avoiding the subject.

'How ... how is she?'

'She's ... she's fine.'

'Look, I know about her illness. I know she ... doesn't have long.'

'No, she's fine. And I mean what I say. She'd be very, very proud of you. What you've done here is truly impressive. You've not only managed to survive against all the odds, you've gone native, a real Viking!' he laughed.

'Yeah, I suppose I am. Odd the Pale, they call me. Who'd have thought? On the subject of which, what's your real name?'

'Today I am Skafti the Sly.'

'No, your real name.'

'I am Agent 07.'

'Well, if you refuse to play ball, I'm going to have to stick with Kaddie.'

'Fine by me, Master Meskitoe.'

'Mister, to you. Remember, I'm a manly man now.'

They laughed and got to their feet.

'So what happens now?' Rib asked.

'We keep our eyes open for anything unusual.'

'Are you expecting Besk to turn up here?'

Kaddie drew a deep breath. 'I have to say there's every chance. The Althing is beyond doubt the best place to seek out intelligence about anything on this island. If he wanted to find out about the Fearance, this would be where he'd start.'

'And one more thing. How come you speak such perfect Viking?'

'Not having the benefit of a leech, you mean?' he smiled. 'I had to do it the hard way. Two week total-immersion course back at base. Locked away for fourteen days with no exposure to anything English at all.'

'Wow, that sounds tough. Two weeks in solitary ...'

'Who said anything about being on my own? I was locked away in a suite with a young Icelandic lecturer called Valla. Valla Olofsdottir. She was a very good teacher.'

'I bet she was!' They both laughed. 'And ... er ... just one more thing, Kaddie.'

'Yes?'

'Thanks for coming to get me.'

'In the words of the Hávamál, "To a true friend lies a trodden road, though his farm lies far away."

The two embraced. The boy didn't want to let go. It was so, so good. He'd been so, so scared …

Odd the Pale and Skafti the Sly went their separate ways, having agreed to meet up again at Karl Lavafield's at noon the next day. The rest of the afternoon passed without event, Rib declining Arvid's invitation to swallow a few horns of Cloudless Swill. Instead, he wandered aimlessly up and down the street, deep in thought. His uneasiness carried through to the evening meal back at the booth, where the brothers were discussing plans for the following day. In the same way as the Las Vegas "conference" delegates feel obliged, just for one day, to take an excursion to the Grand Canyon, so the Hoskuld party felt it was time to take a break from the hurly-burly of the Althing. Having no desire to gaze at glaciers or gawp at geysirs – there being plenty of them back home – they agreed to Skeggi Cod-biter's suggestion of a fishing trip, the Chieftain's eyes gleaming at the prospect of pulling silver char from a mountain tarn.

Knowing full well the young freedman's views on meat and fish, the Cod-biter did not miss the opportunity to taunt, 'Come with us, Odd the Pale, and learn how to be a true man. Or are you still a pup who squirms at the touch of fish skin?'

As founder (and sole) member of the Viking Vegetarian Society, Rib turned down the offer, much to Skeggi's scorn. Tired of their company, he slipped off to bed before the others and slept fitfully, dreaming of riding a golden chariot across the sky, pulled by two golden horses, with a fearsome slavering wolf in close pursuit.

91

He was woken by the morning sun streaming through the open flap of the booth's entrance. For once, the moor of socks – what the Vikings called the bedroom floor – was empty of socks. The others had clearly set off on their fishing trip at the crack of dawn.

There was a commotion outside. Something was happening in the street. Rib stuck his head through the tent flap to see an excited stream of folk heading up the hill towards the Law Court. He ducked back into the booth, quickly threw on his clothes and joined the crowd.

'What's going on?' he asked a boy.

'I am not sure. We have all been summoned to the Law Rock to hear an important speech, that is all I know.'

Arni the Wise was not only a distinguished and highly respected Law Speaker, he was also a tall, imposing figure whose mane of flowing white hair could be seen from afar. But this morning, standing on the mound before the Law Rock, towered a giant of a man, dressed in a black cloak, his head covered by a cowl. Beside him stood a small boy. Arni the Wise, the only man allowed to be on that spot, was nowhere to be seen.

The crowd surged forward, eager to hear the words

of the small boy, who had begun to speak. Rib found himself carried with the crush, ending up about four rows from the front. His knee smacked into one of the stone benches. He swore, rubbed it, then climbed up to get a better view. The small boy was no small boy. No taller than a six year-old, he was a dwarf. A squat hunchback, thick-set and broad-shouldered, with the large head of a man. He was dressed in a full coat of mail and held a gleaming helmet in his short arms. It was difficult to make out what he was saying, his deep, guttural tones carried off on the stiff breeze which had suddenly swept down the plain.

Hideously striking though the dwarf was, Rib's eyes were drawn to the hooded figure. The moment a well-manicured hand slipped out from the folds of the black cloak to pull back the cowl, his worst nightmare came back to haunt him.

Besk!

His heart now racing, he slowly stepped down from the bench to crouch down behind the broad shoulders of a farmer from the Westman Isles. Besk! The man who had come close to killing him and his Gran at the Big Frog. The man who had fired a crossbow bolt through his side at his Mum's refuge. The man who had plunged over the side, encoiled by a python. The man who should be dead.

As if in awe of the raw evil of the man on the mound, the wind dropped. He spoke, interpreted by the dwarf: 'Noble lords, proud chieftains, brave warriors. I stand before you a stranger, yet a friend. I am the bearer of grave news. Your land, Iceland, stands in great peril.' A murmur went round the crowd. 'Amongst you walk frostlings, spies, who wish to steal your most precious wealth.' Besk then spoke a verse:

'I journey to you, worthy men,
To speak from my very heart.
I wish each and every one
Gathered here good health.

I come to play the pale men foul,
Who dare to steal your trove.
May Thor be angered at these foes,
Defilers of this sacred isle.

May their evil deeds
Incur the wrath of Odin.
Noble chieftains, proud Vikings,
I join you in battle!'

The massed ranks cheered loudly, excited at the prospect of a frostling hunt. A couple of berserks at the back began to foam in anticipation. Time to go, decided Rib. If he could slip away through the crowd, make it to the horses without being noticed, then he'd have a fighting chance of escape. The armlock which seized him from behind was as convincing as the cold blade of the dagger pressed against his throat.

'I promised I would be your death shadow. Your time has come, frostling,' a voice growled in his ear. Cod-biter! So that's why he had been so keen to arrange the fishing trip, to get the rest of the clan out of the way, knowing full well he would refuse to join them. The sharp point of the knife pricking into his Adam's-apple argued strongly against struggle and he had no choice but be manhandled by Cod-biter through the crowd to stand before Besk, who signalled the dwarf to step aside.

'Ah, Master Meskitoe, so fortuitous that our paths cross once more. Thank you, Skeggi Hoskuldsson. Your loyalty shall be well-rewarded. Tie the boy's hands!'

Another man stepped out from the crowd with a length of rope to bind Rib's hands tightly behind his back. A kidney-punch from the Cod-biter knocked him to his knees.

Skammel Box-back, Besk's dwarf, then translated his words:

'Brothers, you see before you a traitor, a frostling who has taken on the guise of a Viking. The deceitful actions of this stripling are an insult to the honour of your proud race.'

The crowd responded angrily. 'He must be punished!' shouted one. 'Sacrifice him to the gods!' shouted another.

'... speaking of which, it is now time for me to reveal my true identity,' said Besk, pulling back the cowl and letting the long black cloak slip from his shoulders.

Vikings are not in the habit of taking a step back. Vikings are not in the habit of screaming out loud in horror. Especially when there are seven hundred of them. But that day, in front of the Law Rock, the gathered mass of fearless warriors did both as they recoiled in terror at what they saw.

92

Before them reared up a nightmarish apparition from the darkest depths of Hell, an eight-legged monster with two grasping claws waving in the air, clicking open and shut. Part of the head and one of the arms were all that remained of Hesperus Besk. The rest of the creature was a huge, cybernetic scorpion, covered in sleek skeleto-plates which glinted at the slightest movement. To a man, the retreating mass of Vikings instinctively reached for their axes and swords, forgetting that their arms were piled high on the weapontake tables.

Sensing their fear, the dwarf Box-back moved to reassure them. 'Fear not, it is the god Loki! He has returned to fight with you. He means you no harm!'

A cry went up, 'Yes, see! The mighty Loki has returned!'

'Yes, yes!' shouted the dwarf. 'Your lord and master, the shapeshifter Loki, returns as a … as a …' he hesitated, searching for the Old Norse word for scorpion which did not exist, ' … as a mighty, all-powerful … crayfish!'

The Vikings fell silent and bowed their heads in reverence to the wily Father of Lies, the god who was told to have shape-changed into many creatures – a flea, a salmon, a seal – and now, before their very eyes, a crayfish! Well, sort of …

In one smooth motion, the scorpion fell forward from

its upright standing position, arching its long, segmented tail, a spike at its tip, in a sting-ready curve over its back. On seeing it starting to move down the mound, the crowd – Skeggi included – panicked and retreated, leaving Rib alone to face the approaching monster, its giant claws raised to strike. He closed his eyes.

'I fear we shall not be needing this anymore, shall we?' he heard Besk hiss as one of the pincers lowered onto the top of his bowed head. The claw-tip traced its way down the boy's forehead, followed the ridge of his nose, then moved slowly across to rest on his left cheek. It was warm to the touch. A light vibration hummed against his skin, an almost calming, soothing sensation …

With a sudden jerk, the pincer's jaws opened and snapped onto the leech, ripping it from his earlobe. He screamed out in pain, the soft flange of flesh torn open. Inches before his eyes, his invention crumpled in the claw like a car being crushed in a wreckage yard. A single shaving of cinnamon stick fell to the ground unscathed. The scorpion reared to its full height again, the curved tail serving as a ninth, balancing leg.

'Fear not, brothers, Loki means you no harm,' he spoke via the Box-back.

The massed Vikings were unsure, trapped in fight-or-flee turmoil. It was in their genes to fight, even without weapons, but today they sensed a five-mile run might be just the thing to lift the spirits. Then a bright idea came from someone at the back. 'Let us make a sacrifice to the mighty Loki!' This motion won immediate and overwhelming approval. 'Sacrifice! Sacrifice!' rose the chant.

'Oh, well, if one insists …' simpered Besk.

Up piss-glacier without an ice-axe, thought Rib, as Cod-biter hauled him to his feet.

'To the Plain!' The cry triggered a mass stampede down the path. Tables were overturned, booths flattened by the jostling horde – everyone wanted a front-row seat. After all, it wasn't every day a god returned, the last time being some thousand years ago. Kari the Rune-Carver brought up the rear, tablet of stone under his arm, hammer and chisel at the ready to capture the moment for posterity.

The Cod-biter pushed Odd the Pale roughly out of the Law Court, followed by the god Loki and his dwarf. The alleged frostling knew he was up to his neck in it. His only hope, and it was a long shot, was Kaddie. But, in his heart of hearts, he knew that even an agent of the Protectorate would have trouble getting him out of this one. He hadn't seen him anywhere in the crowd. Maybe he'd slipped away. But surely he wouldn't leave him, would he?

Skeggi shoved, punched and kicked his captive down the track, mocking, goading, cursing him all the way. Of course, Rib now couldn't understand a single word, but he somehow got the drift. When they reached the flat ground at the foot of the slope, they both stopped to look skyward at skein after skein of wild geese flying out towards the sea. Cod-biter encouraged him onward with a scuff to the head, towards the seething throng which had gathered on the plain.

Waist-high standing stones marked a perfect games oval, around which now stood the expectant audience, eagerly awaiting the matinee performance. The crowd parted to allow them through to the field of play. In the middle of the arena stood three stakes driven into the ground. A groan came from Rib's lips. To one of them was tied Kaddie.

'Ah, I see you recognise Agent 07,' said Besk. 'So well-versed in the art of disguise. And now playing the perfect part of a prisoner facing the firing squad. So convincing, is he not? Bind the boy!' he ordered.

His friend seemed badly beaten up. Barely conscious,

his right eye was almost closed, the yellow bruising on his cheekbones already turning a purple hue. A dark trickle of blood ran from a wound in his scalp. His nose looked broken, too. With undisguised enthusiasm, Skeggi Cod-biter tied Rib tightly to the stake, the coarse rope fibres cutting into his wrists and ankles.

'Kaddie,' he whispered. 'Are you all right?'

'Have been better,' came the hoarse answer. He opened his good eye and tried to manage a smile. 'You take care of Besk and the dwarf, and I'll deal with the seven hundred Vikings.'

'Who the hell do you think you are, Butch Cassidy?'

'No, I'm Sundance Kid, the good-looking one. Definitely Sundance ...' he said, wincing at the pain from his broken ribs.

'Excuse me from interrupting this intimate tête-à-tête,' said Besk, 'but we really must have a little chat. I think we all know what is at stake, if you'll excuse the pun.' He paused. 'The Fearance ...'

'You're wasting your time, Besk, if you think we know where it is,' said Kaddie, 'but thanks for letting us know that you don't know where it is, either. You have no idea the comfort that gives me.'

An angry glint came to Besk's eyes. 'Comfort is hardly the word I would use in your situation, Agent 07. And I wonder how many thousands of torture victims have pleaded ignorance at the commencement of their interrogation? The persuasive powers of the rack, removal of fingernails, water-boarding, electrodes attached to the testes, all have a tendency to jog the memory, if I am not right. And, I have to say, gentlemen, that the said implements of torture pale in comparison with the delights I have built into this new body of mine.' On cue, one of the claws flew open with a click and a bright metal shaft emerged. The titanium drill-bit whirred into life.

'Please allow me to introduce the Thriller. Now, Master Meskitoe, would you care to share with me the whereabouts of the Fearance?'

'We've told you,' said Rib through gritted teeth. 'We don't know!'

'As you wish.' The precision-engineered robot claw clicked the bit through three alignments to poise an inch from Rib's right eyeball. The draft from the shaft rotating at 2,000 rpm brought tears to his eyes. Instinctively, he pressed he head back as far as it would go against the rough timber. The bit immediately edged forward to close the gap.

'At this juncture, in the spirit of fair play, I think it only right to inform you of a delicious inbuilt design feature of the Thriller. At the slightest movement, such as the blink of an eyelid, he will automatically revert to default mode and whisk your eyeball to a pulp. Just thought I'd let you know ...'

After 8.4 seconds, Rib lost control of his bladder. After 11.7 seconds, his left leg went into uncontrollable spasm, every fibre of his body focussed on outstaring the drill-bit whirring an inch from his eyeball. But it was no good. He closed his eyes and waited for the pain.

'End of Round One,' said Besk, withdrawing the arm. 'The Thriller ahead by a point, I believe. By the way, it wasn't quite true about the default mode. But thank you, Master Meskitoe, for the tantalising foreplay. Most enjoyable.' The scorpion studied the fingernails of its human hand. 'Now that you are standing comfortably in your soiled underwear, are you absolutely certain that you do not wish to tell me where I might find the Fearance?'

'Cast-iron certain!' spat Rib. His cast-iron certainty was shattered to pieces in one slow-motion second. At the far end of the arena, the crowd parted to reveal a slim figure, trussed hand and foot, being carried by four

Vikings. 'Oh, no. Please, not her. Not her!' He then cast an angry glance across at Kaddie. 'Did you know she was here?'

'She ordered me not to tell you. As soon as she learned you were here, she insisted on coming out. She made me promise ...'

The four men made swift work of tying High Commodore Zeta Meskitoe to the stake. Now Rib knew why there were three poles.

'Gran! Are you all right?'

'I'm so sorry, Rib. It seems that my reactions are not as they once were.'

'Don't worry, Gran. We came through last time, didn't we?'

The old woman slowly shook her head.

'And ... and ... even if it all has to end here, then this is where I'd want to be. With you.'

A tear formed in her eye.

'Oh, so very touching,' said Besk. 'Welcome to our little get-together, High Commodore. So nice of you to join us, albeit a tad late. You would have loved the appetiser, I'm sure. Now, without further ado, we must press on. As you might have noticed, the natives become easily restless. They are expecting a sacrifice and a sacrifice they shall have, unless you reveal to me the precise location of the Fearance. High Commodore, allow me to re-acquaint you with an old friend.' The second arm of the shiny, scaled shell transformed with a soft clunk into something which Rib instantly recognised. The Slayer.

The crossbow which had fired a red-feathered bolt through him.

With a smile, Besk aimed the weapon at Zeta Meskitoe's forehead. 'At our last encounter, if I guess correctly, you dealt me a painful blow – a low, cowardly blow, I have to say. Revenge is a dish best served cold, they say. How appropriate that the opportunity for revenge now presents itself here, in the Land of Ice. Poetic, n'est-ce-pas?'

'You will never prevail,' said Zeta calmly.

'We shall see. We shall see. But before we continue, I must offer my thanks to you all for ... this.' He stroked his left claw in a dramatic sweep along the length of the scorpion body. 'Before our encounter, I was strong. Now, behold, I am ... a god!'

'A god-awful parody of a comic-book villain, that's what you are,' scoffed Zeta. 'A scorpion? Please ...'

'I disagree, High Commodore. The perfect reincarnation for one born under the sign of Scorpio, I would argue. Determined and forceful, emotionally intuitive, powerful and passionate. And of course, my dear, exciting and magnetic.'

Zeta smiled. 'You tell only one side of the story, Hesperus. You omit to mention the darker traits of the sign – resentful, obstinate, compulsive, obsessive.'

Angered at her uninvited use of his first name, he snapped back, 'The world of the Scorpio is black and white, High Commodore. We have little regard for the liberal, grey-wash benevolence of your kind. The Scorpio concerns himself with beginnings and endings. He kills rather than be killed.' With an impatient click of the pincers, he manipulated the Slayer closer to her, its aim still firmly fixed on the spot between her eyes.

'I am going to count to three. If I do not receive the required answer on the whereabouts of the Fearance, from any of you, the High Commodore of CRISP will be history. ONE ... '

Rib's mind raced at a hundred miles an hour. Was this more bluff? This time, something told him he couldn't be sure.

'Say nothing,' said Zeta calmly.

'TWO!'

He couldn't take the risk. He opened his mouth ...

The crossbow bolt stapled Zeta Meskitoe's skull to the stake with a sickening crunch, the red-feather flight protruding from her forehead the sole evidence of the shot. Time stood still. Rib couldn't comprehend what had happened. Her eyes were still wide open, in a look of surprise, staring straight ahead. Then came the stream of blood, dark blood, pulsing from the hole in her head.

'Noooo!' he screamed, straining to tear himself free. 'I will kill you for this, you bastard, do you hear? I will kill you for this!'

'I find the count of three such a tired cliché, do you not?' Besk then raised his eyebrows in mock question. 'But surely, Master Meskitoe, you were not about to give me the answer? That would have been most unfortunate. But, if that were the case, let us try again.' With a click, the Slayer auto-reloaded and took aim at Kaddie. 'ONE!'

The sight of Skammel Box-back flying through the air to land head-first in the dirt in front of Besk took everybody by surprise. The scorpion moved the limp body of the dwarf to one side with its giant pincer before turning to address the intrusion. The crowd roared its approval as a new combatant burst into the arena, announcing his arrival with a blood-curdling howl.

'Is that who I think it is?' asked Kaddie.

Rib nodded.

'I like his sense of timing.'

Too late, Bellower, too late, were the boy's only thoughts.

Grim Hoskuldsson, armed with axe, sword and spear, prowled round the edge of the arena, beating shield against chest. A buzz of excitement filled the air.

'I do believe we have a berserk in the house,' said Besk. 'How fascinating.'

By way of response, Bellower let out a mighty roar and rolled his eyes so that only the whites were visible. He was working himself up to full-on frenzy. Now foaming at the mouth, the shaggy giant made the first move, hurling his spear at the scorpion. Grim's aim was unerringly true, sending the javelin straight as a die towards Besk's head. At the last nano-second, the scorpion plucked the spear from the air with one claw and snapped it in two with the other. The crowd gasped.

'You'll have to do better than that, my hot-tempered friend,' said Besk, before firing off two rapid shots from the Slayer. The Bellower took them both on his shield, then howled his defiance at the monster. The crowd went wild. This was warming up nicely ...

Still circling the scorpion, he reached for his axe. Until that point, Besk had not moved. Now, he too joined in the circular dance. The styles could not have been more contrasting – one partner gliding stealthily over the dance-floor like a stalking panther, the other snorting steam, pawing at the ground like a raging bull. The body-hair of seven hundred Vikings stood on end as the Bellower screamed a blood-curdling roar and charged, axe raised. Had the blow hit home, it would have parted Besk's head cleanly from its scorpion body, Grim would have been declared winner by knockout, Rib and Kaddie would have been cut free, and they all could have gone home. But the blow didn't hit home. One powerful swipe of a claw sent the unblooded axe cartwheeling through the air, over the heads of the crowd, nearly decapitating Kari the Rune-Carver, who by this time was having great difficulty keeping up with the action, his hammer-hand throbbing with blisters.

'Box-back! Wake up!' hissed Besk. 'I wish you to speak with this oaf.' There was no sign of life from the dwarf. If he were still in the land of the living, he was in no mood to let on. Having already been hurled ten spear-lengths in the air by a berserk, he was keeping his head down. Once was more than enough for one day.

In the face of such an awesome demonstration of firepower, a normal man might have backed off, rethought his tactics, maybe even have made a run for it. Grim Hoskuldsson was no normal man. He was a berserk. Not only a berserk, but a really angry berserk. And when a berserk gets really angry, he does one thing. He bites his shield.

Which was rather a shame, because it was a brand new shield, carved from the washed-up mess table from the Lusitanic. Thick as the length of a grown man's thumb, thick enough to withstand two crossbow shots. Grim chewed a chunk out of the top edge as if it were a crispbread wafer. It made a similar sound as he crunched down half the mouthful and spat the other half out. The crowd let out a collective cheer. Now things were going to get really interesting ...

The crazed hulk charged straight at the scorpion, whirling his sword above his head. Besk stood stock still, then at the very last moment stepped to one side in a half-pirouette, the berserk brushing against his side as he rushed headlong past. Hardly able to breathe, Rib watched the deadly battle unfold, sensing something different about this new phase of combat. At first, he couldn't figure it out. Then he realised. It was Besk. His eyes had glazed over, as if in a trance. Yet the scorpion's body movements remained alert, controlled, almost graceful.

At a time when the civilised world had banned bullfighting as a savage bloodsport, a cruel spectacle that had no place in modern society, Hesperus Besk had mourned the demise of what he considered to be a noble craft, an art form, and had been a regular visitor to bullrings – latterly illegal venues – across the length and breadth of Spain. Yes, he derived pleasure from the thrill of the chase as *Dead or Alive* champion, but nothing compared to the pre-Watershed fulfilment he found in the bullring. Yet here, in this most unlikely of locations, in his very own plaza de toros, he was living out his ultimate fantasy. Hesperus Besk became 'Manolete', arguably the greatest bullfighter of all time.

Foaming over with rage, the crazed beast charged and charged again. Besk adopted a bolt-upright stance, lowering his left pincer and turning his profile to the onrushing hulk, to then twist gracefully aside as the berserk swept past. His body hardly moved. It was as if the Bellower were charging round a pole, somehow unable to make contact. After a series of passes, it was clear that Grim was tiring, but he threw away his shield and rushed the scorpion once more, sword raised. This time, the toreador did not pass. With a swipe of his razor-sharp claw, he sliced off the berserk's arm at the elbow. Bellower staggered a few steps, staring at the bloodied stump in disbelief. He then looked up, roared, and charged again. A bolt from the Slayer buried itself in his right thigh. Howling in agony, Grim dropped to his knees. The boy tied to the stake couldn't look any more and stared down at the ground, where an army of ants were filing between his feet in a long line, followed by a colony of spiders, heading in the same direction.

The crowd had gone quiet, knowing that the end was near. The berserk was losing blood fast and, as everybody knew, "he who loses blood loses the battle." With a monumental effort, he staggered to his feet. With a roar, he charged at the scorpion, flailing his sword. Before he could strike, the right pincer dealt him a mighty blow to the head, sending his helmet spinning high in the air over the heads of the audience. The earth shook as he hit the ground.

He lay there without moving. Then, slowly, inch by inch, he raised himself onto his knees. He looked across at the boy. Their eyes met. He slowly shook his head and closed his eyes. Besk lowered the scorpion's shell forward onto all eight legs until it was flat to the ground. The crowd took a step back as he advanced until face to face with his defeated adversary. A long, metal spike whirred from the tip of the scorpion's tail, which then arched high over the top of its body and drove the point down hard between Grim's shoulder blades, right through his heart. It was over. The berserk had bitten his last shield.

'Olé, I believe,' said Besk to the lifeless form, frozen in stone-like crouch. Then he turned to address Rib. 'I suggest the performance merits both ears?' Without waiting for an answer, he snipped off Grim's ears and held them up to the crowd.

There were no cheers, no applause. A silence fell over the arena. Even the tink-tink of chisel against stone stopped. Iceland had lost a brave son. Rib had lost a brother who had given his life trying to save his. "We shall be our brother's defender, our brother's avenger," Grim had sworn. At that moment, Rib knew the name he would give to his dagger. It would be known as Bellower. It would be used to avenge his blood-brother's death ...

93

The dagger! He'd clean forgotten about the slim blade sheathed inside his boot! If he could just reach down ... but he couldn't. There wasn't an inch of give in the ropes tying his wrists and ankles. All the same, he strained to loosen the knots. It was his only chance.

Rib couldn't bring himself to look at his grandmother, standing stiffly to attention, her head pinioned to the stake beside him. Through his tears he tugged and tugged at the ropes, but it was no good. It was his fault. She had wanted to kill Besk under the Big Frog clock. And he had stopped her.

He saw the red flash a second before he heard the roar. The snow-capped mountain at the far end of the Assembly Plain erupted into life, spewing molten rock hundreds of metres into the air. The ground beneath them shook with the tremor, the lake beside the arena started to seethe, jets of scalding steam shot from cracks opening in the earth's surface. Pandemonium broke loose. People were running everywhere in blind panic. A stampede of horses broken loose from the enclosure added to the mayhem.

(Had Tycho-Vikings erected masonry structures on the Assembly Plain, none would have been left standing. Had Tycho-Vikings built steel bridges, they would have been destroyed. And it was just as well that Tycho-Vikings had not invested in an underground railway transit system, for it would have been the end of the line for Law Rock Terminus, its rails twisted, its tunnels collapsed. Such was the onslaught of the earthquake. All because Tycho-Vikings had blissfully set up their parliament bang-slap on the fault line which marked the very spot where the North American and Eurasian tectonic plates rubbed together. Indeed, the Assembly Plain itself had been formed millions of years before, when the tensional stresses between the two continental masses reached the point where they finally fractured and separated, leaving the long, sunken rift valley as legacy of their argument. Almost everywhere on the island, the violent forces of Nature lay boiling and bubbling beneath the thin surface crust. But here, the very place to which the whole male population flocked each year to have a good time, was probably the most precarious point on the whole planet. Had a group of volcanologists been present to witness the scene, they would have asked themselves the chicken or egg question: Did the eruption of Mount Skjaldbreiður trigger the 7.4 Richter Scale earthquake, or vice versa?)

To those actually present, it didn't really matter. It didn't matter at all. At the very second when the shiny, segmented arm of the scorpion aimed the crossbow at Agent 07's head, the whole place blew. The seismic shock of the quake opened up gaping fissures and rifts along the fault line, ripping apart the scarred and twisted lavafields left by the last volcanic episode. Shallow reservoirs of magma burst through the crust in a series of mini-eruptions to join the swarm of secondary quakes moving down the valley.

With a deafening roar, the arena split asunder right down the middle, hurling scores of howling warriors to their death. Kari the Rune-Carver's eye-witness report ended mid-sentence as he plunged into the abyss, a surprised look on his face, hammer and chisel firmly gripped in each hand to the very last. Skammel Box-back made a miraculous recovery and staggered after the scorpion, whose eight legs were desperately trying to secure purchase on the unstable surface in an attempt to make the higher ground. Suddenly, a second massive tremor hit the arena, causing the one half to sink with a juddering spasm, leaving the captives on a sloping slab of rock some five metres beneath the level of the plain. The force of the tremor toppled the stakes, hurling the three – still tightly bound – flat against the rock. The scorpion briefly turned to observe their predicament, smiled and moved on.

'Kaddie!' screamed Rib above the grating roar of the quake. 'Can you get free?'

'No! I still can't move!'

Nor could Rib, straining every sinew to tear himself loose. Skeggi Cod-biter and his crew certainly knew their knots. The old woman had fallen a few metres away and lay, eyes staring up to the heavens, in blissful oblivion to the carnage and mayhem around her. Rib had ended up facing down the sloping slab towards the bottom of the crater, whilst Kaddie's stake had toppled the other way, so that he was looking up towards the top edge of its ridge. The timbers were so heavy that neither could get to their feet.

'No!' gasped Rib.

'What is it?'

The boy couldn't bring himself to answer. All he could do was stare in horror at the red tongue of molten lava licking its way tentatively out of a vent in the bottom of the crater. In a matter of seconds, the trickle became a confident flow which began to fill the basin. Even from twenty metres' distance, he could feel its heat on his face.

'Kaddie, we've got to move! Now! Can you reach my boot?'

In vain, Kaddie strained to shift his position. 'No, it's no good. I can't move an inch!'

Rib stopped struggling. He could only watch in a state of frozen shock as the lava reached the grotesque statue of Grim, still kneeling on all fours. The smell and smoke of burning flesh filled the air as the man they called Bellower, son of Hoskuld the Great, father of Katla the Fair, blood-brother of Odd the Pale, sizzled and spat like an ox on a spit. Still hungry, the tongue of lava licked relentlessly toward them. Ten metres ... nine ... eight ... Rib closed his eyes. Memories flooded through his brain. Mum showing him how to feed the bandicoots for the first time. Gran telling him about Dad by the light of a campfire under an oak tree. Sunset spreading plum jam on his third croissant. Rika ladling out snowgrouse stew and handing him a Koskenkorva. Something tugged at the ropes tying his hands. Kaddie! He must have broken free! He opened his eyes and craned his neck to see Agent 07 still tied to his stake up the slope.

'Ruf!' said the Arctic fox, his razor-sharp teeth biting through the final strands.

'Alf!' Rib pulled his hands free and reached down for the dagger in his boot. Its keen blade made short work of the ropes around his ankles and he quickly slid over to Kaddie to cut him loose. He could feel the heat searing his back. Alf was darting around him, yapping excitedly. A glance over his shoulder told him that the molten lava was now no more than a man's length away.

'Go!' shouted Kaddie. 'Go without me!'

'Never,' said Rib between gritted teeth. Smiðr the Black proved to be the best smith on the island. The slender blade of the dagger bit through the coarse fibres with ease and Rib pulled his friend loose just as the end of his stake burst into flames on contact with the molten mass. He made to move to the third stake, knife drawn to free her body.

'No, Rib, we can't take her with us. She's gone ... '

He pulled away from Kaddie's grasp and knelt beside her still form. The heat was unbearable. His eyebrows started to singe. He placed the back of his hand against her cold cheek in silent farewell before turning away, tears filling his eyes.

'Come on!' screamed Kaddie, following the scurrying figure of the little fox up the side of the crater. Loose scree gave way underfoot as they scrambled up the rock face, so hot it scorched the palms of their hands.

Alf was waiting at the top. 'Grr, rhow, rhow!!'

'What's he saying?'

'Don't ask me. Besk crushed my leech, remember? I think he's probably saying something like let's get out of here.'

Alf the Arctic fox wasn't hanging around to hear the end of the conversation, running full pelt across the smoking plain, skirting round boiling pools, leaping over yawning crevasses, picking his way through jagged splinters of rock. All the time careful to keep his brush erect as a guiding flag for the humans to follow. The terrain was an assault course of nightmares, at each step the rumbling surface threatening to open up. Agitated mud-pots celebrated their coming of age by setting off rockets of magma. Choking, sulphurous steam hissed from every fissure. The whole place felt like it was going to erupt five miles high at any minute.

Kaddie signalled Rib to stop. 'We've got to get to higher ground,' he said, pointing at the steep ridge rising to their left, on the opposite side of the plain from the Law Rock.

'Looks like Alf's got it covered,' shouted Rib, nodding towards the little fox, nose to the ground, zigzagging his way through the smoking field. 'Come on, we mustn't lose him!'

A huge aftershock brought them to their knees. Before their eyes, a whole section of the ridge collapsed in a deafening roar. 'Are you sure this is a good idea?' he screamed.

'We've got to get to the top of that cliff, over there,' shouted Kaddie.

Alf had now come back to circle them, barking furiously. Rib pointed up to the ridge. 'Up, Alf! Up!'

The fox cocked his head to one side. 'Rff?'

'Yes, up!'

94

The three picked their way parallel to the foot of the ridge for some hundred metres, keeping a careful eye upwards for any tell-tale signs of rockfall. Alf suddenly stopped and started yapping, jumping up and down on the spot. They couldn't see what he was getting so excited about, until he scampered up the scree and disappeared into a black slit in the rock face. It was so narrow, they would have missed it.

'Alf!' Rib shouted. There came no answer. The two scrambled up to the cleft. It was barely a foot wide. Big enough for a fox, but for a man? Surely not, they both thought, looking at each other. It would only take the slightest tremor for the rock to close and crush them into two instant fossils, each with the same I-told-you-so look on his face.

'It's our only chance,' said Kaddie, squeezing sideways into the fissure.

Rib followed. The incline was a steep 30 degrees, but worse – far worse – was the sickening wave of claustrophobia which smothered him. He struggled to breathe. He started to panic. 'Kaddie! I can't do this!' he screamed.

'It's OK, it widens out a bit up here! Keep going!'

Alf's muffled barks snapped him out of his frozen fear, encouraging him to breathe deeply and shuffle, inch by inch, up into the blackness, the cold surface of the rock scraping against his forehead and nose. Somehow, he finally made it through.

Kaddie was waiting for him. 'Well done,' he said, placing a hand on his shoulder. They were standing in a ravine, similar to the one above the high pasture at Borg. Rib sucked in deep lungfuls of relief as he craned his neck upwards to see a sliver of bright blue sky. It looked beautiful. A yap told him Alf had come back. To check on him.

Without warning, the ground began to rumble beneath their feet. 'Come on!' screamed Kaddie. They scrambled up the narrow chasm – the two men sometimes on all fours, the fox sometimes on his hind legs – until it opened up onto a broad plateau at the top.

Alf immediately deposited a steaming mound on top of a rocky outcrop to mark the heroic ascent. A little flag would have topped it off nicely. The two men collapsed on the coarse grass, breathing deeply after the exertions of the climb. The panoramic view over the Assembly Plain made them both gasp. Normally a scene of stunning beauty, they saw below them a scene from hell. Scores of ant-like figures staggered aimlessly around the valley floor. Horses galloped wildly in blind panic. There were bodies everywhere. The tongue of lava which had almost consumed them, now greatly swollen in size, was snaking its way down the plain. It didn't need much imagination to see how, if the volcano continued to erupt, the whole valley would soon be flooded with red molten lava. Rib scanned the plain for a giant scorpion, but there was none.

'Keep your eyes peeled for a pigeon,' said Kaddie.

'Pigeon?'

'Yes, a carrier-pigeon with a set of rendez-vous coordinates.'

'Explain.'

'I'm hoping there's a ship of ours somewhere on the other side of that fogbank. But we need the coordinates.'

A rescue-ship! Rib immediately looked to the heavens for any sign of a bird with a little tube attached to one leg. Then something caught the corner of his eye. On the ground. Just in front of him.

Feathers.

Pigeon feathers.

A guilty yelp came from the muzzle of the Arctic fox.

'Alf! You little –'

A zipping sound interrupted him. Kaddie had taken off his tunic, trousers and boots. He was pulling on a skin-tight wetsuit.

'What the ...' mouthed Rib.

'Yours is here,' said Kaddie, patting the flat rucksack which he'd obviously been wearing underneath his tunic.

'We're going swimming?'

'Yes, we have to get to the coast. Just in case you've forgotten, the sea is very cold in these climes. Now put this on.' He tossed a second suit at Rib, who caught it, but made no move to open it. He was staring at Kaddie in disbelief. The man was now removing from the backpack a stretch of turquoise fabric.

'No, please don't say ...' he said, feeling a nauseating rush of déjà vu.

Alf the Arctic fox had edged forward when he saw the man reach into the bag. Maybe it was lunchtime? He quickly leapt back with a snarl as the man pulled out a strange contraption of shining rods, which he swiftly clicked into place to build a frame. He now started strapping on the fabric, testing its tautness as he went along.

'No way, Kaddie, no way! The last time you conned me into flying one of those things, I nearly ended up killing myself! Look at my nose! This is what happens when you fly one of those bastards!'

'It'll be different this time,' said Kaddie, putting the final touch to the wires.

'How so? One turquoise kite equals one crash waiting to happen.'

'Not this time. Last time you messed up. Last time you failed to follow my instructions. This time, I'll be at the controls. This is a tandem glider. Now get your suit on!'

'No way! You're not getting me into that thing. I'll stay here and take my chances.'

'You wouldn't last more than thirty six hours. They'll hunt you down like a wild animal.'

'I don't care. I'm not coming, Kaddie. You go and fetch the cavalry. You'll find me back in the mountains above Borg, holed up in a cave with my mate Alf, OK?'

'No, Rib, that's not going to happen. There will be no cavalry. And do you really want to be alone on this island? With Besk?'

'Besk? How do you even know if he's still alive?'

'Would you bet against it?'

Rib knew the answer.

'And another thing,' said Kaddie. 'The chase is already on.' He pointed down at a group of Vikings making their way across the plain in their direction.

Rib recognised the man in front. 'Cod-biter!' he spat.

'They'll be here within fifteen minutes. Now put that bloody suit on!'

The boy knew he had no choice and did as he was told. When he'd squeezed into the suit and zipped up, he walked over to kneel in front of the little Arctic fox, who had been watching the young human's perplexing performance, head cocked to one side. Rib leaned forward and touched Alf for the first time, stroking the stiff wiry hair on top of his head.

'Bye, little fellah,' he said, choking back a tear.

'Rrrr, grrf, rup, rup, rup!' answered Alf.

Kaddie broke up the farewell scene without ceremony, guided Rib over to the para-glider and strapped him in. He took up position behind him. 'OK, all we have to do is run over the edge of the cliff, holding onto these bars. Then just ease down into a prone position and it's plain sailing from there on in.'

All we have to do is run over the edge of the cliff …

95

The fox barked as the big blue bird disappeared over the cliff. He ran to the edge and watched it swoop down in a deep dive towards the valley floor, before rising to soar higher and higher up into the sky. It circled overhead like an eagle, then flew off towards the middle of the plain. Alf the Arctic fox raised his snout to the air and howled his heart out.

Rib was trying his best to fight back memories of his citidome crash-landing, the rush of warm air in his face not helping one bit. But this time, he wasn't feeling the heat of the sub-tropical rainforest, he was feeling the rising shimmer of hot air from the lavaflow, the boiling lakes and seething mud-pots below. It was hang-glider heaven, as long as the pilot could keep the craft in the air.

Once he realised that they weren't going to be smashed to pieces on the valley floor, he turned to Kaddie and shouted, 'What now?'

'We follow the fault-line. The lift from the heat should keep us up until we reach the sea.'

'And if it doesn't?'

'We can drop in on your farmstead and you can introduce me to that blonde serving maid.'

Rib managed a smile. The plan seemed to be working. Kaddie steered the glider towards the centre of the plain, where it immediately gained height as it met the hot air rising from the lava flow. The hang-glider soared to two hundred metres and started to circle its way down the rift valley towards the coast.

The flight of the big blue bird was watched with a mixture of disbelief and fury by Skeggi Cod-biter. He hurled his spear skyward in a fit of rage before turning on his band of men to curse them for the escape of his quarry. Skeggi's were not the only eyes fixed on the turquoise kite in the sky. Through his high-optic scope, Besk had followed with keen interest his captives' flight across the plain and their launch from the opposite ridge. He had not expected them to survive.

Nevertheless, he allowed himself a smile, a new opportunity now presenting itself. Besk had long realised that his weapon of choice, his beloved Slayer, was not suited to every occasion. Although lethal at close quarters, the crossbow was not designed for distances beyond fifty metres. Built into the scorpion shell was housed a new prototype weapon which Besk had been itching to test in the field. Now was the perfect moment for the maiden voyage of the Banshee. He knew all too well the scientists' sniggers at his namings – Slayer, Thriller, Banshee. He didn't care. They were his only friends. They were his family. He pressed the activate switch and, with a soft whirr, one of the scorpion legs withdrew into its body cavity from which, in its place, emerged a two-metre long carbon tube. The slim barrel shone crimson in the sunlight. Instead of bullets, it fired a 75 cm long arrow. But an arrow with a difference; at its tip, a snubhead engineered to open up in flight into a razor-barbed wheel, which screamed a blood-chilling whine as it rotated. Initially, Besk had wavered over this design feature, but then gradually warmed to the concept of the whistling bomb, whereby the mere sound of its approach strikes terror into the hearts of its intended victims.

Having checked the reading of the compressed air chamber, he took a final glance up at the small dot disappearing into the distance. He had time for only one shot. But one shot would suffice. Two birds with one stone, he smiled, craning his neck forward to take aim at the blue swathe of sail through the telescopic sights. And there they were, two ill-mannered guests leaving the party without so much as a farewell to their host. A stickler for protocol on such occasions, Hesperus Besk insisted on the courtesy of blowing them a goodbye kiss before firing. As only a bounty hunter could, he gently squeezed the trigger. The Banshee screamed into the air, set on a deadly course towards its prey.

Rib heard it coming before he saw it. Instinctively, he reached up with his right hand and jerked downwards on the bar.

'Whoa!' screamed Kaddie in his ear. Followed closely by 'Aaaarghhh!' Fortunately, Rib's evasive action had saved their bacon – the Banshee had been a split second away from reducing their flimsy sail to shreds, sending them plummeting down to a certain death. Less fortunately, Rib's late panic shift to the glider's flight path brought the Banshee into direct contact with Kaddie's left calf. Only a nick, but a nick was enough to rip a three-inch slice from the muscle. Any closer, and it would have taken his leg off at the knee. The kite took a sickening lurch as the pilot clutched at his leg.

'Take the bar,' he groaned.

'Me? You must be joking! I can't fly this thing!'

'Yes you can, just do as I say. I've got to fix my leg, I'm losing blood. Take it!'

Rib grabbed hold of the bar. 'What do I do now?' he shouted.

Kaddie was breathing deeply through his nose, trying to stay conscious. 'To steer, all you do is ... shift your weight in the direction ... you want to ... go. Pull

... pull back on the bar to ... to speed up. Push ... push to slow down. Be careful not to ...'

Nothing.

'Kaddie!'

'Careful not to push ... too hard ... or you'll stall it. When you ... when you feel ... a hot thermal ... use it to gain height. Circle ... circle up within it and look ... look for the next. Birds ... watch for big birds ... do as they do ...'

'Which direction do I take?'

No answer.

'Kaddie, come on, don't go quiet on me now! Which direction do I take?'

The pilot surfaced from the depths. 'Go back ... down valley,' he whispered in Rib's ear. 'Back to ... back to the sea. Must get ... must get ... over fogbank ... fogbank ... '

'Kaddie? Kaddie!' Agent 07 had succumbed to unconsciousness. Rib shifted his weight to the left and the glider responded to the move.

The scorpion swished its metal tail in anger. Besk seethed inside as he watched the blue sail circle upwards out of range. An aftershock sent an avalanche of boulders crashing down to the valley floor. A thick white cloud of hot gas and ash was now sweeping down the plain. It was time to withdraw. He could save Master Meskitoe for another time.

96

As long as he kept directly above the red tongue of lava, he had plenty of lift and managed to make good progress for the first few minutes, circling as high as each thermal would take them before swooping down to find the next. He was surprising himself how quickly he was getting the hang of it. Maybe those wind-surfing lessons on the Middlemedes lake had given him a feel for the sail? The sense of well-being was short-lived once they came to the end of the Assembly Plain. No more lava. The glider immediately began to lose height. Panic, who had been hanging around just in case, made his presence felt.

'Kaddie! Help! We're gonna crash!'

No reply was forthcoming from his instructor, the only sign of life being the steady rhythm of his chest rising and falling against his back. At least he was alive, for all the good it did. Then, something caught his eye, up to his right. Two wheeling buzzards. Watch for big birds, Kaddie had said. He shifted his weight to steer the glider so that it was right beneath the birds. Yes! He felt the warm lift from the ridge below and the kite started to circle slowly upwards within the thermal.

Even though the sun was burning bright in a cloudless sky, the air was becoming cold. Really cold. In spite of the wet-suit, he began to shiver. Black mountain ridges and snow-capped crags stretched into the distance. And beyond them, scarcely visible through

the shimmering haze, he was sure he could see the sea!
But what the hell were they supposed to do once they
got there? He had no idea. One thing at a time. Just the
small matter of getting there first ...

The two buzzards handed over the baton to a lone
osprey, which acted as Rib's guide for the next hour. A
pair of sea-eagles took the final leg, leading him all the
way down the finishing straight to the coast. His whole
body at breaking point, he suddenly recognised below
him a spit of shingle jutting out into the fjord. And, just
inland, a shack. Grim's shack. The cool sea air allowed
him no time to reminisce, the glider lurching into a dive.
He'd run out of lift!

'Kaddie!' Still no reply.

His aching, blistered hands gripped the bar tightly,
steering the kite down the coastline in a long sweeping
glide, over the crest of a familiar hill where he used
to wind-dry cod. Borg farmstead, straight ahead. He
looked left to find Ymir's Milk as dense as ever a few
hundred metres offshore. He'd never make it that far.
He'd never make it over the fogbank. Shit! So near and
yet so far ...

He had to think quickly. If he had to come down
on dry land, here was as good a place as any. But what
sort of reception would he get? Coming out of the sky?
With a man on his back? How was he going to tell
Katla her Dad was dead? And, most worryingly, how
was he going to land this bloody thing? A few snatched
instructions on how to take off, how to climb, how
to follow birds ... that was all he could remember.
Certainly nothing on how to land. In every sense, a
crash-course.

He was now losing height fast. Three, maybe four
sweeps and they'd be hitting the ground. He searched
frantically for the best place to land. The boulder-strew

shoreline was a no-no. And probably not a good idea to try and land on the turf roof of the farmstead.

They'd been spotted. The unmistakable figure of Thorkatla Grimsdottir was standing in the middle of the homefield, pointing skyward and shrieking her head off. More people spilled out of the house. Rib didn't give them a second look – he was now focussing on the final descent. This was where the captain should be initiating landing procedures, lowering the undercarriage, asking the cabin crew to take their seats. But on Flight 13 from Thingvellir to Crash-Mountain, there were no landing wheels and the co-pilot was comatose.

The lush slopes of the upper pasture were his best bet. But he was coming in too fast, far too fast! What had Kaddie said about slowing down? Push the bar! He pushed, but too hard, almost stalling the kite right above the big black rock. He snatched the bar back, fighting to keep the kite airborne, but it had now lost all momentum and hung mid-air in a moment of indecision, in two minds whether to stay up or spiral to the ground.

Boom! Geysir exploded in a plume of steam, its sulphur stench wafting over on the breeze. The geysir! The hot springs! The last throw of the dice. He threw his weight as far over to his right as he could and the kite responded, swooping in a long flat glide towards the raised plateau. A dozen or so women were now running up the slope, shouting and waving their arms. The boy pilot paid them no attention, straining every fibre on keeping the glider steady on its final descent towards the smoking airstrip ahead. Of course, the last thing he wanted to do was actually land there – they'd sizzle like sausages on a griddle. Acrid fumes hit the back of his throat. The Slob spat an angry gobbet of molten mud up at him. He was still coming in too fast!

10 metres ...

5 metres ...

In one final act of desperation, he pushed hard on the bar, trying to force the leading tip of the sail to point skywards. It didn't want to, pulling hard like an Alsatian on a short leash. He felt the searing heat on his front, the rubbery skin of the wetsuit melting against his thighs.

'Aaaarghhh!' He closed his eyes, bracing himself for the crash. But the bubbling heat of the field gave the blue delta sail the lift it hungered for. Rib opened his eyes in disbelief. They were rising! The kite was gaining height!

10 metres ...

20 metres ...

He struggled to keep a straight course right up the middle of the field, wanting to get as much climb as possible. Above the hissing and spitting of the mud-pots, a deep rumbling sound made itself heard. The geysir! He'd forgotten the geysir! And they were heading straight for it! Rib pulled hard on the bar and threw his weight to his left. Nose tip down, the kite accelerated into a steep glide ... BOOM! ... at the very second the dome burst with a roar to send a spout of boiling water high into the air, missing him by inches.

'Aaaargh!' His trailing foot scalded by the spray, Agent 07 briefly rejoined the land of the living before slipping back into unconsciousness.

Sweat now pouring from every pore, Rib steered back over the field, gaining height all the time. And at once, as if by magic, they were inside the thermal column and rose, circling slowly, high above the hot springs, the homestead, the pasture, the shieling, the sheepshed. The sound of women's cries, the thump of the geysir, the wash of waves breaking on the shore melted into the muffled distance behind him. Two huge black birds came from nowhere, screeching loudly as they wheeled above. Then, as quickly as they had appeared, they peeled off into a long glide over the bay, over Ymir's Milk and out to sea. The boy flying the blue glider leaned to his left and followed them ...

98

A light drizzle was drifting in from the Brickhills. High Commodore Angela Munroe stared out from the Library window over the manicured lawns of the Mansion. In her hand she held a small scroll, newly delivered by carrier-pigeon. She wiped the tears from her eyes, unfurled the message and read it for a second time.

Classified Information. Subject: The Fearance

I can confirm that Protectorate Vessel Intrepid has picked up Agent 07 and expedition member R Meskitoe from the sea off the south-west coast of Iceland. Both were suffering from hypothermia. Agent 07 also suffered severe laceration to his left calf and scalding to his left foot. Both have been placed under medical surveillance and are expected to make a full recovery.

The two have been held in separate quarters for debriefing. The following summary is taken from Agent 07's account. Meskitoe has refused to comply with questioning.

1. *Agent 07 and Meskitoe are the sole survivors of the Expedition. All other members of the crew were lost in combat against a hostile native*

population. The Lusitanic lies at the bottom of the Borgarfjord.

2. *Praecox Magister Besk's suspected presence on Iceland is confirmed. He is heavily armed, having taken the form of a cybernetic scorpion with unknown power source.*

3. *It is my sad duty to report the death of High Commodore Zeta Meskitoe at the hands of Besk.*

4. *Agent 07 is unable to confirm the location of the Fearance.*

The Intrepid is due to dock at Liverpool within two days. Arrangements are in place to return Agent 07 to base for a full debrief. I await your instructions with regards to Meskitoe.

Your humble servant

Captain David Marshall

Angela Munroe rang the polished brass bell on her desk to summon her assistant. 'I want this sent to Captain Marshall immediately,' she said. Taking a sheet of blue paper from the desk drawer, she unscrewed the cap from her Mont Blanc and scratched four words in reply.

Let the boy go.

EPILOGUE

He was the old man who drank Coke on the rocks alone in the bar shack on the beach. He had now gone eighty-four days without a drink. A real drink. Doctor's orders. Doctor's last orders.

The old man was all skin and bone. His leathery skin tanned taut by the tropical sea-breeze, he stared without expression at the colony of liver spots on the back of his hand, the broken finger nails almost orange against the darkness of his skin. He raised his left hand and held it horizontally some six inches before his eyes. His fingers trembled uncontrollably. Even after eighty-four days. He let out a deep sigh and took a reluctant sip from the tumbler. He grimaced. It put his teeth on edge.

The sound of breaking waves faded gently into the distance. The old man closed his eyes and surrendered to the cotton-wool embrace of afternoon sleep. He drifted into dreams not of his manhood. No longer did he dream the adventures of fear and flight. No longer did he dream of his wife, the woman he'd wed at the age of eighteen, the woman he hadn't seen for forty long years. Instead, he dreamed boyhood dreams, of Africa. He heard the surf roar and saw the reed-slender native boats slicing their way through. He dreamed of lions on the beach, the cubs still playing at dusk.

A paper bag blowing across the doorway of the bar woke him, signalling a sudden change in the wind, followed almost at once by the smell from the shark factory across the harbour. The old man got up from his chair and walked out stiffly onto the terrace. The sand whipped up against his bare legs and he knew that a storm was brewing. He wondered whether he could make the twenty minutes' walk along the beach back to his hut before the storm broke. Or should he weather it out, here in the bar? In the cold company of Coke.

Still half-asleep, the old man was struggling to make up his mind when something caught his eye, out at sea. It was a dinghy, its light-blue sail billowing in flight from the oncoming rollers. The small boat bobbed bright against the black backdrop of the gathering clouds. The sailor knew his stuff, thought the old man, as he watched him outrun the storm. The skiff ran easily with the herd of white horses doing their best to buffet him to the point of capsizing. He finally broke free, sailed cleanly into the lagoon and up onto the narrow stretch of shingle below the rocks. The sailor stepped out, pulled the boat up onto the shore and made her fast. The slim figure padded back to the boat, as if in a hurry, unstepped the mask, furled the sail and tied it. He then turned to set off in a loping run up the beach, towards the old man standing unsteadily on the terrace of the bar shack.

At about thirty paces, the slim figure slowed to a walk, as if unsure what to do next. Only then could the old man make out his features: skin colour too light for these parts; long, fair hair, but dreadlocked even so. The young man's pale blue eyes bore deep into his soul. Only then, in the flashflood of a single tear, did the old man know who he was and why he was there. They embraced without a word and the old man led his grandson into the shack, motioning him to sit at the small round table at the back. He went behind the empty bar, took two glasses and a bottle of dark rum from the shelf. He uncorked the bottle and threw the top through the doorway. The cork bounced once on the wooden terrace before landing upright in the sand.

www.ingramcontent.com/pod-product-compliance
Lightning Source LLC
Chambersburg PA
CBHW070829260626
47170CB00007B/2314